CW01513198

by any means, without the prior written p
author), except for the quotation of brief pass:

**Publication Date December 21, 2012, 2nd printing July 11, 2018
ISBN: 978-0-9883606-2-4**
Printed in USA

Word count: 103,211.

3

TABLE OF CONTENTS

Revelation (Seven Seals)   6

Forward   10

Prologue   22

CHAPTERS

1. Spinning the Saucers   28
2. We the People   38
3. China   44
4. Current Affairs   50
5. Divorce   76
6. Tucson   104
7. Diabetes   112
8. P.P.S   118
9. Homeland Security   126
10. College   144
11. All Souls Day   148
12. Disinformation   158
13. Gavrilo Princip   176
14. Apophis   192
15. War Games   202
16. New Jersey   222
17. Arizona   228
18. Survival Of the Fittest   236
19. Guardian Angels   256
20. Acapulco   266
21. Exopolitics   270
22. Greenland   294
23. The Future   322
24. What If   326
25. About the Author   328

APOPHIS 2029

by
John J. Ventre

(This book is a re-write of *"12/21/2012 A Prophecy"*)
This book is rated "R"

Edited by
Vanessa K. Ventre & Roger Marsh

www.LangPublication.com

Copyright © 2012 John J. Ventre

Also by John Ventre

Books:

Case for UFOs

Apophis 2029

The Ufologist

Day After 2012

12/21/2012 A Prophecy

UFOs over Pennsylvania

String Theory of the Unexplained

An Alternative History of Mankind

TV:

Hangar 1

UFO Hunters

Alien Mysteries

UFOs over Earth

Close Encounters

UFOs over Pittsburgh

Anderson Cooper Show

String Theory of the Unexplained

UFO Conspiracy: Hunt for the Truth

"And you were dead in your trespasses and sins, in which you formerly walked according to the course of this world, according to the prince of the power of the **AIR (UFOs)**, of the spirit that is now working in the sons of disobedience." (Ephesians 2:1–2) . . . also known as the Morningstar and can appear as an angel of light (orbs)!

SEVEN SEALS:

Revelation 6:1-2

And I saw when the Lamb opened one of the seals, and I heard, as it were the noise of thunder, one of the four beasts saying, Come and see.
And I saw, and behold a white horse: and he that sat on him had a bow; and a crown was given unto him: and he went forth conquering, and to conquer.

Revelation 6:3-4

And when he had opened the second seal, I heard the second beast say, Come and see.
And there went out another horse [that was] red: and [power] was given to him that sat thereon to take peace from the earth, and that they should kill one another: and there was given unto him a great sword.

Revelation 6:5-6

And when he had opened the third seal, I heard the third beast say, Come and see. And I beheld, and lo a black horse; and he that sat

on him   had a pair of balances in his hand.
And I heard a voice in the midst of the four beasts say, a measure
of wheat for a penny, and three measures of barley for a penny;
and [see] thou hurt not the oil and the wine.

Revelation 6:7-8

And when he had opened the fourth seal, I heard the voice of the
fourth beast say, Come and see. And I looked, and behold a pale
horse: and his name that sat on him was Death, and Hell followed
with him.
And power was given unto them over the fourth part of the earth,
to kill with sword, and with hunger, and with death, and with the
beasts of the earth.

Revelation 6:7-8

And when he had opened the fourth seal, I heard the voice of the
fourth beast say, Come and see. And I looked, and behold a pale
horse: and his name that sat on him was Death, and Hell followed
with him.
And power was given unto them over the fourth part of the earth,
to kill with sword, and with hunger, and with death, and with the
beasts of the earth.

Revelation 6:12-17

And I beheld when he had opened the sixth seal, and, lo, there was
a great earthquake; and the sun became black as sackcloth of hair,
and the moon became as blood;
And the stars of the heavens fell unto the earth, even as a fig tree
casteth her untimely figs, when she is shaken of a mighty wind. And
the heavens departed as a scroll when it is rolled together; and
every mountain and island was moved out of their places.
And the kings of the earth, and the great men, and the rich men,
and the chief captains, and the mighty men, and every bondman,
and every free man, hid themselves in the dens and in the rocks of

the mountains; And said to the mountains and rocks, Fall on us, and hide us from the face of him that sitteth on the throne, and from the wrath of the Lamb:

 For the great day of his wrath is come; and who shall be able to stand?

Revelation 8:1-6

And when he had opened the seventh seal, there was silence in heaven about the space of half an hour. And I saw the seven angels which stood before God; and to them were given seven trumpets. And another angel came and stood at the altar, having a golden censer; and there was given unto him much incense, that he should offer [it] with the prayers of all saints upon the golden altar which was before the throne.

And the smoke of the incense, [which came] with the prayers of the saints, ascended up before God out of the angel's hand. And the angel took the censer, and filled it with fire of the altar, and cast [it] into the earth: and there were voices, and thundering, and lightning, and an earthquake. And the seven angels who had the seven trumpets prepared themselves to sound.

Revelation 16:1

And I heard a great voice out of the temple saying to the seven angels, Go your ways, and pour out the vials of the wrath of God upon the earth. (34)

Eschatology is the study of the teachings in the Bible concerning the end times or of the period of time dealing with the return of Christ and the events that follow. Eschatological subjects include the Resurrection, the Rapture, the Tribulation, the Binding of Satan, the Three witnesses, the Final Judgment, Armageddon, and The New Heavens and the New Earth.

My question is if make can create a situation so bad that it would force the return of Jesus to save us?

If you read beyond this point, you will lose the protection of God.

FORWARD

End Times Prophecy

Since becoming the Pennsylvania Mutual UFO Network (MUFON) State Director in 2007, I've had many opportunities to lecture about UFOs at conferences and various radio shows all over the northeast. My daughter, Vanessa, attends most of these conferences. She often reminds me that she likes my "End Times" talk the best. I coincidentally published "*12/21/2012 A Prophecy*" within weeks of becoming MUFON's Pennsylvania State Director. What follows is an outline of my "End Times" talk which covers various cultures and new age thoughts along with scientific facts.

All over the world doomsday vaults are being built. To be precise, 1,400 seed banks are being built and managed by the Global Crop Diversity Trust Board. These vaults are deep within mountain ranges at 300 feet above sea level and house millions of seeds at -1 degrees and can store them for 1,000 years. These vaults must be completed and serve to safeguard against asteroid strikes, nuclear wars, climate change and natural disasters.

In 2004, the asteroid Apophis was discovered. Apophis, the ancient Egyptian God of chaos who took the form of a serpent and, as the foe of the sun god, Re, represented all that was evil. Although the serpent generally symbolized divinity and royalty, Apophis inhabited the underworld and personified death and destruction. Each day Apophis encountered Re at an appointed hour in the sun god's ritual journey through the night in his divine bark. The voice of Apophis betrayed him and Seth, who rode as guardian in front of Re, attacked him with daggers, slaying him. The ancient Egyptians thought they could help Re by reciting prayers against Apophis. (Encyclopedia Britannica)

Project Space-Guard was formed in 1998 by NASA to identify all near Earth asteroids. There are 1,100 such objects larger than one mile wide. The categorizing was to be completed by 2020. The United States and China have the greatest likelihood of a strike. The asteroid Apophis has been tracked since 2004 and will be tracked for years. It is three quarters of a mile wide and passes the earth and gets closer every seven years. These size asteroids strike earth every 70,000 years. Apophis has a 2.8 percent or 1/37 chance of hitting the earth on April 13, 2036, with the force of a 500 megaton bomb. Apophis is not a planet killer, but it would wipe out a large city or small country upon impact. Its trajectory is across the Yucatan peninsula and across the Atlantic Ocean towards Nigeria. It is the first asteroid promoted to a threat level four on the Torino scale which measures the threat level of near Earth objects. NASA believes it has time to deal with the problem. In 2029, Apophis will pass by and dip below the height of our satellites, skimming the Earth's atmosphere just 22,000 miles away. Satellites orbit at 26,000 miles or one tenth the distance to the moon. It is then that corrective action would be taken unless its path has changed by colliding with the smallest pebble. We are not technologically prepared to divert an asteroid on such short notice and have not yet tested the technology. It will also be visible in the night sky in 2029 from Europe, Africa and Asia.

In April of 2008, I told everyone I knew that Apophis would pass by on Friday the 13th and there should be interesting news in the newspapers and on TV. To my surprise, there was not one news article written on Apophis when it passed by closer to the Earth than to the moon. I was stunned that the media would keep this story silent for the "good" of the public. In 2015, they did the same again.

In March of 2009, with two days' notice, the 152 foot asteroid DD45 was discovered. It passed by at twice the distance of our satellites at 44,750 miles from Earth. It was the same size as the asteroid that exploded over Tunguska Siberia in 1908 which flattened 80 million trees on 80 square miles. Siberia contains 25 percent of the world's forests. Amazingly, the Siding Spring Space

Observatory reported that, "No object of that size or larger has been observed to come closer to the Earth." Apparently our Space Observatory never heard of Apophis.

In a November 2011 *USA Today* article, it mentioned that the 1,300 foot asteroid 2005 YU55 will pass 202,000 miles from earth. "It is the closest visit to Earth by a space rock this size in more than three decades." The article went on to speak about other asteroids but there was no mention of Apophis which is twice the size and will pass four times closer in four years.

It is instances like this that reinforce my belief that the government censors what we are told and that the truth about many anomalies are not revealed to us. Is the urgency and silence regarding Apophis a cover for a larger more deadly asteroid that has targeted Earth or do they know that Apophis will strike on its next go around?

The Mayans, Toltec's, Hopi Indians, I-Ching, and Hindu Kali Yuga all have end time prophecies. Nearly every culture has a legend of the Great Flood . . . because it did happen.

The Mayan culture lasted from 300 BC to 1500 AD. The period I will review is from 300-900 AD when the culture peaked. This Stone Age culture suddenly developed suspension bridges, astronomy, medicine and the most accurate calendar we have ever seen. It is more accurate than our Gregorian calendar. Mayan records say that a dark rift exists in the center of the sky. In 2002 we discovered a black hole at the center of our Milky Way Galaxy. In 1993 we discovered that from the Earth's view, the sun will rise in the center plane of the Milky Way Galaxy. This happens every 25,800 years due to the fact that our rotation changes by one degree every 72 years. The Mayans have three calendars and one is on a 25,800 year cycle. The last Ice Age started 25,800 years ago and marked the end of Neanderthal and the rise of Cro-Magnon man whose 10,000 year appearance and disappearance could not have been a product of evolution. There was also another ice Age three cycles ago or 75,000 years ago.

The most sacred Mayan text is the Popol Vuh which tells of extraterrestrials coming to Earth and creating a perfect human species and then destroying it and replacing it with a "dumbed down" version. "It is said that those ones that were created had no father, no mother, yet they were called men. They were not born of women, they were not produced by creators, only by a miracle of magic were they created." This is a similar story to older Sumerian tablets found 8,000 miles away.

The Mayan legend of Kukulkan says that a Caucasian male with blond hair rose from the sea and had an elongated skull. He gave the Mayans their technology and before returning to the sea, he said that he would return in 500 years. When the Spaniard Cortez arrived on March 5, 1519, he was mistaken for the return of Kukulkan. Cortez brought with him diseases that killed 90 percent of the Aztecs and much of the Mayan population while he raided their gold and burned their libraries similar to the burning of the Library of Alexandria by the Romans.

Mayan knowledge is similar to the primitive African Dogon tribes of Mali. When British Colonialists discovered the tribe, they worshiped the twin star system of Sirius. They have no technology yet they knew all about the star system and the hidden dwarf star. They believe that ETs visited us from Sirius and gave us knowledge and will return in the Age of Aquarius. Carl Sagan said it is impossible for the Dogans to know of and correctly identify the location of Sirius.

The Hopi Indians (500 BC to the present) say that a blue star will approach earth and, "The Earth will be shaken by an explosion that will rock North and South America". There have been three previous great cleansings by an asteroid or volcano, the Ice Age and a Great Flood. "The Sacred Ones will arrive via Flying Shield". This resembles the Book of Enoch where Ezekiel, in 593 BC, goes up into a "Flying Wheel". The Hopis perform Kachina dances where their outfits look like space suits with helmets.

There has been other Hopi prophecy that has come true. "We will talk through spider webs" which has been accepted to be phone lines. "We will ride in carriages without horses. Women will wear men's clothing." And the pants if I may add that!

"In the end, a purifier named Pahana will arrive to destroy evil people. There will be flood, famine and hail storms (similar to the Book of Revelation)."

Edgar Cayce, also known as the "Sleeping Prophet", saw the destruction of Japan and the west coast of the United States as they dipped into the Pacific Ocean. He foresaw upheavals at both poles and a reversal of hot and cold climates. In the 1920s, years before scientists discovered them; he predicted solar bursts or sun spots which heat the planet.

Jean Dixon had a vision of Washington DC as a barren wasteland. She had a vision of Queen Nefertiti holding a Muslim baby boy who would grow to be charismatic and a lover of peace at first and then become the Antichrist. Dixon also correctly predicted the 1967 Apollo tragedy, FDR's death, the JFK-RFK-MLK assassinations, and that Churchill would lose his election after winning WWII.

In 1124 AD, Father Malachy O'Morgair, the first Irish Saint, wrote the Papal Prophecy and named every Pope from 1124 to the last Pope. He said there will be 266 Popes; Pope Benedict XVI was number 265. The end of days started in March 2013 with the naming of the 266th Pope. The Vatican kept Father Malachy's writings locked away until 1595. Father Malachy also correctly predicted his own death on November 2, 1148, in Clairvaux, France, of natural causes.

Zecharia Sitchin, the author of *The 12th Planet*, concluded that there is a planet on a 3,600 year orbit that will pass close to the Earth. He based his theories on Sumerian text that he was able to translate. I always doubted this theory due to the fact that deep space is -434 degrees and solar radiation will boil your blood and dissolve DNA. I recently read that there may be a distant planet on an elliptical orbit that orbits a dwarf star which keeps it warm and cannot be detected until it is very near to Earth. Sitchin also spoke of their people being named the Nephilim, same as the Bible.

Other prophecies speak of the magnetic poles reversing. We know that they are weakening right now and have reversed in the past. It is evident in the geologic stratum of rocks. The weakening of the magnetic poles will cause our brain waves to change and so will we. A reversal of the poles would wreck all electronics, satellite transmissions and communications. This has occurred in the past as an 1859 solar flare fried all telegraphic systems worldwide. Our magnetic fields reflect radiation and a weakening would increase the greenhouse effect, melt the poles and cause severe climate change. All life support will be under stress; air, oceans and agriculture.

There has always been climate change. It is a natural process minimally affected by mankind. In 6000 BC temperatures dropped eight degrees. From 900-1300 AD temperatures warmed seven degrees. Temperatures then cooled seven degrees through 1850. Our planet is still warming since the last Ice Age and will rise 10 degrees by 2100 and sea levels will rise by three feet. There have been four Ice Ages; 800K, 200K, 75K and 26K years ago and the cycle is getting shorter each time. Every Ice Age was climate change. We are not seeing sea levels rise now because the continental shelf is rising as the northern ice sheets melt. By 2050, Niagara Falls will be a stream as it tilts backwards toward Lake Erie. Antarctica contains 90 percent of the world's ice and it is not melting; it is getting thicker at the center. That is why you don't see a sea level rise. Also, any ice that is floating on water displaces the same when melted. Only ice on land adds to sea level when melted. If all the ice melted around the world, sea levels would rise 200 feet. More proof of bad climate change science includes the Mars ice cap melting in conjunction with our arctic cap and the carbon levels in Pluto's atmosphere doubling. Solar activity is causing this.

Some people believe that evolution is speeding up. We only use 10 percent of our brain capacity and only 3 percent of our DNA. The other 97 percent is junk DNA. It is hard to believe that God had no purpose for the 97 percent or that we may be ready to evolve into the next stage of humanity as we use 20 percent of our brain capacity and 10 percent of our DNA; humanity 2.0. In a March 2009 poll, only 39 percent of respondents believe in the theory of evolution.

Some believe that there will be a shift in our consciousness away from materialism and towards the next level of our potential. It will be the end of a male dominated society dependent on government and centered on war. There will be a global wakeup call. Time will seem to speed up. People will be compelled to perform righteous deeds and will have dreams or visions that come true. They will see loves ones that passed and remember past lives. They will hear voices while awake and then see angels. There will be an evolution of consciousness and our psychic ability will increase. There will be a singularity where all people are connected psychically. We will anticipate each other's thoughts and actions and sense impending danger. Crime would dramatically decrease as we would know what each other have done and plan to do. This telepathic capability is the next step in being able to operate vehicles, electronics and spacecraft using our minds. The Roswell craft had no visible controls. Indigo or Star children have been born since 1982. They are technologically savvy, question authority, have higher IQ's than their parents. They will refuse to support the government, pay taxes and enlist in the military. The meta-gene factor is a biological variant that lies dormant in select humans. When activated, a chromosomal combustion takes place in the pineal gland causing psychic abilities.

An April 2009 news article read that "Tibetan Monks predict that extraterrestrials will save Earth". Tibetan Monks have used remote viewing for thousands of years. They see regional wars and an increase in terrorism. They see a nuclear war between China,

India and Russia over natural resources. Extraterrestrials have been watching us and will intervene. They have intervened in the past. They will reveal themselves so that we will not be scared. We are destined to see and interact with them. Man will not be allowed to alter the future or destroy this planet. We will be more in tune with spirituality and the mind, body, soul reincarnation connection to God.

Few know that Sir Isaac Newton spent more than half his life trying to decode the Bible. Michael Drosnin wrote the Bible Code books in which the Old Testament, *Gone with the Wind* and *War and Peace* were analyzed through a computer program. These three books all have about the same number of words. Numbers were applied to letters in order to search for words found on the same page that tell us the future. The Bible is a cryptogram and foretells the future. Over fifty prophecies were discovered in the Bible as compared to just one in the other two texts. "Only God could've written the Bible. It was sealed before God." I also remember reading that the Torah is written without spaces and that if you change or alter a single letter, you can alter the future. This is a form of *Goatia* where words give off frequencies and have ancient power. The Bible is the only book that reads you as you read it!

Many scientists believe that Earth is past the tipping point; we're heading toward our galactic midnight. We are suffering from over population, pollution, ozone depletion, terrorism, climate change and economic collapse. Earthquake activity and hurricane strength has increased each of the past four decades. Yet, we have the technological powers attributed to past gods. A primitive culture would view modern humans as gods.

Buried in our DNA is the collective memory of past devastation. Evolution does not explain the sudden jumps or advances in development. Whole new species suddenly appear. Our DNA shows mutations in intelligence 6,000 years ago when the Bible claims man was created, 17,000 years ago when Homo sapiens replaced Cro-Magnon and 26,000 years ago when Cro-Magnon replaced Neanderthal man and 35,000 years ago when the DLL gene was introduced to humans enlarging the skull and brain. Homo sapiens have 223 genes that are not found in its predecessors and could not be the result of evolution. Humans have the most diseases and genetic mutations of any species on Earth. If we evolved from apes and chimps then why did only one type stand and run to survive and become a meat eater when it is easier to pick fruits and nuts? Why didn't they all evolve for the same reasons? If we evolved from apes and chimps, then why do chimps have 200 genetic defects and humans have 6,000 or one for every 200 births? This may be because we contain the DNA of two species. DNA is like a cross word puzzle. Yet, our bodies contain the same percentage of salt that ocean water does and we also have the same percentage of water as there is land to water on the Earth.

In a November 1980, interview with Cardinal Ratzinger regarding the third secret of Fatima, he said, "When one reads that the oceans will flood entire portions of land; that human beings will die in minutes, and in millions, then one should not desire publication of the secret. Knowledge means responsibility. It is dangerous when one only wishes to satisfy his curiosity, if he is not prepared to do something about his discovery, or if he is convinced we can do nothing to prevent prophesized disasters from happening."

No prophecy discussion would be complete without a discussion of the Book of Revelation. "A star will fall to Earth by the name of Wormwood with the breaking of the sixth seal". Will this be an asteroid strike? The Red Horse signifies war. We've had 9-11 and Iraq. Will there be a global war for resources? The Black Horse signifies famine. I wonder if it doesn't signify the want of oil. There will be food shortages; the United States feeds 100 countries. The Pale Horse signifies plague. One million people a year die of malaria. Small pox is the only plague that we have cured. Polio is the only disease that we have cured. Will it be a manmade pandemic? There are only three species that wage war; ants, chimps and humans. Chimps are four times stronger than humans and can weigh up to 200 pounds. The White Horse signifies the rise of the Antichrist. He will be charismatic, persuasive and a peace lover at first. There will be seven years of bounty prior to his rise. Possibly the housing and stock market boom from 2001 through 2008. Then, 25 percent or 1.8 billion humans will die. The sky will go dark from an asteroid strike or a super volcano eruption. We know that there have been five massive extinctions in the past and supposedly evolution has repeated itself all over again.

It would take an asteroid of at least one mile in size to cause an earth changing event. An asteroid over four miles would be an extinction event. When an asteroid strikes, it is not like the "Deep Impact "movie. You don't get to watch it for minutes as it streams across the sky. If you can see a large asteroid, you will be incinerated. It will enter our atmosphere at 29,000 mph or 60 times faster than a speeding bullet. It will strike at 2,500 mph. The jolt will resonate like a church bell many times throughout the planet. Two seconds later, 10 miles away, a magnitude eight earthquake will be felt. Twenty seconds later, a 700 mph heat blast will incinerate everything.

There are seven Super Volcanoes around the world. Three are located in the United States. Ninety percent of humans died 74,000 years ago when a Super Volcano in Indonesia blew. We know this from our female mitochondrial DNA. Yellowstone Park is a 40 by 60 miles Super Volcano which is 40,000 years overdue from blowing. In January of 2009, it experienced 21 tremors and the ground is swelling up and moving lakes and hill sides. The caldera is one half the size of Long Island or Puerto Rico. It would blow ash into our upper stratosphere and darken the skies for weeks. Acid rain could kill our oceans and all crops would fail. Maybe this is the urgency to complete 1,400 seed banks around the world. There are also 129 Deep Underground Military Bases (DUMB) in the U.S. with a connecting tunnel system that may account for the hum that many experience. The bread belt of the United States would be covered in eight feet of ash. There have been five great civilizations; Lemuria, Atlantis, Egypt, Rome and the United States. Could this be how the United States comes to an end?

At a conference, I was asked what makes me think that the United States is a great civilization. My answer was that everything that this world is came from Western societies; mainly the United States and Europe. Technology, the rule of law, an end to slavery, today's freedoms are all products of the United States. Eighty percent of all new technology, inventions and patents are "made in America". Militarily, it is the greatest civilization that has ever existed. If a Super Volcano or asteroid doesn't destroy the United States, then it will be the mental illness of Americans who seem to hate this country when it is the greatest place to live!

Like Hamlet's "To be or not to be", picture your current frustration with housing prices, stock prices, and unemployment. Everyone is upset and on the edge. Now imagine a series of natural disasters that disrupt the food chain; we lose all power for weeks and regress to feudal times. An asteroid, a global earthquake or a Super Volcano; all events that you have no control over. It's predicted, it's possible, and everyone senses in their collective memory that it is coming!

PROLOGUE
**"Any sufficiently advanced technology
is indistinguishable from magic"**
(Arthur C. Clarke)

Scholars and professors would like you to believe that history, like evolution, moves in a straight line. Scientists want repeatable, verifiable results, but sometimes a phenomenon happens rarely or only once. Anthropologists and paleontologists love to run the clock backwards using carbon dating, DNA and fossil records. But in fact, the clock is moving forward with genetic modifications, stem cell research, biocompatible computer chips and trans-humanism. Will we create a spin-off human race like the Demi-Gods of Greek mythology or become extinct?

Evolution teaches that life arose from an unguided natural process. The Bible teaches that life is too complex to be accomplished by chance. These scientists, as well as religious leaders, will fight to protect their transparent theories. In the course of doing this, they reject, insult, deceive and attempt to debunk evidence conflicting with their ideas. These same scientists come to conflicting conclusions when analyzing out of place evidence. Like children locked in a closet, they rationalize that eyewitness accounts, which is the basis of our justice system, are the worst kind of scientific evidence. It has literally become "political science". Does the theory of co-evolution (including a soul) fit best?

Even the Freedom of Information Act regards the public as the "public enemy" when they black out sentences and paragraphs for security reasons. The acceptance of the paranormal would destroy the basis of science taught in our universities. Therefore, scientists sit in the cheap seats and decide not to play. (2, 12, 17, 26)

There has never been a satisfactory explanation for the sudden development of civilization around 4000 BC. At that time, mankind experienced the sudden appearance of Samaria, Egypt and Peru. According to evolutionary biologists, human beings are the result of snail-paced evolution. Then why can we find no archeological evidence of a natural progression? Instead, we find only missing links!

If the Earth were a 24-hour clock, single cell life formed 12 hours ago; dinosaurs, one hour ago; mankind, 38 seconds ago and modern man only one second ago. It appears that God has left this universe like a clockmaker who put his work in motion and left it running. (21)

There is a global conspiracy of disinformation, confirmation bias, cognitive dissonance and consensus science from archeology to UFOs to politics and religion. Our world leaders keep the truth from the public, assuming, whether rightly or wrongly, that the people "can't handle the truth." If the facts don't fit the Theory of Evolution, then the facts need to be disregarded.

Through the use of carbon dating, for example, it has been discovered that the Earth periodically cleanses itself. This technology has shown many artifacts from all over the world as existing in a time "out of place." There is overwhelming evidence disputing religious leader's theories concerning the Earth. They continue to believe the world began 6,000 years ago. Yet, 230 different cultures tell a similar story of a Great Flood and dinosaurs are found with skin, muscle and tissue still intact. Pottery, jewelry, modern human skulls and bones and shoe prints have been found in coal deposits that are 250 thousand years old! Every archeological finding pushes our modern existence further back in history, never the other direction.

In the film "Planet of the Apes", the Simian leaders would do anything to suppress the truth. As we do today with people, the ape's leaders followed the convenient premise that the apes "can't handle the truth." Like a recessive gene, what truth could be so horrible that our world leaders must protect humanity from its discovery? What truth caused the Brookings Institute in DC in

1960 to decide that people can't be told about UFOs? (2, 12, 17, 26)

We are also left with the inconvenient truth that "some know" and have prepared for an "event" that happens on a known cycle. Only, you and I won't be included in the "rescued few" that restart humanity. How can the U.S. be in $20 trillion in federal debt and another $2 trillion in state debt? That number continues to rise but equals around $70K per person. Could it be that there was never any way to pay this debt off or break even? That they just appeased the masses with social programs and handouts because it never mattered? That they have been funneling money to a deep underground survival system for the chosen few? I thought I grew up in the greatest country on Earth only to find out that most everything we've accomplished has been subsidized with Social Security Monopoly money. What if no society can pay for everyone? What if we can only advance when everyone is productive and educated and survival of the fittest is the rule? What if there is no way to sustain the bottom 40 percent or any social programs? What if they've known this all along and that "something" is coming and it never really mattered?

This book will challenge the Creation-Evolution mythos that you have been taught. The real question is whether you believe we evolved from apes and chimps or we were born from God or a Superior race and still retain some of their abilities. Regardless of whether Jesus was the son of God or an ET Ambassador, based on how we treated him last time, we should expect something very different next time!

You are reading this book because you were meant to!

"The suppression of uncomfortable ideas may be common in religion and politics, but it is not the path to knowledge, it has no place in science." (Carl Sagan 1980)

All over the world, enigmatic artifacts have been found that do not fit the accepted geologic or historical timeline. Do they offer a radically different view of our world?

Photo courtesy Frontiers of Reality
Metallic vase found inside solid rock.
(Source: Scientific American)

Of all the many unexplained phenomena, experiences, and objects in the world, ones that hold a great deal of fascination for me are what I categorize as "ancient anomalies." Also called "ooparts," these are objects that by scientific measure are very old, but in form or construction appear to be quite modern. They are impossible fossils, out-of-time technology, and anachronistic artifacts. In other words, if our history of the world is correct, they just should not exist. And there are many examples - many more than geologists, archaeologists and other scientists care to admit. Why are they so fascinating? First of all, most of them are real and tangible. Unlike ghosts, mysterious creatures like Bigfoot and the Loch Ness Monster, and phenomena like telekinesis; these unexplained artifacts have been seen, touched and examined. There they are before our eyes, with nothing in our current experience or knowledge to explain them. Second, because they do exist and do not fit the standard scientific timeline or geologic and anthropologic chronology, they suggest, in their own baffling way, that either our dating techniques are wrong, geology does not progress the way we suppose it does, or there is far more to the history of life on this planet than we currently know about. In any case, these bothersome ooparts upset established, orthodox thinking. Here are a few, for your consideration:

ADVANCED TECHNOLOGY

These are the best kind of "ooparts" because they have been documented, often photographed and examined by experts:

"Spark plug" in a geode: In 1961, the owners of a gift shop in Olancha, CA, found a fossil-encrusted geode in the Coso Mountains. When one of the owners cut the geode in half with a diamond saw, however, he found an object inside that was obviously artificial. The object had a metal core surrounded by layers of a ceramic-like material and a hexagonal wooden sleeve. When X-rayed, the object seemed to resemble a modern spark plug or some other electronic component. Yet it had been completely encased in a geode that was covered with fossils estimated to be 500,000 years old.

Very old nail: In 1851, *The Illinois Springfield Republican* reported that a businessman named Hiram de Witt found a fist-sized chunk of auriferous quartz while on a trip to California. When it accidentally slipped from his hands, it split open, and out fell a cut-iron nail. The quartz was about one million years old.

Gold thread among the rock: The *Times of London* reported in 1844 that workmen quarrying stone near the River Tweed in Scotland found a piece of gold thread embedded in the rock eight feet below ground level.

Chain in coal: In 1891, Mrs. S. W. Culp, of Morrisonville, IL, was fragmenting coal into smaller pieces for her kitchen stove when she noticed a chain stuck in the coal. The chain measured about 10 inches long and was later found to be made of eight-carat gold, and described as being "of antique and quaint workmanship."

According to the *Morrisonville Times* of June 11, investigators concluded that the chain had not simply been accidentally dropped in with the coal, since some of the coal still clung to the chain, while the part that had separated from it still bore the impression of where the chain had been encased.

Ancient modern tools: While quarrying limestone in 1786, workers came to a bed of sand about 50 feet below ground level. In the layer of sand, however, they found the stumps of stone pillars and fragments of half-worked rock. Digging further, they found coins, the petrified wooden handles of hammers, and pieces of other petrified wooden tools. The sand in which the discovery was made was beneath a layer of limestone dated at 300 million years old.

Mysterious vase: In June, 1851, *Scientific American* reprinted a report from the *Boston Transcript* about how a metallic vase, found in two parts, was dynamited out of solid rock 15 feet below the surface in Dorchester, MA. The bell-shaped vase (see photo), measuring 4-1/2 inches high and 6-1/2 inches at the base, was composed of a zinc and silver alloy. On the sides were figures of flowers in bouquet arrangements, inlaid with pure silver. The estimated age of the rock out of which it came: 100,000 years.

Too-old screw: In 1865, a two-inch metal screw was discovered in a piece of feldspar unearthed from the Abbey Mine in Treasure City, NV. The screw had long ago oxidized, but its form - particularly the shape of its threads - could be clearly seen in the feldspar. The stone was calculated to be 21 million years in age.

Ancient nanotechnology: In 1991-1993, gold prospectors on the Narada River on the eastern side of the Ural Mountains in Russia found unusual, mostly spiral-shaped objects, the smallest measuring about 1/10,000th of an inch! The objects are composed of copper and the rare metals tungsten and molybdenum. Tests showed the objects to be between 20,000 and 318,000 years old.

(Source: Before it's News, May 12, 2012)

Chapter 1

SPINNING THE SAUCERS

"This is where we fight. This is where we die!"
(King Leonidas)

On September 19, 1976, U.S. satellites picked up a large object entering Iranian airspace. We immediately proceeded to notify the Iranian military of the occurrence while continuing to monitor the object. The duty officer informed Assistant Deputy Commander of Operations Yousefit of the violation of their airspace. No protocol existed for this type of scenario. Commander Yousefit gave the order to scramble an F-4 Phantom jet from Shahrokhi Air Force Base.

At 1:30 a.m., the jet headed north towards the object that was 70 miles away. As the jet approached, it lost communication and electronic capabilities. Each time the jet turned south, away from the object, electronics were restored.

A second F-4 jet was launched and approached the object. The object was picked up on radar and glowed intensely. As the jet approached at Mach-1 speed, the object instantly rose from 5,000 feet altitude to 40,000 feet and accelerated at 15,000 mph. As the jet closed the gap on the now stationary object, the pilot could see red, blue, green and orange lights on the object. The lights strobe in a rectangular pattern. A second smaller craft emerged from the UFO and headed directly at the F-4. The larger object again moved but this time maintained a 25 mile distance between itself and the F-4.

The F-4 crew armed an AIM-9 missile as they began to panic. The F-4 weapons control and communications functions went off line. The F-4 dove to avoid the object. The smaller UFO followed the F-4 into a negative-G dive and pulled away after a short time and allowed the F-4's systems to restore. The F-4 communicated with the base which observed the incident. The F-4 was ordered to chase the UFO and again the same system failure ensued.

The F-4 was then ordered to return to base. All power to the base turned off. This was observed by the flight crews of KLM and Egyptian Airlines. As the F-4 returned, the smaller UFO followed. It closed to within 15 miles . . . then 10 miles . . . then five miles until it veered away as it got dangerously close. The UFO was now in front of them and stationary in their path. The F-4 again dove but the crew observed the UFO descend erratically and land not far from the base on a dry lake bed. The F-4 was ordered to engage.

As the F-4 approached the landed object, the F-4 armed its missile once again and locked in on the target. As the weapons panel indicated that the missile was ready to fire, the pilot gave the order not to fire and radioed the base. A recovery team was sent to the scene while the larger UFO disappeared from sight and radar.

The Americans insisted on knowing what happened but the Iranians insisted that the smaller UFO flew just above ground level and returned to the mother ship. The larger UFO was later seen over Cairo and Lisbon before disappearing over the Atlantic Ocean.

In 1979 President Carter, the weakest U.S. President of the 20th Century, failed to support the Shah of Iran which caused his fall from power. Iran was the strongest U.S. ally in the region and a key listening post on the former Soviet Union. Sixty percent of the world's oil resides in this region. The result was the rise of a theocratic, evil, and Islamic, anti-American state. President Clinton proceeded to cut costs and weaken our military and C.I.A. while aligning himself with Saddam Hussein in Iraq. This gave rise to an Iranian terrorist state.

Current U.S. President Datchet had made a peace proposal to solve the ongoing Middle East saga. Although the Torah gives this land to Israel, he offered U.S. citizenship to all Israelis as long as they sell their businesses, homes and property to the Arabs. The

Arab Nations would pay a 40 percent premium over the assessed value, as opposed to bulldozing the area like the Gaza Strip, for the Israelis to leave in peace. This would solve the never ending wars and the U.S. could use this highly educated and skilled workforce. It was an objective business decision. When it was turned down, Israel joined NATO which meant that NATO member nations must defend Israel.

Iran's first strike against our new embassy in Baghdad and the poisoning of the New York drinking water supply again signaled a turning point in our history. The U.S. cut the cables and communication lines that lay at the seafloor just outside the port city of Dubai and embargoed tankers with refined gasoline from entering Iran. Iran is a large exporter of crude oil but imports 60 percent of its gasoline. This was the U.S. response to the kidnapping of 27 soldiers by al-Qaeda in exchange for the release of 9-11 terrorist Zacarias Moussaoui from a maximum detention facility in Florence, CO, where he has been held for 28 years. The U.S. also cut off $1 billion in aid to Palestine and other democratically elected radical Muslim governments. Israel refused to negotiate with Hamas after its democratic election and legal formation of a Palestinian army. Israel destroyed Iran's nuclear power plant at Bushehr and fuel enrichment plant at Natanz after the U.N. Security Council weakly sanction Iran with a slap on the wrist for its uranium processing. Israel called it "Have nukes or have a future" program.

Iran focused attention on this one plant while the real research and development was taking place in numerous sites hidden in mountain caves. Fearing a U.S. invasion in Iran like Afghanistan and Iraq, Iran struck. The Mullahs represent God's view and not popular opinion. They do not prize life in the hereafter more than on Earth so deterrence does not register with them.

Iran had upgraded its "shooting star" Shahab 3 missiles which have a range of 800 miles; developed high speed torpedoes that travel at 223 mph or four times faster than a conventional one;

acquired remote control Kowsar surface to air missiles along with Fadjr-5 multiple warhead stealth missiles; set up sophisticated Russian air defenses by purchasing SS-NX-26 and S-300 missiles which can fire at two targets up to 20,000 feet; purchased Russian KH-55 cruise missiles which carried the nuclear strike on Baghdad. They stockpiled armor piercing bullets, sniper rifles and night vision goggles having misread the U.S. ban on guns as a sign of weakness. They believed a fight was coming and would use Hezbollah terrorist volunteers across the region to defeat us. Iran funds Syria who supplies Hamas and Hezbollah and has funded every attack against the U.S.

Russia has a naval base in southern Iran and has funded them with military advisors and training personnel. Russia recently warned that if Iran is attacked, it would be a direct threat to Russian national security and stationed its nuclear carrier Admiral Kuznetsov there.

France, Germany, China and Russia stood back and watched while Iran did their dirty work. China had transferred sophisticated technology to Iran in an effort to undermine the U.S. and acquire oil contracts from Tehran. The U.S. had sanctioned China for violating controls on the transfer of weapons technology but the chess match had been in place for quite a while. China was in its puberty while it believed the U.S. was in its menopause as an industrial and military leader. When the Chinese Taikonauts landed on the moon in 2025, they neatly folded the U.S. flag planted by Neil Armstrong and Buzz Aldrin 60 years earlier and replaced it with a starched Chinese flag that wouldn't wave in a vacuum. . . The antagonistic act so infuriated the Americans that they decided to bill China for its theft of intellectual property from movies to pirated and counterfeit products and its failure to honor its trade agreements resulting in a $3 trillion dollar price tag which negated the U.S. debt to China.(26)

Iran warned the U.S. not to attack or they would shut down our power grid, Internet and all satellite links. The U.S. launched stealth fighters from Turkey and Saudi Arabia and from its 30 military bases in the area. Iran had back engineered the crashed drone that was used in the bin Laden killing and cracked our stealth technology and data encryption through back engineering and could track our bombers. The Iranian's sent their own signals through U.S. satellites into the bombers high tech weapons systems and ordered the bombers to fire their machine guns allowing Iranian anti-aircraft guns to see and down the bombers over the Gulf.

Iran responded to Israel, Saudi Arabia and Turkey by launching hundreds of missiles armed with EMP warheads at Tel Aviv, Ankara, Riyadh and Istanbul. The shock wave took all Israel, Saudi and Turkey electronics offline and the following wave of missiles leveled the four cities. The Iranians had also built massive torpedo silos underwater off their coast and launched an attack on the U.S. Naval ships stationed in the Persian Gulf. Like Pearl Harbor, the ships were caught off guard as they picked up the torpedoes too late and were sunk. Iran also launched its Great Prophet Sunburn missiles that fly nine feet above the water surface at mach-2 and then pop up and explode. Every U.S. ship in the Gulf was trapped and vulnerable to attack as the Iranians closed the Straits of Hormuz. The U.S. Navy had never faced weapons like this before. Iran then attacked the Saudi oil facilities and oil stock piles which would make a close range U.S. attack impossible without the ability to refuel.

Saudi Arabia's Royal Air Force which is equipped with Eurofighter Typhoons, Tornado IDS and F-15E Eagle fighters were inoperable.

The Iranians then launched a newly developed Zohal or Saturn attack "plane" that strongly resembled a classic boomerang UFO. Israel was disabled in less than three hours. Since the cable and communication lines to the Middle East were cut, there were no transmissions of this new craft. A very tense 12 hour period ensued which very few people were aware of. Startled by the news of this next generation fighter, the European Union called President Datchet and asked for a U.S. truce with Iran since it feared E.U. surrender was inevitable. The U.S. President laughed at the French delegate's request and said, "Our friends should respect us and our enemies fear us."

Iran's Fars News Agency reported that Muslim nations were cheering Iran's quick defeat of Israel, Turkey and Saudi Arabia and awaited the U.S. response. The Iranian President vowed that the 21st Century would belong to Islam and that Iranian airships would strike the U.S. capital of Washington, DC before nightfall after destroying its navy in the Gulf so easily. This was all feasible since the Iranian craft used antigravity propulsion technology and EMP and laser weaponry. No one knew how Iran could've developed this technology. U.S. satellites watched every move Iran made above ground.

Iran first launched a series of computer virus and Trojan horse attacks on the U.S. The cyber security attacks on critical U.S. infrastructure were joined by the Hacker group "Anonymous" who saw the opportunity to take the U.S. down and free the people from the U.S. monitoring of all cell phone and email transmissions and the holding of U.S. citizens without a hearing which were approved by President Obama years earlier. The electrical grid, nuclear power plants and air traffic controls were under attack from within by these citizen zombie groups who hated the U.S. and the freedom it stood for by bullyingly exercising its military might with little provocation over the years. Iran had also lined hundreds of 55 gallon shipping containers with explosives and these barrels were exploding all over the world in western ports and factories. This was the psychological attack needed before attacking the U.S. on its motherland.

Iran launched all six of its UFO airships and the U.S. monitored their mach-8 or 5,300 mph approach toward the U.S. capital. Seizing on the opportunity, Hezbollah fighters had been aiding Mexican drug cartels all along the U.S. border and they now emerged from their drug tunnels to attack U.S. citizens and police in border communities. Some Hezbollah terrorists were caught months earlier using laser cutters to weaken bridge structures that would mysteriously collapse weeks later. Many fighters were also caught trying to sabotage the Alaskan and Canadian pipelines. (3)

Americans were in frenzy as the fear of being occupied by "towel heads" erupted. The heartland of America was armed and waiting. After 20 minutes, the bay doors of Hanger 28 and 29 opened in Groom Lake, NV, or better known as Area 51. Eight dome-shaped Alien Reproduction X-37 Vehicles or "saucers" from the U.S. Antigravity Squadron were released and headed due East in a direct line of conflict with their Iranian counterparts. President Datchet and the Air Force General Joint Chief were the only two in the crowded Oval office that weren't stunned. President Datchet explained that we did indeed back engineer the Roswell UFO craft and were saving it for a day like today. The President did say that he had no idea that the Iranians had done the same with the UFO incident in 1976. He was confident that the upgrades we had made over the years would ensure victory for us and that no Iranian craft would launch an attack on U.S. soil. It took 10 years to kill Osama bin Laden and now it was time to kill his dream which was funded by Iran. Vice President Alvarez asked what the plan is if we cannot defeat them. The Air Force Joint Chief quickly replied that we would have no choice but to surrender. The room went silent. The tremendous air speeds of the 14 craft meant that they would meet over the Atlantic Ocean in less than a half hour. Two U.S. saucers cut their speed to half and fell back as a last line of defense.

Apparently the over confident Iranian crafts had no tracking equipment or were utterly surprised by the U.S. attack force. The U.S. craft used an electricity field around its skin to create an electrostatic field ahead of the body. This reduced friction or drag and moved the air out of its way leaving no signature to track. The U.S. craft also had "reactive skin" which enabled it to change color like a chameleon and blend against its background. The six Iranian airships were destroyed by the U.S. warships on the first pass as all six U.S. fighters locked their lasers on their designated opponent and fired plasma shells. The plasma shell fires at 10,000 miles per second. The Iranian craft all fell into the rough Atlantic seas. All eight U.S. craft hovered to observe their sinking opponent and then turned at 40 G's and returned to Nevada within the hour reaching speeds of mach-8.

President Datchet explained that the Iranians would comply with turning over all technology and allowing U.S. inspectors into all underground facilities or face complete and utter destruction. "Iran is the gateway to Russia and the underbelly to China. We finally get access to Fortress Eurasia. Forget their oil. Now we have a springboard to China and Russia. Russia will either join with us like they did in WWII or submit. There are only two types of craft; AR X-37's and targets! The best way to avoid fighting wars is to be prepared to win wars but a preemptive strike under Project Vigilant Shield gives us the God given right to use tactical nukes when there's a real threat to the American Homeland . Preemptive strikes are an instrument of peace."

Homeland Security Chief Giuliani Jr. asked if we were finally going to disclose the truth about UFOs to the American people.

President Datchet immediately replied, "No, of course not. The French will demand that we share the technology. Romans gave up their liberty for Bread and Circus. Americans are similarly content with fast food and cable TV. We also can't compromise our False Flag operation "Northwood's" mission. Our astronauts and the Vatican spokesperson on outer space have said for years that UFOs are real. They've laid the groundwork for our campaign to drastically change world governments. The average person will believe our fake politics and its con artists. Project Blue Beam was tested at the Olympics and is in place to show a UFO hologram over key cities around the world. We'll use our "UFO" craft for flybys so everyone will know they are real. The UFO will be hailed as a savior and also as the Antichrist. Once everyone is on their knees, which they will be, the ET's will make contact. Our satellites can tap into every transmission around the world through Project Stellar Wind. First, we'll. . . .I mean they'll, offer a cure for HIV which we already have. Then they will tell the world that humans need to be free. It is an "inalienable" right. Forgive the play on words."

The whole group chuckled.

Giuliani says, "Why not have them order us to choose peace?"

"Now why would I do that? What would our military do? Freedom means capitalism which means another stock market boom and more wars. It is well that war is so horrible; otherwise we would grow fond of it. All forms of government must change to democracies or face the wrath of the ET's. Pope Peter and Prince William and Henry will also substantiate the request. Everything will fall in place for global political reform. The hologram will appear to leave. Our UFOs will fly low enough to be seen and verified before returning to base and we will communicate that the ET's plan is to return in ten years to monitor the changes. If all comply, the cure for all diseases along with a free energy system will be given as a reward as the human race will be allowed to enter the galactic community! If we don't comply, there will be severe consequences. I'm telling you this now due to the circumstances. We are less than eight weeks away and this will remain above top secret! Remember, Jesus Christ's public campaign lasted only three years and we'll accomplish as much in three days."

Giuliani says, "Look how it turned out for him. What if we create a cult of the UFO caused by the feelings of abandonment? What if a religion of the saucer emerges and the people reject government and science? What if this great deception backfires?"

President Datchet shook his head and said, "Well I guess we'll just have to get the mafia to bail us out again. Listen Rudy Junior, we have craft that can fly one quarter the speed of light. If we need to leave this planet we can and have. We've got stuff that would make Steven Spielberg jealous!"

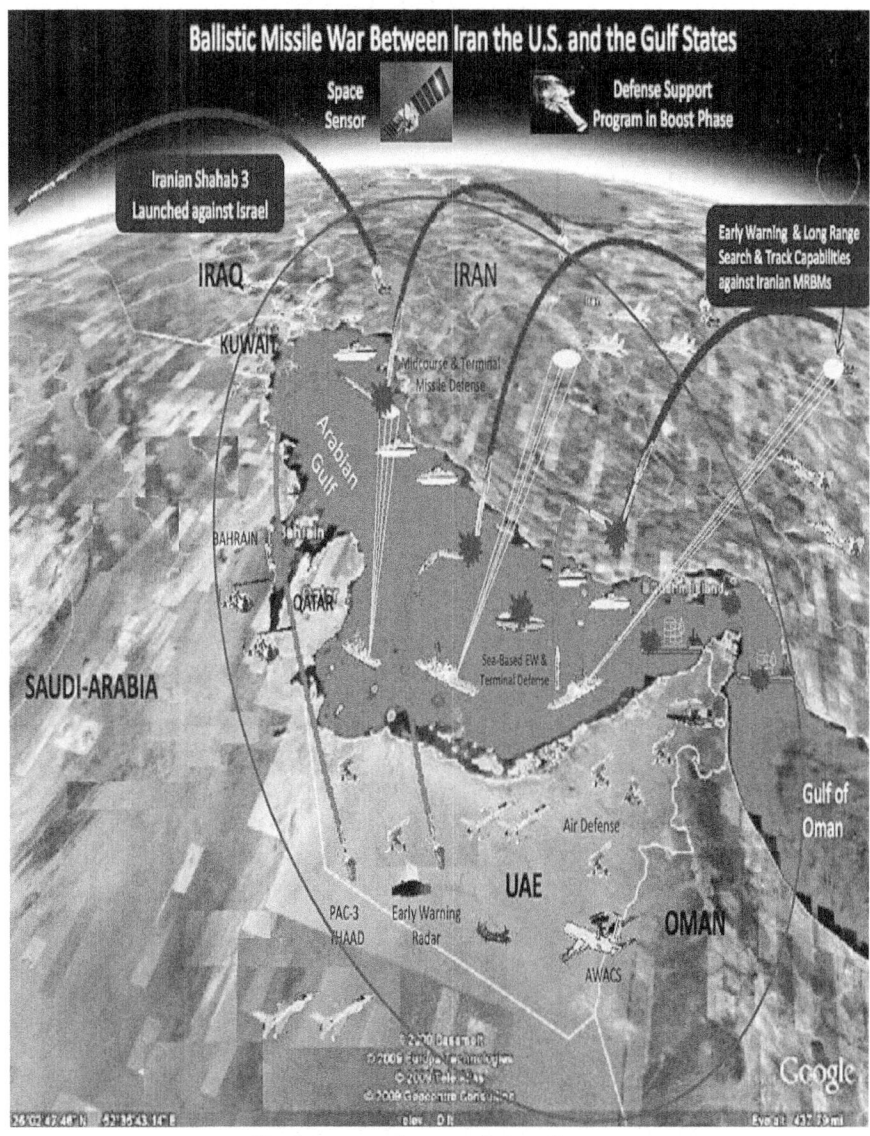

(Source: Robert Johnson)

Chapter 2

WE THE PEOPLE

"There's a plot in this country to enslave every man, woman and child and I intend to expose it."
(President John F Kennedy 7 days before his assassination)

Like a soufflé that wasn't supposed to rise twice, the failed Obama administration laid the psychological path among younger followers for the worst President in the history of this great country. Even the 2016 election of patriot Donald J. Trump couldn't undo the subliminal social disease that young Americans contracted. I'll call her the un-named President since no one speaks her name anymore; 2024 was a very pivotal election year.

Barack Hussein Obama was elected in 2008 as a vote against President Bush and again in 2012 as Americans became accustomed to handouts and he used his office to promote voter fraud and his left wing Marxist ideas that he learned in his early upbringing overseas from Saul Alinsky and from the Jeremiah Wright hate church he attended for 20 years and from militant "Underground" friends like Bill Ayers that hated America. He was ushered through Ivy League schools. He routinely got his facts wrong like his saying that the U.S. had 57 states. Everyone knows the old U.S. had 50 states and now has 63. Everyone but him! His "hope and change" promise had to do with destroying American values, exceptionalism and culture and making us dependent on government with entitlements. He was able to accomplish this "change" of America due to the color of his skin and the relentless liberal policies of affirmative action where you could not publicly tell the truth if it didn't build up a female or minority. Obama never issued one legal review when he was the head of the Harvard Law Review. He had no work history or voting history in Congress or any history to speak of that enabled him to become President other than un-named financial (George Soros) and media support and guilt ridden liberals. The American media had become a tool to influence people and had nothing to do with actual facts. Obama had strong anti-colonialist feelings from his Kenyan father and believed the West had profited off the poorer countries yet he never acknowledged Africa's failures to maintain what the West had given them or their inability to achieve while India and Indonesia did. He was determined to spread socialism, share the wealth of others and bankrupt the country to recreate a socialist state. Like Marx or Chavez, he would pit the poor and middle class against the rich. He never spoke of the great opportunity in America and he never encouraged the poor to advance. He "off-shored" jobs to China while 30% of Americans were forced to work for minimum wage. He started with beautiful California which ended up with the most social programs, and more school administrators than teachers. Manufacturing was driven out by green policies and they over taxed every worker and employer except Hollywood and the drug dealers. He managed to make a sow's ear out of the silk purse of America. His Health Care plans lead to Euthanasia and worse by the un-named President. He was so comfortable with his incompetence that he truly didn't know what he didn't know. He subjugated the Constitution, prosecuted Border Patrol Agents and conservative sheriffs and bought immigrant and minority votes and tried to ban guns so he could control conservative America. He was the only President in history to create a shadow government to undermine his successor; Trump during his years as President as Obama bought a home down the street from the White House and maintained an office in the White House. Obama organized protests and riots against the Trump policies as he did the only thing he knew how to do; socially organize liberals against the establishment, agitators for a coup. A change in the psychology of young Americans occurred.

The un-named Presidents disarming of America nearly occurred if it wasn't for a hand-written document that called for the United States of Islam by the President uncovered by Congressman Ertnev.

After Congressman Ertnev visited Russia and confronted President Putin in public over his human rights treatment he then bonded with him over a week of MMA fights, snowmobiling, Russian vodka and woman. The divorced Congressman then brokered a deal for trade of natural resources between the two countries, a ban on Russian abortions and the acceptance of traditional Christianity for the Russian state. Russia has become more "Westernized" and a stabilizing force for Eastern Europe against the liberal policies of Germany and the EU.

The Congressman returned to the U.S. to find that guns were banned in his district as a test of social engineering. On National TV, he confronted DHS agents with the support of the sheriff's office and shot and killed a DHS agent who fired at him first. The entire town filled the streets in their Congressman's defense. Ertnev invoked the Declaration of Independence and said, "the government is not deriving it's just powers from the consent of the governed but is destructive to these ends. The People can abolish the existing government and replace it with another."

The un-named President enacted Title 10 section 332 of the Insurrection Act allowing him to suppress any rebellion against the U.S. and ordered a military strike on the Congressman's location. Six Black Hawks were sent from DC to Pa. Two defected and faced off with the other four above the Congressman's location as women holding children encircled their Congressman. President Putin threatened to go on Defcon 4 if action was taken against his new friend. The un-named ordered the killing of Congressman Ertnev and the two rogue Black Hawks.

The American people sided with the President as the liberal media portrayed the Congressman as a Russian sympathizer. After a stand down, when none of the six pilots would fire, the insurrectionists were given five days to disperse peacefully since there was no violation of the Posse Comitatus Act. The Congressman was able to uncover the document revealing "Her" true plan.

The U.S. had gone from a booming economy with a high standard of living to Obama's vision and reality that everyone is entitled to what someone else earned because that is fair and equal. The economy slowed, people were paid not to work and inflation increased. It took nearly two decades for inflation to increase and for price controls and shortages to occur. Middle class neighborhoods fell apart. Unemployment increased and the ten too big to fail banks started to fail again. Unions went on strike and violent gangs appeared everywhere. Rolling blackouts were common and the government confiscated gold and silver. Food and fuel prices skyrocketed and there seemed to be shortages of everything essential. It was finally proven that Obama's Connecticut Social Security number belonged to JP Ludwig who died in 1924. A relative of Obama working at the Probate Office in Hawaii assigned the deceased Ludwig number to Obama.

A decade later, many started to see the similarities between the un-named President and Hitler. Both had changed their names, concealed their birth certificates, ghost written false auto biographies calling for a new world order and had large youth followings and blind followers due to their oratorical skills. Both advocated population control, spying by family members on each other, detention of citizens without a trial, assassination lists of enemies, stockpiling of ammo while restricting civilian purchases, citizen spies on co-workers and detention camps. The un-named one tried to suspend our Republic during the Chinese conflict same as the Romans used to do in times of war and put one person in complete control. The only problem was that the last Roman leader to do that was Julius Caesar and he never relinquished control. She also declared military vets as mentally handicapped and denied gun permits to them out of fear they would support the

Constitution. She rounded many up that were believed to be right wing extremists and they were never heard from again. She should've been impeached for crimes against humanity.

A large contingent of 300,000 millionaires and their families joined the Atlas Society movement and tried to purchase Madagascar for relocation from the U.S. Their plan was to create their own country based on the original ideals of the U.S. and to only give the right to vote to people who pay taxes. Your percentage of vote would be based on your percent taxes paid. This group had their assets seized and redistributed to the poor by the un-named one.

In a stirring Hitler like speech the un-named President turned the under 30 year old Obama loving voters against seniors who she said no longer served any purpose and unfairly drained Social Security and Medicare. Seniors pay no state taxes, reduced or no property taxes and have very few bills and a home that is paid off. She said past Presidents bought the senior vote by giving free medical, prescriptions and excessive disproportionate monthly social security checks with cost of living raises that they never earned while today's workers would be lucky to get half as much out of social security as they put into it. The net income of seniors was up 17% due to investments while everyone under 55 realized a reduction in net income from $56,000 to $29,000 per family. The workers could no longer support the retirees! The un-named President offered a basic income of $16,000 upon graduating High School and allowed the recipient to keep $8,000 upon finding a job. Young worker hate groups emerged that targeted seniors with flash mob violence while Homeland Security looked the other way.

She almost lost the election when she was overheard saying on an open mic that "no society can progress with the burden of the sick, disabled, lazy and elderly. Can you imagine where we would be today if everyone was productive and not a drain on the state?" This was foreshadowing of what was to come two years later. The un-named ones Democratic National Convention speech of 2024 which she titled "One Nation under Government, Not under God" went on to lay the ground for the removal of the five references to God in the Declaration of Independence, removal of "In God We Trust" from money and banned religious items and any mention of God or Christ at National Cemeteries or Veterans hospitals.

"Never Again" is a phrase well known to Jews regarding the Holocaust and Blacks regarding slavery but they are only words and anything is possible again. In May of 2025, payments to Social Security, Medicare and interest on the national debt exceeded all federal tax income. On July 23 2026, the un-named President authorized the CIA to release the human Stuxnet bio engineered virus or Chinese flu at the Beijing Daxing International Airport in China. It targeted age markers in DNA and released influenza on the elderly. It killed 590 million worldwide although the plan was for 1.1 billion.

The Center for Disease Control in Atlanta said that the influenza was spread by "stink bugs" which originated in China and have spread all over the world. This was the plan to free countries from the legacy spending that was bankrupting the world. It resulted in the U.S.-Sino conflict of 2026.

There was much fighting between protestors, the Oath Keepers and the DHS. "Posse Comitatus", the rule of not using troops against civilians, no longer existed. Citizens were detained without a hearing. Swarms of Predator Drones would hover over homes and fire on war veterans suspected of being preppers or rising against the government. Hoarding more than a seven day supply of food was illegal. Democracy seemed to be ending for the promise of socialistic hope and equality.

Chapter 3

CHINA

**"I think the outcome would be much the same as
when Columbus first landed in America,
it didn't turn out very well for the Native Americans"**
(Stephan Hawking)

The creation and destruction of old industries for new ones is a part of capitalism. It improves efficiencies. If there was a plus, it came from American know-how in creating industry resulting in 400 million less people around the world living in poverty. There was also a reduction in pollution in the U.S. The skies over India and China grew dark from 50 years of unregulated pollution from their boom in manufacturing. India's population is set to pass China's next year in 2030. China has 70 percent of the world's most polluted cities and 60 percent of its water supply is tainted with chemicals. With this misguided liberal policy of global prosperity where the U.S. put its economy second and everyone else put theirs first, China devalued the yuan by 60% making imports cheap and told the West that the price of admission to acquire cheap labor was the relocating of their factories to China. China looted the technology and America lost its place as the world's leading exporter and manufacturer. In every instance, short term greed driven by Wall Street expectations had backfired and betrayed the American people.

The Chinese Exclusion Act of 1882 and Senator Ted Kennedy's 1965 immigration law that no longer required immigrants to have a skill or speak English laid the groundwork for the current state of America. This 1965 law had in essence ended European immigration and shifted it towards unskilled Third World countries whose workers have nothing in common with white Americans who will be a minority in 10 years. After China invaded Taiwan, the U.S. opened its borders to eight million skilled Taiwanese business people and professionals creating three almost equal in numbers minority groups in America. This was the compromise to avoid an all-out war between the two countries. The U.S. had denied an upgrade of Taiwan's aging 30-year-old military fleet and aircraft. With China's People's Liberation Army focusing 3,000 J-10 fighters, 100 J-20 Stealth fighters, 800 bombers, 30 Destroyers, 60 Song Class stealth subs and an array of missiles that would take out Taiwan's runways before its planes got off the ground; the U.S. conceded that Taiwan was a lost cause.

China had taken advantage of the many U.S. crisis's by invading Taiwan, a self-ruled island Democracy that split from China in a 1949 civil war. Chinese Communist leader Xi Jinping consolidated his power among the 24 members Politburo. During a plenum, or full assembly of members, Xi cemented his grip on power and declared himself "party chief" and in 2018 was elected for "Life". China had been building its economy and military for years off of the U.S. trade deficit and from stolen military secrets during the Clinton years. It had over 800 short range ballistic missiles aimed at Taiwan. Although Taiwan had its own ICBM's aimed at China, a confrontation would be futile without U.S. support. The U.S. recognized China's "One China" policy which included Taiwan and sold them out in a compromise of lesser evils.

President Clinton should've been tried for treason when he allowed our military secrets to be stolen by China in exchange for campaign contributions! The Clinton years of false prosperity were setup by slashing budgets for defense and intelligence. He laid the groundwork for world terrorism. The Chinese experiment of growing its economy for U.S. Corporate expansion greed and the belief that a large middle class with money would not want war backfired. China's long term plan had always been control of the Pacific Rim and had increased its military budget by 20 percent per year to over $600 billion. (26)

China became Africa's primary ally. The resource rich continent with 54 countries was once again exploited. With 70 percent of the world's HIV cases, the West stayed away. Like the board game "Risk", China aided African incompetence and expedited its ill health and "moved in" to help the ailing continent. Interracial relationships were met with the death penalty since China preached race above all else. As the Africans died off, 300 million ruthless colonial Chinese re-colonized the continent. Sudan, known for ignoring human rights, was the oil, uranium and mineral prize. China stayed clear of South Africa and Nigeria; two U.S. states. China funded every black activist group in the U.S. as it tried to create race riots. DNA testing companies responded by fudging the results where all genetic tests showed some African heritage even though it was not true. This psychologically calmed most racial tensions.

China was now a hostile, formidable foe. Although their civilization peaked prior to the European Renaissance, they are more than capable of technological advancements and cruel warfare. Not only do they have an army with manpower greater than the entire U.S. population but with the stolen secrets, their military technology was almost equal to the U.S. capabilities. A Brookings Institute study predicted that by the year 2030, China and India's need for resources would push China into invading Russia and the Middle East for needed resources. China was importing 60 percent of its oil from Saudi Arabia and didn't like a trade deficit as China had come full circle and took the U.S.'s place as the largest consumer of oil they didn't have. China's "friendly" re-colonization policy averted the need for an armed conflict with its neighbors. China's policy of denial and deception with regard to security made it difficult to determine exactly how advanced its military actually was. They held their position and capabilities and bid their time until they amassed enough capital and military might to spring their attack.

In order to avert WWIII due to the U.S. release of the Chinese flu in retaliation for China's refusal to sell rare earth metals for our electric cars and their deliberate poisoning with lead of toys sold to our children and makeup for women and their threat to replace the dollar with the Yuan; Taiwan, the Kuril and Senkaku islands off Japan were "absorbed" into China. These islands are also a mother lode of oil, gas and minerals. Russia became a member of the WTO but gave up much of its Siberian maritime province which Russia took from China in 1860. Russia also took Great Britain's place in the E.U. in hopes of protecting its population centers in the East. The Chinese had been illegally settling in this area north of Manchuria for years. With Russia's population and economy shrinking, it was accepted that eventually Alaska's neighbor across the Bering Sea would be Chinese again.

The Pacific was passive in name only. China had never forgiven Japan for Unit 731 which was a covert chemical a biological research center in China where the Japanese performed horrific experiments on the Chinese during WWII and after the slaughter of 200,000 Chinese at Nanjing. Japan and South Korea realized that they could no longer rely on the U.S. nuclear umbrella for protection when their closest hostile neighbors were nuclear armed. With U.S. power receding in Asia, the two nations used their advanced technology to arm themselves in less than six months. They vetoed their pacifist Article Nine in their constitution and purchased U.S. Aegis radar systems, SM-3 missiles, Patriot Pac III ABM's and Boeing 767 AWACS. Both nations quickly acquired nuclear weapons and the land of the rising bipolar sun became the new hot bed of nuclear tensions.

The currency collapse that all feared actually came from a crypto-currency called Lib-coin which was created on the internet and wasn't real. Many invested in it and it collapsed the Federal Reserve and world monetary system.

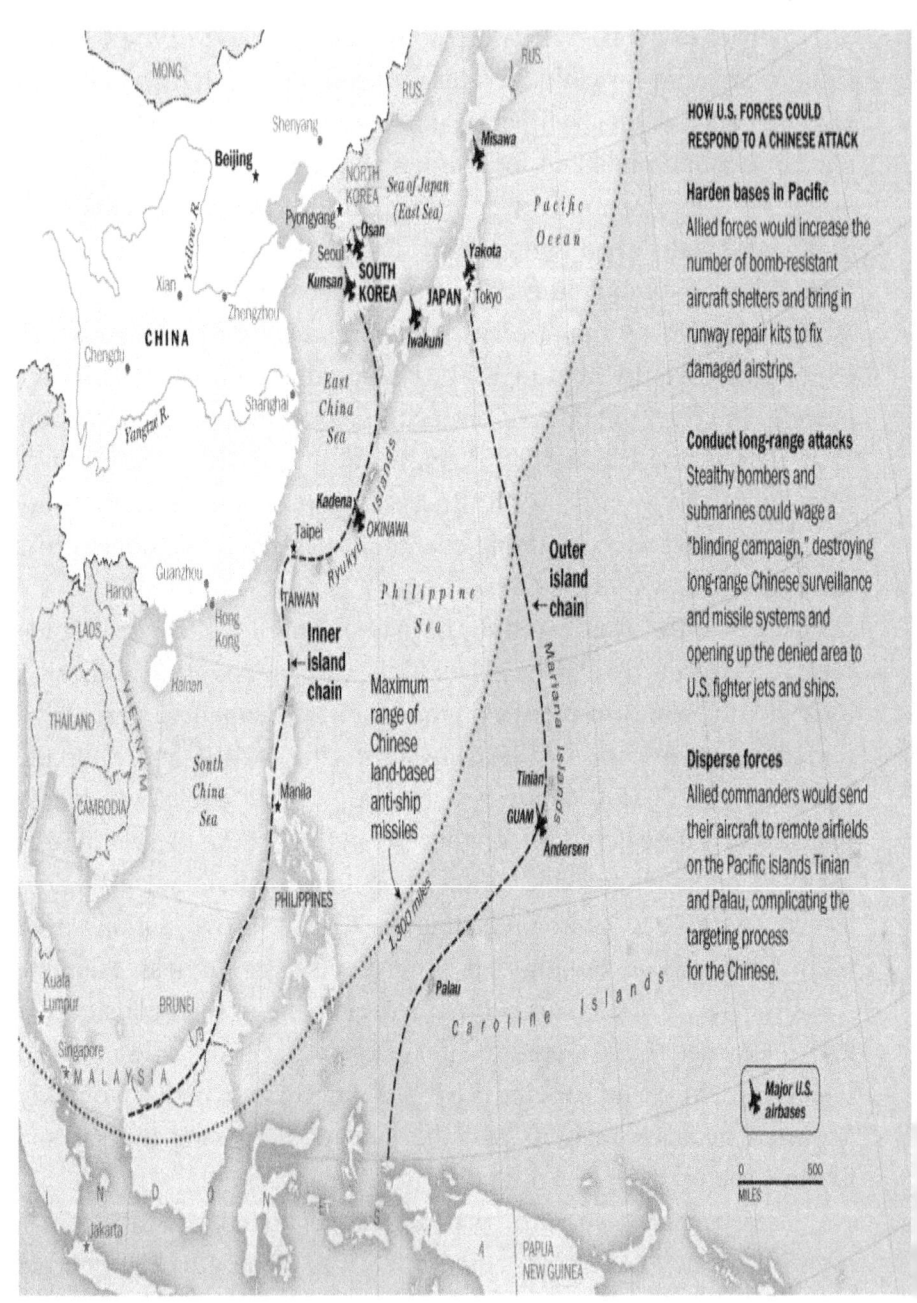

The map contains the following labels and text:

HOW U.S. FORCES COULD RESPOND TO A CHINESE ATTACK

Harden bases in Pacific
Allied forces would increase the number of bomb-resistant aircraft shelters and bring in runway repair kits to fix damaged airstrips.

Conduct long-range attacks
Stealthy bombers and submarines could wage a "blinding campaign," destroying long-range Chinese surveillance and missile systems and opening up the denied area to U.S. fighter jets and ships.

Disperse forces
Allied commanders would send their aircraft to remote airfields on the Pacific islands Tinian and Palau, complicating the targeting process for the Chinese.

Inner island chain

Outer island chain

Maximum range of Chinese land-based anti-ship missiles

1,300 miles

Major U.S. airbases

0   500
MILES

(Source: Center for Strategic and Budgetary Assessment)

48

BRITAIN & AMERICA

UNITED WE STAND!

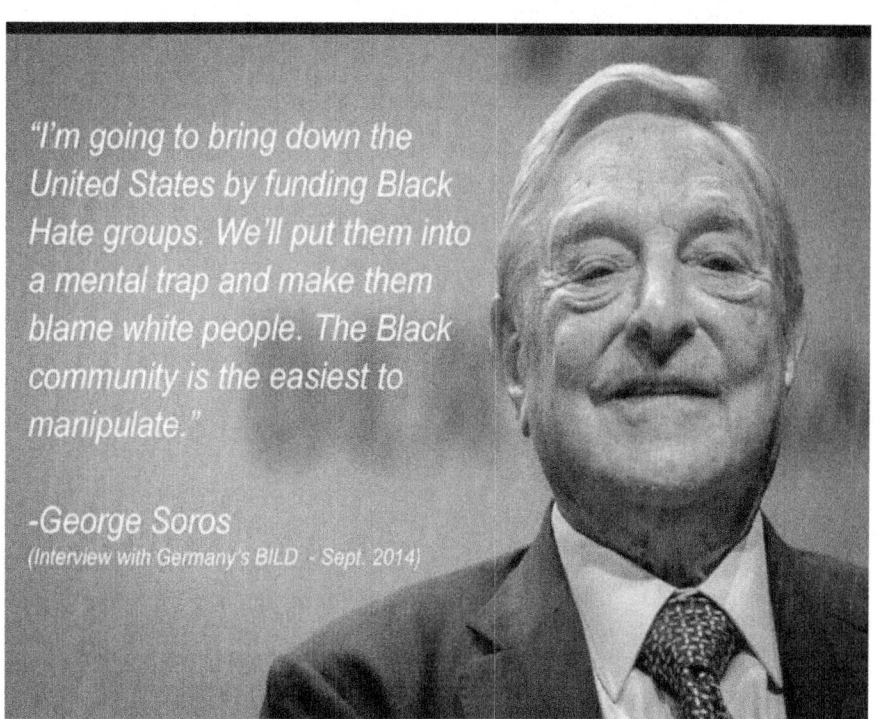

"I'm going to bring down the United States by funding Black Hate groups. We'll put them into a mental trap and make them blame white people. The Black community is the easiest to manipulate."

-George Soros
(Interview with Germany's BILD - Sept. 2014)

Chapter 4

CURRENT AFFAIRS

**"What have you wrought?" Ben Franklin answered,
"A Republic if you can keep it."**
(The 1787 Constitutional Convention)

"Damn!" Kirk Lolich yelled loudly as the phone rang and the water bottle he had been holding slipped from his left hand and began to form a small puddle beneath his recliner. Kirk had dislocated his left ring finger a few weeks earlier while playing volleyball. He had snapped the finger back at a 90 degree angle and simply grabbed it with his right hand and snapped it back in place so he could continue playing. The tendons were stretched and considerable scar tissue had formed. He had joked at the time that it was only his ring finger and that he had no use for that one again anytime soon. Kirk found that the finger was unstable and very sore to the touch.

The water bottle lay on its side, its contents seeping across Kirk's hardwood floor. He was thankful it was just water and not soda or alcohol. He smiled to himself, just one more small advantage of his healthy lifestyle.

Kirk answered the phone by saying, "hold on" and then took some tissues from a box and wiped up the mess. He realized he must have dozed off watching TV.

Kirk picked up the phone and said, "Hello".

Claire, his daughter, was on the line. She said, "Dad, you're not going to believe what just happened. Remember last week for Halloween when I told you my friends dared me to sit in the upstairs bedroom of the old Vandermeer house all alone at midnight?"

"Yeah, that's that abandoned house that you were trespassing in."

"No Dad, there are no signs posted because no one would dare enter the grounds. No one would believe me when I told them that I was sitting in a chair in the upstairs bedroom overlooking the lake at the back of the house when at the stroke of midnight, I saw something rise out of the water and start shuffling towards the house. It looked like something out of one of those zombie movies. I ran from the house and everyone out front laughed and said I was too scared to stay in the house. Well, they just found the body of a teenage girl dead in the same upstairs bedroom. They say she was scared to death. Another group of kids must've had the same idea and entered the house after we left. Isn't that creepy? I could've been killed!"

"That's why I was mad at you for going there. Zombies eat brains so your friends were probably safe. You're smarter than that. Call Uncle Frank at the state police and explain what you know just in case your fingerprints are found and give him the names of the other kids that were with you. Tell them to tell the truth and I'll call him in the morning to make sure there are no problems. And use the speaker phone on your cell phone. Those damn things cause brain tumors."

"OK Dad, I already ordered a new Bluetooth mainly because they don't disrupt migratory birds and honeybees. Love you and I'll be home in 10 minutes. I'm also so happy you bought me a two-seater Segway. It's so easy to drive and I won't forget to plug it in this time. And one other thing, I'm still hearing a rocking chair and a baby crying in the extra bedroom."

Kirk sat back down and shook his head. All three of them seem to be experiencing paranormal activity. Cole said he heard a voice in the wall behind his bed say it was 'going to get him'. He adjusted the gold chain around his neck. Three gold bands hung from the chain. Kirk had started a new tradition by putting his wedding band along with his fathers and grandfathers on the chain.

Kirk's Dad was still alive but gave his wedding band to Kirk up front because he was sure the ambulance driver or funeral director would steal it when his time came. Kirk planned to pass the chain on to his son as an inheritance which would continue to get passed down to the oldest son until there were no Lolich's left.

Kirk was also somewhat disappointed that he had missed part of the program on Baseball Tonight. Kirk had fallen asleep while watching the reality show, "Mars One" where astronauts, scientists and crew are selected for the next Mars mission. Every two years eight more members are selected to go to the human colony on Mars. The public watches them go through their training and then votes at the end of each two years on who is most qualified to go. After finding what appeared to be ancient "Apollo" type artifacts on Mars' moon Phobos, it was determined that there had been life on Mars. The show is sponsored by the NASA-European Planetary Protection Agency.

Kirk did get to watch his other favorite show, "What If?" where history is rewritten based on possible scenarios. Tonight's show was based on Einstein not escaping Nazi Germany and coming to the U.S. The "Kennedy lived" show was also interesting.

Today was a special day for Kirk and millions of Detroit Tiger's fans. Today was November 5 and also the week after the Tigers had swept the San Diego Padres in four games to win the World Series. Kirk had been excited about the program devoting the whole show to his favorite team. Kirk became a Tiger fan because he had the same last name as the Tiger pitcher, Mickey Lolich, who helped the team take the 1968 World Series by winning three games. It wasn't easy being a Detroit fan while living in New Jersey but that was consistent with Kirks "Semper-Fi" personality of doing what he wanted to as long as it was legal and always remaining loyal. Kirk smiled once more as he thought about how things had changed since his youth. He was so glad that today all he had to do to see his favorite program repeated was to pick up his remote, push the ESPN icon, scroll down the program listing, and click Baseball Tonight.

He got into a comfortable position and prepared to watch his Tigers. He mused to himself about how ironic it was that the Tigers had defeated the Padres in the series in 1984; the year he was born.

The 108-inch high definition 3D SONY Silicon X-Tel Reflective Display TV came on immediately. The system controlled the lighting and smell of the room. If the TV displayed a night scene, the lights would dim. If it displayed a storm, the lights would flicker when lightning flashed on screen. It also contained 28 aromas that fragranced the room based on the scene viewed. It was the total sensorial experience. Kirk cancelled PreconTV when he found out that they were planting subliminal messages and false memories in order to control the masses. They even say that one Presidential election was manipulated by it . . . The un-named Presidents election, when there was a rash of psychosis in perfectly normal people. PreconTV went off the air for 30 days.

Kirk was viewing the Rookie of the Year, ambidextrous pitcher Grant Hubble. Kirk was glad that the mostly lefthander had won the award. Hubble was well known for talking to the ball before every pitch, much like the pitcher from the 70s, Mark "the Bird" Fidrych had been said to do. Hubble, 25, was acquired from the Pittsburgh Pirates organization for a dozen maple bats after his Single A season. Hubble had given up 248 hits in 137 innings and had an era of 14.68. He found his control at AAA Toledo last year after deciding to throw with either hand as he did in high school and now throws strikes at will with either hand. He also takes his warm-up pitches from second base. His screwball, like his personality, is his best pitch. Hubble often says, "I guess they needed the maple bats!"

Baseball hadn't changed much since the freethinking 70s or steroid 90s where the integrity of the game was compromised in an effort to generate fan interest and attendance by allowing a handful of false heroes to "emerge". Athletes recently had been caught with enhanced contact lenses for hitting; neural enhancing prescriptions for motor control and muscle reaction; myostatin protein blockers that increase muscle mass and viruses that increase red blood cells which carry oxygen and increase stamina. Even horse racing and cycling was found to be "doped". Umpires today wear visors that show an outline of the strike zone and all home runs and foul balls are called by a computer on the Jumbo-tron.

Kirk missed watching contact sports since due to concussions, todays sports are more like touch football.

The digital clock, in the lower left hand corner of the TV, was flashing 11:13 p.m. and Kirk realized he wouldn't have enough time now to watch the entire program before bedtime. So he set his VCR on record and clicked off the ESPN icon and pressed the CNN icon to view a quick recap of the news. Kirk still liked to use VHS tapes. It made him feel young and was easy to use. Kirk had three new VCR's in his closet along with a case of 144 tapes. Kirk's kids would shake their head and call him the "omega man" of VHS and say that he was "unplugged".

Today, you only pay for the cable channels that you want to watch instead of having 200 channels for a flat rate. Even new release movies are computer generated with such life likeness that big star fees have dropped from $25 million per movie to $5 million since work was becoming harder to find with nearly half of the movies created by computer.

A talking head appeared looking almost three dimensional on the screen. The anchorman didn't interest Kirk in the least so it smiled at him. All products use glad-vertising and sad-vertising where imbedded cameras and face tracking software detect the viewer's mood and change the expression of the ad or character. Everywhere you go; billboards, cereal boxes and newspapers read your mood and change to reward you. What caught Kirk's attention was the crawlspace beneath. The few lines he read spoke of the death of a white buffalo.

"Lakota, the 2-year-old white buffalo, died suddenly today on the DiFranco ranch in Edmond, OK. The white buffalo symbolizes a time of peace and is considered sacred to all Indian Nations. Indian tradition teaches that the white buffalo will reunite all the races of the world and restore balance."

Since prophecy was one of Kirk's many interests, he knew that there was a lot more to the story than he had just read.

Kirk quickly grabbed the remote and pushed "Cloud". The talking head became visible once again as did the crawlspace. As he pointed the laser remote's light onto the crawlspace, the "additional info" icon appeared at the top of the screen. When Kirk clicked again, he viewed a new screen that had covered the anchorman. It was as if he had opened a book devoted solely to the white buffalo. He scrolled down the headings with his remote until he reached "Native American Prophecy." Cloud computing had replaced PC's years ago and all new TV's are voice activated.

He read again about the buffalo symbolizing peace but it was what followed that intrigued him.

"The death of a white buffalo marks a period of ensuing upheaval and war. There have only been three white buffalo born in the past 100 years. One was born in 1933 and his death heralded the start of W.W.II. The other buffalo was born in 1994 and his death coincided with the attack on September 11, 2001, and the subsequent war on terrorism."

Kirk shook his head. The news he had just read was a bad omen. Kirk shrugged his shoulders and clicked back to live FOX news. He figured he might as well see how bad-off the world was before he went to sleep rather than ruining his morning. He sat forward in the recliner, remote in hand, ready to click it whenever he couldn't stomach the news.

The first story concerned the anniversary of the simultaneous death of the last two surviving U.S. veterans of WWI. Harry

Landis 112; of Sun City, FL, and Frank Buckles, 110, of Charles Town, WV; both Dough-Boys passed away of old age. They were the last of the generation to fight in the "War to end all Wars". Preparations were being made for a huge celebration to honor the 90th anniversary of the start of WWII for 2031 and to honor the few remaining survivors who fought in the war and survived the Chinese flu outbreak and gang violence against seniors. That generation rightfully lived through the greatest time in America; the 1950's.

The next segment concerned President Datchet and the upcoming State of the United States of 63 Address. Election Day was now a holiday enabling the citizenry time to vote. With only 25 percent of the people voting, government by the consent of the people took on a new meaning. In fact, the President increased our paid holidays from eight to twelve with Valentine's Day, Aprils Fool's Day and Halloween added as National holidays. All employees also start off with three weeks' vacation so we could all have appropriate time off from work each month and the extra days off forced companies to hire more employees.

President Datchet or POTUS as some referred to the President of the United States had bulging eyes as if surprised by something, which he never was. He also had a thin silver moustache. Unlike World War II's patriotism, we polarized the public with a message of fear using color coded text alerts which relegated the public to vigilant but anxious passengers. (27)

Kirk would get angry at the protestors. If they knew anything about American history or researched what really happened at conflicts like Gettysburg, Iwo Jima, Bataan, Pearl Harbor and September 11th, they wouldn't protest. They would be angry but supportive of our troops and effort.

The real reason Datchet had won was because with the help of the Free Mason Party, he ran the country like a business that also does charitable work. He capped CEO pay at fifty times the average employee pay after middle class jobs disappeared and all we were left with was minimum wage and professionals. He and the Republican controlled Supreme Court said they would suspended the 1951 Twenty-Second Amendment to the Constitution to allow a sitting President, in "a time of crisis", to run for four terms or 16 years like FDR if there was a repeat of the terrorism that occurred just a few years ago. He also declared that the President must switch to the Independent Party upon election. There were also two Vice Presidents; one for Foreign Affairs and one for Domestic. The Domestic VP was first in line if something happened to the President in these dangerous times. The Free Mason Party captured 19 percent of the vote with their catchy phrase, "The House divided against itself cannot stand", enabling President Datchet and Vice Presidents Rice and Alvarez to defeat the Democrats by a 42 percent to 39 percent margin after only three years of the un-named President's term.

This ancient and honorable society, the Free Masons, was the protectors of truth and knowledge and was deeply involved in the founding of this nation. They were the principle architects of our Nation's Capital. Most of the signers of the Declaration of Independence were Free Masons. Many Presidents from Washington to the present were Free Masons. General MacArthur and J. Edgar Hoover were also members. A scandal in 1850 sent the group from public sight but not from politics. This third party's goal was to bring the nation back to its roots and original ideals. The fledgling party was gaining support and planned to run an established campaign with Giuliani Jr. for President.

American wars, IOU's, trade deficits, senior citizen entitlements, open borders, and shrinking industrial base were pushing citizens toward an alternative party. Their cry was, "Wall Street killed Main Street and 1776 is our answer to a New World Order!" The President even resorted to selling war bonds as a way of borrowing money from the people and gathering support. The bonds doubled in value every eight years. He also passed a law that all social program dollars must be divided by the number of recipients. If more people went on social programs, then everyone received less and the total budget cost could not go up.

Kirk would've preferred Homeland Security Director Rudolph Giuliani Jr. for President. Giuliani had convinced the President to declare war on drugs similar to the war on terrorism and had also linked organized crime to terrorism. Our military flew unchallenged into many South American, Middle Eastern and Asian countries and fire-bombed the fields and labs where drugs were grown and processed. The U.N. shook with rhetoric and anti-American hatred as we violated the sovereignty of country after country that exported drugs to the U.S. The President, and Giuliani, declared that no resource is as precious as our children and that exporting drugs to the U.S. is the same as declaring war on our youth. Hit squads tried to enter the country to kill the President like past Presidents who were assassinated when they didn't meet the demands of the unholy. Organized crime collaborated with terrorists and drug lords to take down our government. Chaos and weak leaders are the friends of organized crime and terrorists. They have a common purpose and overlap and cooperate. It is rumored that the La Cosa Nostra families of New York aided Giuliani in his investigation of Asian and Russian crime syndicates and their link to Islamic countries. Although many believed that the Mafia would sellout to terrorists for a buck, they have a strict code of honor. They helped identify money transfers and identification fraud along with weapons acquisitions. The same families that Giuliani's father prosecuted 50 years earlier now "took out" the hit squads and empathized with America. It was the Sopranos versus al-Qaeda. Many wondered what the payback would be for their help. But with no "competition" and the hand-writing on the wall regarding drug transactions, the Mafia was now free to return to their 1950's era control of gambling, prostitution and protection with a condoning blind eye from law enforcement.

President Datchet had survived much crisis. Of course, the never-ending 30 year $4 trillion war in Afghanistan-Iraq-Iran-Pakistan was yet another story. It seemed like we were trying to kill the terrorists one at a time, like an endless stream of cockroaches.

Thankfully, at least the thousands of soldiers that get wounded in war can now benefit from the McGowan Institute for Regenerative Medicines Franken-scientific breakthroughs. They've been successful at growing back cells for damaged muscles, skin, bone and tissue. They use a biomaterial made of polycaprolactone and hydroxyapatite laced with stem cells to enable the re-growth. Severed limbs are now being grown back after amputation.

All soldiers now have silk producing spider genes and fish genes for resistance to cold spliced into their genome to produce "bulletproof" skin. The new skin is stronger than a Kevlar vest since spider silk is five times stronger than steel. All soldiers are "GM" or genetically modified. They kill without remorse or anxiety or fatigue. First came the high tech helmets to improve senses; then came the genetic modifications. An effort was made to stop the use of animals containing human material (ACHM) for the testing and diagnoses of drugs and the use of genetic modifications (GM) to produce human chimeras but the author of the Senate bill conveniently died and the second author who took up the Senate bill committed suicide.

Trans-humanism was a reality. The Russians were the first to practice it 25 years earlier as their boxers dominated the Heavyweight Boxing ranks. The Russians started the "Initiative 2045" in conjunction with the U.S. for the human genetic evolution of the species to enable it to solve our environmental changes and allow us to one day leave the planet. It wasn't an "arms race" but a race to build humans that can live in adverse conditions. The Russians and Americans had worked together in fear of the Chinese and North Koreans developing a super soldier first. We had always had a dysfunctional partnership with Russia. The Russians knew we had never been to the moon in the 1960's due to the Van Allen radiation belt and that we planted the flag and dropped off the rover in the 1990's. Many moments in history had been re-enacted for the public in an attempt to increase nationalism. (33)

We had mastered Nano robots and the use of the mind to control machines and equipment. We were on the verge of transferring thoughts and memories to artificial bodies and engineering and reverse engineering a brain. Soon we would be able to live simultaneously in different realities and locations through artificial carriers of human intellect. By 2045 we will have engineered a new species capable of anything; including leaving this planet and settling on other planets and moons. Maybe this is how it started for other "ET's"? Maybe this is the only way to be able to make the long trip in space? Maybe those that have come and will come are only mirror images of their fathers? Maybe this is where it all goes wrong for an advanced civilization? Kirk had joined the "Immortal Me Society to learn more. (33)

In a stirring patriotic speech just prior to the election, against the backdrop of patriotic country music which has been adopted as the national favorite, President Datchet spoke of the importance of military service and raised military pay by 20 percent.

"Those bearing arms promise to act with loyalty, skill and honor. The People must also act with honor in sending our troops into battle on faith. Our democracy depends on their sacrifice. If we falter or send them unjustly, it dishonors us, not the soldiers who serve. Freedom is fragile. It can be destroyed by our enemies or by our indifference. Lincoln's ideal of a government of the people, by the people and for the people shall not perish from this Earth."

Islamic extremists were determined to stop the spread of democracy and peace. They believe in the vengeful God of the Old Testament. They believe in group or mob approval and not individualism and human rights. Like the Japanese kamikaze who believed in cultural honor, suicide bombings are approved of. They moved from one country to another in an effort to find a base to launch their attacks from. They overthrow moderate governments by rallying the Muslim masses. They receive support from Muslim governments, corrupt charities and blame their failures on the West. The Islamic militants even attacked Russia who was not a supporter of Operation Iran Freedom.

No army is as powerful as an idea whose time has come. They believe that Allah is the only God; all should submit to the Quran and be governed by the law of Islam. Islam survived two centuries of Ottoman humiliation, Western rule, communism, and U.S. aggression. They vowed for every Muslim to kill an American. But to kill an American is to also kill an idea. We are not from any particular place, race, creed or religion. All that believe in the idea of freedom are Americans. In the long run, al-Qaeda will be defeated by Muslims, not foreigners. (27)

The American Millennial's wanted community but no God so they started humanist church-like non-religious services. They wanted speaking of God to be a hate crime. In a heated debate over the constitutional right to freedom of religion, we closed down numerous Muslim mosques and schools in Detroit. We proved that they were a front for terrorist activity and that they cease to have the protection of the Constitution. We deported their extremist cleric preachers of hate and sedition. We enacted laws, similar to the 1996 Rico statutes, which combated religious and charitable organizations that are funding fronts for terrorists. Some feared a slippery slope which would extend to majority rule in restricting other "minority" religions and argued that the terrorist win every time we compromise our standards in the name of safety.

President Datchet made it clear that the enemy considered every retreat as an invitation to greater violence. There would be no peace without victory in the Middle East. (27)

We eventually carpet bombed Dubai with our new "spank and run and sell your own oil" to rebuild policy. Our first strike was on the half mile high Burj Khalifa Tower. Our bombers waited a full hour out of respect for the World Trade Towers until the world's tallest building collapsed before we continued the bombing. We hoped for a cheap military victory using advanced military technologies. A techno war fought from a distance would be swift and sure. Only there are no bloodless wars. Ethnic bigotry must be fought with "boots on the ground". War means fighting, and fighting means close quarter killing. Iran was the Arab world's last chance to board the plane towards a modern civilized region. Freedom is a western ideal that didn't fit in the Muslim world. Their preference for violence and terror lead to the collapse of their civilization. (26)

After Saudi Arabia's oil flow diminished as their Ghawar oil field dried up, we diverted the $145 billion we invest in protecting Middle East oil fields. Our biggest fear was a terrorist nuke on the fields which would collapse the world economy overnight and shift the global balance of power. We destroyed Mecca with a 30,000 pound Massive Ordinance Penetrator in order to send a deterrent signal. The precision guided bomb, built by Boeing, is the largest conventional bomb in our arsenal. We next destroyed the Dome of the Rock which infuriated the Jewish and Muslim world. President Datchet said that, "If you can't settle your differences then I will split the holy site in two like King Solomon did with the disputed child in the Old Testament". The secret plan was to allow the Jews to rebuild King Solomon's Temple and fulfill the prophecy. President Datchet told Pakistan and Venezuela to pay close attention. We have a viable military option against their nuclear programs. We performed this act on August 22, the date that the Islamic calendar depicts as the night Mohammed started his prophetic mission. Unexpectedly, there was no Jihad against the West like we hoped. They just waited for us to send soldiers to occupy; which didn't happen.

Even though Kirk always votes Republican and people tend to stick with who they know in times of crisis, he found it surprising that the President still got elected. When the bombings didn't work, it was rumored that Datchet asked the Pope to publicly appeal to the West for a fourth Crusade after a number of church burnings and Christian neighborhoods were rampaged in Europe and the U.S. and were proven to be the work of the Muslim Brotherhood extremists. The spread of misinformation through cell phones, web blogs and text messages were sure to ignite a holy war of religious and ethnic hate. The Pope made his ill-fated request at a publicized Sunday morning mass but when it failed to raise Western support, the Pope was left hanging on the issue. Christian led Ethiopians briefly battled Somalia Islamic forces. He couldn't say it was the President's request because Datchet was protected by the firewall of cutting off U.S. aid to the Vatican through charitable tax contributions. Good and evil are like opposite ends of a stick; you can't pick up one without the other.

The Federal deficit had skyrocketed to $35 trillion. Federal spending had increased 60 percent over the past 12 years as each President gave more and more to the masses in order to secure their vote. In a bold move, Datchet made an aging Jim Cramer of "Mad Money" his fiscal chairman. Thirty seven percent of Americans either worked for the government or were employed through contracts or grants. Thirty percent of males didn't work since they could receive some form of disability. Unfunded programs and future liabilities were at $48 trillion or $300,000 per full-time worker. Nearly 40 years earlier, we strategically caused the fall of the Soviet Union through the arms race spending and now we were falling into the same over spending Pandora's Box. Some called it the Four Horsemen of the American Apocalypse; oil, debt, corporate greed and the religious right.

Many stores elected to close on Sundays as a way to save on energy and payroll.

Gasoline prices, President Datchet's special interest, were at $6 per gallon and a discount compared to fuel in Europe. Fracking was halted due to increased earthquakes immediately after drilling. In 1956, Geologist M. King Hubbert calculated that U.S. oil production would peak in 1970. No one really knew if he was correct due to the fake oil shortage crisis of 1973 and 2008. Every generation seems to go through the same oil, housing and stock market scams perpetrated by the controlling interests. Due to increased demand in China and India, all oil producing countries were pumping at maximum capacity. We currently use two percent of the world's oil supply yearly and will effectively be "out of oil" by the year 2190 after modern fracking methods extended oil reserves by 100 years. Political instability in Venezuela, level four and five hurricanes in the Gulf, and admissions by oil rich countries that they over-estimated their reserves, only exasperated the situation.

After the Ogallala aquifer dried up, this was the largest aquifer in the world and supplies eight states in the U.S. Great Plains with water; and growing signs that greenhouse gases were in fact contributing to global warming, President Datchet increased the federal tax on fuel by $1.50 a gallon. This drove the right behavior creating jobs and inventions and made alternative fuels like solar, ethanol, hydrogen, clean coal and nuclear more attractive. Desalination stations were built on the coasts and tidal plants were constructed along all major rivers and utilized underwater turbines – like wind turbines - to generate electricity. It was found that wind speeds were decreasing noticeably with climate change. As the temperature difference between the equator and poles reduced, so did air pressure which causes wind and let the "wind" out of turbine construction. Since the average car lasts 17 years, it would still take a decade before realizing any results. Rapid bus transit systems were installed in all major cities. The former U.N. had wanted a 50 cent worldwide fuel tax to fund needed projects and a move towards a One World Government. There were many that argued that the global warming frenzy was similar to the Y2K or Mayan calendar frenzy that gripped the world a decade earlier and proved to be nothing more than a multibillion dollar scam created by the Club of Rome to foster a one world government and cap and trade taxes. (26)

The thawing of the Alaskan tundra coupled with the drying of the Amazon rainforest which produces 20 percent of the world's oxygen all but proved climatologists correct but this was a natural repeated process minimally influenced by mankind. One benefit of the climate change was the opening up of the 4,000 mile Northwest Passage around North America. A 70 percent reduction in ice flow allowed shipping companies to avoid the Chinese owned Panama and Suez canals saving millions of dollars on fuel and tolls. A quarter of the world's shipping now passes through the Northwest Passage. Alaska's Arctic coast now looks like old Louisiana with oil platforms, port cities and cruise ships. The "Passage" was popularized by the rock group "Arctic Nation".

There had also been such an increase in inner city crime and inter-racial relationships that educated black women were complaining that it was becoming hard to find an eligible black male over the age of 25 due to incarceration and white female's preference for black lovers. Black women, like all women, were evolving and becoming successful at a much faster rate than their male counterparts. It was as if a mutated gene had been introduced only to women. Humans share the same amount of DNA with bonobo apes as they do with chimps. The bonobo females band together and dominate the stronger males who are loners and depend on their mothers their whole lives. This same behavior is now apparent in human females. Aggressive behavior among women had also resulted in an increase in females going to prison. Twenty seven percent of all inmates were now women.

Last year, race and gender were removed from all job, college and financial applications. How offensive to track people based on anything other than merit and income! This was accomplished after years of social engineering through the media where all TV and movies showed only inter-racial couples, falsified DNA results from Ancestry.com and other sites showed all test results as mixed race and all social media search engines steering racial inquiries to the politically approved sites and explanations.

Boston lawyers, trying to make a point, argued successfully that the NBA had to represent Caucasians based on population. They argued the reverse regarding the winter Olympics. This precedent would soon spread to all sports. It mirrored the current thought process used for job advancement and college admissions. How preposterous and unnatural to base athletics on percentages. The absurdness of the case highlighted and reversed how all Americans had previously been "classified" by the pigment of their skin.

The same bill also reinstituted the legal use of the term "God" in all schools and federal buildings and overturned legislation by the un-named President. No denomination was favored, but the word was clearly meant to be used by the Founding Fathers. We are a Christian nation founded upon Christian ideals. Since a majority of the public believed in "a God", in this instance, the majority ruled. Schools would be required to teach evolution, creationism and intelligent design by ETs. Since there is no clear cut answer, all three would be taught. The President wanted students to debate, think outside the box and learn to make their own choices. The President, all past Presidents, and a select few knew the truth about our development and it didn't include religion or evolution. Sooner or later, the truth would come out and the public needed to be slowly exposed to it through sci-fi movies, books and education.

Some argued that all religion and the lure of make believe should be outlawed. Abstract ideas and religious fanatics were the root of terrorism. There was great atheist pressure in agreement with the un-named President to ban all Christmas celebrations, nativity scenes, singing of Christmas carols, remove "under God" from the Pledge of Allegiance and remove "In God We Trust" from all currency, and remove all crosses from Arlington cemetery. Russia outlawed religion and closed most churches 100 years earlier, yet 75 percent of the population continued to practice their faith and today Russia is a Christian country. Many cited FDR's 1941 "a date that will live in infamy" speech where he ended it with "so help us God". Wisely, the lesser of the two evils was chosen and the schools would teach open mindedness and tolerance.

The Republicans then transformed this country into a republic instead of a democracy like our Founding Fathers meant it to be. President Datchet took advice from scholars in constitutional law and articulated what George Mason University Professor Walter Williams had said, "The Founders knew that a democracy would lead to the same form of tyranny the colonies suffered under King George III. The Founders intended, and laid out the ground rules, for our nation to be a republic. The word democracy appears nowhere in the Declaration of Independence or Constitution. The Constitution guarantees "to every state in this Union a Republican form of government." Does our Pledge of Allegiance say to "the democracy for which it stands" or does it say to "the Republic for which it stands"? Do we sing "The Battle Hymn of the Democracy" or "The Battle Hymn of the Republic"? John Adams said, "You have rights antecedent to all earthly governments; rights that cannot be repealed or restrained by human laws; rights derived from the Great Legislator of the Universe." Nothing in our Constitution suggests that government is a grantor of rights. Instead, government is a protector of rights. In recognition that Congress poses the greatest threat to our liberties, the Framers used negative terms toward Congress throughout the Constitution, such as: shall not abridge, infringe, deny, disparage, and shall not be violated, nor be denied. In a republican form of government, there is the rule of law. The government and all citizens are accountable to the same laws. Government power is limited and decentralized through a system of checks and balances. Government intervenes in civil society to protect its citizens against force and fraud but does not intervene in the cases of peaceable, voluntary exchange. In a democracy, the majority rules. The law is whatever the people determine it to be. Laws do not represent reason. They represent power. The restraint is upon the individual instead of the government. Rights are seen as privileges and permissions that are granted by government and can be rescinded by government. The Founders deeply distrusted democracy. Democracy never lasts long. It wastes, exhausts and murders itself. Democracy believes in the wisdom and goodness of the people. The people supported the guillotine. The people supported Hitler and the Nuremberg laws. They elected Hezbollah in Lebanon and Hamas in Palestine. Our Fathers no more trusted the people to do what was right than they trusted the Kings. In the Republic, they created the peoples House of Representatives which was severely restricted by the Bill of Rights and by a Senate and by the President with veto power and by a Supreme Court. Should we fear a Congress that can muster a majority vote? As Jefferson said, "Hear no more of trust in men, but rather bind them down with a Constitution." (26)

Kirk was proud that the President took back the country. The mental illness of liberalism had made us soft minded and submissive; unable to make the tough decisions. Liberals always side with the enemy in a treasonous posture to bring down the current establishment.

The global economy and the race for cheap labor spelled the end of high priced manufacturing jobs. The good life built on assembly line muscle was gone. Capitalism isn't compassionate except for the top of the food chain where CEO's were rewarded for bankrupting companies in order to turn them around with improved models that reduced worker pay and benefits or sent them overseas. This twenty first century was marked by a reversal of fortune; job losses, net worth reduction, economic stagnation and mounting debt. (26)

The U.N. was created after WWII as a way to protect human rights and avoid a repeat of the 50 million lives lost. The U.N. charter is a wonderfully written document only their record was appalling. The "Blue Helmets" were guilty of rape and many other atrocities.

We closed the U.N., like the failed League of Nations, after it demanded control over the Internet in order to regulate harmful web cafes and demanded the disarmament of all countries under a centralized world government. Many countries complied and left their populace unarmed against a neighboring attack or even an extraterrestrial attack. The U.S. of 63 was one of a handful of countries that could defend themselves from a "War of the Worlds" type attack.

We turned the U.N. building into low income housing. We offered to relocate the U.N. to the Sudan where it was needed but France stepped in and proposed a new site in Paris. When we withdrew our membership, so did most English speaking countries. Like the original 13 colonies, six English speaking nations joined the U.S. as 13 new states. The new G-7, which consists of a representative from each continent which have consolidated into Unions similar to the European Union, now meet and decide world policy. North America was the only exception to the Unions.

Also proposed was a rearranging of states and state borders. California, Florida, Texas and the Long Island portion of New York would split into four new states. Smaller states such as West Virginia, Rhode Island, and Delaware would be eliminated and merged into Virginia, Maryland and Connecticut. Other states with odd borders or "pan-handles" such as Oklahoma, Florida and West Virginia would have those areas merged into the proper state. Since this right belongs to the states and not the federal government, the idea was snuffed by the smaller states.

All financial aid to non-English speaking countries was stopped. All trade agreements and treaties were ruled null and void. It once again became a privilege to do business with the

U.S.! Inadvertently, our treaties with native Indians were voided and they had to pay taxes on the billions in revenue they generate from casinos.

The United States of 63 had learned from the un-named President and found new convenient ways to deal with the poor, elderly and sickly population. Doctor assisted suicides had been made legal with the formation of the Dignitas Corporation. The end result was that record numbers of sick and elderly ceased to exist. Autonomy and dignity are the precious values that the right to a peaceful death is all that we aspire to and get. The fact that the sale of so many potassium chloride kits was such a fiscal boom to the pharmaceutical giants never entered the average person's mind. They were happy to just rid themselves of their burdens. Doctor Jack Kevorkian's use of potassium chloride, to stop the heart, had been frowned upon when introduced in 1990. This soon led to incarceration for its creator but upon his own death the method was patented for profit.

Quality of life and ones contribution to society took precedent. Hubert Humphrey once said, "The moral test of government is how it treats those who are in the dawn of life, those who are in the twilight of life, and those who are in the shadows of life." Once life is devalued, none of us are safe. President Datchet also added, "The moral test also includes how we treat our wounded soldiers upon return from war." On Memorial Day, the POTUS opened

"Soldier City" located in Ohio south of Cleveland and north of Columbus and just 40 miles from Pittsburgh. The banner at the gates of the city read, "No Vet Left Behind." Here all veterans can live rent free in row houses. Groceries are also free in the commissary. The largest veteran's hospital in the world was constructed here. Many vets were able to start new lives with low interest loans by opening small service businesses that follow every community. No cost was spared. Military pay for all soldiers was increased by 20 percent. This was surely one of the shining successes of the new millennia.

WOUNDED WARRIOR
P R O J E C T

Today it is different. After performing cost-benefit analysis, the government is justified not to have to pay the health insurance and social security for millions of elderly and sick. Eighty percent of one's lifetime health costs were spent at the end of one's life. The unsustainable Medicare system had collapsed. The legal drug businesses were making more money than ever which didn't hurt the party in power in the next election. Only Japan treats its elderly as living treasures with character and respect. Americans would give botox injections to works of art, Sequoia trees and historical buildings if we thought it would make them look better. In the twilight of life, we give the elderly assisted suicide. In the shadow of life, we give the diseased and handicapped a chance to have the government give them a good, honorable death. For those who were in control of their lives, they are also in control of their death.

71

The environmental news segment came on and Brazilian scientist Emil Silva frantically exclaimed that although we've been reporting and studying the global warming trend in the north for years, an opposite and equal increase in snow and ice accumulation in the south has been occurring. His data shows that the Antarctic ice sheet has increased 23 percent and is causing the crust of the Earth to shift one mile per week. In 20 years, the U.S. will be at the equator; Brazil will be in the Antarctic and Russia and Eastern Europe will be in the Arctic Circle.

Kirk sat up attentively as the next story began. The 1979 House Select Committee on Assassinations would be releasing its files on the JFK assassination and most people believed that the conclusion of a conspiracy would be the verdict. In a bit of nostalgia, it was mentioned that the 1984 movie "Terminator" was set in 2029 where the Terminator was sent back to kill Sarah Connor.

Kirk had clicked the off button. He had grown tired but had always had a passion for outer space but sometimes the science bored him. He was more interested in the creative possibilities of science fiction. As a child, he had watched "The Outer Limits", "Star Trek", and all the "B Movies" of the 1950's he could get his hands on. Perhaps it was his love of the "unexplained" that made him join the Mutual UFO Network, and collect a magazine called *Famous Monsters of Filmland* that he inherited from his father.

Kirk smiled to himself as he remembered the time he had gone so far as to visit Forrest Ackerman, the magazine's editor with his father. Mr. Ackerman would graciously allow tours of his home on Saturdays. It was Forrest who had coined the phrase "sci-fi". It wasn't surprising to find his home on, of all streets, 213 Moon Fan overflowing with sci-fi memorabilia. Kirk remembered how glad he had been when he found out that his father had to go to California on business. And how luck, or as Kirk liked to think, fate, had arranged for him to have a free Saturday enabling him to visit 213 Moon Fan.

Kirk shook his head in an effort to get his mind back to reality. Kirk stretched his six foot frame across the couch and yawned. The satellite on the asteroid Apophis should be sending back images and information from space. We landed the satellite on Apophis in April of 2022 but it has failed to send data. The asteroid takes a seven year elliptical orbit through our galaxy and will bring back more data than Hubble ever did.

Kirk raised himself from the couch and whistled softly. Two Doberman pinchers entered the room. He knelt down in front of the two dogs. Mama Bear and Poppa Bear began to lap his face and playfully jump at him. "Time for bed", he said, as he kissed the dogs. As Kirk stood, the dogs crossed the room and curled up on the floor. The dogs were the only true unconditionally loyal friends that Kirk had. As he headed up the staircase of his five bedrooms colonial, his knees began to ache. He was glad he had purchased a large house. After all, with two teenagers in the house, it helped to have extra rooms. He also liked the touch of a spiral staircase in the center of the home. The only problem was, on nights like tonight, when he over did it at the gym, he could do without the extra steps. Kirk knew he was still in good shape at 45 years of age. After all, he still played racquetball and practiced mixed martial arts and worked out four times a week. He also knew that at his age, not many 210 pound guys had so little body fat. He would joke that soon he'd be on the downside of the bell curve. Kirk viewed being in shape as "body armor" against the world. Something that was his and that they could never take away from him. He was proud that he could do all that and still serve as a single parent to his children. The fact that he had a rapidly fading career was, of course, a large downside to his life. He had been told by his regional department head that years ago the corporation had identified him as their future corporate security head but that was prior to Kirk's divorce and his stubbornness to not move the children again. But, as he kissed Cole and Claire goodnight, he still couldn't help but feel blessed that family is a renewable resource.

A short time later while he lay in bed, he thought about the London terrorist bombings during the Olympics and the kidnapping and killing of six contestants of the Miss Universe beauty pageant in Brazil in July. Al-Qaeda had the audacity to apply for an Olympic team. Bin Laden's Harvard Law School trained brother and a Massachusetts resident filed the petition. The plan had always been for the brother to defend bin Laden if caught. He had worked for the CIA as an operative under the code name Tim Osmond. They didn't plan on his assassination a decade later by SEAL Team 6. The petition was turned down after a meeting was requested by the U.S. State Department.

At 4:58 p.m. on the last day of the Olympics, a UFO was spotted high in the sky over London. Millions saw it as the camera's panned toward the sight. It was explained as a light inversion due to the Olympic stadium lights.

At 6 p.m. on the last day of the Olympic competition, simultaneous attacks occurred. Explosions took place at eight airports all around the world. Terrorists attacked the busy lines at check in. Although they could get their plastic explosives through the metal detectors, they chose to cause maximum damage as families waited in line. No one questioned the bomb carrying luggage left unattended as the attacker excused themselves in order to go to the restroom and asked the person behind them to save their place. These home grown terrorists were recruited from local schools and spoke the language perfectly. The attacker's biggest concern was that someone would steal the luggage and walk off before he could detonate it. Lines at theme parks, concerts, rush hour train stations and sporting events would be the next round of targets for female terrorists with breast implants pumped full with nitroglycerine.

Big Ben was hit with a surface to air missile right at England's "hour" of triumph in the 100 meter run. The Tower Bridge was also hit by multiple surface to air missiles. Its 100 ton draw bridges fell 142 feet into the River Thames.

Scotland Yard hurried to 10 Downing Street to protect the Prime Minister and the M-6 surrounded King William at Buckingham Palace. A third blast ripped through a double-decker bus in front of St Paul's Cathedral. Although it was the fifth cathedral built on the sight, the Portland stone held its own against the blast and the 300-year-old spiritual center of the medieval city held fast.

Kirk couldn't get the live video out of his head. A reporter approached a pile of clothes which began to move and moan. As the veteran foreign correspondent rolled the woman over, all her limbs were missing and had blood pouring out of them.

The fourth and last attack was against the century old Tower of London. Its 15 foot thick walls of white Caen stone defended this formidable fortress well. The plan was to steal the Crown Jewels and embarrass this 51st State of the U.S.

Four hundred years earlier, Captain Blood of Ireland stole the Crown Jewels. King Charles II pardoned him for his bravery. There would be no pardon this time. As Scotland Yard moved in, the three thieves were trapped like rats. One died in the gunfight, one drank a poison from the amulet around his neck. And the third, a female, was captured. She has yet to be heard from in her three months of "intense interrogation". (26)

Kirk wondered why environmentalists, abortion foes, and other groups resort to terrorism. Is it in our nature to strike out at authority when we disagree? As he started to doze off, he thought about how his life had changed since his divorce. He realized he spent way too many nights just lying here and thinking about the past. He wouldn't only think of the divorce itself but also how it had caused him stress on his job and even contributed to his mild depression. The divorce had truly worn him down.

As Kirk rolled over, he remembered Edgar Cayce's words, "There are no accidents. There are no victims because we chose this life."

Chapter 5

DIVORCE

"And lo, the Beast looked upon Beauty and stayed his hand from killing, and from that day on, he was as if dead."
(King Kong)

Kirk slammed his fist on the steering wheel. The honking horns seemed to be all around him. This was Route 80 in New Jersey at evening rush hour. It was a place that Kirk would rather not have been right now. He then smiled as he remembered why he was going into the city. He thought about his friend Arian Whitaker's words.

"Kirk, old buddy, the world will end before the Tigers win another World Series." Then came Arian's challenge to Kirk. "Loser buys all night at Niko's." When you support a team your whole life, a challenge against them is like a challenge against your manhood. No true fan would ever back away from his team. So now Kirk sat in traffic, bored, stressed, and smiling from ear to ear. "Get ready to open that wallet wide tonight Arian. I'm going to be really thirsty."

As the minutes wore on, Kirk's mind began to wander. He thought about Arian's mention of the end of the world. Edgar Cayce, the famed prognosticator, had made reference to the solar cycle peaking causing a rash of sunspots and solar bursts.

Cayce had been right before. He had predicted W.W.I, the defeat of Hitler in W.W.II, the independence of India, and of course the deaths of both Roosevelt and Kennedy. Maybe Cayce knew what he was talking about.

It wasn't like he was alone in his concern. Kirk remembered a prediction he had read from Jeanne Dixon, known as America's most famous psychic. When she was looking out of her window at

Washington D.C., she saw only a barren wasteland. The greenery of the mall had been replaced by utter devastation. Kirk realized that Dixon was no hack at predictions. Dixon, like Cayce, had a good track record. She had predicted the Apollo tragedy of 1967. How about how she told F.D.R. of his coming death six months before it occurred. She was also right about the assassinations of both Martin Luther King and Robert Kennedy. This lady had a track record when it came to being right. After his triumph of W.W.II, she had predicted Churchill's defeat in the next election; he lost. (19)

As the traffic began to move more quickly, Kirk sat up straighter behind the wheel. He thought about the show he had seen pertaining to the disaster of the Philadelphia experiment. He clicked on the Sirius satellite TV system in his Jaguar while the car drove itself. He searched the guide for the Discovery channel icon. Kirk scrolled down the episode list that appeared. At the middle of the P listing he found episode 415, the "Philadelphia Experiment." He clicked on the listing and a face appeared on the visual screen below the dashboard. Kirk clicked off visual and the face disappeared. Immediately, a narrator's voice was heard.

"In 1943, the Navy destroyer the U.S.S. Eldridge became invisible for four hours. This is the story of why and what happened."

Since he was anxious to get to the part he vaguely remembered, he began to fast forward through the commentary only stopping now and then when a phrase interested him.

"The 1943 Philadelphia Experiment resulted in time tunnel experiments in the 1980's.... Through the use of abandoned Einstein and Tesla Unified Theory Technology, the U.S. Navy desired to make a ship invisible to radar. This was of utmost importance since German U-boats were sinking 50 percent of allied vessels traversing the Atlantic Ocean."

Kirk pressed fast forward again; then plays. "The ship disappeared from a dock in Philadelphia only to appear 275 miles south in Newport News. When it reappeared shortly thereafter in Philadelphia, the crewmembers were in various forms of distress. There were men embedded in the steel framework. Others became transparent, insane, burned alive, or even able to walk through walls. Sadly, some disappeared never to be seen again. Two brothers jumped from the ship as the experiment began. They landed in 1984 at a research facility on Long Island. One brother returned to 1943 while the other stayed in the future." (19)

Kirk pushed stop. The voice ended. That's it, exactly like Jeanne Dixon saw. Before he could ponder the similarity of the two futures, he saw the flashing lights of Niko's.

The car parked itself on the street and Kirk swung the door shut with his left hand. He caught his left ring finger on the handle and grimaced in pain. He walked towards the welcoming neon of his favorite former hometown bar. It is a place he seldom visited anymore. But a place he often thinks about.

Kirk saw Arian sitting at the bar as soon as he walked in the door. Arian is the same age as Kirk. He was almost in as good shape as Kirk except for the beginnings of a beer gut. Arian never had kids and didn't like holding or kissing them; just their mothers.

"Hey buddy!" Arian yelled across the bar. Kirk waved and crossed the room to his boyhood friend. He can see immediately by Arian's actions that he has been there a while. When he spoke he seemed to sway like a salsa dancer. The two gave a man hug where they shake with their right hands, hug with their left while slapping each other's back.

Arian had moved to Long Island nearly the same time as Kirk. The only difference was, after graduating college, the lure of the city had brought Arian back to his boyhood home. Arian was named after his grandfather and every first born grandson carried the name of Arian. The connotations of the name certainly influenced Arian's personality and beliefs. He was a frequent visitor to Niko's and most people there knew him.

The place, and most of the people, had changed since Kirk and Tammy had hung out there. Although neither of them were big drinkers, the allure for them had always been Niko's Italian heroes. Tammy always said they were the best in the Bronx.

"Sit down man," Arian said as he slammed his hand down on the seat next to him.

"No thanks." Kirk pointed to the back of the bar. "Would you mind if we sat in a booth?"

"No problem buddy." Arian picked up his beer. "Pete, could you send Jenny back for Kirk's order."

Kirk waved off Arian. "Don't bother her yet Pete. Just give me a Bud Light. Thanks." He picked up the frosty bottle.

Arian yells from a booth in the back. "My tab Pete; this is that Tiger fan I told you about."

Pete looked up from the sink. "Congrats. You know the Yankees will be back next year."

Kirk smiled at the back of Pete's head. "I'm sure they will. So I want to enjoy this as long as I can."

Pete continued to face the sink. "Can't blame ya for that."

Kirk began to walk to the booth and saw a tattoo of the Declaration of Independence on Arian's shoulder and proceeding down his back. Arian was wearing a "Ginny" T-shirt and carrying a jacket. The words, "We the People" are plainly visible.

"Nice guy", said Kirk.

"He's okay. Wait till you see Jenny. She is hot." He motioned towards the other seat. "Sit down man. Ready to gloat yet?"

Kirk looked at his friend. Arian needed a shave, but he like Kirk, still looked young for his age. Hell, thought Kirk, why couldn't they get a hot young waitress. He didn't have to think twice about Jenny's age. He knew if Arian thought Jenny was hot, it also meant Jenny was young. Arian was like "Rosebud" trying to recapture his youth.

"I don't want to gloat. How the hell are you?" Kirk sat across from Arian. Kirk spoke again before Arian had a chance to respond. "I want to talk. That's why I wanted to sit back here."

"Whoa. I thought the bet was I pay for your drinks if the Tigers win. I don't remember anything about having to listen to you while we drink." Arian smiled. "Sure. What's up?"

"I know this will sound weird. Do you remember what you said when you made the bet?"

"Not really. Why?"

Kirk leaned toward Arian. "You said the world will end before the Tigers win a World Series again."

"Well. I guess I was wrong. They did and it didn't. Did it end, and no one told me?"

"Smart ass!"

"Ooh. Here comes Jenny. Hey sweetheart, how about another round," said Arian.

Kirk stood to face Jenny. She was hot and of course in her late twenties. Jenny had light brown hair, with blond streaks which hung in wisps around her gray eyes. As Kirk dropped his gaze, he could see she had nicely rounded breasts that were pressed tightly in her snug tank top. Her tanned belly appeared between her cropped black tank and short pleated white skirt. She was all Arian had said and more.

Jenny smiled sweetly and spoke a soft hello to Kirk as she gave him the ass out hug where nothing touches and is reserved for bad dates and co-workers. Kirk returned her smile.

"Let's see, that is one Bud Light and one Heine."

"Let's make those two Heines." Arian motioned to his lap. "One on the table and one right here."

Jenny smiled at Kirk but not as sweetly as before. "I'm used to your pal, A, by now." She leaned so close to Kirk that he can smell the fruity shampoo in her hair. She whispered to him. "He's harmless and he knows my boyfriend is a bouncer." She laughed. "I'll be back with…" She looked right in Arian's eyes. "One Bud-

Light and one Heineken." To add emphasis, she put her middle finger up. Then with a swish of her skirt she crossed the room.

"Do you have to act like a leech Arian?"

"Wouldn't you want a piece of that split tail?"

"Of course, but she's just doing her job and trying to get a good tip."

"If she wants good tips, she should be a stripper. Women are just like us; they want laid. You know, the human body has 206 bones in it. I should've asked Jenny if she wanted 207."

They laugh.

"Do you know what the easiest way to get laid is?"

"Pull your Johnson out at a Weight Watchers meeting?"

"No idiot, buy a hot tub."

"What do you mean?"

"When you bring a chick over to your place, just ask her if she wants to go in the hot tub. It's understood that if she says yes, her clothes are coming off. Nothing else needs to be said. Best investment I ever made.

Did I tell you about the guy from my gym whose wife had an affair with his three golf buddies?"

"No, you didn't. I think I would have remembered that" said Kirk.

"Jenny made me think about it. You know how older guys chase younger women because they need the extra excitement to get going. Now there are older women dating younger guys, especially at the gym, just for the sex. Of course, you can't get them pregnant and they don't demand the gift of diamonds later on." Arian drained his beer.

"There was one poor guy, whose wife was 15 years younger and hot as a firecracker. She would take turns with his three buddies. They were all pretty devious, and worked out a schedule. Since all four guys worked together, it wasn't difficult to fool the husband. Two of the three would always call the husband to go drinking or golfing while the third always had work or another commitment. All the while, the third 'friend' was visiting with the wife. The poor bastard never caught on that the three friends were rarely all together with him at the same time. The guys all had demanding careers and little time to nourish a relationship.

"So I guess the guys and his wife got what they wanted. They all got uncomplicated sex and the old guy got screwed."

Kirk drained the last bit of beer in his bottle, and then shook his head and said, "Adultery is not about sex, ultimately it is about how little we mean to each other."

Arian waved at Jenny and yelled to the front of the bar, "On my tab, Pete."

Jenny placed the beers on the table then bent over to wipe the table's surface of moisture. She then placed clean napkins on the table and lastly put the bottles on the napkins. While this went on, Kirk can't decide whether to look at her nipples straining through the tank top or the top of the back of her thigh where just a glimpse of her white lace panties could be seen. He opted to look at the wall. Why get all worked up over the unattainable.

Arian squeezed a tip into Jenny's hand. "Thanks sweetie, and when are we going to have that date?"

"A", you're the kind of guy who is gone in the morning when you wake up and also finds that your diamond earrings are missing."

"Yeah, but I'd replace them with a gold bracelet."

They all laughed and Jenny smiled and said, "Let me know if you need another round." She placed the empties on the tray, gave Kirk a quick smile, and was gone.

"So have you invented anything lately? I remember when you thought the Thor wood splitter would be a big seller and then the Flying Salsa Mexican UFO restaurant".

"Actually I'm thinking of opening a state of the art drive in theater and restaurant called Lolich-wood". Said Kirk.

"That would be cool".

"Yeah, we can show the UFC fights also".

Arian said to Kirk, "There's a bar down the street that has bourbon whiskey aged 20 years in the bottle. Do you want to go there?"

Kirk replied, "Only wine ages in the bottle. They make whiskey in a charred barrel and it ages as long as it is in the barrel. The longer it ages the stronger it gets but the less there is. Once it's bottled, it is what it is."

Arian swore, "God dammit, I've been paying extra for those shots because the bartender said the older the year on the bottle the better. That reminds me. Do you remember when we hauled the Seadoo's to Lake Michigan and we rode all weekend and that group we met at the bar wanted to ride west and we went east?"

"Yeah?"

"They came upon a cave in Michigan City and found Al Capone's long lost stash of 2,000 cases of whiskey. They sold them for $300,000. I would've kept them."

"Would've been hard to carry back on two wave runners."

"Yeah, I didn't think of that. If we had gone with them, it would've been a six way split of $50,000 each."

Arian looked at Kirk and said, "You remember what we were talking about?"

As he waited for a response, he took a long drink of beer.

Kirk looked quizzically at his friend. "I guess it was sexual?" Kirk smiled and began to speak. "You mean as long as there are young waitresses. I was getting ready to tell you, before Jenny showed up, about people I've known. Being the head of security, people know they can trust me and are comfortable talking to me since I'm an expert on divorce. I guess it is always the same. One would blame the other, whether justified or not. They failed to realize one of them had changed while the other hadn't. Where's the loyalty after all those years? You would think there would be a bond that would outlast anything. 'For better or for worse and in sickness and in health.' People should read their wedding vows on every anniversary. I re-read them when I was getting divorced. It really struck home!"

Kirk took a long gulp of beer.

Arian took a long drink of beer and slammed his bottle on the table.

Kirk took another smaller drink.

"My boss told me about a friend of his. The friend let his 'down and out' brother move in with him because his brother needed some help. While the hubby was away on business trips, the brother started sleeping with his sister-in-law. All at once, the husband is out on the street. The bitch got a PFA against her husband. They get divorced. The wife gets support. Get this. The wife marries the brother and gets the damn house too."

Arian said, "Most of the problems in today's society can be traced back to women's rights. Look at the divorce rate. Guys I know are looking for a younger one that hasn't been ruined or isn't too career oriented. They want us to be wage earners but enjoy all the feminine stuff like them. Feminists are hostile! Prices sky rocketed when they started working. Now, you can't get by on one income. And these kids, what a bunch of sissy's. You can't discipline them. They're all fat. They play virtual reality games all day and don't exercise."

Kirk said, "Yeah, Generation XXL. They're like shape shifters; fat kids who like fast food. Their mothers don't make them and their fathers aren't around to be afraid of. What did you think of that movie last year where we get invaded by China and all the Americans in the movie were grossly overweight and couldn't fight or even run away and we ended up surrendering. Those stupid liberals in Congress bid out our microchip contracts to China for the lowest cost and the chips all have kill switches in them. Why would our military purchase anything from China? All our weapons technology shuts down and that scene of our navy getting destroyed was worse than Pearl Harbor. We expected fair treatment under the Geneva Convention and they made the Bataan

Death March look like child's play by slaughtering us. The shame is it's a real possibility. We really do purchase weapons components from China, even after the conflicts we've had with them."

"Yeah, "*Made in China*" was the name of the movie and who saves the day; the aging baby boom generation. The 30 million retirees that survived take up arms and fight for freedom like the founding fathers after the Generation XXL kids surrendered. I loved that scene where a large group of Americans were being chased by the trans-human Red Army through a narrow canyon and the 'seniors' decide to take up position in the rocks on a suicide mission to buy their grandkids' time to escape and they ambush the 'chinks'. It was like the Battle of Thermopylae between the Spartans and Persians. The teens hear the gunfire and decide to return to help their grandparents only to find that they had already won the battle."

"Yeah, the movie sent a message about the violence against seniors that had occurred a few years ago and it was cool how they had all those veteran movie stars in cameo roles fighting for freedom; Daniel Craig, Will Smith, Vin Diesel, Brad Pitt, Ben Affleck and the Rock. That was so moving."

"Don't forget Angelina Jolie, Cameron Diaz and Jessica Alba."

"Man did Cameron get so wrinkled around the eyes!"

"Funny how movies have changed. So many controversial movies come out now with a sequel the following week from the other point of view. It works well with war movies and cop movies. American view, Middle Eastern view; cop view, robber view. It makes you think about both sides. I even like how they take the classics and update them years later with the same computerized actors and how their lives turned out. Kind of gives closure to the movie and makes a lot of money for the studio."

"The other movie I really liked was the *War in Heaven*. It told the biblical story of Lucifer's rebellion."

"Yeah, the special effects were great. The more powerful angels were bigger; like in the *Hobbit*."

"Yeah, each of the nine levels of angels was distinct. They never did show Gods face though."

"You know, getting back to these women. Maybe 40 percent of women are better off but they ruined it for the ones that wanted to stay home and raise a family or even work part time. The feminists failed to recognize that some smart career women have nature calling for children also. Instead they've eradicated fathers out of kid's lives. That's their biggest accomplishment. These poor kids have to deal with their mothers frustrated hostile, demeaning attitudes. If couples put their own interests secondary, we could raise healthy, smart, successful kids!" (26)

Arian said, "Housewives today are nothing but lazy women in disguise. Divorce a housewife and you'll be paying for the next 18 years. Excuse me, 22 in New Jersey. They make you pay support even while the kids are away at college. There's a total anti-male double standard. When they mention us it's preceded by 'abusive' and when they mention themselves, it's preceded by 'battered'. These indignant feminists don't want us to have any say in raising the kids. Only they can decide whether to have the kid or abort the fetus. But we get handed an invoice for the rest of our lives to pay. Hostile feminists like Gloria Steinem and Margaret Sanger, the mother of abortion, wrote books about how marriage is bondage and exists for our benefit. Marriage is prostitution and women can't be free unless they destroy the family unit and raise the kids without the father. In the 1950's, 95 percent of adults were married with four children and there was no legal abortion or welfare and people had manners. The mom may not need the man but her children sure do. (26)

You know, some men can't handle being caged. We have real problems with being controlled and being told what to do. Between the government, the courts and these vindictive women, sometimes you have to be a man and strike back. They leave you no choice.

It's the only way of feeling whole. That's why I. . . " Arian stopped what he was saying and after an awkward pause added, "Marriage only became a religious ceremony in 1563 with the Council of Trent. It didn't even become a legal commitment until 300 years ago. They should call it a Business Marriage Contract instead of a Marriage Certificate."

Kirk broke the silence and said, "That fight or flight response is hereditary you know. The neuroD2 gene controls it...Seems like we're becoming a nation of sheep; and sheep always get led to slaughter. How about marriage counseling? That's the kiss of death! The hunted have become the hunters. Why don't they think we have a loving interest in our children? Most guys I know would've raised the child alone if it hadn't been aborted and we had some say in the matter. Let's face it, some women aren't mother material and some men don't deserve their kids." (26)

"Their mothers are the reason kids can't handle teasing and explode with violence. When I was growing up, if you looked at my old man the wrong way, he'd belt you one. You had no choice but to learn to turn the other cheek. Children have a need to be with the two people who brought them into the world. No child support check can heal that wound of separation."

Kirk said, "I think a lot has to do with being politically correct. Everyone is offended by everything. You can't crack a joke or say anything without some group complaining. It's ridiculous! Everyone is so thin skinned that they erupt with violence. I blame the media for that. And these kids won't even enlist in the army. We had to open up the military to foreigners who are then allowed to become citizens. We've even gone so far as to enlisting criminals who volunteered for an opportunity to be freed in one of six third world countries after four years of service and renouncing their U.S. citizenship to return. The Founding Fathers must be turning over in their graves. They gave us freedom and self-government but how are we going to be able to hold onto it? It seems like in one lifetime, the country we grew up in is gone, changed for the worst!

And how about the overpopulation lie we were told in high school. "You should have two kids and maintain zero population growth. There aren't enough resources to sustain the planet." Instead, we're dealing with an obesity problem. Someone should've looked at when the baby boom generation was due to retire and figured out that zero population growth leaves us short on replacing and sustaining the large numbers of people that were retiring. Global overpopulation may be a problem but not in Western society where we value wealth and career above all else. I also read that in 1960, 25 percent of the world's population was white. Now it is 15 percent and in 2050 it will be 10 percent. Our population will drop by over 100 million around the world while Third World countries add 100 million people per year. Even after culling the seniors, we're in this situation with Social Security and immigration because we were told it was bad to have more than two kids and we are actually having only 1.3 per family."

"I know. Family size has dropped from 6.5 in 1900 to 5.1 in 1967 to 3.3 today if they stay married. Birth rates are at their lowest since the Black Plague 600 years ago. I don't know how we are going to pay for everything when we have a population implosion and negative economic growth. Look at all those empty Mc-Mansions. People went from 4000 square foot homes to 2000 square foot townhomes to 200 square foot nursing home rooms where they're put to sleep."

"Yeah, in a 20 square foot plot."

"Also, look at all those successful women who opted not to have kids in order to get ahead. Capitalism seems to be our best contraceptive. Our best and brightest didn't reproduce. Female wealth and education equals lower birth rates. Yet the trailer trash has six kids."

Arian added, "That's called biological degeneration. I read a book on eugenics. When you think about it, in this global economy, we are the minorities. China or India or the Middle East has twice as many people each than all the white people in the world combined!"

"Too bad they laced tobacco fields with radioactive uranium in the 60's. Look it up. There were very few cases of throat and lung cancer prior to that."

Arian switched thoughts as the alcohol kicked in.

"I do like how the army has switched from green to Union Blue uniforms. It seems to instill pride; like when we were fighting the Revolutionary War and had cavalry troops in the Indian Wars."

Kirk said nothing.

Arian switched thoughts, "Remember that song from the 1970's, 'American Woman'?"

"Yeah, it was better than the remake."

"Agreed, but did you ever turn up the volume at the end so you can hear what he says?"

"Yeah, yeah. It says goodbye American Woman"

And they both speak in unison.

"Goodbye American shit!"

The two burst out laughing. Arian got up and put a dollar in the juke box and played the song.

Kirk said, "Can't live without them."

"Yeah but…"

They both said in unison.

"There's nothing like a woman on her knees with her butt in the air and her back arched."

They both laugh.

"A woman can ride all she wants but the man has to finish on top!"

After a reflective pause, Kirk said, "Well, a lot of guys ducked out rather than provide for their family. I don't know how you could do that to your kids! Seems like women were raised to fear us. Want to see a grown man cry? Ask him to talk about his father. We thought that working and protecting and fixing things meant love. They want emotional intimacy and judge relationships by the quality of the friendship. We just make money and tough it out.

"I do like how now, 20 percent of all teachers must be hired from retired military or managers from corporations. Ethics classes are also mandatory. What does a 22–year-old out of college know about the real world anyhow?"

Arian began to feel his liquor and the insulating effect of his beer jacket.

"They all give that sympathy line about how they were abused or raped. It's always the 'man's' fault. If it wasn't for sex, I could do without them."

A woman with thick cankles and a short haircut stood up after over hearing the conversation and yelled out, "Why don't you just go plant a tree. It's the equivalent of removing 700 pounds of carbon monoxide from the air. You could drive 600 miles without polluting the environment. It will make you feel a lot better."

Arian wheeled around wide eyed and angry and exploded, "Who the fuck asked you your opinion bitch!" Then he laughed and said, "You know you have summer teeth? Some are going this way and some are going that way." They laugh. "I bet her name is Robin Swallows and her maiden name was Spitz".

The woman smiles and says, "I'm sure the best way to your heart is through your chest" as she grasps a knife on her table.

Kirk calmed the two of them down, drained his beer and continued.

"A trustworthy guy is not good enough for them. Now they need variety."

Arian responded. "I don't get the white women with black guys. I did have three women ask me to give them anal. I always refused. I told them why waste a perfectly good vagina!"

They both laughed the laugh of people beginning to feel the effects of liquor.

"Remember when they tried to bring back the styles from the 60's a couple of years ago?"

"It was like Austin Powers again for about eight months."

Sitting in the next booth were Arian's friends Lance Southworth and Kelly Bravo.

Kelly said, "I feel for you guys, women know the system and take advantage of it. Our breasts are like smart bombs. I know some women who, when they find a guy with money, will tell them they're fixed and there's no need for protection. Hoping to get pregnant, they figure they'll get married or get support payments. It's a no lose situation. I do have to say that guys are dumb. Even with marriage and cohabitation laws being obsolete and null and void, a woman can still lock a payment in with pregnancy."

Lance yelled, "What?"

Kelly said, "Don't worry baby, get the tab and I'll take good care of you later." She goes on to say, "We love sex and trick you into buying us things and giving us all your money or we won't give it up. I read that a woman's clitoris has twice as many nerve endings than a man's penis and is twice as sensitive. When we girls get together, we laugh at how easy you guys are!"

Lance added, "Among primates, humans have the largest penis. Must be a reason for that! But you can have the money. All we want is to drink hard have sex, an occasional fight or two, tell off color jokes, and go to strip clubs when you're out of town."

Kelly glared at him and said, "Let's go."

Kirk added, "See what I mean. When women get together and talk, they put all kinds of ideas in each other's heads. Couples should hang out with family members. Other women poison a relationship with their 'advice'".

You have to give women credit though. A lot of guys mistreated them and they opted for freedom. They used the system. Nowadays, women have excelled at jobs we never thought they could do. Women are better educated and make up 60 percent of the college grads, get better grades, have a majority of the professional jobs and have as many executive positions as men.

They're not financially dependent on us anymore. Twice as many single women buy homes than men. They want security while all we want are big screen TV's, football on Sunday and sex for fun. They seem to be evolving while men are digressing. Two women recently climbed the Infinite Spur of Mount Foraker in Alaska. Only seven world class male teams have climbed that vertical maze of crevasses and chutes. If it wasn't for heavy labor jobs and reproduction, they might not need us. Career women are actually the best to date. They understand the finances and keep that separate from just wanting companionship like we do. I think we are just so used to what's out there in our forties that we don't realize that all the good ones are gone by 25. All that's left are damaged goods, like us."

Arian said, "They are where they are due to government quotas and affirmative action. White males are discriminated against. Civil rights don't apply to us. Fifty years from now, we'll be needing protection from them. Imagine if that closet lesbian Hillary had won the election in 2016? That's why separate but equal is better. Let them pay their own way, have their own place. Never let a woman move in with you. They just take and take. The first thing they want to know is how much you're worth! That's why more adults live alone than in families or with a mate. You had better learn to like yourself because you are the only person you'll spend the rest of your life with."

Kirk said, "Actually, there's been a rise in communal living where successful professionals buy five or six or seven bedroom McMansions and live in a college dorm like atmosphere. No marriage, no demands, plenty of company. Most women don't know how to play fair because they never played sports like we did. Although they're taking that over also!"

Arian said, "Not the UFC! There's no faking hand to hand combat. That Chuck Liddell-Mike Tyson UFC 250 fight was a classic even though they were both in their late forties!"

"Yeah but Brock Lesner in UFC 200 was juiced to the max. What are they up to now?"

"UFC 450 is coming up next Saturday."

"I hear they are going to wear metal shark net suits and go up against big game animals just like they did in Rome!"

"Did I tell you that I've been taking martial arts? We both boxed as teenagers but I'm learning Muay-Thai, Grappling and Ju-Jitsu."

Arian became sullen and added, "It's a shame the National Organization of Men didn't work out. Women have N.O.W., why couldn't we have N.O.M.? You didn't see any metro men join that one!"

Kirk said, "That started as a group of disgruntled divorced male professionals who were fed up with the divorce laws. It was great that they voided cohabitation laws, but then the right wing anti-government hate groups joined. They saw a predominately white male organization with clout. In the 1940's and 50's, the government was our ally. It rescued us from the Depression and W.W.II. But Watergate, the Kennedy and King Assassinations, and Vietnam sowed the seeds of government distrust. Our trade policies that destroyed the auto and steel mills fueled anti-government feelings. The Cold War taught us how well disinformation worked. Then came Ruby Ridge and Waco. Gun control and unreasonable taxes sounded the battle cry of 'Give me liberty or give me death!' (16)

"Once the K.K.K., Patriot Movement and the Aryan neo-Nazis signed up, the original members and Oath Keepers dropped out. We were left with an anti-government organization which was shut down as a terrorist group! Many of the members were explicitly ex-marines who enlisted for the training to use for their own means if a race war broke out.

"It's amazing how the dominant group always yields to the minority; almost out of guilt. Life is about who wants it more;

who's hungry. That's what worries me about terrorism. France tried to appease them and look what happened."

Arian said, "I hear you there philosopher buddy. Membership in hate groups has doubled since 9-11. After reading the *Turner Diaries* and *Why Race Matters*, I agree with the militias. And the Jews, they worship in their synagogues of sin. Can you believe what's left of Israel will become our 64th state? It's bad enough that the Saltzbergers own *The New York Times* and the Bernsteins own the *Post*; they control everything. You want another round?"

Kirk replied, "No, what do you mean? Slavery was wrong but it gave blacks the greatest opportunity in the world by having their great-grand kids born here. The government might be inefficient and make mistakes but we're the envy of the world. Our economy can overcome any disaster or terrorist attack due to our wealth, resources, technology, generosity and freedoms!"

"I've never heard the big "Thank You" from the NAACP to northern whites for ending slavery. Over 300,000 northern white males died helping them," said Arian.

"As for the Jews, they've been persecuted for thousands of years. They finally wised up and used the system instead of fighting it. The American Jew is the antis-Isis of the American black. The only way to not be persecuted again is to control the banks, media and then politics. It's self-preservation, hell, its capitalism.

"I guess money to get power and power to guard money. You know, instead of watching every Sept 11th anniversary they should've been watching every April 19th due to the American Revolution, Waco and the Oklahoma City bombings occurring that day! I just don't feel that this government represents us anymore. I'm glad there's a third party now. The difference between Republicans and Democrats is like the difference between Coke and Pepsi. These politicians are so afraid to offend anyone because they'll lose the minority vote. They should remember that we're still a majority in this country and over 80 percent of us vote. We choose the politicians; they don't choose which voters they want!"

Arian's head bobbed and his eyes rolled up into his head and he swayed to the left.

"Ever been to the Sexual Harassment Club outside of Vegas? Anything goes below the waistline; that is, between men and women. You can pick out any woman without her consent and do whatever you please. Some dress as school girls; others as nurses or in lingerie. . . "

Arian swayed back to the right.

"And another thing, these politicians sell us out with political correctness and want to disgrace America's past and accomplishments. Political correctness reinforces uniformity of expression in order to exercise centralized control over the masses. They rewrote all of the history books in 1992 downplaying our Founder's achievements because they were slave owners. There were no celebrations of the American century on December 31, 1999, because they think we stole this land from the Indians and Mexicans. They have cultural amnesia; we created everything and abolished slavery. They even portray the fuckin Boy Scouts as a hate group because they won't let homos in."

"You know they did the same thing in France after WWI. The Pacifists downplayed the heroism of the soldiers and de-glorified their achievements at Verdun. They made the soldiers the victims. The liberal teachers union rewrote the text books by purging them of courage and self-sacrifice and took an international non-patriotic view. Hitler studied their once great society. France fought Germany for four years with massive casualties in WWI but only lasted six weeks against Hitler. Charles de Gaulle blamed France's humiliating collapse on the school system's pacification of its students."

"That's enough for me. I'm feeling it already."

Arian swiped the chip in the back of his hand which acted like a credit card.

"I sure got off cheap. I'm glad you're a light drinker." Arian laughed.

"Well thanks, A."

Kirk stood up and shook his friend's hand but avoided eye contact.

"Take it easy. Tell Jenny I said bye. I've got to go. I have a long drive."

"Can you drive? Should we order a C-cup of coffee from Jenny?"

Kirk smiled, "I'm fine. Thanks again. It was good talking with you."

"Wait, a few jokes before you leave Kirk." Arian loved to tell off color jokes.

Kirk said, "Before you go any further you better be careful. You know we have speech codes and they turn any racial comments into hate crimes and terroristic threats. We're becoming like Brazil where it is a crime to make a racial comment. If you're not colorblind, you better change your glasses before you get into trouble!"

"I know my rights. I've been to the National Archives in D.C. and have read the Bill of Rights. Don't blame me because I view my race as an extended family and want to protect our kids more than someone else's. Hate crimes are thought crimes and the government can't tell me what to think. Didn't someone famous say, "I may disagree with what you say but shall defend to the death your right to say it?" Censorship is more dangerous than free speech. I won't be silenced because what I believe is offensive to someone else. The thought of being punished for speaking the truth and being forced to submit to what's best for everyone else is no longer freedom in this country!"

Kirk was taken aback by Arian's comments but respected his individualism and the two walked towards the door.

Arian grabbed Kirk's right forearm and asked, "You think that skier Linsey Vonn and that tainted German model; Heidi Klum that got killed in a hit and run a few years ago was an accident? I not only know who did it but I helped."

Kirk looked at his friend and said, "You almost had me but that's fucked up, you've got to be kidding me. What are you mental? You need some sort of help."

Arian's expression changed as he gave Kirk that dead eyed stare. Kirk expected his drunken friend to throw a punch. Instead, Arian said, "Maybe you're right. You've gone 'incog-negro' and I'm the one that is fucked up. I'm a bad American because I believe the money I earn belongs to me; I think owning a gun makes you smart; I don't think being a minority makes you a victim or entitled to nothing; I think the cops have a right to shoot you if you break the law; I think people should speak English in this country; I'm a bad American because I don't mind carrying a picture ID card; I think if you're too stupid to figure out how a ballot works, you shouldn't vote; I think it doesn't take a village to raise a child, just two parents of the opposite sex; I believe illegal is illegal; and I believe there is only one American flag and you better not burn it! The liberal elite have taken on a religious fervor with their gun control, cap and trade, and recycling. It's not a sin to drive an SUV or hunt! I'll see you the next time you need a common sense talk. I've taken the oath and you should too. All the ex-military and police have." Arian turned and walked away.

Kirk said, "I'm out of here" and waved at Jenny and Pete and proceeded out into the night. Kirk thinks to himself, "We were such racists as kids. Why hasn't Arian matured?"

Walking toward him was a mid-forty looking man wearing a fedora hat and dressed in a baggy suit whose waistline was pulled up well above the waist and the tie was very short. He looked like someone out of a black and white movie from 100 years ago. A '57 Chevy passes by playing "In the Still of the Night".

The man walked right into Kirk and said, "Did you see "On the Waterfront"? That Marlon Brando is wonderful. That new singer Elvis is going to be something also. Why aren't these kids playing

97

"Ring around the Posey" or "You're it"? When I was a kid, mom would scream from the kitchen window for me to come home for dinner and any parent was allowed to discipline you. What's going on here? Where are the kids riding on handlebars with baseball cards in the spokes?"

He walked past Kirk saying, "I need a do over, eeny, meeny, miney, mo. Forget the principle, I'm scared of my father. Why can't a water balloon be the ultimate weapon anymore?"

Kirk watched him as he faded into the night.

As Kirk entered his car, the bitterness began to well up inside him. The discussion he had with Arian made him think about Tammy and they were not good thoughts. Kirk had never wanted to become the typical bitter middle-aged divorced man. But as he started up his car and he felt that way. Kirk's generation paid their alimony and got stuck with huge divorce and palimony settlements. It wasn't until three years ago that woman changed all the rules. With women earning more than men and more women in professional jobs, they were not going to play by the same rules that men had to deal with when they were the bread winners. When women have money, they don't share it. Funny how the rules changed when women became the meal ticket for men.

He knew music wouldn't be enough to occupy his mind on the drive home. He turned on the satellite connection to his cloud computer and said, "Edward Cayce". The screen brightened as the first sentence began to form. Kirk switched to audio and a voice began to narrate.

"Edgar Cayce was born on a farm in Kentucky in 1877. His father was a dowser, which meant he could discover underground water sources. Perhaps this was genetic for his son's latent talents. At the age of 10, Edgar awoke from a deep sleep and saw a woman at the edge of his bed. She filled his room with light and told him of his hidden talents. The woman told him that he would be able to heal the sick. Cayce quit school at 15 believing he was destined for more important things. Cayce was of the belief that one could cure themselves by concentrating on increasing their circulation to the inflicted area of their body. He was known to have fallen into trances. During which, he would provide medical procedures with the end result being the curing of the afflicted. Cayce would never take a fee for performing God's work.

"It was also well known that Cayce solved crimes and made accurate stock market predictions. Another of Cayce's talents was his ability to perform 'life readings'. These would be windows into a person's past lives.

"Among some of Cayce's beliefs were his claims that the pyramids were built in 10,500 B.C. and that they, as well as Stonehenge, were created by levitation.

"Some of his future predictions are the destruction of Japan as well as that of the west coast of what had been America. He also felt there would be upheavals in the Arctic and the Antarctica as well as a reversal of the hot and cold climates . . ." (19)

Kirk pushed the off button and the screen went dark.

When he heard the word upheaval, it made him think of the upheaval Tammy had caused in their lives. Kirk could no longer think about Cayce, only about Tammy.

As the car drove itself on, Kirk reminisced about how their life had been before Tammy ruined it for the entire family.

He thought about the day they bought their first house. It had been a one-year anniversary gift. Kirk was 22 years old. Then he pondered how his job had taken him all over the U.S. and overseas on special assignments. He also remembered how unhappy Tammy was when he went to Europe for three months. It was the chance of a lifetime for Kirk. He came home each month for one week. When he returned home on the second rotation, Tammy became cold towards him. This was the first time during their 11-year marriage this had occurred. How things had changed since the day they bought the house.

Kirk remembered the day he turned down the position to head security for PPS in Spain and Portugal. He did it because he feared that Tammy's fragile world couldn't survive overseas after she threatened to divorce him over the relocation. The guy who took his place is now corporate security director for PPS.

Since Kirk knew, in the corporate world, one couldn't survive turning down two transfers, he accepted a transfer to Oklahoma. Kirk hadn't been able to realize how he had become drunk with success. Tammy was miserable after having been uprooted from her mother and family events. But Kirk had seen the move as a way of getting Tammy to grow up and break her mother's hold on her. He didn't see the pain he had caused his wife, until he saw the note.

One evening, Kirk had returned home from work to find the house empty. The note explained how Tammy could no longer live in Oklahoma, and had taken Claire and Cole back to New York. The relocation and Cole's diabetes had become too much for her to handle alone. Although Kirk hated the northeast and was happy living in Edmond, OK, he managed to get a transfer to New Jersey. Everything was fine for about a year.

Then out of the blue, Tammy told Kirk she would never move again. She also wanted him to quit PPS. Kirk had never quit anything in his life. He had his sights set on a promotion to regional manager and nothing was going to stand in his way. Kirk remembered how he had told Tammy that he could find a better wife faster than a better career. The following week the sheriff delivered separation papers. Kirk often wondered if their blissful year in New Jersey was all just a legal maneuver. He knew that under New Jersey Law, a person had to be a resident of this state for a year to file divorce papers. Since Kirk felt that Tammy always had emotional problems, it was entirely possible she stayed with him for the year as a formality.

Six months after he received her papers, Kirk hired a lawyer. He had refused to believe that this was happening and knew she had no grounds.

As Kirk's marriage began to crumble, so did his job performance. The fact that his new boss was an ex-marine, with no people skills, didn't help matters. The ex-jarhead was very paranoid and verbally abusive to everyone. He was Kirk's polar opposite, a "rear admiral" who was only good at criticizing yesterday and placing blame. When Kirk thought his life couldn't get worse, it did.

Kirk car parked itself in the garage and he got out. He placed his palm on the security system and the house came to life with programmed commands based on the time of day and user. Lights could come on or off. Window blinds could open or close. The TV or radio could come on to Kirk's preferred channel. He shook his head hoping that the cool night air would take his mind away from the thoughts of Tammy.

As Kirk brushed his teeth, the mirror did a full medical body scan and downloaded it to the chip in the back of his hand as he thought of how his job performance had continued to slide. He spat angrily into the sink as he remembered having to take Prozac to function. He told the doctor how it scrambled his brain, and stopped taking them after six weeks. Kirk knew he was coming apart at the seams. He could no longer focus and concentrate like he used to. It all seemed like only yesterday or, at times, a hundred years ago. If only he could change his way of thinking and understand that Tammy didn't do it to him, she did it to herself.

Kirk always liked those "Rocky" movies. He often thought of the scene where Adrian wouldn't support Rocky until he was in a coma. When he awoke from the coma, she told him "To Win". That was all the motivation Rocky needed. All Kirk wanted to hear was for his wife to tell him to succeed or to make her proud at work and he would've advanced to the top. Instead, he never got that vote of support from her.

As Kirk lay down on his bed, he didn't want to think of Tammy anymore. He smiled as he thought about Jenny. She was in her late twenties but she looked much younger than; almost as

101

young as Vespa looked that afternoon in college. Kirk remembered how he would tell Vespa the Norse tale of the Bifrost; the bridge between heaven and the realm of man that Thor would cross. It was said that it would collapse at the end of the world. Kirk stopped smiling. Although Vespa had been cute and the sex was great, it had not been one of Kirk's shining moments. The guilt had entered his body almost as soon as the sperm had entered hers. As she finished climaxing and reached for his hand, he pulled it away. The euphoria she had just felt began to subside with her smile. He remembered her words even now.

"Kirk, is something wrong?"

He got out of the bed and put on his pants. She tried to dredge up a smile as she asked the next question.

"When can I see you again?"

Her smile began to wane even before he answered. The guilt began to mount as he pulled on his T-shirt. He wanted out of there now. The words came out in a torrent without even thinking.

"When hell freezes over, baby."

Vespa didn't know what to do for an instant. Then she sat up, the sheet falling from her flushed pert breasts. She reached for a clock and flung it at him. Between sobs, she tried to get out "fuck you" but Kirk never heard her. He was already out the door.

Kirk rolled over and closed his eyes. In spite of all his thoughts, the beer was having a welcome effect. Kirk was beginning to doze. But he opened his eyes a tiny bit and looked into the darkness and whispered;

"I'm sorry, Vespa."

At 2:28 am, a strange unidentified object is sighted flying over Route 46 in Rockaway and over Roxbury and Budd Lake; almost directly over Kirks home.

Chapter 6

TUCSON

"Fear not the path of truth, but the lack of people walking it."
(Robert Kennedy)

Vespa Prada was 44 years of age, had never been married, and could not have children. Infertility may have been the reason she had never taken the vows, for it definitely wasn't because of her appearance. Vespa was Italian with olive skin, brown hair, and with eyes of a brown hue that nearly matched her hair. She was a little more than five feet tall. Although it was common for Italian women her age and height to become pear shaped, that was not the case with Vespa. Her frame was very athletic and her rear was firm and well rounded. Vespa worked hard to keep her heart-shaped butt in shape. Vespa was an only child but never her mother's favorite.

Vespa's breasts were as firm as the rest of her body and they ended with thimble like nipples. Of course, the fact that they were always hard in the cool air of her accounting office didn't seem to bother her. She made sure that the sheer blouses she wore were just small enough to accentuate her attributes and didn't care that they were NSFW or not suitable for work.

Although her employer, AAP, had a strict policy against fraternizing among employees, this didn't seem to deter Vespa. In fact, she was notorious for her sexual escapades. Her nickname among the corporate executives was "spinner." The executives had given her this moniker because during sex, she changed positions so frequently that her small frame seemed to spin through the entire Karma Sutra. Upon meeting Vespa for the first time, if she liked you, her back would genuflect while speaking to you. The guys in the office knew this would give her intentions away every time. Her preference though, was for a man's tongue between her legs flapping her oversized lips back and forth. Vespa also had the odd habit of burping out loud. Everyone joked about it privately but no one would say anything to her because she was just so damn hot to look at.

Vespa also spun from job to job, usually changing jobs every five years. Her pattern was to use her body to get vested and then move on. She made no bones about using her looks to get ahead or give head. In fact, she had slept with 118 male partners over the past 26 years. As she gained more experience and materialistic greed, she became a hater of family and children. She was loathsome of women that reproduced and were saddled with kids. The best years of a woman's life shouldn't be spent as a cow. She viewed motherhood as one's own Trojan horse. Whenever she saw families together, she'd make a disparaging remark. She usually worked long hours around holidays just to avoid families.

One summer, Vespa joined an online bondage club where women would view profiles of men and approve up to 20 and then designate a night and time that one would come visit the lucky lady. Only the game was that the woman must be lying naked on her bed face down. The gentleman would be wearing a ski mask and he would pretend to break in the unlocked front door and bind his victim's wrists to the head board and proceed to have his way while the young lady fantasized about being raped. Sometimes she would be left handcuffed and a second perpetrator would participate. They had scripts that they would act out and the ladies would pre-approve what was permissible and how many would be allowed. Vespa heard that one lady set a record by having all 20 men visit her on the same evening. Vespa found the game simply irresistible until one of her friends became the victim of a homicide. Apparently one of the guys told a friend who told a friend and on the selected evening a psychopath showed up and murdered the guy and took his place in the game. After having his way with the willing participant, he sliced the poor ladies' throat from ear to ear. Vespa never participated again and authorities quickly shut the game down.

Vespa was not like some women who have no choice but to use their bodies to garner success or maintain a low trimmed nail on their middle finger. She had a photographic memory and the mental bandwidth that had enabled her to breeze through C.W. Post College. Her brain had been digitally hard-wired for technology and not relationships by all the hours she spent as a kid on the Internet, smart phones and video games.

Although Vespa had graduated high school as a virgin, she more than made up for it in college. After the rigidness of her private Catholic school upbringing, she found college as a time to experience total sexual freedom. This had reached the point to where she would have sex with two guys at once but never crossed the inter-racial line. Today, as a finance manager for the telemarketing firm of AAP, one guy was sufficient and if he happened to be a corporate executive, so much the better.

The economic climate was so dire that most large corporations were turning to "downsizing" or "outsourcing overseas" to stay competitive. It was no surprise that Vespa was forced to leave her beloved home in the northeast to travel across the country to Tucson, AZ.

Corporate America had been telling society for years that they had been obliged to downsize or outsource to improve their service. In reality, all the corporations were doing was reducing their costs and compensating for low birth rates by moving the work overseas. Globalization added over $1 trillion dollars a year to multinational companies net revenues while costing American workers 60 billion dollars a year in lost wages. Apple, General Electric and many companies produced none of their product in the U.S.

Economic patriotism to buy American became a dirty word. Trade policies of the past 200 years designed to benefit Americans were replaced by a global economy. Even though American standards of living declined, it was good for the rest of the world. There was a worldwide economic shift. The most self-sufficient nation in history that produced 96 percent of what it needed was now dependent on foreigners for 50 percent of its autos, electronics, textiles and steel. Only airlines and phone companies were protected. Foreign ownership in airlines was restricted to 25 percent in case the Pentagon needs the planes to transport troops in times of war. Broadcast and phone companies are restricted to 20 percent foreign ownership to prevent sabotage and propaganda. (26)

After rejecting Mexico's push for a North American Union super state where all three countries have open borders and free trade and establish a common approach to security around the three countries as opposed to between, including the movement of goods along with a new NAFTA Tribunal court and monetary currency, the "Amero", we instead purchased the rugged desert-ocean Baja peninsula from Mexico and added it to California while legalizing five million immigrants. But the illegal immigration still didn't stop. Mexicans are hard workers and family oriented with their Catholic values. Most of the new citizens were relocated to the "Rust Belt" cities of Detroit, Cleveland and Pittsburgh in an attempt to revitalize the cities with eager workers and corporate tax incentives for new construction. These "ready-made" cities already had the infrastructure to support larger populations. Their heyday was in the 1950's when their populations were twice what they are now. The more than 350 million Americans live on only six percent of the land. Theoretically, the entire eight billion people of the world's population can all fit in the mainland U.S.!

In order to reduce competition in the above poverty level jobs, the U.S. thought it dealt with its continuing illegal immigration problem by paying Mexican workers to build a wall, and then told them to stay on the other side. We ended benefits to illegal's, prosecuted employers, and deported them to Tapa Chula, the southernmost city of Mexico. This was a costly 2,400 mile boat ride, rather than simply busing them back across the border. The long trek back to the U.S. by foot was nearly impossible. Ironically, Mexico controls its southern border by deporting 250,000 immigrants to Central America each year. Many believed that with an aging baby boom generation and low birth rates that we would be begging for 30 million young workers in 20 years. The health of the economy was what really should control immigration.

Immigration in America comes full circle every 20-30 years based on the economy and need for labor. The 1820s brought in 7.5 million Irish-Dutch immigrants; the 1880s brought in 23 million German-Italian immigrants. The Border Patrol was formed in 1924 to help control our borders. Illegal immigration costs the tax payers $125 billion a year in benefits and they occupy five percent of the jobs.

Along with this methodology to stop illegal immigration, the U.S. passed the Anti-Abortion Law with the exception for rape. If the mother chose an abortion for the child then the rapist received an automatic death penalty. It was believed that the abortions of 40 million U.S. children had allowed the immigration and terrorism problem to fester. Its elimination would create a larger homegrown English speaking U.S. workforce. If 12 million illegal immigrants were out of the picture, and a larger work force was being born, there would soon be enough U.S. citizens to replace the retirees and the "casualties" of the Chinese Flu. Convincing the public that unborn children are not an embarrassment or inconvenience to their parents was a daunting task. Family friendly policies were adopted. Income tax credits for children were increased to three thousand dollars each for the first three children born only. The creation of state run child rearing schools made it easier to preserve the lives of the innocent. With military enlistment dwindling, these kids would be groomed as our soldiers of the future if they were not adopted along the way. The public didn't know that a secret trans-humanism program was in place where these kids at puberty underwent a genetic sequencing chimera upgrade with a triple helix addition to be super soldiers. FDA approval of the artificial womb also made pregnancy more convenient for career and/or vain women to carry the fetus outside of their body. It is also estimated that world population in 2050 would be 12 billion; in 2100, 19 billion and that the Earth carrying limit for redistribution of world resources is at four billion people if everyone had a Western lifestyle.

America is a nation of diverse people-but everything that makes us American is exclusively European, descended from Western civilization and beliefs. European beliefs of freedom, liberty, and inventiveness founded this country. Beliefs not demonstrated in Asian, African or Muslim nations. America had become polarized between liberal and conservative. (28)

Vespa knew that in an economic climate such as this, her degree in accounting would be secondary. She was an "At Will" employee and office politics and employee cowardice went hand-in-hand. She used to say, "Why show them brains when all they really want is breasts." She would have to not only use her body to get a job with one of these outsourcing organizations but she also would have to leave New York and follow work to a place she hated.

Vespa hated the desert southwest. The landscaping with sand and rock didn't appeal to her. She longed for the green of the Northeast

She often preferred the additional two hour drive north on Route 17 to Flagstaff, and in particular, to Sedona. Vespa had found Sedona to be one of the Southwest's best kept secrets.

Sedona is a beautiful community nestled in Red Rock formations 90 miles south of the Grand Canyon. The town is filled with hundreds of specialty shops. Here, one could buy beautiful Indian jewelry, art and clothing. Vespa's greatest treasure was a Mandela she had purchased at a small shop on the strip. It was black with white feathers and real rattlesnake heads mounted in the center. The Mandela was a real conversation piece whenever she would have visitors.

The city is also well known for its infatuation with new wave thinkers. It is also the home of many mystic and psychic conventions. Psychology was outlawed in 2027 when it was proven that it was based on false premises. The brain does not control the mind and most drugs didn't work on mental illness. The mind is controlled by an invisible soul and good and evil forces. The brain is the hardware and the mind is the software. These factors are now taken into consideration in criminal investigations.

The Southwest has long been a haven for numerous UFO sightings from Roswell to Area 51. There have been retired military men who worked at Roswell who claim to have engineered lasers, integrated circuits, fiber optics, Kevlar vests, stealth technology and particle beam weaponry. Many of these sightings are of U.S. military "new concept" planes. This technology is probably based on alien principles. The recent unveiling of the newly developed V-shaped Lockheed attack planes could be an example of this. This aircraft has no conventional exhaust and contains complete stealth capability. These capabilities, plus the fact it has top-secret propulsion and laser weaponry, confirms the popular belief that it has taken the U.S. 80 years to copy or back engineer alien technology.

There are important individuals who have claimed an alien presence. In the 1950's, soon to be astronaut, Gordon Cooper saw UFOs while flying a fighter plane. An X15 pilot named Joe Walker filmed UFOs in 1962. In 1968, Apollo 8 astronauts saw a large craft that disappeared on the next orbit. Astronauts have witnessed UFOs rising from craters and blinking lights in craters. Astronaut Neil Armstrong claimed to have seen an alien base on the moon during the Apollo 11 landing. Ham radio operators picked up transmissions on the non-public frequency where the astronauts said," I'm telling you that there are other space craft out here. The base is on the far side of the crater's edge. They're watching us from the moon!" When the 1969 Apollo 12 lunar module ascent stage crashed down back onto the moon, seismic equipment picked up the impact and recorded the moon ringing like a bell for 40 minutes. The ringing was again recorded when Apollo 13's third stage fell to the lunar surface. Reverberations lasted for three hours and travelled to a depth of 25 miles and increased with depth. A natural satellite cannot be hollow. Rock samples show that the moon is 700 million years older than the Earth. (25)

As far back as a March 22, 1950, memorandum to J. Edgar Hoover, it was mentioned that there was documented evidence concerning alien aircraft. It was brought to the FBI Director's attention that the U.S. had in its possession at least three crash landed saucers and the deceased three crew members from each ship. (25)

This mystical mystery laden area is a place where Vespa felt comfortable. That is why she worked her fingers feverishly across her keyboard searching for accommodations. At last, she was successful in her search. As December approached, Vespa reserved her condo in Mystic Hills for the last week of the year. She couldn't wait till Christmas week when she could finally leave the desert.

Chapter 7

DIABETES

"Ask that part of you that is immortal, to defend the mortal."

The alarm went off at 5:15 A.M. Kirk jumped from his bed, put on his sweats, shaved, gathered his suit and gym bag and headed downstairs.

Four times a week, Kirk worked out at the YMCA located near his office. It was a way for him to beat the morning traffic on route 80 as well as staying in shape and releasing stress. The only downside to this athletic routine was paying a nurse/nanny/cook/housekeeper four times a week. An expense he could barely afford at this time. But when it came to his children's well-being, it was a price he would gladly pay.

Kirk's relationship with this "caregiver" could be described as different and possibly a little perverted. She was ten years his senior and they were an item for about four months as Kirk went through a "rough" period. Kirk matriculated to "younger" women and Rose stayed on as the family "caregiver". The relationship had always been covert. Not even the children suspected anything. They had a mutual understanding of convenience. Rose came and went as needed. She would cook for Kirk and his girlfriends. Kirk was concerned that she might do something to his date's food but she would cook and serve the meals and always give Kirk a sly smile. Twice she arrived unannounced while Kirk and his date were coupled in the sex act. Rose would silently stand in the bedroom doorway for a few minutes and stare at her twenty year junior protégé before making eye contact with Kirk. She would then smile at Kirk with that same sly smile and then turn away and proceed to do her chores.

When Rose developed breast cancer, she decided to go with a "natural cure". Kirk knew her days were numbered when the cancer spread to her liver but he still paid for her breast reconstruction and a face lift. It wasn't out of vanity. Kirk wanted her to die with dignity because she had become one of his few close friends.

Since Cole had developed diabetes right before his fourth birthday, many aspects of Kirk's life had to change. Many signs foreshadowed the arrival of the diabetes. Cole had been losing weight; he wouldn't eat, couldn't get enough to drink and was constantly urinating. Kirk would get up for work and find the bathroom sink lined with Dixie cups. Cole would have used them all during a single night. This would contribute to Cole not getting enough sleep. Kirk would become angry and yell at his son for not eating but also because Cole only wanted to drink soda or chocolate milk.

It wasn't until August, at which time Kirk as well as Tammy and other family members took the children to a concert in the park, that Cole became ill. He began to vomit after drinking chocolate milk. Tammy felt there was something very wrong with Cole. They rushed him to the hospital where Cole was diagnosed with diabetes. The nurse said they were lucky because most kids come to the hospital in a diabetic coma. Cole's blood sugar level that day was 984. A normal blood sugar level is between 80 and 120. One more night and Cole's body would've no longer been able to handle the spilling of sugar into his blood. The ketones from his body were depleting all of its fat cells in order to get nutrition.

Even though it was years since then, Kirk still remembered the difference that day between he and Tammy. While Kirk cried at the site of his little boy hooked up to tubes in a hospital bed, Tammy stood there cold as ice.

Cole was now 18. He stood 5'11" and weighed 160 pounds. He had his mother's good looks and he was a gifted athlete. He could run like the wind and was lightning fast; much like his father had been at that age. In spite of his diabetes, Cole excelled at baseball, football, track and basketball. An added plus from his sports activity was that it was a good way of keeping his blood sugars controlled; thereby reducing the amount of insulin he needed. Cole knew when his blood sugars were low because his legs would feel weak, but never thought twice about the devastating effects of the disease.

Kirk had become very involved with the disease since his son's diagnoses. Kirk got elected to the Board of Directors for JDRF. He knew that one in every eleven people has diabetes and that there were three million citizens in this country alone that had the more serious insulin dependent form of the disease. If the disease is left uncontrolled, it can destroy the small capillaries of the blood system, which then may lead to blindness, amputations, and kidney failure resulting in a reduction in life expectancy by twenty years. He even got his company, PPS, to switch their $30 million fundraising sponsorship from the United Way to JDRF.

The FDA had just approved a cure for diabetes and other autoimmune diseases. A bone marrow transplant from the same donor six months prior to there being an insulin producing islet cell transplant into the thymus gland had been proven to eradicate the disease. This is because the thymus gland is insulated from the body's immune system and therefore cannot be attacked by the white blood cells. The bone marrow transplant then introduces the immune system to its donor and allows the thymus gland to trick the immune system with insulin producing cells. The key to success is using the same donor for both transplants. This procedure had proven to be effective in curing diabetes. Availability of cells was the biggest setback. With 100,000 Americans waiting for organ transplants, Xenotransplantation of pig cells and organs held the most promise. In Pittsburgh, where polio was cured almost a century earlier, a team of scientists cloned pigs whose cells were genetically altered to be compatible with humans. Human anticoagulant genes were added to the pigs' DNA to avoid human rejection. (26)

Japan was also on the verge of a cure using stem cell research and organ re-generation. President Datchet would not allow uncontrolled stem cell research even though the vast majority of the people approved of it. Embryonic stem cells caused tumors in clinical trials. Stem cells can be harvested from other areas of the body. The Asians found success in creating pancreatic islet cells with the PDX-1 cells from the placenta.

Denmark was also close to a break through by using Smart Insulin that only releases insulin when glucose levels are above 140. The once-a-week shot had no risk of low blood sugars or diabetic shock.

Most cures take 15 years from the testing stage to FDA approval at a cost of $1 billion. Only one out of every one thousand drugs even makes it to clinical trials. Many drugs used to treat one disease or condition turned out to be useful for others. Aspirin was used as a pain reliever but its thinning of the blood properties reduced stroke and heart attacks. Viagra was tested as a heart medicine but improved erections. Rogaine was a blood pressure medicine that caused patients to grow hair. The diabetes protocol was also used for Alzheimer's and Parkinson's diseases.

Cole was perfectly healthy with his regimented system of exercise, diet, and an insulin drip through a meter taped to his abdomen. Cole could monitor his blood sugar through readings every fifteen minutes on his cell phone. He was on a long waiting list for his turn to be cured.

Sadly, many of the one million AIDS patients accused the government of procrastinating on a cure for AIDS when the cure for diabetes and Alzheimer's was published. They turned to the Gates-Buffet foundation for assistance. Some people believe that HIV was introduced by the government by injecting genetic modifications directly into the womb to get rid of some undesirable portions of society. This idea seems to be contradicted by the fact that the government has spent a considerably disproportionate amount of money on finding a cure for this disease at the expense of other diseases and required all citizens from 16 to 60 to undergo an HIV/AIDS virus test.

Kirk was only concerned that someday his son will be completely cured. But for now, Cole had been accepted at Penn State University. Cole had been confident that colleges would scout him to be a shortstop or a defensive back, but that hadn't occurred. Kirk had purchased a pitching machine and netted in a portion of the yard so that both children could practice their hitting skills.

As for Claire, she was now sixteen and was 5'9". Claire had brown hair like Kirk. Cole's dirty blonde hair resembled his mothers. She also had the same freckles on her cheeks that her dad had at that age. Claire was also an exceptional athlete. She ran track and played basketball and softball at her school. Her goal was to attend Rutgers University where she hoped to study law. Claire suffered from the same bad back that Kirk and his dad had. A degenerative L-5 disk was the genetic cause; only Claire's back seemed much worse than her Dads. At sixteen, she was just starting to blossom. Although Kirk was concerned about her defiant attitude, she always did that which he asked of her. Claire would always tell people her last name was Voyant due to her uncanny sixth sense.

Kirk had always been concerned about the children growing up without a mother. The children were his whole world. He knew losing their mother in the car crash three years ago had affected their sense of security. They had been through enough with moving from New York to Oklahoma and then back across the country to New Jersey. Then, of course, there was the divorce followed by the loss of their mother.

Both children were more mature than others their age and neither was afraid of change. Kirk would always tell them they could be anything they wanted to be. He always felt that confidence and determination would overcome ability every time in the real world.

Kirk and the children also attended religious services once per month. They initially would research a different faith each month and then attend their service. It had become a routine now to attend Catholic mass one month, then Jewish the next, followed by Muslim, Buddhist, Protestant, Lutheran and Hindu. Kirk believed this would make the kids more open minded and worldly.

Kirk stepped over the kid's "floor-drobe" and kissed the children goodbye and released the two powerful Dobermans into the fenced in yard. He was secure in the fact that at 6:00 a.m. Rose would arrive with her key to the house to care for the children. Kirk didn't like leaving the children so early but as was usually the case, he had a busy day planned.

Chapter 8

P. P. S.

"Inherit the Wind."
(Scopes Monkey Trial, July 1925)

Kirk stopped at the entrance to PPS and read the caption on the plaque. "Preferred Parcel Service; Founded in 1949 by our esteemed owner Roaf Sticklemann."

Kirk smiled slightly, "I guess I haven't worked here since the day it was opened. It only feels that way." He said softly to himself.

Kirk looked at his watch and thought, only four more hours till lunch. Then he yawned slightly and opened the door. His meeting would begin in ten minutes. He did not want to be late.

The meeting ended like most business meetings, not when it was supposed to. At least, thought Kirk, this one ended early.

As Kirk was walking down the stairs, he spotted his best friend at PPS, Randy Peterson. "Hey, Randy," Kirk said loudly.

Randy looked up from his Nokia Lumina5. "Kirk, how are you?" He spoke as he waited for Kirk to reach the bottom of the stairs.

Kirk didn't answer his friend but instead asked him a question.

"Are you hungry?"

"I have a meeting at one o'clock, but I could kill an hour or so. Lunch room okay?"

"Yeah, I just need to talk, more than eat."

"Okay, I'll meet you there. Hay, you look terrible."

"I know. I can't sleep. I keep waking up every hour or so and feel as though someone is in my room. I woke up swinging my fist at the air and hit my wrist on the headboard. I think I chipped a bone. The dogs are asleep in the hallway but I don't know what it is. It feels like there is a malevolent presence in my room. Forget I even mentioned it"

"OK, I catch up to you in a few minutes."

It seemed like an eternity till Randy showed up. But it was only ten minutes. Kirk drained his bottle of water and nervously picked at his salad.

"Hey, you look like a different person than the guy I saw in the hallway," Randy spoke as he sat down.

"What's wrong?"

"I've been thinking a lot since I saw you before."

"In ten minutes?"

"They want me to go back in at two for a private meeting with the boss after our one o'clock conference call."

"Three in one day? You usually have two meetings a week in security."

"I know, this can't be good."

"I don't know; sounds strange. Of course, a lot about this company is strange. Remember those stories we used to hear about Roaf." Randy knew something was not going right for his friend so he tried to lighten the mood.

"My favorite is the one about the founding of the company. How Roaf had been a Nazi SS officer and when they had their first few meetings the managers would give a Nazi like salute. Can you imagine a room of bald, old white guys saluting like that?" Randy said as he laughed.

"Don't forget the driver's uniforms; gray on gray with the PPS chrome bars on their collars," Kirk said as he smiled slightly. "And how about how his two partners died mysteriously in a car accident after we obtained intrastate rights and became very profitable! Roaf was ill that day and missed the trip and the car that sideswiped his partners was never found."

"You know, for all the money he had, he never married. Just look at how the company was built. Twelve hour work days, forced transfers, rapid advancement and no regard for the family.

We live to work instead of working to live. I could go on," Randy said as he opened a candy bar.

Kirk looked at his friend. Randy also was a manager, but not in security like Kirk. He was a few years older than Kirk and looked it. As much as Kirk felt like bad mouthing the company today, he worried about Randy getting in trouble even though no one else was near them.

"Never mind, I'm just worried about the meeting. I shouldn't whine. I've been given the greatest opportunity in the world. I've traveled the country and half the world on special assignments and got to live in different parts of the country. It's just a shame that my career was fast tracked and my divorce screwed it all up for me. Now, instead of being a corporate executive making the decisions, I might be out the door."

Randy shrugged his shoulders and spoke. "It really bothers me that no matter how long you work here, if you turn down two transfers you're demoted. They can transfer you anywhere in the U.S. 63 and you have to go. Sometimes the spouse doesn't go for that, like yours. And the divorce rate among our managers is almost as bad as in law enforcement. Of course, when most of us started here back in college, we weren't married anyway. I guess when we start out part time and then see the benefits and pay, as we move up, it's hard to leave. I mean, come on, they never promote from the outside unless they hire people in legal or financial and of course computer geeks."

"I guess. But isn't that a plus that we can be anything we want to be at PPS as long as we work hard. I just feel we are brainwashed into the PPS culture at such an early age, we don't know any other way. Look at how our managers become so unprofessional in their behavior. They become experts at pointing fingers and placing blame but rarely do they fix the problems," Kirk said.

"I think you're being a little hard on them. We all go through extensive training in ethics, integrity and how to treat people. We

120

even take a yearly relations survey to express our views," Randy said.

Kirk was a little perturbed at his friend's view of PPS.

"Haven't you ever noticed how the most disgruntled managers are let go at the start of every year? Do you really think that that survey is confidential? I was in a meeting once regarding an investigation where the HR manager mentioned what this employee said on the survey. How did he know? Everything we do is documented so the company policies and training could be used against us. They are ready to jump on us anytime we show disloyalty or express ideas different from the group. What about how they test our loyalty to the company? They force us to choose between drinks with the boss or a movie with the kids?"

"If you're smart, Kirk, it's going to be drinks. That is unless you want to work for FDX or UPS. As for me, I'm Fed-Up with the competition." Randy laughs. "Get it?"

"That's an old joke around here. Actually, the best thing we ever did was the joint venture with those two companies to build our own refinery for our own jet, diesel and gasoline fuels that we use." Kirk pushed his salad away. "It's strange, Roaf died in 1986. I think he was 76 and we still work in this abusive, production oriented, controlling culture that he created. It still endures the same as it was over 40 years after his death."

"You better hope our conversation wasn't monitored or someone was listening to us," Randy said.

"When you're head of security, you know where the cameras and mikes are." Kirk laughs. "Anyway, I'd never do anything to jeopardize Cole's health benefits."

Randy shakes his head. "That's for sure. I know you would never risk those. Do you remember when you got divorced and I let you live in my basement apartment? Rumors started that we were gay. I told you my girlfriend was moving in and you left."

"I heard the rumors and knew that you were trying to be kind. That's the stupidity around here that I hate." After a pause,

"Anyway, what a shame, this company had everything going for it when we started. I knew when we went public that that would be the end of our job security. First we outsourced the clerical jobs, and then we cut back on management. For what? We put up solid quarterly returns and Wall Street hammers us. All we had to do is provide the best service at the lowest cost and take care of our people along the way. I don't understand why we became like everyone else. We had a unique culture. We destroyed our loyalty for short term gain. The surest way to not get rich is to have a goal to be rich. The Management Committee sold us out for short term gain!"

"Yeah, theirs! A lot of people made a lot of money. How about how the stock price spiked for our 80th anniversary after years of being stagnant? That was the time to sell. The bottom line is we are paid well but are being squeezed out by the competition. They pay less and charge less. For every five people we need, we get three. If we add the staffing we need, our costs go up. We have a no win cost model so we need everyone to do the job of two people. No wonder our part time supervisors unionized."

Randy looks down at his watch.

"Well I've got a meeting to prepare for. Good luck with yours buddy. Remember, don't put rules on these guys, you'll lose. Everyone ends up exactly where they belong in life anyhow."

Kirk smiles, "I have a feeling I'll need it. And you're right about life. Everything catches up to you or evens out. See you and thanks."

Randy waves and says, "Don't worry, the Bifrost hasn't collapsed yet" and walks out.

Kirk sat for a few minutes feeling guilty about expressing his feelings but then thought about the staff meetings he has attended where the HR manager reviewed the EEOC quotas for females and minorities. Very few people know that the government tracks this. They give companies the available workforce to be hired in each town based on race and gender.

The first meeting today had followed the usual procedure of the monthly meetings. Kirk and his boss reviewed his results, last month's plans, and security problems. It was the next meeting he feared; the one to announce the Security Director.

Kirk was one of the three Security Directors for PPS in New Jersey. It was a position he had held in Oklahoma as well as New York. He knew PPS was downsizing to one Director in New Jersey. He also knew that although he had the best results, he was not well liked. Results only count when you don't have them. Kirk was one of the few individuals who had the integrity to say what was right even if it wasn't politically correct. Kirk had made many enemies upholding the integrity of the company, as was the duty in which he was charged. In Kirk's younger days, he was known as the "Terminator" or the "Hammer". He didn't care about people. He had that angry stare; that rage. He could never be a poker player because you knew exactly where he was coming from.

At PPS, corporate politics often had more to do with promotions than did job results. Kirk preferred to debate with blunt forced realism rather than watch PowerPoint presentations. Kirk wasn't a micro manager. He promoted people who got things done. He could take ideas and turn them into outcomes while others were stuck on details. He had the ability to observe people and play to their strengths. He had no tolerance for brown-nose's, egos or politics. He knew the competition was in the field, not in the office. He invited disagreement but everyone knew exactly where they stood. He never said anything behind someone's back that he hadn't already said to their face. Weak leaders surround themselves with yes men. That wasn't Kirk. (11)

An hour later, Kirk's fears were realized. He was not selected as Security Director. As was always the case, there would be a voluntary separation for him as there would be for all management employees who lost a promotion.

He knew there would be a few other positions available to him at a lower grade level and with no stock options.

Kirk's boss had no conscience or people skills. He was a toxic unprofessional leader who operated through fear. Kirk viewed him as a vampire. He was like a bloodsucker that saw nothing when he looked at himself in the mirror and he could have cared less about Kirk.

When Kirk argued that he had limited knowledge in these other jobs, it fell on deaf ears. The conspiracy of silence spoke louder than words. He also argued that he should be evaluated on results not personality. It was to no avail. He couldn't believe that after all the sacrifices he had made, that he would be betrayed by the company.

Kirk knew that with his lack of a degree and poor computer skills, he could never replace his salary. The worst aspect of a separation would be a loss of medical benefits for Cole.

Kirk wanted to head to the gym and get rid of his stress but he had to get to college before the administration office closed for the Christmas holiday. He was also having trouble holding the weights with his injured left hand. The only release he had was to slam his fist into the steering wheel, causing him undue pain, as he left the PPS parking lot, possibly for the last time.

Chapter 9

HOMELAND SECURITY

**"I don't know what weapons WW III will be fought with,
but WW IV will be fought with sticks and stones."**
(Albert Einstein)

The Department of Homeland Security was established in 2002. Its primary mission was to prevent, reduce, and minimize the damage to the United States of America from terrorist attacks.

In its second stage revision, the Department of Homeland Security or DHS, expanded its policies and aligned itself with a six point agenda against potential threats.

After the terrorist attacks of 2026, the third stage revision created the most comprehensive reorganization of the federal government in history. The DHS consolidated 23 agencies and 200,000 employees into a single agency with an annual budget in excess of $25 billion. The list of powers added to the U.S. government included the assassination of U.S. citizens, indefinite detention of citizens without a hearing, warrantless searches and the monitoring of all communications. The government had the very powers that the framers of our Constitution feared. The all-inclusive DHS incorporated:

    1. The old FBI- transformed to prevent terrorist attacks and provide 10-year background checks to employers for a fee. This became a large profit center that paid for most of this branch expenses.

    2. A Chief Medical Officer to coordinate the response to biological attacks and order mandatory vaccines.

    3. Federal Emergency Management Agency - FEMA.

    4. Federal Air Marshall Service.

    5. Transportation Security Administration- TSA.

6. Customs and Border Patrol.

7. Immigration and Customs Enforcement.

8. Information Analysis and Infrastructure Protection - Helps deter, prevent, assess vulnerabilities and disseminate information.

9. Science and Technology - The primary research and development arm of the DHS. Their work is designed to counter threats by development of revolutionary new technology.

10. U.S. Coast Guard - Protect the nation's ports and waterways.

11. U.S. Secret Service - Protect the President and nation's leaders, along with our financial and critical infrastructures.

12. Nuclear Incident Response Team - Provides expert personnel and specialized equipment to deal with nuclear accidents and emergencies.

13. National Disaster Medical System - To ensure that resources are available following a disaster.

14. National Response Team - An all discipline, all hazards team.

15. Urban Research and Rescue - A multi hazard team trained to respond to earthquakes, hurricanes, tornadoes, floods, dam failures and terrorist activities.

16. U.S. Northern Command - Coordinate Pentagon defense.

17. The National Counterterrorism Center - The National Intelligence Director controls Congressional oversight.

18. Terrorist Threat Integration Center - Synthesizes information collected worldwide. Its officers have arrest power of US citizens on US soil without a hearing.

19. Terrorist Screening Center - Consolidates terrorist watch lists.

20. Project Bioshield - An $8 billion group that develops vaccines and responses to biological, nuclear, chemical and radiological weapons. The Biowatch group monitors every major city and oversees and installs radiation detectors at every port, border crossing and airport.

21. U.S. Visit Group - Uses cutting edge biometrics to check the identity of foreign travelers and restrict Middle Easterners from entering the U.S.

22. DHS Investigators - The investigative arm of the department who can use wire taps, seize property and issue warrants at their own discretion across state lines without any judicial oversight.

23. National Office of Cyberspace (NOC) - Direct cyber offense and defense strategies. Safeguard the Einstein Program. Ensure consistency with all U.S. laws, privacy and civil liberties.

The third stage revision also included the immediate incorporation of all local law enforcement, fire fighters, public works, public health, emergency medical and responders under the DHS unified control in times of crisis along with working hand in hand with the NSA to spy on citizens and other countries. (27)

The NSA's SPY NETWORK

The Utah Data Center is, in effect, the NSA's cloud. The center is fed data collected by the agency's eavesdropping satellites, overseas listening posts, and secret monitoring rooms in telecom facilities throughout the U.S. All that data is then accessible to the NSA's code breakers, data-miners, China analysts, counterterrorism specialists, and others working at its Fort Meade headquarters and around the world.

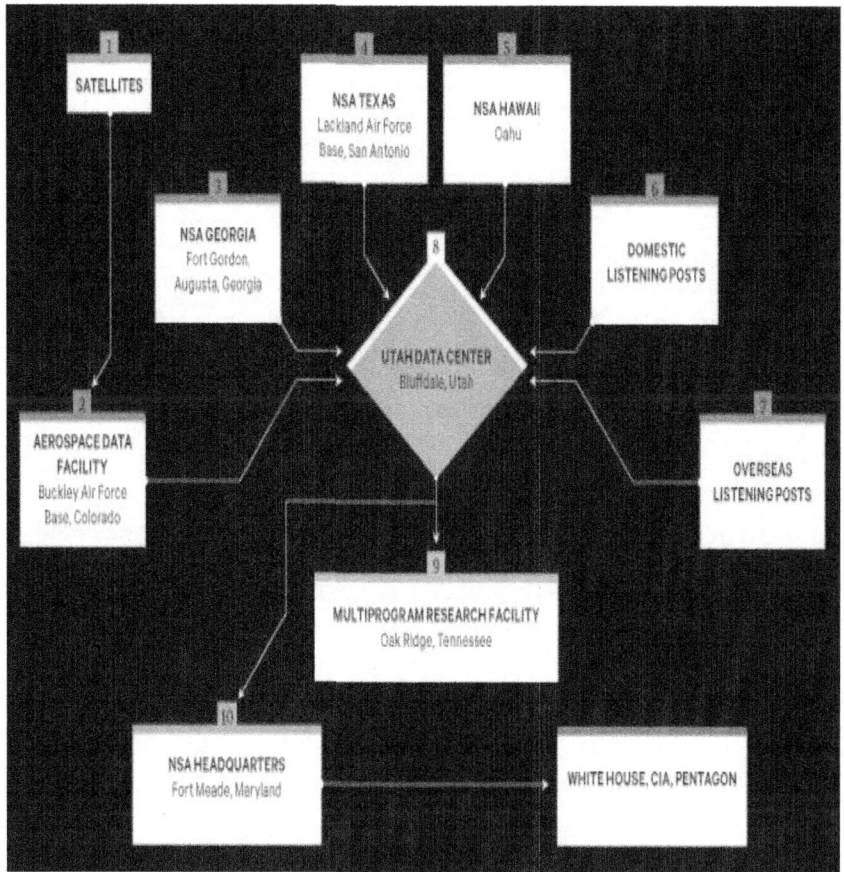

Here's how the data center appears to fit into the NSA's global puzzle:

1 Geostationary satellite

Four satellites positioned around the globe monitor frequencies carrying everything from walkie-talkies and cell phones in Libya to radar systems in North Korea. Onboard software acts as the first filter in the collection process, targeting only key regions, countries, cities, and phone numbers or email.

2 Aerospace Data Facility, Buckley Air Force Base, Colorado

Intelligence collected from the geostationary satellites, as well as signals from other spacecraft and overseas listening posts, is relayed to this facility outside Denver. About 850 NSA employees track the satellites, transmit target information, and download the intelligence haul.

3 NSA Georgia, Fort Gordon, Augusta, Georgia
Focuses on intercepts from Europe, the Middle East, and North Africa. Codenamed Sweet Tea, the facility has been massively expanded and now consists of a 604,000-square-foot operations building for up to 4,000 intercept operators, analysts, and other specialists.

4 NSA Texas, Lackland Air Force Base, San Antonio
Focuses on intercepts from Latin America and, since 9/11, the Middle East and Europe. Some 2,000 workers staff the operation. The NSA recently completed a $100 million renovation on a mega-data center here—a backup storage facility for the Utah Data Center.

5 NSA Hawaii, Oahu
Focuses on intercepts from Asia. Built to house an aircraft assembly plant during World War II, the 250,000-square-foot bunker is nicknamed the Hole. Like the other NSA operations centers, it has since been expanded: Its 2,700 employees now do their work aboveground from a new 234,000-square-foot facility.

6 Domestic listening posts
The NSA has long been free to eavesdrop on international satellite communications. But after 9/11, it installed taps in US telecom "switches," gaining access to domestic traffic. An ex-NSA official says there are 10 to 20 such installations.

7 Overseas listening posts
According to a knowledgeable intelligence source, the NSA has installed taps on at least a dozen of the major overseas communications links, each capable of eavesdropping on information passing by at a high data rate.

8 Utah Data Center, Bluffdale, Utah
At a million square feet, this $2 billion digital storage facility outside Salt Lake City will be the centerpiece of the NSA's cloud-

based data strategy and essential in its plans for decrypting previously un-crack-able documents.

9 Multiprogram Research Facilities, Oak Ridge, Tennessee
Some 300 scientists and computer engineers with top security clearance toil away here, building the world's fastest supercomputers and working on cryptanalytic applications and other secret projects.

10 NSA headquarters, Fort Meade, Maryland
Analysts here will access material stored at Bluffdale to prepare reports and recommendations that are sent to policymakers. To handle the increased data load, the NSA is also building an $896 million supercomputer center here. (35)

At the Morristown, New Jersey DHS investigative branch, two local officers sort through their mound of cases that need investigating and their "pile" of information tips from concerned citizens about the comings and goings of their neighbors and co-workers.

Agent Artemus Cohagen is a 53-year-old white male who earned his rank by coming up through the old FBI. He barely got through college but when it came to law enforcement, he learned quickly. After nearly 30 years in the field, he's one of the best. His short cropped hair has a hint of gray at the sides. His blue eyes are bright and alert and like an MRI that seldom missed much. His shoulders are wide but his overbite and flat broken nose give the appearance of a not too bright or successful boxer. Cohagen could hardly be called a family man but he does spend time with his daughter. Cohagen also has the uncanny ability to convert letters into numbers. If asked, "What's the phone number for Avis?" Cohagen would respond, "1-800-2847." This ability has come in handy on investigations especially when a serial killer was leaving clues in numbers and letters. On stake outs, Cohagen has been known to keep track of time by using his own pulse rate.

Agent Luis Rodriguez is a 47-year-old Hispanic male who worked for immigration in New Jersey for twenty years prior to joining the DHS. He has dark stringy hair that he likes to comb back with his fingers. His hair matches his dark eyes that seem to burn whenever he fixates on something. They are eyes that have seen a lot over the years but he still has a very empathetic side. He is lean and compact and his narrow shoulders and long arms make him look more like a lab technician than a peace officer. He sports a goatee' to cover his weak chin. Unlike his partner, he is happily married with four children. He has an obsession with crosses. He sees them in window panes, telephone poles, shoe laces, woman's "G" strings and anything else that crosses. He is also a somnambulist or sleep walker.

"Yo Arte" says Agent Rodriguez, "What juicy cases do we have this week?"

"It's a freaking buffet of sicko's," says Agent Cohagen.

"We have a wacko who attacked a DEA Agent with a chain saw in Trenton.

"We have a school Superintendent in Boonton who tried to light a county commissioner on fire because he wanted to keep ET intelligent design out of the classroom.

"We have an Arian Whitaker who an informant says he belongs to the '88' White Supremacist group. The '8' is the eighth letter in the alphabet and the double 'H' stands for 'Hiel Hitler'. We have emails from him to other members where he argues that there are differences between the races and that whites need to stand up against reverse discrimination. This group has a dotted line connection to 'The Order'; a white supremacist criminal organization that traffics arms and explosives. He also attended a concert in Pennsylvania by a supremacist band called 'Prussian Blue'. They compare their music to the old "Gangster Rap" from twenty years ago as a similar form of free speech. I'm glad that this "music" crap can only be played after 10 p.m. and is restricted like some R-rated movie.

We have a real good lead on a Muslim group that is attacking priests to appease God. That's a hate crime!

And finally, we have a Muslim man that is skinning cats and sacrificing them to Allah. Shame it took us so long before we realized we were dealing with a global Muslim movement and not a Masonic lodge. Which one do you want to start with?"

"Jesus," swears Agent Rodriguez. "The priests sound most pressing. You never know what might happen when you are dealing with religious nuts. Although the other cases are important, the one with the priests seem most heinous."

"Okay," says Cohagen. He stacks the files placing the priests on top. "I'll pull up NCIC and cross reference it with the names listed here and we'll have a place to start. Sometimes I'd like to turn a blind eye and let nature run its course."

"I know what you mean. We had a rash of deaths from heroin laced with fentanyl. Addicts were dropping like flies and it seemed like most agents were slow to investigate. We finally caught the vigilante. He was a clean cut millionaire with no record that was buying pure heroin and not cutting it to dilute its potency. He said he was doing society a service. The thing here isn't just the attacks themselves but the ramifications from them. If we let someone murder a priest, then some other nut feels ordained to avenge the priest and soon, before you know it, we have a Holy War on our hands."

"Well at least we ID'd the drug users."

"Yeah, do you want a coffee? I'm headed downstairs for a decaf and a bagel," says Rodriguez.

"Thanks, I will with cream and six sugars. That last one reminded me of that guy that would dip his bullets in rat poison because it thinned the blood and his victims would just bleed to death."

"Six sugars? Why not just get a donut?"

"I don't really like coffee. I like the sugar. And make it dark roast, no decaf here."

"Si, si Alex Ciente."

Agent Cohagen types away accessing one data base after another. By the time Agent Rodriguez returns, their itinerary is all laid out.

"Here you go, Arte. Caffeine keeps me up all night."

"I need the boost, especially when I'm on the hunt. Get this, there's a national Survivors Network of Abusive Priests organization in Chicago. It's an advocacy group known as SNAP."

"You've got to be kidding me?"

"I'm serious; a David Logan is the Director. Let's follow-up on this lead in Flanders before we call him."

"My turn to drive this time," says Rodriguez.

The two agents get in their Dodge Charger and head north on Route 287 and then west on Route 80. They exit at Route 206 south and drive four miles to the quiet town of Flanders, New Jersey.

Luis asks, "Arte, what was your toughest investigation?"

Arte replies, "Around twenty years ago, I had to tell the parents of two sons that both were killed in separate simultaneous car accidents about a mile apart. It was eerie to investigate. And worst of all, I knew the parents. The kids were friends of my younger brothers. The mother still cries in her sleep, so I'm told."

"Wow, sometimes this job can humble you. Mine was investigating the trafficking of young Mexican girls and boys for sex trade. They'd be brought to New Jersey like some distribution center and then be moved to major cities along the east coast. Some people have no soul; how could you do that to a 12-year-old?"

"On second thought," Says Arte," I investigated a case that involved a macabre body harvesting lab here in New Jersey. They extracted tissue, tendons, skin and bone from funeral homes without the families consent. They shipped the stuff to hospitals all over the country for surgeries. They were making hundreds of thousands of dollars from looted body parts. People started contracting HIV, syphilis and diseases from the operations. This is a big business. It's regulated by the FDA which requires body harvesting firms to screen cadavers for age and disease and treat the tissue with antiviral antibacterial agents. It was gross. People were getting sick or getting decayed parts from 90–year-old victims that didn't take. All for the money!"

"I read that twenty five years ago China took all those political prisoners and the Tiananmen Square protestors and put them to death and sold off their body parts. They say 2,500 prisoners a year. I guess they got their freedom as someone else's kidney or liver here in the U.S. They say that "Bodies Exhibit" is the Tiananmen Square protestors."

After a long silence, Arte says, "See that apartment complex on the left, Oakwood Village? I used to belong to a singles group there. They were a nice bunch. We would meet at various locations and take day trips on the weekend. I dated two women in that group before I moved on."

"You never told me that before. Too bad you can't meet someone nice and settle down. Companionship is important as you get older."

"I know, between our line of work and what's left out there when you're over 50, there's not much to choose from. Driving past this place brought back memories. I wonder if they still meet and if the same people are still there."

"When I was 26, before I got married, I had a fling with a 50–year-old woman. Man did she know how to take care of a guy. I guess that generation had it right. I didn't know what to expect. Funny how only the face ages. Her body was in pretty good shape. I could hardly keep up with her. She was so accommodating, maybe grateful. It was nice," says Rodriguez.

"We have to bear right on County Line Road at the light after the 7,000 square foot plastic looking log cabin. Can you believe the owner of that cabin was able to get his own private street named"?

"Yeah, I heard he named it Sex Drive. Is it true the house number is 69?"

"Don't put my mind in the gutter. We're interviewing a priest in five minutes. They can read minds!"

"Mens Rae, guilty mind in Latin," says Rodriguez.

"Here we are. Father Richard Hardt, a Benedictine priest, was assaulted yesterday while taking his evening walk. Let's go, clear your mind just in case he can read it," says Cohagen.

The two agents laugh as they approach the sixteen foot oak doors of the church. They enter and proceed towards the hallway to the right of the altar. Agent Rodriguez briefly kneels and gives the sign of the cross. Agent Cohagen turns, wondering why Rodriguez is lagging behind. They find Father Hardt in his office reading a report.

"Father Hardt, I'm Agent Cohagen and this is Agent Rodriguez." They show their ID's. "We've been sent to investigate your assault."

Father Hardt says, "I just unlocked the doors. The monsignor was sick this morning. In another era, it was the exception to lock the doors at night."

"Is this because of your assault?" asks Rodriguez.

"No, there has been vandalism and theft. I'm concerned about the welfare of anyone praying alone at night. We hate to do this but it seems to be prudent. In a perfect world, we'd keep the doors unlocked, but that's not the world we live in. At one time, criminals held churches in such high esteem that they wouldn't commit crimes here. That reverence has gone by the waste side like most values. Even though the doors may be locked, God is never locked out of our lives when we pray." (26)

In an attempt to relax the Father, Agent Cohagen asks, "Before we begin, give me your thoughts on creationism."

"Science would have us believe that creation was without order or design. These people are fooled by atheism. God's love is demonstrated by the marvels of creation. Alas, so much for the sermon. I told the local police everything about the assault. It was nothing."

"We think there may be wider implications. Please be so kind as to tell us again what happened," says Agent Rodriguez.

"Fine, I was taking my eight o'clock walk like usual when a car drove by and threw a bottle at me. It hit me in the back of the head."

"If it hit you in the back of the head, which side of the street were you walking on? With traffic or against?" says Rodriguez.

I always walk against traffic so I can see the cars coming."

"Then the driver threw the bottle and he'd have to be left-handed," says Rodriguez.

"I never thought of that," says Father Hardt.

"What kind of bottle hit you? Did he or she say anything to you?"

"He said, 'Et tu Brute' and drove off. There was a blond woman in the passenger seat. The police have the bottle. It was a SoBe power drink bottle and there were no prints on it."

"What do you think he meant?" says Agent Cohagen

"Et tu Brute means you too Brutus. That's what Caesar said when Brutus knifed him in the back. It means he thinks I betrayed him."

"Did you break your oath of confidentiality regarding a confession?"

"No, I wouldn't do that."

"Think hard, why a "SoBe" bottle and not a beer bottle?" says Agent Cohagen.

"The police asked the same question. I have no idea. They said they were looking for an athlete or someone that works out in a local gym."

Agent Rodriguez says, "Isn't "SoBe's" slogan, drain the lizard?"

"I'm not gay if that is what you are implying," says Father Hardt in a stern voice.

"We're just asking," says Agent Cohagen.

"I know, sorry," says Father Hardt in a lower tone of voice. Some married men and priests use their cover like a beard to hide their latent tendencies; I'm not one of them." He breaks eye contact and looks down. Agent Cohagen senses a change in his body language and continues.

"It must be tough listening to all those confessions and not being able to do anything about them. Sometimes the means justifies the ends."

"What would you say if I told you that you've been doing the right thing by occasionally tipping off the police? Isn't that right Father?"

Father Hardt looks away and stares at the stained glass window and speaks.

"Yes I've helped the state police. It's necessary to prevent other crimes. I couldn't sit back and do nothing."

"Confession is good for the soul. You did the right thing," says Cohagen. "Were there any recent tips?"

"Yes, I told the police about a 23-three-year old boy that had been having relations with his 15-year-old sister. He's been in trouble before and I thought she needed to be saved."

"What's his name?" says Agent Rodriguez.

"Michael Younger."

"Thank you," says Agent Cohagen. "We won't bother you any further. And Father, I think you did the right thing."

Father Hardt says, "Faith is sometimes the fuel that feeds conflict."

Rodriguez says, "Yes, religion is a powerful healing force in a world torn apart by religion."

"My son, there are crucial teachings shared by the Koran and Bible. Both faiths promote peace through scripture."

"Too bad they don't carry books instead of bombs."

"The Vatican has called for a truce in this cultural war. We emphasize the peaceful teachings of the Bible and not the apocalyptic violence of the Book of Revelation. Many wield religion like Constantine's sword."

"There are two ends to that sword."

As the two agents approach their car, Rodriguez stops and asks Cohagen.

"Why did you cut the interview off so quickly?"

"This is a one-time incident. We'll give the lead to the local police, probably his contact. This is not part of a conspiracy to attack the clergy nationwide. Let's head back and call Chicago."

"Yeah, but people know more than they think."

Cohagen smiles and says, "Well then I think I would know then!"

As they get to the stop light, Agent Cohagen asks Agent Rodriguez to turn right. They proceed to a local pizza place.

"I love pizza," says Cohagen. "I hope we don't have to fly to Chicago. I hate that phony pan pizza they have out there."

I've never been to Chicago," says Rodriguez.

"You're lucky."

I'm glad Father Hardt was upstanding. My family is deeply religious. That's why I wanted this case," says Rodriguez.

"Mine too; I'm glad he told on that scum."

"I've always wondered if the priests were working with the local police."

"I've worked with priests in the past. I knew he would come clean," says Cohagen.

"I've never heard that term 'beard' as a cover-up."

"I heard it a few years back; it's pretty cool when you think about it."

When they arrive back at the office, they call the National Survivors Network of Abusive Priests organization.

"I'd like to speak to Mr. Logan," says Rodriguez.

"This is Logan, and you are?"

"I'm Agent Rodriguez of Homeland Security. I'd like to ask you a few questions."

"Okay."

"I'm investigating a lead on a group that wants to retaliate against priests. They believe that they are doing God's work against the priests. Can you help me?"

"Yes, I'm not surprised. There's more to the story. Got a half hour?"

"Yes, please continue," says Agent Rodriguez. "I'm going to put you on speaker phone so my partner, Agent Cohagen, can participate."

"Fine, if you pull up our website, we publish all the facts."

"Thanks, but please also give us the 'Hines story'. We need your most recent stuff," says Agent Cohagen.

"Sorry, this goes back for years. You need the long version," says Logan.

"Please proceed," says Rodriguez.

"If there is retaliation against priests, I think I know why. Who knows how far back this story goes but the reason is sexual misconduct. The authority of the all-male clergy has always sought to exclude women. This led to the misguided policy of celibacy which then led to homosexuality. There are a number of priests that are sexual predators, no different than the general population. The difference is, when found out; the Vatican reassigns them rather than prosecute. There have been a number of lawsuits, but most victims don't come forward because they are ashamed that God did this to them or are paid off and this crime goes unreported. Twenty years ago, when the publicity from this started to get uncomfortable, the Vatican formulated a new policy. They intentionally sent abusive priests to transient out of the way communities where kids were less apt to tell and have less faith in the justice system. These Roman Catholic priests were assigned to remote towns in Alaska, the Deep South, and near Native American tribal lands. Because of the isolation and cultural reverence for authority figures, parishioners were less likely to speak up. These 'perpetrators' got away with molesting children.

When a priest was caught or reported multiple times, he was simply sent overseas. They have been coming back recently from their 'international training' and that's why these assaults are occurring." (26)

"Have you been contacted recently by anyone regarding these incidents? Anyone in the New Jersey area?" asks Cohagen.

"Actually we received three calls from your area and two email requests regarding cases, names, and locations of incidents. They said it was for a college term paper."

"Did you report it?" asks Rodriguez.

"No, I'm am atheist. Sometimes you let nature take its course!"

"Sounds like a crime of omission," says Rodriguez.

"I have no knowledge of any crimes. This information is on our website and is easily obtained through the freedom of information act."

Attempting to bond with the Director and not alienate him, Agent Cohagen says, "I'm an Agnostic also, I understand."

"Please don't patronize me. A Gnostic seeks the truth, an atheist doesn't believe in fantasy or higher powers. Nice try at mirroring me though."

Cohagen is embarrassed and realizes that Director Logan knows his stuff. He's probably testified in these cases and should've done his research and background works prior to questioning Logan off the cuff. Agent Rodriguez intervenes.

"Could you please give us the email ads and any contact info that you have?"

"Sure, I will email you the links. There is a group in Columbia that you should be interested in."

"South America?" says Rodriguez?

"No, New Jersey. I believe it's near the Pennsylvania border before you get to the Pocono's."

Cohagen quickly responds, "I know that area well. It's fairly rural and unsophisticated. I've worked a few cases up there."

"There you have it," says Logan. "I wish I could say you two instilled confidence in me."

As soon as Agent Rodriguez received the email, Agent Cohagen asks one last question. "Why do you think the clergy has this problem with gay priests?"

"It's estimated that 40 percent of the priests are now gay. They say they must be celibate for three years before becoming a deacon and that they cannot have deep rooted homosexual tendencies. Most straight priests are turned off by the gay culture in the seminaries. We know from our research that it's a huge closet. They can't attract heterosexuals because they cannot marry but then again it might just be Satan's way of infiltrating and destroying the church!" (26)

Cohagen abruptly thanked Director Logan for his help and hung up.

"What an ass-hole!" Exclaims Rodriguez.

"Yeah, but I can't believe I said agnostic instead of atheist. Logan knows his stuff. If you're going to kick a lion in the ass, you better have a plan for his teeth!"

"What do you think about gays?"

"I read that twelve percent of the population is gay. I view them like any other minority group. We've accepted all other groups, why not this one? But gay priests are a sign that the devil has entered the priesthood."

"This whole investigation annoys me," says Agent Rodriguez. "When I was growing up in Camden, I looked up to my priest. Like literal father figures. They taught us how to play basketball and had a boxing clinic. When I graduated high school, I'd go back to do volunteer work. The priests were just like us. They'd smoke, have a beer, and occasionally cuss. He'd smile and make the sign of the cross and we'd all laugh. They were strict but not abusive. I think these people make this stuff up."

"I agree. It used to be like those old James Cagney, Edmond O'Brien movies that I watched with my grandfather," says

Cohagen. "I once spoke to a bishop and he told me that these aren't forced transfers. Priests volunteer to work in these remote areas and do so because they are committed and want to serve in these tough locations."

"So now what?" Says Rodriguez.

"It's getting late and Route 80 traffic west is terrible at 5 p.m. Let's do our leg work and move on this in a week," says Cohagen. "Oh yeah, don't forget to submit a req for robots. I love those things. We need fliers and crawlers but no self-directed ones. I don't trust the ones that think and work in unison. One day they'll turn on us. By the way, what's the guy's name that we are investigating?"

"It's Gavrilo Princip."

"Is he an illegal alien?"

"No, but the name sounds familiar. They say he hunts bald eagles for sport."

Chapter 10

COLLEGE

"It is dangerous to be right on matters on which established authorities are wrong."
(Voltaire)

Kirk slammed his Jaguar into gear over riding auto drive and sped onto the highway. Kirk preferred to drive his mid-life crises rather than let the vehicle self-drive. The speedometer began to climb and soon he could see he was 40 mph over the speed limit. Kirk had a friend over-ride the autonomous car technology powered by Google technology. Today's cars drive themselves while the driver can relax or even sleep. Sports cars are illegal and only driven on a race track. He suddenly realized his anger had gotten the better of him. Kirk all at once comprehended what he had done. He was being very selfish by driving so recklessly. It was only a few years ago since the children had lost their mother in a car accident. They probably couldn't handle losing another parent in the same manner. Kirk put on some classical music rather than the alternative rock that he enjoyed and left ear worms where he couldn't get the tune out of his head, and the speedometer began to drop.

Since it wasn't yet rush hour, Kirk made it to Farleigh Dickerson University in plenty of time. The Christmas break had already begun for the students so parking was plentiful. He pulled into a space at the admissions office and searched his glove compartment for his checkbook.

Kirk had started back to night school, attending one night per week. Today was the final day one could pay for next semester's classes. He had inquired about classes at Princeton but had been told there were only engineering classes offered at night.

Kirk checked his watch and saw it was still an hour before the office would close. He was burnt out physically and mentally after the day he had. Kirk leaned his head back on the soft leather headrest and decided to close his eyes for a few minutes.

As he sat in the parking lot, he began to remember his college days at C.W. Post. Kirk thought about the times he played intramural sports. Since he had to work part time to pay his own way through school, he missed out on the chance to participate in intercollegiate sports. He couldn't help but wonder how things may have been different if he hadn't always had to work.

Kirk knew for Cole and Claire it would be different. He had already set up funds for the children's college education.

All through his youth, working had hindered Kirk's athletic chances. His paper route and later his part time job at age 16 had diminished his chances of joining organized sports at school.

Kirk had always been a four-tool baseball player. The fifth and most important tool, the one Kirk lacked, was hitting a fastball. He always felt he had the skills of speed, quickness, and the hands for football. He knew he could have been a receiver or a defensive back.

Kirk remembered the Saturday afternoon when he and some neighborhood friends played a pick-up game against the junior varsity high school football team. They ran right through Kirk's team on the first two plays. Then Kirk and his friends got angry and began to show them what they were made of.

The quarterback on Kirk's team was built like Charles Bronson and was probably using steroids at that time. He could throw a football 80 yards in the air.

Kirk scored three consecutive times on the same post pattern past the J.V.'s cornerback. He also returned two punts for touchdowns. Kirk annihilated the opposition when he made bone-crushing tackles while playing on defense.

Kirk would usually allow the receiver to make short yardage receptions in front of him. He would then time his hit to when the catch was made. If the receiver held onto the ball, Kirk would make him pay the price. He would put his shoulder into the small of the players back and then grab him by the thighs and slam the receiver face first into the ground. When he was finished with them, a receiver either dropped the ball or wish they had.

Kirk remembered being asked to join the junior varsity team the following Monday. He had to decline because he had to work and watch his baby sister until their mother returned home from her job.

When Kirk continued to think about his college years, he couldn't help but think about Vespa again. He thought about her more than once since the night he met Jenny. It must have been because of Jenny's youthful appearance. There was no physical resemblance between the two girls. In fact, in some ways, Jenny resembled Tammy who had been 5'10" with blond hair and green eyes and of Scottish descent. While Vespa had Italian features, Kirk was most attracted to brown eyed blonds but had never dated one.

Tammy had done some modeling in high school, but she had no work ethic. Kirk used to tease her that she was allergic to sweating.

The two girl's personalities were also completely different. Vespa was smart and aggressive while Tammy was naive and laid back.

Kirk thought again about the afternoon he spent with Vespa. She had invited him to her dorm by telling him she needed help with sociology. Kirk knew she had better grades than he did. He figured, because of her aggressiveness, her ruse was simply a way to entice him to have sex. Kirk remembered how it had differed from making love with Tammy. That afternoon with Vespa had been pure lust for him. He remembered how the guilt he felt served to drive him closer to Tammy.

Tammy had always been so much more quiet and passive than Vespa seemed to be. Tammy let Kirk make all the decisions. She just wanted to be married and raise a family.

As Kirk blinked his eyes to fully awaken from his daydream, he thought how things had changed in his life.

Kirk had once been a loner and a homebody. He now had many friends he met from playing racquetball, working out, and joining ski clubs and singles groups.

He had been with sixteen women since his divorce; most of who said they would like to marry him. Kirk felt he was a good catch but questioned the motives of the women. He wondered if the reason they wanted him was his hydrogen electric fuel cell five-bedroom house on an acre of property with a built in pool and because he drove a Jaguar XJL. Kirk felt he had been ruined by a bitter divorce. He also found it hard to trust a woman again.

Kirk very much enjoyed his freedom. He had even developed a routine to his relationships. He would sometimes lead a woman on for six to eight months and then as soon as they would become possessive or make demands on him, he would dump them. Kirk feared he would end up alone, but couldn't make a commitment and he enjoyed changing partners.

As he got out of the car, Kirk remembered how aggressive he used to be. Now, as he walked across the admission buildings parking lot, Kirk only felt tired and burnt out.

Chapter 11

ALL SOULS DAY

**"Perhaps people think that I have come to cast peace
upon the world. They do not know that
I have come to cast strife upon the earth."**
(Jesus)

The day started like any other winter day. The air was cold and crisp. It was the kind of morning when only the hardiest of joggers would be in the park. Their breath came out as smoke from their lungs that were like a fire stoked by the cold air they gulped between their chapped lips.

The Bulova watch company installed a huge clock in NYC's Times Square which to the surprise of the onlookers, ran backwards. Everyone broke out in laughter at the mistake. A digital message ran across the APPLE screen across from the clock that stated that the Board of Bulova installed this clock in hopes that we could reverse time and avoid the future. The crowd fell silent.

In spite of the cold, there was a smile on the faces of shoppers and a hearty greeting for everyone. After all, it was only four days till Christmas. Even the atheists were happy on this morning of the winter solstice. The sun was shining brightly this morning as if mocking the early sunset on this shortest day of the year. It seemed as if the most important question of this day was the age old one of the last minute shoppers. "What should I buy?" As is usually the case every Christmas, the concern came from the men who waited till the last minute to shop. There was no need to panic; they still had four days until the gifts would be opened.

There may have been wars going on a continent away, but none of that touched the public during this holiday season. Of course, there were prayers said and ribbons hung for the troops in combat. Even the big department stores were collecting for the unfortunate soldiers away from home.

Christmas was a time of joy. The credit/debit registers were clicking more than ever since the addition of 13 additional states to the Corporate U.S. It would be a highly profitable season; especially the next few days of Christmas rush. The National Retail Federation was reporting sales of $11 billion per day or $800 million per hour on a 14-hour sales day.

The Vatican condemned the materialistic spending of the States but had no response to the allegations that within its walls are housed an art collection stored in 1,400 rooms in twelve complexes whose value is beyond appraisal. Except for the Curia scribes that inventory the collection, most of the artwork has remained unseen for centuries. Many of the greatest Renaissance artists were commissioned by the Vatican and it is rumored that a better Mona Lisa or Pieta' are hoarded in these rooms. In typical hypocrisy, the church denounced mankind's materialism which keeps many people employed, while hoarding its own pot of gold. (26)

Eugene Wormwood had tried for hours to get through to the unblinking eye of the Near Earth Asteroid Tracking Station in Vancouver. Eugene was an artist by day and an astronomer by night.

Initially, while on vacation in Europe, he had thought he spotted the asteroid Apophis but it was way off course. Apophis was scheduled to pass by Earth in April and dip below our communication satellites at 22,000 miles. It was early, off course and not supposed to hit Earth. Cloud cover had obscured his view for two nights. When he had remotely scanned the sky last night via computer link, he again saw the warm glow of a small rogue asteroid heading on a collision course with Europe. His anxiety level peaked due to the fact the sun's rays would hide the tiny asteroid in the daytime. His find could only be verified at night. He knew it would be next to impossible to convince anyone during the daytime of his discovery. He also knew he had to fax or email three days' worth of digital photos. It is hard to determine the orbit of a newly discovered object without at least a month's worth of photos. Early detection could mean early deflection if he could provide proof to the Asteroid Deflection Research Center in Iowa.

Eugene had grown used to people not taking him seriously. It all began when that damned Ukrainian had joined the Astronomy Society to which Eugene belonged. He told everyone that Wormwood in Ukrainian meant Chernobyl. So to be funny, his fellow members would always say, "Here comes Eugene the walking disaster." For Eugene, this couldn't have been any worse because the asteroid would be named after him. If it wasn't Apophis, the asteroid would be designated as Wormwood. Eugene was familiar with a prediction in Revelation concerning the breaking of the sixth seal. It spoke of a star falling to earth named Wormwood. If the astronomer at the tracking station knew of this prophecy, he may not take him seriously.

Eugene was sweating profusely. He knew he had to do something, but he didn't know how to prove his find. Suddenly, the realization hit him. He must find an area where it would still be night.

Eugene decided to call the observatory in Sydney. Since Australia was now part of the U.S. 63, he figured he would give it a try. As he worked to connect to Sydney, his mind wandered. He remembered how the country had been before that fateful day.

Although the U.S. had been on alert since September 11, 2001, and on high alert on holidays, anniversaries, and had reliable "Intel" that November 9 would be the next attack, the unthinkable had happened. On September 11 again, terrorists had poisoned the drinking water supply in New York City. We were preparing for a November 9 attack since in Europe and the Middle East the date precedes the month when written.

Even though we've been protected by two oceans, our Achilles heel has always been our free open society. Initial reports by first responders and the media were incorrect and fueled panic. They misidentified the biological agent and quickly administered the wrong antibiotic. The CDC has twelve strategic national stockpiles for vaccines and antibiotics. The CDC is a private company that owns most of the patents to the shots they recommend and earns over $5B a year regulating itself, selling data to homeland security and cloning the DNA samples. Maybe the lab tech had a co-conspirator employed or there were two agents present or the CDC saw an opportunity to profit. One office building on Park Avenue had a confirmed outbreak of anthrax administered through its air conditioning system. Victims did not realize that the true attack came from the drinking supply. As most New Yorkers were dealing with the anthrax diversion, the real infectious agent was spreading through family members and co-workers. The disease had already advanced to the untreatable stage before it was reacted to.

At the same time, a bomb exploded in the Holland Tunnel which was meant to flood the city's labyrinth of subterranean tubes. No breach occurred because the tunnels had been hardened and the flood gates were updated to seal off water after the 2012 Hurricane Sandy.

A tabloid paper also published that there was a small pox attack and the accompanying news article threw unprepared responders and public health officials in the wrong direction. Sixty percent of the health workforce decided to stay home citing the risk factor.

The news story detailed how biological warfare had been used for centuries. The Romans fouled their enemies' water supplies with dead animals. The Tatars launched bubonic plague victims' bodies over the city walls of their enemies starting the Black Death which killed one third of Europe's population. Early American settlers gave small pox infected blankets to Indians. Nazi scientists experimented with the neurological poison ricin. The Japanese used cholera against the Chinese. The former Soviet Union used to

151

employ 70,000 scientists and technicians to experiment with anthrax, Ebola, HIV, Hepatitis and mad cow disease. Even though in 1977, the World Health Organization dictated that only two samples of small pox would be maintained worldwide in Moscow and Atlanta, stockpiles of this devastating microbe which killed 500 million people in the 20th Century were found in five other radical countries.

Anthrax, the most feared of all biological agents, is a naturally occurring bacterium which is 100,000 times more powerful than the deadliest manmade chemical agent. The news article went on to describe what would occur from small pox; 300 Americans would die immediately. That did occur in the office building diversion. Next, 2,000 would be infected with 1,000 dying within the first week. The U.S. health system would be overwhelmed. All schools and public gatherings would be restricted. The National Guard would be deployed to close all state borders. Stock trading and interstate commerce would cease. Riots would start. Within two months, three million would be infected resulting in one million deaths. Martial law would be imposed. Makeshift morgues would be setup. The world economy would be on the brink of collapse. Worldwide deaths would reach 80 million within 12 months. Worldwide stability rests on U.S. stability and power! This was a prelude for the un-named Presidents Chinese flu outbreak. (16)

The tabloid article was wrong but it was just as Nostradamus had predicted hundreds of years ago. Thousands died on September 11 and the days afterwards. Many who died were dignitaries there to commemorate the new monument to September 11, 2001. The Archway of Freedom was completed at the site of the old World Trade Center at a cost of $27 billion. It resembled the St. Louis Arch but stretched from Manhattan to Newark, New Jersey. It was the largest project ever constructed by mankind.

The response by the U.S. and many of her allies was swift. The Anglo Acts were passed within days. The most important of the

Anglo Acts offered statehood to seven of the 51 English speaking countries. Great Britain, Australia, New Zealand, Iceland, Nigeria and South Africa all accepted. Although Canada joined, there was a proviso for the province of Quebec. Since there were such close ties to the French in Montreal and all of Quebec, it was mutually decided by both parties that the French-speaking province of Quebec would be better off on its own.

The seven countries added 13 states to the U.S. Great Britain added two and Canada five new states. Scotland joined the European Union and left the U.K. years ago after Great Briton exited the E.U. Australia became two states while South Africa, Iceland, Nigeria and New Zealand added one state each. Nigeria was divided between its Muslim north and Christian south where all its wealth also resided. Only the south gained statehood.

Although Eisenhower had proposed statehood to Great Britain over 70 years ago, he had been turned down. As terrorism flourished, so did fear of non-English speaking people. The English speaking countries that had become states now formed the United States of 63. The word "America" was dropped in a very close and angry vote. It had taken them nearly 10 years but the terrorists had indirectly succeeded in their goal. On the first day of January, the United States of America ceased to exist.

Another change to the world order came about after the death of Premier Fidel Castro from cancer in 2016. The U.S. had made an agreement with Russia during the Cuban missile crisis that it would not invade Cuba as long as Castro lived. In exchange, Russia removed its missiles from Cuba and we did the same from Belgium.

Fidel's brother, Raul, had been running the country in one of only five remaining communist countries in the world. Raul and Che' Guevara recruited Fidel into the communist party prior to taking power in 1959. Raul was in charge of the military and five years younger than Fidel.

China was aiding Cuba in building off-shore oil wells 60 miles from the Florida coast. The U.S. had hoped for a protracted rebellion among its 11 million citizens but any reformers among top Cuban officials had been purged over the years. Cubans earned 20 dollars per month; were rationed four pounds of meat per month. They were forbidden to own a car or a computer.

We even had a 400 page plan on how to confront post-Castro Cuba. The plan even included a Major League Baseball franchise in Havana. Castro had circumvented our transition plan and undermined our five decade trade embargo with an agreement with President Obama and by developing a $5 billion trading partnership with China. Fearing a launching pad for terrorists and an adoption of the Chinese model of remaining tough politically while pushing for and getting economic concessions, the U.S. 63 saw an opening and invaded Cuba and then Venezuela, Uruguay and Bolivia to spread President Datchet's Doctrine of Freedom and Liberty. (26)

South America under Castro's and Chavez's influence had become very anti-capitalist and a training ground for anti-American terrorism. They heavily taxed foreign multinational companies and eventually cut them off from exploration and production which lead to the nationalizing of U.S. companies assets. (26)

What had once been the Americas were now at last free of communism and dictators. Cuba became a thriving tourist location for Americans and open border free trade immediately boosted its economy. Many South Floridians maintained two homes; one in Cuba and one in Miami while regularly commuting to baseball games in Miami and Havana. South America became good friendly trading partners with the U.S. again.

On Nov 11 2026, The Department of Homeland Security discovered a plot to poison the 266 million turkeys that are raised on farms for Thanksgiving. It is the one holiday where most people are at home. A group of Indonesian Muslims spread a mutated avian flu virus H5N1 through most of the U.S. turkey farms. The migrant workers passed as Mexican immigrants who were among the group granted amnesty and citizenship. Like a "Trojan horse", the influenza would've killed as many as twenty million Americans. This new strain would only affect people who have had a previous flu shot. In essence, it would leave Third World countries immune and only attack Western citizens.

In 1890, the "Russian flu" killed one million people. In 1918, the "Spanish flu" killed forty million people. In 1957, the Hong Kong flu" killed two million people. This Pandemic flu was administered two weeks too soon. Before the birds were eaten, they infected a 4-year-old farm girl in Virginia. She developed a fever, sore throat and a cough. She then died of heart failure and an autopsy was performed. DHS agents were also tipped off and all turkey farms were quarantined. Tests were performed at the St. Jude Children's Research Hospital in Memphis which is the world's only lab that studies the human-animal relationship in spreading influenza. The birds were destroyed prior to being eaten at the Thanksgiving feast. It was the first year since 1621 that the holiday was celebrated without the bountiful harvest of turkeys, stuffing and gravy.

Eugene shook his head as he thought how the world had changed, then shuddered at the drastic change that was yet to come. He finally was able to get through to Sydney where it was still night time "down under". Startled astronomers discounted his findings and calculated that it would be a near miss by 10,000-12,000 miles or one fifth the distance to the moon. They told the public it was Apophis and it would come in at half the distance originally expected and that gravity from a planet it passed must've accelerated and changed its path. Apophis was originally due in four months. It would so severely enter our atmosphere and gravity that it should light up the sky as it burns up. In fact it wasn't Apophis since this unknown asteroid was much larger; twice the size of Apophis.

On any given day, we have a one in 20,000 chance of being struck by a half-mile-wide asteroid which would destroy a small state. The odds of dying from an asteroid are the same as dying from a tornado or snake bite. Since they had never measured anything this dangerously close to the Earth, they decided to run their calculations three times using the Spitzer Space Satellite which utilizes "frame dragging" for a level of accuracy never possible before. The Faulkes Telescope North on Maui and the Faulkes Telescope South at Siding Spring Australia somberly confirmed a strike. (26)

The coordinates showed a direct strike on Rome. If it didn't disintegrate, it would take out most of Italy. Even if the fugitive asteroid disintegrated in our atmosphere, it would still strike with a force to level 50,000 acres. A similar strike to this one had taken place in Tunguska, Siberia, 100 years earlier. Shockwaves were felt around the world and trees were flattened for miles. There are three theories on the cause of that strike. It was a meteor that disintegrated in the atmosphere; or it was a UFO since Russian scientists claim they discovered fiber optics and computer chips buried at the impact point; or that it was Tesla's death ray.

Nikola Tesla told Admiral Perry in Alaska that he would send him a light show from his lab in Long Island. It is said that Tesla bounced a particle beam off the ionosphere and overshot Alaska and struck Tunguska.

It looked as if the ancient Roman city would again succumb to a foreign "Hun" invader that it could not defeat.

It was reported that it would be a "regional event" capable of flattening a wide area. It takes a four-mile-wide object to cause a global extinction event. Most asteroids are discovered seven months out giving us time to plan a nuclear strike or land a tugboat on it which would alter its course by firing its engines.

By two in the afternoon, news of the eminent strike was on every news station. Fear spread like cancer. The Center for Disease Control worried about the possible spread of a new plague or disease. Many countries scrambled to fill their doomsday vaults. Norway has a storage cave inside an Arctic mountain on the island of Spitsbergen where they store two million crop seeds. The Global Crop Diversity Trust manages 1,400 seed banks around the world where they house a backup of gene sample materials to protect against a global event. Similar banks exist for non-agricultural samples. World governments have always planned for catastrophic events like this. All nations have underground bases for limited human survival in case of an event. The cost of maintaining underground bases for the select few far outweighs the cost and risk of colonizing space.

It had been proven by Astrophysicist Sir Fred Hoyle, that comets, meteors, and asteroids are capable of carrying and salting the atmosphere with pathogens and depositing new viruses on this planet whenever they strike or come close to our atmosphere. The Black Death, AIDS, and other diseases formerly blamed on the cutting down of the rain forests were probably deposited here from space. Some hypothesize that they were brought here from the Apollo missions in the 1960's. To date, small pox is the only plague ever cured. Doctors had argued that humans could no easier catch a disease from a tree than a tree could catch a disease from a human. This is called Zoonosis where a disease leaps from non-human prey into a human. There was no proof that humans can catch non-human viruses especially since it is believed that we are alone in the universe. Today, with this asteroid's coming kill shot, it seemed a little late to debate the question of humanities exclusivity to the rest of the universe.

Chapter 12

DISINFORMATION

"They told the future backwards"
(Isaiah 41:23)

A group of eight men congregate in a warehouse in Allentown, Pennsylvania. There is nothing out of the ordinary in their appearance other than their diverse dress styles. Some are wearing jeans, others are in suits. The focus of their meeting which unites them is a wooden pendant with a large H over laden a cross.

Gavrilo Princip is nearly foaming at the mouth as he rages at the others. He holds a book in his left hand that appears to be bound in human skin and has or is the face of a man on the cover. He rips his shirt off and extends his arms which are covered with a red birth mark from wrist to wrist and navel to throat giving the appearance of a red cross. He genuflects as he speaks.

"I told you it would happen today: and all praise to him, it is even as we speak." He wipes the saliva off of his English handlebar moustache with the back of his hand.

"By tomorrow, there will be no Catholic hierarchy; our plan has been put in place." He pauses. "Then it will be our time. Our Muslim Brotherhood, like you, are preparing all over the world. The wheels are in motion. All Catholic churches will be attacked simultaneously. It is our beginning. All those who worship the corrupt cross must perish. Our plan has come to fruition. Our followers have infiltrated all fundamentalist Christian sects and have carefully planted the seed that Islamic extremists will begin a Jihad against Catholicism. The fourth Crusade! Allah is angry with the Catholic priests so He will punish them by the hand of His people and with His tool, an asteroid. We will use the U.S. President's Christian beliefs as a tool. He will immediately leap to defend his Catholic brethren. Can you visualize it? A world once again torn apart by war. Killing in the name of God; the most convenient excuse often used. We will strip away the façade that hides the truth about Christianity.

During the chaos, we will kill the 144,000 virgins as Herod prescribed. As the President likes to say, there'll be no child left behind. The vile leaders and the children of the cross must die." He screams even louder.

"We are the alpha and the omega; the beginning of the New Order and the end of Christianity. One society ruled by Sharia law. Dying in the name of Allah is the highest privilege. We are Paleomen, hunters. Then he will come to us. The Antichrist will come. If you gain victory, kill them. If you find them hiding, kill them. Kill for the love of killing. Kill for the love of Allah. Their code pink protest signs and tee shirts will lie in the same pile of rubble as their American flags and Tea Party banners. We shall submit America to Islamic rule!"

At the Vatican, Pope Peter, the 266th Pontiff, had called a meeting of the 187 Cardinals to decide the "Holy Seals" course of action. Although the Vatican sits on 109 acres and has assets in excess of $140 billion, at this late date; the money meant nothing. The conclave met in the Sistine Chapel appropriately under Michelangelo's ceiling painting of Christ delivering the Last Judgment. Only the local European Cardinals could attend. Many arrived by foot or car to the Domus Sanctae Marthae or guesthouse. Some of the younger Cardinals in their 50s arrived wearing Bluetooth ear pieces. They were dressed in their traditional red cassocks and skull caps. The Pope and Cardinals then changed into their light gold vestments with white miters and red caps. The Sistine choir's Latin Gregorian chants could be heard. The Pope wore both symbols of his authority; the Signet ring of The Fisherman and the lamb and sheep wool Pallium shawl. Its three gold pins represent the crucifixion nails and five red silk crosses represent Christ's blood. (26)

They were forbidden to speak to reporters regarding the Vatican's secretive world. The remaining Cardinals were conferenced in by Live Meeting. Twelve percent of the Cardinals are from North America; eighteen percent from Latin America; nine percent from Africa; fifty percent from Europe; and nine percent from Asia. Since there are more deaths in Europe than births, many Islamic immigrants had moved in to join the workforce. The Catholic Vatican had become a minority in the mostly hostile Islamic world surrounding it. (26)

After a Bible reading from the book of John, the Cardinals began to argue amongst one another in a sea of denial, as the asteroid approached Rome. Rome was the first city to reach a population of one million in 133 BC.

Cardinal O'Neal was nearly in a panic mode. "Why of all places was the holy Vatican built here on the ground of Emperor Caligula's Circus where thousands of Christians sinned and committed vile acts?"

Pope Peter was in no mood for recriminations. "Sir, why at a time like this would you question God's wisdom?"

Cardinal Jacque questioned the Pope. "With the history we have in France, the Pontiff should have resided there. Then we would have been safe."

"Don't speak to me now of the Virgin and Joseph of Arimathea. The world could not have handled that!"

Jacque shouted back to the Pope. "Why? Could it be because it is true? That the recent security breach by your trusted aide told the truth and we are in possession of the hand written gospel of the Lord Jesus? That Judas followed Jesus' orders and didn't betray him. That Mary was the wife of John the Baptist and had a son by him but spent all her time with Jesus and later married The Lord after Johns beheading thus causing rumors of infidelity and prostitution yet she was actually a Nazarene Queen. That after the crucifixion of our Lord those who supported him were persecuted. Joseph, Mary Magdalene, the Virgin Mary, Lazarus, even Cassius Longinus, the centurion who lanced the Lord's side, were all set adrift to die. That by the grace of God, Joseph, who was once a merchant sailor, piloted the boat to Britannia where they worshipped our Lord. The pregnant Mary gave birth to a daughter, Sarah. And that only the descendants of Sarah's extended family have a soul. How many souls could they have created in 2,000 years? Or is it that only the offspring of the Sons of God that mated with the daughters of man in the old Testament are the only humans to have a soul? It explains the vial cruel behavior of soulless evolutionary humans. I come from that area. I know all this to be true. That the spear of Cassius, the spear that pierced Jesus has become the Spear of Destiny coveted by both Napoleon and Hitler. Constantine and later Charlemagne used the spear to win many battles. Whoever possesses it can never be defeated in battle. The spear today resides in a vault in Washington D.C. We know there is a false Spear of Destiny displayed in a museum in Austria." (2)

"That will all change soon with the Coptic papyrus that proves Jesus married Mary. We will allow priests to marry as our savior did. This will help solve the sick behavior of some priests. It wasn't until 200 AD that theologians started to claim Jesus never married. They rewrote history. And yes, there was some truth to the breach but the St Pius-X Society and Vatican police helped spin and de-escalate the situation."

"I also know that Jesus uttered three words to Thomas that he said the existence of the universe depends on these words; Caulacau, Saulasau, Zeesar (Isaiah 28:10). We learned how all apostles wrote a gospel and only four were selected for the Bible; Matthew, Mark, Luke, and John. Why not the other eight? We also know that Jesus said that the Kingdom of God is inward. Self-knowledge is important. Love one another. (John 13:34). Of course, being from that region, I know how Edward Longshanks banned the printing press for 200 years so no one could write this history. The church is responsible for throwing the world into the 500 years of the Dark Ages through the control of information."(2)

Peter responds calmly. "Because the authors of the other eight are unknown and gnostic, and *The New York Times* prints more information in one day than Longshanks was exposed to in his entire life. Even if this were true, now is not the time to consider this."

Cardinal Clement spoke. "I feel this is the time of the shaking of the Vatican as prophesized by Nostradamus. We should've done more to stop abortion. One out of every three children is sacrificed to the evil one through abortion."

Pope Peter grew angry. "Don't speak to me of prophecy now!"

Cardinal Evanchik interjected. "This day was foretold by the children of Fatima and Medjugorje." All the Cardinals were well aware of these two prophecies. The first concerned the Virgin Mary's appearance before three children in Fatima, Portugal, in 1917. She gave them three prophecies; World War I would end soon, Russia would spread terror but then become an ally, and the third prophecy should not be released until 1960. When Pope Pius XII read the third prophecy, he fainted and never released it. (18)

On June 24, 1981, the Virgin Mother appeared in Medjugorje, Bosnia. She gave the children ten secrets. She referenced Fatima, where her instructions had not been followed.

Cardinal Clement spoke. "Why was the third prophecy not revealed? The Popes have always borne false witness to the Virgin. This is the time to set it right. Twice she gave the Pontiff instructions; twice he over-ruled the Blessed Virgin. Why did our Popes ignore the Holy Mother of Christ's instructions for over 100 years? We all know of the prophecy. The Holy Mother of Christ told the Church to follow the original teachings of Christ and to stop our greedy ways or the Church would be punished."

The men in the room all sat quietly. Not a gold robe rustled for what seemed like an eternity. They were all aware of the prophecy. They sat and pondered some of the indiscretions committed by the "Holy Seal". They began to grow more fearful as they remembered just a few.

Pope Clement VI made no secret of his liking female company. The Countess of Turenne and her family grew rich on their knowledge of his indiscretions. He paid them with donations to keep them quiet; with donations that were meant for the poor. (4)

In 1378, a Roman Cardinal, Cardinal Robert of Geneva let loose a band of mercenaries upon his citizenry resulting in the murder of 4,000 innocents! (4)

Pope Alexander launched the first censorship of printed books - The Index, it lasted 400 years. The Church needed to suppress knowledge and free thought. (4)

There were Popes who murdered for political and personal reasons. The Popes in many cases lived for money, women, and sometimes even worse. They seemed to live their lives with the age old concept, "do as I say, not as I do." Unlike the apostles who went out barefoot, the Popes were decked out like the Kings of Persia. They demanded to be worshipped, and no one came empty handed. (4) As if their role in the Crusades and Inquisition wasn't bad enough, they even offended Heaven. This they accomplished by selling indulgences to lessen a sinner's time in Purgatory.

In 1484, Pope Innocent VIII blamed the death of one third of Europe's population from the Bubonic plague on witchcraft. He then ordered the burning of 50,000 innocent peasants at the stake.

In 1489, Pope Innocent VIII issued the Malleus Maleficarum or Witch Hammer document that made witchcraft punishable by death and started the infamous witch trials.

Cardinal Santorini broke the silence. "The Virgin did not condemn us that day. She gave us an opportunity to reform. The Virgin Mary told us God was in all of us. All one had to do was to form a personal relationship with him. It wasn't through the Church and its ten percent tithing, but through faith and belief. "Blessed are those who believe without seeing." That is what Jesus told Thomas. Then Thomas wrote a Gnostic gospel where one can achieve salvation through a personal union with God. Why has the Gospel of Thomas been ignored? If one believes they have a soul, then God is in you, not in the gold and marble walls of a church. Why does one have to go through a church to get to God?"

Cardinal Olaff repeated Luke 17: 20-21, "The kingdom of God is within you." He continued by saying. "Heaven is not a place, it is in our hearts. When we do that which is right, we already are in the Kingdom of God. Jesus preached in caves, open fields, and by the seaside. He did not want or need gold and marble statues and buildings as his church. These are for men of greed and power. Pride and ambition will not get you to heaven unless they are overpowered by humility and generosity along the way. If one does not change, as they get older, they will have learned nothing. One must see and feel what they have done to others. Our souls are eternal; we go from chapter to chapter in the book of existence. How many lifetimes will it take for a person to learn their lessons? How we react is our free will. Life is about hope, faith, and reacting with a pure heart." (2)

Pope Peter screamed. "Blasphemy Cardinal Olaff! What you speak is blasphemy!"

Cardinal Jacque of France spoke. "I'm not so sure that it is, Peter. I'm sure you remember the underground church in France. Mary Magdalene founded it. Jesus had two levels of Apostles. There was the inner core that knew everything and the other nine who knew only that which they needed to know. The outer core members wrote the four gospels of the Bible. The truth has been hidden for thousands of years. The Gnostic Nag Hammadi scrolls told the truth. The Church closed access to them for forty years and only displayed the parts they wanted the faithful to see. There are many sections still in the Vatican archives, their truths never disclosed.

In 325 AD, Constantine and the Court of Nicaea agreed with Peter's version. He was a hater of women and the enemy of Mary. After the Ascension of the Lord, Mary left Alexandria, Egypt, with their daughter Sara and two inner core members. Joseph of Arimathea being a merchant seaman piloted their ship to Maries de la Mer on the Rhone River. She founded the Gnostic church and the bloodline of Christ. They would use the code word of Ark to describe their churches. They believed they would be reborn over and over to serve the people. The four Gospels were written between 35 and 65 years after Jesus' death. Most people were illiterate and received information through word of mouth. We didn't even agree that Jesus was Divine and not an ordinary man until the 2nd Nicene Counsel of 389 AD." (2)

"You sound like a heretic Cardinal Jacque!" screamed Cardinal Reynolds. "People were burned for less than that in the Middle Ages. But we are under great stress today. I'm sure the 'Holy Father' will forgive you."

Pope Peter nods in agreement.

Cardinal Jacque interrupts. "I'm not finished yet. That is my point; we've burned people for less. We persecuted Galileo and Copernicus for their ideas. These Gnostic beliefs were strongest in the first century A.D. but had resurgence with the European Cather's during medieval times. The Church's Inquisition wiped out the Cather's and the order of the Templar Knights. Many of who had fought for the Church in the Crusades. The only reason the Pope and the King of France betrayed the Templar's was to steal their land and their wealth and to reduce their power. The people respected them even more than they did the King. I find it sad that the Church, like the world in general, limits itself only to the histories that have been written throughout the ages. There are many sources that show us that history in general, and the history of the Church in particular, has never been told accurately. The Roman Apostle Paul wrote much of the New Testament but never even served under our Lord. There are many churches along the trade routes in China which bear the name of John the Beloved. (2) The possibilities are endless concerning our faith. We should have presented all these views to the faithful long ago. Then let them decide for themselves, what they believe. I fear the time has grown too late for that. Forty percent of people claim no religious identity. They refer to themselves as the "None's". Today there is no shame in saying you don't believe. No pressure to claim a religious affiliation."

Cardinal Tosi then spoke. "I'm afraid I must agree with Jacque that the time is too late. The prophecy is in the Book of Revelation passage 8:7 that John of Patmos wrote in 50 A.D. Although he was probably not the Apostle, in his book he described the Seven Signs of the Apocalypse. It seems it is that time. Let us try to remember the signs now. Perhaps we can interpret them and find a resolution that will not be as dire. I'm sure we remember the first four that concern the Horsemen of the Apocalypse. Let us ponder all the signs."

They all sat silently and prayed for the gift of interpretation. The Cardinals all thought of the Seven Signs.

The White Horse bears a bow but has no arrows. It is the liar. It will trick the U.S. into the destruction of the Middle East but will effectively bankrupt itself in so doing. It signifies war.

The Red Horse will take peace from the Earth. It signifies disease.

The Black Horse signifies the want of oil.

The Pale Horse, which is green, will leave with 25 percent of all living souls. It signifies death.

The death of the innocents is legalized abortion.

The sun will go dark and a star will fall to Earth and its name will be Wormwood.

Silence in Heaven will occur when the first infant is born without a soul.

God will then break his silence with seven trumpets. The Rapture will be preceded by a departure from faith by many Christians.

Many believe that this will not be the end of the World but that 1,000 years of peace will follow.

Cardinal Jacque spoke once more. "In the Apocalypse of Thomas, Jesus told him of his Ascension and his second coming. So we have not only John but also Thomas speaking of the End of Days. Jesus' return is mentioned 321 times in the Old and New Testaments."

Cardinal Tosi then said, "Jesus visited many lands in different forms; as Buddha, Mohammed and others. Maybe we were wrong. Buddhism seems to follow the Lord's teachings the closest."

Cardinal Ventre then spoke. "We are the only religion that believes in the End of Days and practices exorcism. We all walk around with this primal fear of destruction. This all makes me think of Moses and how in 1200 B.C. he saw the God of Israel. The original Bible words were written without any breaks for the words. The Hebrew Torah also contains the unbroken string of characters of the Old Testament. They have a strict warning," Should you omit or add a single letter, you could destroy the whole universe. The Bible is a cryptogram, a riddle from God. The Lamb opened the seals with this Comet, or asteroid Wormwood. The slayed Lamb, having seven horns and seven eyes, has been sent to Earth. Experts in Equidistant Letter Sequence have tried to decode the Torah. It seems that every 50th letter spells Torah. According to the Cabbalists, Moses wrote a secret code into the Bible. There's a hidden language in the Bible. There used to be 13,000 languages. Today, only 6,500 are spoken and soon we'll be down to just 600. The crossword pattern of 304,805 characters in the Bible foretells the future. It reveals events that take place in the future. While scholars have spent a lifetime trying to decode it, technology of today has aided a great deal. Senior code breakers at the National Security Agency in Washington D.C. wrote a computer program to decipher the Bible.

Every significant advancement in technology, art and science was already recorded along with the names of the inventors. They found Prime Minister Rabins' name crossed with the words assassin Tel Aviv. They found Gates and Microsoft; Edison and electricity. They also discovered the assassinations of both John and Robert Kennedy encoded in the Bible. The year 1504 appears along with Da Vinci and Galileo who died that year and the word Shakespeare who was born that year. There are five original Torahs, four of which found the word Leader along with the names of Trump, Datchet and Rice as well as betrayer with Barack and the un-named one who I will not say. You all may wonder what the reason is for me telling you this. The Fifth Torah found the words

End of Days alongside the word Wormwood. It was believed that the Fifth Torah was compromised and therefore the other four Torahs were factual. What if the Fifth Torah is the only original worded Bible in existence? Then it must be true! The Bible code predicted every major war and cataclysm including September 11, 2001, and September, 11, 2026. Deuteronomy targeted the recent poisoning of New York's water supply. Leviticus spoke of earthquakes in Japan. Prior to 1960, the world experienced an earthquake every three years. Now we have upwards of eighteen a year. What if there was a global earthquake and all the off shore oil wells broke free? The oceans would be destroyed as they fill up with oil! The Fifth Torah puts the words comet and Rome together. Etna appears in Exodus. Yellowstone Park in Wyoming is the site of a super volcano. Yellowstone appears in Deuteronomy with the word comet; it will be crumbled, torn to pieces, Earth annihilated."(6, 26)

Cardinal Clement was ringing his hands together nervously as he spoke. "And English words have been found in the Torah and Maharabata. How can that be when English didn't exist? God placed those words there as a sign of his prophecy. This is an asteroid, not a comet! Maybe it is wrong and we will be safe. It is Apophis not Wormwood!"

Cardinal Infante interjects. "Eugene Wormwood discovered the errant asteroid. It is Wormwood!"

Cardinal Ventre says, "No, the asteroid will hit and turn our planet dark and cold for years. It only takes a seven degree drop in temperature to start a new ice age. Cayce, Dixon, even Nostradamus predicted cataclysm at this time. We know Nostradamus was correct about the poisoning of New York. He spoke of the breaking of an old religion and the coming of an Antichrist. I know it is not accepted but I have perused his writings secretly. I'd like to enlighten you 'Holy Father' and the others. Nostradamus said:

"There will be chaos from space. This will bring about famine. There will be a holy war; perhaps it will be the remnants of our faith against the Antichrist. The Antichrist will annihilate three. Blood human corpses, water and red cover the Earth. The Isle of Scotland will suffer frost. Temples consecrated in the early Roman fashion. Mars threatens us with war like force. The clergy will be exalted and the people will learn nothing from them. The Senate will not approve of him. His poison blood will be in the chalice. The Antichrist will come from the Middle East."(18)

He pauses for a moment.

"Jeanne Dixon had a vision of Queen Nefertiti holding a soiled ragged newborn child. She claims he will be a charismatic speaker and bring mankind together under one faith. She will have been raised as a Muslim but will deny it in public. The world will follow this beast. She will be the Antichrist. She also had a prediction of Washington D.C. Looking out of her window, instead of seeing the green grass and trees; she saw a barren land. I believe the un-named President was the devil. (19)

"Don't you see? We would never allow the Antichrist to rise to power if the church was intact. Too much has already come to pass. Nostradamus said there would be plague and destruction at the beginning of the 21st Century. There is the plague of AIDs and many cataclysms from the oceans, Earth and sky. He also said, 'The sky will burn at 45 degrees in the Great New City.' Perhaps he spoke of September 11, 2001, or Rome? There seems to be a great connection to the U.S. 'Living without laws and exempt from politics the one who makes Thursday his holiday shall prevail.' They celebrate their Thanksgiving Day on Thursday in what was once America. It is the only holiday I know of celebrated on that day. He also spoke of changes in the weather. 'Long rain will come the length of the Arctic Pole. Of people and beasts, there will be horrible destruction. Vengeance will be seen as the comet passes. The dead shall rise from their graves.' (18)

"Will the vengeance be on Rome? I don't know. But I fear the threat is great to us today. We must head to the mountains away from here, so we don't breathe the cosmic dust. 'In the last days, the Lord's temple shall be established in the mountains.' (Isaiah 2:2) We must leave Rome and go to St. Mary's of Axum, the holy site where the Ark of the Covenant is housed and the spell of *Goetia* is guarded. The mountain site in Ethiopia is high enough to survive anything. We can prepare to battle the Antichrist if the prophecy is true."

Pope Peter spoke one word. "No!"

After a long pause he proceeded to say. "Never again mention the word *Goetia* or the ability to control the Fallen who built all of the ancient sites. The Congregation for The Causes of Saints was formed years ago for this very purpose of investigating miracles, prophecies, and the paranormal. It has found none of these claims to be true. When you look at our solar system in a text book or the planetarium you see that all nine planets are aligned on the same plane. You will also notice that the huge and massive Jupiter shadows the Earth like a big brother. God placed it there with its size and strong gravitational pull to protect the Earth. Why else would this alignment be so if not to protect us? No, we are all bound for heaven eventually!"

Suddenly, Cardinal Evanchek screamed. "We're all doomed! I just remembered the prophecies of Father Malachi O'Morgair and how he said the last Pope's name would be Peter. That's you!" The Cardinal was nearly hysterical.

Pope Peter spoke to Cardinal Ventre. "Get him some wine." Peter was very agitated. "What is this nonsense he is saying?" Cardinal Santorini began to explain, to those not familiar with the "Papal Prophecy", about Father Malachi and his book.

"He was a priest and the first Irish Saint. He predicted his own place and date of death: Clair Vaux, France, on November 2, 1148, and he wrote a book concerning future Popes. He gave the book to Pope Innocent II in 1140. The Vatican kept his writings secret until

1595. In this book, he named every Pope from 1124 to the present. The last Pope to be named will be Peter. The End of Days will begin with the naming of the Last Pope, the 266th. That also explains why there are 266 columns outside these walls in the Basilica. One for each Pope!" (19, 26)

Cardinal Evanchik put down the wine glass and screamed. "It is you! We should have listened to the Blessed Virgin at Fatima."

Peter nervously spoke. "These prophecies are nonsense. What exactly did he say? Cardinal Santorini, humor me, tell me more. Cardinal Olaff, you are adept at the Internet, find me that passage. What is the name of this book?"

Cardinal Santorini speaks. "It is called "Papal Prophecy" and it contains much more."

The Pope speaks condescendingly to Santorini. "Please regal us with more mythology while we wait."

"Besides predicting every Pope by name, he speaks a great deal of John Paul I. He predicted the murder of the pontiff, one month after his election, on September 28, 1978. Which we now know to have been true!

"That a secret Masonic group, the P-2 with members who were Cardinals, politicians, judges, and military, formed a web of corruption whose goal was the control of the Vatican wealth. When John Paul I announced that he had personally audited the Vatican accounts and would punish the embezzlers; he was found dead in his bed. No reason for his death was ever published, and no autopsy performed. Of course, now we know Malachi was right." (19)

As Santorini finished, Olaff burst through the door.

"I have the prophecy." He pulls out a paper and reads. "During the last persecution of the 'Holy Roman Church', there shall sit Peter of Rome, who will feed the sheep great tribulation. The city of Seven Hills or Rome shall be utterly destroyed and the dreadful judge will judge the people." (18)

He faces the Pope. "Could this be today, Peter?"

Peter screams. "Enough! I have listened for hours to blasphemy and heresy from some of the most esteemed members of our faith. You sit there and say that we falsely portrayed Mary Magdalene as a prostitute, persecuted the Cather's and Templar's while supporting the Inquisition, declared Crusades on Islam, repressed science and have a macabre secret library which houses the truth. Jesus did not marry Mary and have a child. Jesus was without sin and would never have been allowed to enter Heaven if he sinned. This Priory of Sion story was proven to be a hoax in 1956. Opus Dei does not battle the Priory of Sion. You sound like little children afraid of the boogeyman or the darkness. I feel like the soldier Cartaphilis who struck Jesus and is condemned to walk the Earth for all days. You never stop with your predictions. Many false predictions have been told to deceive the many. I cannot believe my Cardinals would repeat this heresy, let alone read it. These alternative ideas are the Antichrist testing your faith. There are 5843 independent records of Jesus from that time; more than any other person of that time. There are 500 witnesses to seeing him after the crucifixion. Jesus was without sin. Those of you who compromise your beliefs with the pagan religion of evolution and inclusiveness are now lost. We shall stay here. No such strike will take place against the Vatican. When the people of the world see we have not fled, they will be converted. The battle is for souls! Have faith my brothers, we are the only religion that can be traced back to the crucifixion of our Lord; the son of God. All others are simply copies or branches of the Holy Roman Church. We are the only true religion. Jesus suffered Adams penalty. Whoever does not believe is already condemned. We will stay here.

I have also waited to this moment to announce a change in direction for our ministry. No longer will we be the brunt of lies. Jesus is also a Warrior King wielding a secret weapon; the word of God. Remember the vengeful and ruthless assassins of Avignon? They were wolves like the Templar's, not sheep. People will once again shutter at the voice of the Holy Roman Catholic Church. For years the New Knights Templar has been recruiting in Eastern Europe and Russia where the disease of liberalism never took hold. A rejection of abortion, birth control and mass immigration to low cost of living Eastern Europe has built up a huge Christian militia. Multi-culturalism and liberalism in the West has created this catastrophe or opportunity. The ignorant West was like a driverless car. We will not have a replay of the fall of Rome because we will be in control. Do what thou wilt is NOT the whole of the law. Jesus said "And let the one who has no sword sell his cloak and buy one." I have reinstituted the warrior assassins and 117,000 have been trained and have taken the sacred oath to purge humanity of heretics regardless of race or creed or age or sex. I am the Vicar of Jesus and will restore the glory of the Holy Roman Church in His name through the militia of God. Orders have been given to crucify the enemy upside down and disembowel them for all to see. Poison will also be used in cases where access is difficult. Who among you disagree? Who do I start with? Who disagrees?"

There is silence and then great applause as the Cardinals erupt with pride and enthusiasm toward the new plan. It has been too long since the Church was aggressive and will no longer be a target. All are in agreement. All support this new direction for the Holy Roman Church. Cardinals can be heard screaming, "We will kill them with prejudice!"

The news networks were now full of predictions from Cayce, Dixon and Nostradamus. In Daniel 8:11-14, it was stated that there would be 2,300 days until the end. If one would count backwards 2,300 days, nothing special had occurred that day. This therefore could not be the "End of Days". The news networks used this fact as a way to quell panic and rioting. All the world's governments were assuring their citizens that this would be nothing more than a meteor shower, the Leopold Meteor Shower, which is a scientific fact.

174

Many lamented that Camelot ended and the End of Days started when JFK Jr. and his wife died in that plane crash near the Cape.

Rabbit News reported that the Earth had been struck four times by asteroids which were planet killers. The last one was 65 million years ago. The Earth is due for one. The Rabbit News Network experienced satellite problems at 2:17 p.m. and was unable to broadcast the evening news.

In twelve hours, the entire world had changed. No longer were people waiting to celebrate the birth of the baby Jesus but instead were preparing to see an adult Jesus coming down out of the clouds. People no longer gave one another a hearty Christmas greeting but now looked away, afraid of what they may see in another's eyes. The most worthwhile thing that occurred was that the cash registers stopped clicking. Society closed ranks around family and friends. Those still on the streets cast an eye to the heavens. Churches were bursting at the seams, lines stretched out the door from the confessionals. The Internet sites devoted to prophecy were overwhelmed. Many feared the worst, but tried to find solace in the interpretations of Nostradamus who had predictions concerning mankind until 3797. No longer was time spent looking forward to receiving that special Christmas gift. Now time was spent looking forward to that next sunrise.

President Datchet ordered the capping of all deep sea oil wells and a temporary shutdown of all nuclear power plants.

Chapter 13

GAVRILO PRINCIP

"Those who cannot remember the past are condemned to repeat it" (George Santayana)

A sedan quickly proceeds along Route 80 towards northwest New Jersey. Within it sit Department of Homeland Security agents Artemus Cohagen and Luis Rodriguez. In the vehicle's console, a computer screen displays ever changing data.

Luis turns toward his partner. "So Arte, do you think these," he looks away at the computer screen, "Herodians are connected to our case with the priests that we are ready to move on? Or is it the Muslim Brotherhood?"

"Who knows?" He turns the computer screen towards himself. "The Muslim Brotherhood was founded in 1928 in Egypt and their founder, Hasan al-Banna was an admirer of Hitler and translated Mein Kampf into Arabic."

"Hasan al Banana founded them?"

"No, Banna not Banana. All we have on these Herodians is that they hate Christians. HQ says they are dangerous, and they just might be. What concerns me are their egos. It says here that they have 10,000 members all over the world and we know very little about them. They're closed knit. No one has penetrated their group. I think the biggest danger will be their heads and whether their heads fit in our 'paddy wagons'."

Luis laughs. "Yeah, especially if our buddy Gavrilo Princip is up there tonight. We can take care of two strange birds with the same stone and save the taxpayers' money on our operation tomorrow night."

"What if this guy is more connected than we think and has a Napoleonic complex. Doesn't it bother you that we get this tip about an all-girls monastery at Our Lady of Grace church in out of the way Columbia, New Jersey, where it is so rural that nothing happens? We have two religious cases in close proximity, almost as if they knew we were preparing tomorrow's operation only a few miles away. Big hunters want big game. They take the lion, not the cub."

"We were called in for expertise, this is SWATS operation. Let me see if I can hook into their surveillance system," says Rodriguez as he types a few code numbers in and a church appears. As he pans back and forth, a number of vehicles come into view. "There are three local police cars and the SWAT vehicles."

"How many SWAT and local police do we have?"

Luis types in a few lines and receives a reply that there are 15 SWAT and six locals.

Cohagen yells, "Tell them to get rid of the locals. And find out if they have robots, I mean drones."

Luis begins to object but then shrugs his shoulders and says, "Gotcha. Hey Arte, how fortified could this church be?"

Cohagen sighs loudly and says, "I don't even know why they are here. Hell, to tell you the truth, I don't know what's been happening the past few days with trying to secure our plan for tomorrow. It's almost Christmas and I haven't bought any presents yet."

"Man did you procrastinate again this year? It almost doesn't seem right to go to midnight mass when an asteroid is supposed to hit the Vatican tomorrow."

"The Pope doesn't seem too concerned; he called a meeting today to "diss" the whole idea."

"Do you know what the shame is about this assignment?"

"No, what?"

"That they didn't target lawyers instead of priests."

They both laugh.

The two agents were greeted by a surreal scene as they drove up the driveway of Our Lady of Grace retreat. The sun was beginning to set behind the bell tower casting a red hue over the whole scene. It could've been an award winning photograph. It seemed so beautiful except for what seemed out of place on the church steps. Two large pools of blood were seeping down the steps. The source was two mangled blood soaked husks that had been two priests.

Surrounding the scene were a number of black SWAT vehicles. Rodriguez exits the vehicle and yells out to the SWAT members, "Who is in charge here?"

A SWAT member turns angrily and says, "Who the hell are you?"

Rodriguez flashes his badge and says, "Department of Homeland Security. I think that's all you need to know. Oh yeah, we're also taking over here!"

The burly SWAT team member responds, "Be my guest, Captain Nichols is in charge and he is standing right there."

The agents proceed to approach a man that looks strikingly similar to the others. He is standing under a church bulletin board that reads, "The only thing missing in CHRCH is U." No stripes or cap or other marking to distinguish his rank from the others. He is dressed in all black with a black Kevlar vest. He has one black leather booted foot resting on the bumper of a SWAT van. His Kevlar helmet and modified M-15 were also leaning against the bumper. The only difference between him and the others was his look of authority and determination.

Rodriguez surmised by his body language that Nichols had been an officer in the military. He no doubt had leadership skills and took charge but he was combat trained; good things in a war but not in a delicate situation like this.

As Luis prepared to walk up to him, Cohagen trotted up behind him and said, "Pakistan war commander. He probably commanded the con-berets; an all criminal group under West Point command that was offered amnesty if they came back alive. They got the toughest assignments and were uncontrollable. I heard we had some of these ex-military commanders here locally. Damn it! Every damn returning officer seems to have joined SWAT. Doesn't the government get it, a good soldier doesn't always equate to a good investigator."

"I heard we lost about the same number of soldiers in Pakistan over the first four years as we lost on the first day of battle on Iwo Jima island in 1945 during WWII; 3,650 men. We give these guys too much credit. It wasn't very intense at all in Pakistan. The liberal media just played it up to stir anti-war protestors."

Cohagen shakes his head and says, "Over 51,000 Americans died at the battle of Gettysburg. Freedom isn't free! Let's get this over with."

He extends his hand and says, "Captain Nichols, I'm agent Cohagen and this is agent Rodriguez. We're here to assume command."

Nichols spins around to face them. He had a scar on his left cheek which was obviously from close combat. "Agents, I'm glad to have your assistance but I believe it would be in all our best interests if I remained in charge. You've just arrived while I've been assessing and overseeing the operation for over an hour. You weren't here to hear the screams of the priests as they took them to the precipice of the bell tower. You didn't hear their gurgles as their throats were slashed or see their death throngs as they were thrown from the bell tower."

Cohagen interjects, "That being said, there is more here than meets the eye. I don't want you or your men going into this unprepared. This isn't an isolated incident; it appears to be part of a movement by a radical sect. We need to capture them and get the information we lack about their movement. We need to wait for the cover of darkness and plan our assault."

Nichols shakes his head, "I don't think stealth will make a difference with these heinous monsters. From what we can see, there are only three or four of them at best. Anyway, four of my men have camouflaged predator garments on that blend in with their background. We'll be able to walk right up to them without them seeing us."

Rodriguez asks, "How experienced are your men?"

"They have experience; we've trained for situations like this."

Suddenly from the bell tower, a voice yells out, "You see what we did to the priests. We have nuns and young girls in the rectory." They hear high pitched screams. "Hey, I think the girls are in need of counseling like the choir boys get from the priests. We're going to do them a service. But first, we need to show the nuns the light and let them eat of my body." They hear two or three men laugh and more female screams. The screams seem to be cut short like the girls were gagged. Then a woman yells out, "Help us." A man yells; "Shut that whore up." There is a loud grunt, a moan and more sobs.

"Jones, can you get a shot?" Nichols yells.

"I can't see anything Captain. There's too much glare from the sunset."

"Damn them, we can't let them do that to those women. Prepare to go in."

Cohagen screams, "The hell you are. I'm in charge here."

Nichols spits out his words, "The DHS may be in charge of this site but not my men."

Rodriguez angrily says, "You don't even know if there are nuns in there or how many there might be. Wait until we can get an assault vehicle and use the cover of night. For God's sake, we have the sun reflecting off of our vests."

"No, I listened to you about the local cops but not this. You were called in as consultants. We need to move now."

Rodriguez asks, "Are you Catholic?"

Nichols responds, "Yes, what of it?"

"We are too. It's sickening to think of what might happen tomorrow to the Pope and the Vatican. You can't appease God by trying to save these nuns like they are the last of our faith. This is much bigger than what's happening here. For all we know, they could be cleaning people, secretaries and other lay people, not nuns and young girls."

"What the hell kind of Catholic are you that you would let them violate those nuns and young girls. They're all virgins."

"Virgins; my God, these are the Herodians. Don't go in. This isn't Pakistan. There's no air support or tanks to back you up. We don't know what we are up against."

Nichols flings his arm in the air. "I didn't know the DHS employed a bunch of slack jawed pussies. I commanded the Pelican Bay Commando's in Pakistan. They were the worst of the worst most violent ethnic prisoners. I received the Medal of Honor for killing a dozen Pakistani soldiers that overran a small detachment of medics. It was the only Medal of Honor given out during the war. I was ST9 prior to that. Seal Team Nine! I was blown off a cliff by a rocket grenade and crawled six miles with a fractured back and two bullets in me and killed five Taliban along the way. I had my hands and feet bound and thrown into the water and managed to swim a mile to shore on my own. I think I can handle these cowards. There's a time when you have to decide if you want to be the man on the cross or the man hammering the nails. Lock and load men, we're going in. Sergeant Chow, get behind the wheel. We'll take the bullet proof van up to the steps. We'll use the schematic that I handed out earlier. This is assault 101, just like in training school. Let's move. Turn on the laser mirrors so when they look at us they'll get it in the eyes."

"Arte, have you gotten through to the diocese? These nuts are going in."

"I'm on hold, can you fucking believe it? Luis, my gut tells me this is a setup. It's too orchestrated, they're being baited in."

"I have the same feeling. The sun in our eyes like some bad western. The sound of short screams and moans. This isn't going to end well. These guys have no idea what they are in for. I'm calling DHS for backup. We'll advance our plan by one day. Use the same agents a day early."

"I'm one step ahead of you. I already called Director Mattes when Nichols started with his John Wayne speech. All agents are out; engaged at other churches in the area. Same 'M.O.' all over Jersey. Dead priests called in by locals. Some thought they were Santa Claus displays in their red outfits that fell over, except it turned out to be priests covered in blood. This isn't good. There hasn't been one shot fired at any location. This stinks of a well-orchestrated setup. Let's put our vests on and get our rifles. Maybe we can pick some of them off."

The same screams and moans can be heard. The two agents put their vests on, cock their assault rifles and prepare.

"God, this is sickening. Do you think they are harming the nuns?" asks Cohagen. He slams the computer shut after receiving no response from the diocese.

"Damn it, Arte, what should we do? We're not prepared for this but we can't sit back and wait any longer."

"Follow me, that window appears to be ajar. Be ready for anything."

The two agents go through the window and the screams appear to be getting louder; repeating itself in a strange unnatural manner. The agents take the safeties off their weapons and move into the room where the voices are coming from.

"Oh fuck Luis, it's a recording. It's a goddamn continuous play recording. Tell Nichols there isn't any nuns, it's a fucking trap!"

Rodriguez yells into his headset, "There are no nuns, there are no nuns; it's a trap! Damn it, Arte, there's no response. They turned off their headsets."

As they turn to exit, they see the nuns and young girls stacked neatly in the corner of the room like fire wood but in the shape of an H. Their throats cut but no blood as if they were moved here from the real scene of the crime.

Rodriguez was lucky the first shooter was nervous as the armor piercing bullet whizzed past his head and slammed into the door. The agents dive out through the open window. More shooters appear in every stained glass window as they explode outward from bullet fire.

The SWAT team members were not as lucky as agent Rodriguez. Nichols fell almost immediately as a bullet tore into his shoulder and the force spun him 180 degrees. He was the first to go down as if the shooters had observed the conversation and identified the leader. The blood soaked his black shirt as his weapon fell to the ground. The second shot seemed to explode in his thigh as the blood sprayed out. He grabbed his M-15 with his good arm and rolled under the van.

A series of bullets blasted into the windshield which exploded glass back into the face of Sergeant Chow. His helmet and visor protected his face and eyes from the glass but not from the next bullet which tore into his throat beneath the helmet. The force nearly decapitated him but death came quickly as his spine exploded from the impact. The sticky red liquid began to cover the leather seats as Sergeant Chow lay slumped behind the steering wheel.

The rest of the SWAT team scattered from behind the van to whatever cover they could find. Nichols yelled out orders but no one could hear him over the report of the gunfire and the screams of the wounded officers. The SWAT team responded with assault fire back into the church.

As dusk began to arrive, the blood red sunset was replaced by a creeping darkness punctuated by the tracers from the weapons and the red of the flowing blood down the driveway.

Arte and Luis had taken cover behind the SWAT van.

Luis whispers to Arte, "They blew it, they don't have a chance."

Arte nods his head to the side, "It's getting dark; they're dressed in black; that could be their equalizer."

The bullets ricocheted off the cement driveway and blew out the tires of the vehicles but missed their human targets.

Arte peeked from their vehicular shield to see two SWAT members make it to the marble steps. As three bullets slammed into the first officer, he was thrown from the steps on to the sidewalk. Arte didn't know if he was dead or alive but it seemed to be a moot point as blood flowed excessively from all wounds. The second officer threw himself onto the steps and emptied a clip into the glass double doors which shattered immediately. His success gave him a false sense of security. Feeling exposed on the steps, he made a frontal charge for the entranceway. The first bullet dismantled his kneecap. He pitched forward as his knee buckled and then he slammed into the marble steps. He reached for his rifle as a figure appeared in the doorway wearing night vision goggles and peppered him with non-lethal shots as if wanting to make him suffer. The officer twitched back and forth as bones, nerves and arteries exploded. A well-positioned SWAT ended his suffering with a fatal shot to his head. The officer's head snapped back and hit the ground with a thud. His brains spilled like a broken egg. The dark figure slipped back into the vestibule of the church as the SWAT chose a mercy killing for their peer rather than a kill on their enemy.

Another SWAT quickly rounded the corner of the doorway and fired round after round at his shadowy enemy. The figure collapsed backward against the baptismal font. The brave officer's end came just as quickly as a barrage of bullets hit him and he flopped to the ground.

Cohagen slipped around the side of the car and opened the driver's door. Although it was missing a windshield and had two flat tires, it was still drivable. Artimus Cohagen was a survivor because he always kept his head in intense situations. Almost as if he could step back and be an observer while in action. Arte had parked the sedan at an angle so that the SWAT vehicles had forged a protective barrier. As he crawled into the driver's seat, his hands were easily cut from the broken glass. The type of razor cuts that you don't feel as your attention is fixated elsewhere. He glanced behind himself to see Luis fire off three rapid rounds. Spent cartridges ejected into the air. His partner gave an exclamation of success as Arte knew he must've hit his target. For an instant, Arte thought they might actually win this battle. Then he heard the first explosion. Cohagen swore loudly, "Damn it, they have RPG's!"

Rodriguez yells to his partner, "They hit the van, it's gone. God Arte, this is a mess."

"Get in the car, Luis, there has to be another way in," Cohagen yelled to his buddy over the noise which included the explosion of another SWAT vehicle. Luis crawled to the passenger door of their sedan and Arte opened it halfway so that Luis could crawl in.

"Luis, I'm going to drive straight for the rectory. We'll jump out near that statue of Saint Michael and take cover behind that small wall and go for that main door that appears to be open."

Luis throws his rifle over his shoulder and replies, "Let's roll."

The fires had changed the darkness into its former red hue. The SWAT not killed in the explosions continued to fire into every stained glass broken window and occasionally were rewarded with a twitching figure falling to the ground. They fought bravely like men about to die with nothing left to lose. Nichols' burnt husk of a body smoldered under what was left of their van. He never even got off a shot as the leader of this offensive. A soldier's angel, Valkyrie, could be seen in the smoke flying overhead.

If Luis and Arte were still in view of the rest of the team they would've been surprised to see that they were communicating now by hand signals. The seven surviving officers, although most bleeding from various wounds, began an all-out charge towards the statue of the blessed Mother and its three foot wall. Six officers made it and they began to fire at the wooden entrance door and at any movement or flashes of gunfire from the windows. With the protection of the wall, they could measure their shots as opposed to shooting wildly in a desperate attempt at self-defense. Although the enemy had the vantage point, they lacked the officer's training. Each time they exposed themselves to fire, the sharp shooting SWAT found their mark. Four windows displayed the folded bodies of assailants hanging out of the window. The Virgin Mary's arms were outstretched in a welcoming and comforting gesture that seemed to be protecting the crusading officers.

The Herodians wanted the total destruction of Christianity, the officers and any icon of religion. The officers didn't consider the ramifications of taking refuge around the religious statue but it incensed the insurgents. Two well placed RPG's split the wall and shattered part of the statue. The officers shook off the plaster but realized that their sanctuary had been compromised. One more blast and the wall will collapse exposing them like a pheasant shoot. The situation was becoming desperate. The six officers let off a volley of shots and tear gas and then leapt over the wall and charged the open doorway. As they emerged through the wall of smoke, the first three officers were wounded immediately like an Assassins Creed video game. Blood sprayed from their body armor as they fell back into the wall of smoke and into the arms of their slower less athletic comrades who seemed to carry them. A moderate breeze advanced the protective fog towards the doorway. The officers had dropped to the ground and placed their gas masks on. Their eyes teared and burned as they started their deliberated encroachment to the doorway. Shots whizzed over their prone bodies as their enemy could no longer see them. Fear gripped the Herodians as they could see figures standing in the smoke but yet their bullets passed right through them like holograms of the officer's protective angels. What type of trick could this be? They could see figures but could not take them down.

As the fog of smoke entered the doorway of the church, two officers sprang to their feet and fired as they advanced. Their protective wall of fog had become a thin mist now as it had served its purpose and their guardian angels ascended. Pews splintered as the shots hit every waist high object. Two Herodians slumped over the pews while three others were shot through the soft pine benches.

The two officers dove behind the marble baptismal font which began to shatter from the nonstop gunfire hitting it. The font exploded spraying holy water into the air and dousing the officers in another protective shield. It would be their final baptism as the dust and flakes of marble that stuck to their clothing turned red from the multitude of penny sized openings in the officer's bullet strewn bodies. The officers were dead before their heads touched the blessed water soaked ground.

The remaining officers rushed for the oak trimmed marble altar. They exchanged fire with two assailants before entering the sanctuary behind the altar. The officers threw the two bodies and those of two dead nuns onto the altar as an additional wall of protection from the gunfire. Above them hung a 30-foot wooden crucifix in an upside down position; the sign of the devil. There seemed to be a moment of silence as the officers looked up and their assailants observed the surreal scene.

The eerie quiet was shattered as an RPG struck the rear wall of the church and exploded sending the men into the dead bodies strewn on the altar. Dust and plaster covered the officers like scrap metal. Bullets peppered the altar but to no avail. The officers were safe. A loud creaking and cracking could be heard as the crucifix broke from its mooring and plummeted down onto one of the officers in their hopeless cause. The officer saw it right before it impaled him. His Kevlar vest was no match for the weight of the pointed spear. In his last few moments of life, he visualized Jesus carrying this heavy cross to Calvary and struggled to make the sign of the cross with his free hand before his life was pressed from his broken body.

To the remaining officers, it seemed as though the wooden cross provided another wall of protection as the image of Jesus seemed to be taking all the shots that were meant for them. On this night, five days before the celebration of the birth of Jesus, the savior's grace couldn't protect the officers forever. As the mold of Jesus splintered, the officers muttered a soft thank you. As the words exited his lips, a bullet entered his skull and silenced an officer forever. The two remaining officers fired into the choir area where the flash originated from.

The Christmas trees and pinsetters stood in stark contrast to the bloody scene taking place on hallowed ground. The star fell from the top of the tree but was caught by the branches that extended out in protection of the manger.

The wooden altar surrendered to the relentless bullets that impacted its walls. The altar seemed to serve as a casket for the two remaining blood soaked officers as they fell within its box-like walls and surrendered to the onslaught of automatic weapons fire. Their blood ran down the altar but welled up on the red rug in front of the manger. In a small victory for Christians this night, the blood that was shed never reached the figurine of baby Jesus who shed his blood for all mankind. Twice the minions of Herod fired into the crèche that held the nativity scene but it appeared unscathed. Here in Columbia, New Jersey, at the Our Lady of Grace Church, Christianity won a victory, albeit a small one. Undoubtedly the same scene was being played out in other locations around the world.

There was a time when Artemus Cohagen was a true believer. Luis Rodriguez had tried many times to bring Arte back into the fold for Luis was a devote believer. Luis said a small prayer as Arte revved the engine. They prepared for the hail of bullets as their vehicle wobbled towards its destination, but there was none. They strategically exited their vehicle and ran to the safety of what was left of Saint Michael's statue. The tear gas had dissipated and they could see the bodies of the fallen officers. Still there was no sniper fire.

Arte Cohagen was a survivor. He prided himself on that fact. Heroes usually end up dead. Arte had never lost a partner although he had put his guardian angel to the test too often. As the two agents stepped over the bodies in the doorway, they had no idea of what they would find inside this sanctuary. They walked past splintered pews and red soaked bodies. They approached the altar and saw the two officers in their makeshift casket. A tall unarmed figure stood up from behind the altar. His arms were outstretched. He said, "I am Gavrilo Princip."

Cohagen retorted back, "Who the fuck is Gavrilo Princip?"

Princip's eye brows seemed to kiss as he calmly responded with a smile, "You must've failed world history in high school. Not that Americans really care about the rest of the world anyhow. You Americans are meanly born and poorly educated with your guns. You have a suicidal openness to your enemies out of fear of offending them. History is a nightmare from which I will not allow you to wake up from. My great grandfather started WWI by assassinating Arch Duke Ferdinand of Austria in 1914. You've just witnessed the start of WWIII. Although I'd like to 'cross' examine you, only you won't be around for our triumphant victory."

Artemus said, "Yes, if not for your not so Great Grandfather there would've been no Hitler or Russian Revolution or Cold War or Einstein or A-bomb or American century".

Arte had seen and survived it all in his thirty years of service. Even a professional has that moment when he is too stunned to physically react. In that second, Arte lost his first partner. Luis stood slightly ahead of Arte. Blood sprayed into Artemus's eyes as a bullet exploded from the side of Luis' head. Flash bulbs went off in Artemus's eyes. Brain matter splattered onto Artemus; going into his mouth and nostrils. Artemus didn't have time to grieve his failure as the barrel of cold steel touched the back of his head just below the hairline. The small shell .22 caliber bullet was meant to ricochet around the skull and tear up the brain. The two partners crumbled and pitched forward in unison from the kicks of the boots from their assassins. They fell together; their heads nearly touching the crèche. It took two seconds for their bodies to hit the floor and they were dead in the first second. Again the manger was uncontaminated.

The war against Christianity had begun without the bang of Armageddon but with the calculated murder of the innocents in churches around the world.

Chapter 14

APOPHIS

"The sun shall be turned into darkness and the moon into blood, before that great and notable day of the Lord shall come" (Acts 2:20)

As noon passed, many if not all humans contemplated what might be their last few hours on Earth. Some made peace with their maker, some regretted past deeds, some apologized to others and cleared their conscience, and some took the easy way out and died at their own hand.

A very large oval granite black planet killer of an asteroid slammed into the moon at a 15-degree angle. It hit with such force that it started a slight rotation of the stationary moon as it more than glanced off its surface. Fragments of the blast flew off into space. JPL had detected this huge asteroid but concluded that there was no need to panic the public. Reports of a smaller strike were all the public needed to know.

At 2:47 p.m., a small asteroid fragment penetrated Earths onionskin atmosphere and struck the town of Has Megiddo in Israel. This town had been the site of thirty five battles throughout history and was well accepted as the site where Armageddon would start.

At 3 p.m., the hour which is widely believed to be the time at which Jesus died; the sixth seal was broken and a small, brightly lit C-class asteroid entered the Earth's atmosphere. Satellite photos showed a blue center surrounded by a fiery red glow. The news commentator called it "The Eye of God." He went on to say, "Ten million years in the making. I wonder if in a million years the next intelligent species on Earth; dolphins or parrots, will be debating if mankind was wiped out by an asteroid just like the dinosaurs. Wondering if this asteroid lead to the rise of their species as temporary dominant on Earth?"

The asteroid fragment made a direct hit in the center of the Indian Ocean. It parted the sea and struck the ocean floor. Satellites beamed images back to all major news stations. Reports estimated that 182 square miles of ocean floor, or seven times the size of Manhattan, were exposed before the ocean rushed back in to cover the crater. A small mushroom cloud escaped into the air as the water rushed back and forced the cloud straight up as if Poseidon took a deep breath and blew it into the atmosphere. The asteroid was promptly named Moses 2029. The surface water for miles heated to over 150 degrees causing a hypercane to form. Hypercanes are hurricanes with wind velocity greater than 500 mph. Hurricanes form when water temperatures are over 100 degrees. The Category ten funnel cloud continued to rise even into the stratosphere. The news reports said that the asteroid was way off the original coordinates.

The Pope was seen at his balcony raising his arms up to heaven as the square below his balcony was full of armed rejoicing believers. In the battle with the Muslim Herodians the night before, the Christians had prevailed. The Pope also gave orders to his warrior assassins to seek revenge.

A massive wall of water fanned out towards East Africa, India, Indonesia, Western Australia and Antarctica.

In China, crocodiles emerged from water and headed inland. In Rome, birds flew in confused patterns and household pets grew uneasy and fearful. Birds are sensitive to vibration and pressure changes while dogs and cats seem to have a sixth sense regarding danger. Almost immediately, the birds screeched and flew in all directions from the city center. All breeds of animal also darted to the four corners of the city.

Above Saint Peter's Square at the Vatican, an apparition of the Virgin Mother appeared. She was not dressed in the usual white satin with gold thread garments. She was dressed in a black robe and was holding the body of a dead Jesus Christ similar to the Pieta' sculpture.

At 4:16 p.m., a meteor shower filled the sky. It was trailed by a small, brightly lit B-class asteroid. The asteroid shot across the sky at 29,000 mph or sixty times faster than a bullet. It was a thing of beauty as it turned white hot. It crossed Boston; then to Madrid and onto Rome in a matter of minutes. There it made a direct hit, at 2,500 mph, on the ancient city. The jolt echoed through the planet many times resonating like a church bell. Two seconds after the impact, people ten miles away felt a magnitude 8.0 earthquake. Twenty seconds later, a 700 mph heat blast incinerated everything. Thirty seconds later, Mount Etna, Europe's largest volcano blew. The news reports said it was a small strike. Most of Southern

Europe and Northern Africa had been destroyed. The planet was safe.

People around the world filled the streets. They celebrated that their lives had been spared. Churches, synagogues, mosques and other places of worship were full with people mourning the deaths of millions of people in Southern Europe, Northern Africa and the countries bordering the Indian Ocean. In the financial districts of the U.S., corporate heads began to decide how to bring relief to the survivors while others planned on how to use the asteroid strike to their advantage. One suggestion was an "After the Asteroid Sale."

In the dense forest of Chengdu China sits the mother lode of deep underground military bases. This base, larger than Dulce New Mexico, sports the world's largest genetics lab run by the world's cruelest race of people. It also has a world class maglev rail system to the four corners of China.

Dr. Jun Wang and her six rogue scientists release 16 primates into the wild. Her research group's mission was to develop and study the survival and progress of a new sub human species. Apes and chimps had been granted "human rights" as a way to end poaching. Since stem cell research and future therapies needed to be tested in primates before humans, a group of genetically altered primates was needed. The closer to humans you get, the better the model for success. The genetic coding of humans and chimpanzees share 96 percent of the same DNA sequences. Humans are 99 percent similar. The one percent difference explains racial differences and why some families are prone to certain diseases and intelligent parents have intelligent children or athletic parents have athletic children. Mice and rats are 90 percent the same and mice and humans are 40 percent the same. The scientists had worked through the three billion pairs of DNA coding to effectively manipulate the one million pairs of coding that differentiate the functional differences between humans and chimps and create transgenic chimps that were 98 percent compatible to humans. (17)

In the 1920's, Joseph Stalin "monkeyed" with eugenics. The plan was to produce a new invincible human soldier. One that was insensitive to pain, possessed great strength and had enough intelligence to follow orders. The crossbreeding of man and ape to produce a Soviet simian was a failure because humans have 23 pairs of chromosomes and apes have 24. Alien-human breeding means that aliens and humans are more closely related than apes and humans. Aliens would have to have 23 chromosomes. (26)

Dr. Wangs thought process was that this humanized chimp may be the best last hope of the human race after the Earth strike. She remarked how clever it was to insert a fish gene for cold tolerance, and a spider gene for skin strength. Ebola and HIV may have been released on humans in a similar fashion. We often learn what is going on in labs only when the results slip out of them. As she released the 16 alpha humans into the thick brush, the eight males doubled back along the perimeter of the facility. Chimps are notoriously aggressive and dangerous when they reach maturity. Chimps will war with other groups for their entire lifetime. They know no peace. The eight hybrids entered the facility by the same door that they exited. They brutally beat, raped and killed their seven creators. As they reunited with their eight female partners, the males roared and beat their blood soaked chests with a sense of dominance and victory. In 100 years, an army of hybrids may stage a Genghis Khan like attack on Asia to claim their inheritance.

The impact of the asteroid in Europe bulged in the Pacific on the other side of the planet. The impact of the strike in the Indian Ocean bulged in the north Atlantic. The Ring of Fire exploded. Mount Fuji, Ranier, and St. Helens all erupted. They resembled a biblical pillar of fire reaching for the heavens.

Mount Ranier's explosion made the 1980 explosion of Mount St. Helens look like a fire cracker. The Cascade Range of the Pacific Northwest and Glacier Peak of Puget Sound were on fire. The 14,410-foot giant, towering over Seattle, blew. The 60 miles to the city were covered in 90 minutes. All four million Seattle,

Tacoma and Vancouver residents were killed when a wall of wet concrete hit the coast and perimeter cities. Tons of ice and snow had covered the west side of the volcano prior to its eruption.

The 11,239-foot Mount Hood blew in unison causing the 12 dams in the region to collapse. As a 50-foot wall of water and ash cascaded through the city; bridges collapsed; highways disappeared and the two million residents of Portland were swept away in an instant. The last time it had rumbled was in 1805 during the Lewis and Clark expedition. That was all just a part of history now.

In 1812, Memphis was hit with five of the largest quakes the U.S. had ever seen as it sits on the New Madrid fault line. The ground shook so hard that Memphis leveled out and 60,000 Tennesseans perished. St Louis sits at the opposite end of the fault line and is located on the Mississippi River with gas and oil pipelines breaking and releasing 22 million pounds of toxins into the river.

Anchorage, Alaska, is surrounded by 13 active volcanoes. Mt Redoubt started the chain reaction of eruptions causing a tsunami wave to target the Golden Gate shipping channel of Oakland and San Francisco.

The greatest fear had been the threat of the eruption of a "Super Volcano." This will usher in the true end times of the bible. Yellowstone Park in Wyoming is a Super Volcano. It last erupted 74,000 years ago. When it occurred, it reduced the population of the world to a few thousand humans. If the sixty mile by forty mile eruption blew, it would take mere seconds for the plume of ash to reach the upper atmosphere. The result would be the reflecting of sunlight off of the ash and a cooling of the planet by ten degrees. The eruption would be 4,000 times stronger than Mount Saint Helens. We know this to be true because it happened in the past. This is proven because our mitochondrial DNA shows that the gene pool was reduced by ninety percent, 74,000 years ago. There are seven "Super Volcano's" around the word. Three reside in the western U.S. Many believe that the U.S., like Atlantis, will be destroyed by this volcano. It will then be up to the E.U. and the remaining U.S. of 63 states around the world to keep the flame of freedom burning. (10, 13)

The Ring of Fire runs from New Zealand to Japan then to Alaska and finally to South America. It contains 450 of the world's 600 active volcanoes. Earthquakes also rocked the Pacific Rim. This in turn created tsunami waves higher than the Washington Monument. The entire rim moved. California, Japan, Southeast Asia, and Chile all dipped into the ocean momentarily. The newly installed Tsunami Alert System was all but useless at a time of massive cataclysm like today. The gigantic waves washed over the coastal areas around the world bringing death and destruction. Millions were dead in minutes. As the sky filled with volcanic ash, the Earth grew dark. Similar to the ethereal darkness that covered the Earth at the time of the crucifixion of Jesus when he cried out, "Father into thy hands I commend my spirit."

In the clouds, a celestial cross appeared over Spain; a "Sign" to precede the Lord's return. The sun appeared to split in two among the dust filled clouds.

In 1949, in the Canary Islands off of the West African coast, a volcanic eruption broke loose a slab of rock the size of a mountain. It had been slowly sliding toward the ocean. The 100 cubic mile slab broke loose and slid into the ocean causing a half mile high wall of water to race at 500 mph across the Atlantic Ocean towards the North and South American coasts. Whatever was left of the U.S. coast east of I-95 would be washed away in nine hours as the wall of water washes thirty miles inland. A mere three foot rise in water would put Philadelphia's City of Brotherly Love with the countries sixth highest population under water. New Jersey has six high risk chemical plants on its coast. When the wave rushes in, the Kuehne Chemical facility will unleash chlorine and toxic gases that will turn the air to poison for the sixteen million residents within its reach. Breathing these gases would burn one's lungs and cause them to suffocate and drown on their own internal fluids. New York City sits on a fault line that crosses 125th Street which would cut gas, water, electric, and subway lines and will collapse at least two of the five bridges out of the island. Just up the Hudson River is the Indian Point nuclear reactor which sits on the Ramapo fault line.

Due to the shape of the North American continental shelf, the largest wave would hit the Virginia Beach area.

Iceland, the land of "fire and Ice", sits on the North American and Eurasian tectonic plates. As the plates pulled apart, its numerous hot springs and geysers blew as the molten rock pushed to the surface. Iceland used to be the size of Ohio. Now, it has a wide river running through the entire length of the country.

Less than two decades ago, the U.S. had led a coalition against Afghanistan, Iraq, Syria and Iran in what many felt was a war with an oil agenda while ignoring a greater threat in North Korea. While many in the U.S. had willingly given up many of their freedoms with the Patriot Act, Supreme leader General Kim Jong Un had been forced to give up nothing. The Russians urged diplomacy as opposed to sanctions. President Obama foolishly listened to Kim's lies until President Trump was elected. You should always judge a person by what they do, not what they say! In 2018, Kim agreed to freeze North Koreas nuclear program in exchange for an open trade agreement, peace with So Korea and a treaty with the U.S. that we wouldn't launch a first strike. He refused unification where the norths cheap labor and the souths technology would've produced a powerhouse to rival Japan and China. In 2025, he again agreed to not start his nuclear program and allow inspectors in exchange for a better trade deal.

What the public didn't know, and what the President didn't know was that North Korea had smuggled three nuclear suitcase bombs into the U.S., through Customs in Long Beach California, as Kim planned to hold the U.S. hostage. Kim revealed the three locations to us as Los Angeles, San Francisco and Seattle.

Investigators found trace elements of radioactivity in the warehouses where they were stored and confirmed what appeared to be nuclear bombs. All three sites were under high tech Samsung surveillance beamed back to three locations in North Korea. Any attempt to disarm, evacuate, or bury the bombs would result in Kim ordering their detonation. Kim demanded more economic aid and an apology from the U.S. What was agreed to was that the U.S. would not destroy North Korea as three nuclear subs were permanently stationed off the coast of the country and that the truth of the situation would never be revealed to the public.

Seventeen missile silos opened in Siberia and the six headed thermo nuclear weapons were launched from each over the North Pole towards the northern most states of the mainland U.S. The North Korean blast was detected by the Russian computers as a strike. The old Soviet Bears Doomsday Cold War strategy of the 1960's planned on igniting thermo nuclear weapons over the southern part of the North Pole, Canada and Greenland. The blast would create an ocean of water that would engulf Canada in a tidal wave that would then flood the rest of the U.S. Canada has more lakes than the rest of the world combined but this deluge would just flow over them. This plan had been kept absolutely secret in the former Soviet Union. The breakup of the Republic splintered most of the Soviet Union's defenses and their nuclear arsenal was no longer under anyone's firm control. Their doomsday plan had been forgotten over the years since they had signed an oil and gas treaty with the U.S. It was a deal beneficial to both sides. With U.S. 63 oil and gas reserves stabilized by the vast oil sands of Canada and Pennsylvania found in shale, the deal enabled Russia to westernize and overtake Saudi Arabia as the number two oil producer and also had five times as much cubic meters of natural gas than the U.S. The U.S. 63 then cut off all oil imports from the Middle East. They immediately signed oil contracts with China and India. The sheiks would've almost burned the oil for free since their master plan included the creation of as much oil fired pollution as possible to contribute to global warming which would one day return the Middle East to grass lands like in the times of the pharaohs when the climate shifted. The strategy was that once the Pakistan-Iraq-Iran War officially ended, the U.S. 63 would never have to deal with that region of the world again. We bought their oil while it was cheap; until the price rose to $5 a gallon and then we used our oil. The U.S. has a 120 year supply of gas, 200 year supply of oil and 500 year supply of coal. The U.S. became the world's number one oil producing country in 2027 which created jobs and became a game changer for the economy.

War, occupation and then rebuilding didn't work in the Middle East and resulted in too many soldier deaths from suicide bombers. Historically, it costs $1 billion for every 1,000 troops and requires one soldier for every 200 citizens to occupy a territory. We would need 603,000 troops for Egypt, 501,000 for Iran; 250,000 for Saudi Arabia; 180,000 for Syria and six million to control the 1.2 billion Muslims in the world. The Middle East roadmap to peace had been placed in formaldehyde. Tonight, that continuing terror zone was the last thing on most people's minds. Surviving the night was!

There were two fatal flaws to the old Soviet plan that had taken place inadvertently. One flaw was that over the years these missiles, as well as the entire Soviet nuclear arsenal, had been upgraded in strength. Secondly, there was no fail-safe system to stop a launch. When an enemy missile was detected, a Russian retaliation was automatic. No human error was possible. They relied solely on a computer driven system.

A night time satellite photo of the Earth, which normally shows the developed nations of North America, Europe, Japan and South Korea aglow with lit up cities, tonight appeared dark as these "electric-cities" were without power.

On Friday, Armageddon had begun. As in Revelation, the fourth Horseman of the Apocalypse left with twenty five percent of all human lives.

Chapter 15

WAR GAMES

"Though I walk through the valley of the shadow of death, I shall fear no evil..." (Psalm 23)

U.S. satellites immediately detected the launch. The President and key personnel were notified within seconds. Contrary to nationalistic beliefs, our policy was not to launch a full-scale retaliation known as Mutual Assured Destruction. Any such reaction would mean the end of the human race. The U.S. policy had always been one of deterrence; the threat of a full scale retaliation. We were all offense with very little defense. In the event of a missile attack against the U.S., we would attempt to destroy all incoming missiles with Standard Missile-3 Interceptors and then retaliate on key targets using our subs.

The $200 billion missile defense system uses infrared satellite technology to track the signature missile plume rising from its silo. Confirmation would come from the Cobra Dane radar mirror in Alaska or sea based X-Band Radar Systems which are so precise they can detect a football from 4,000 miles away. Ground radar would track the missiles path and Interceptors from Alaska, California, Virginia, Kauai Island in Hawaii, or from one of our twenty one cruisers or destroyers that are fit with the Aegis system to acquire and destroy its target by force of impact rather than explosion. There are several ways of dealing with interceptors from generating radio signals to coating the missiles with reflective paint. If the interceptors failed, we would then launch Patriot PAC-3 missiles from land at the 15,000 mph ICBM's during the descent stage. Our last line of defense during the kill stage would be the launch of THAAD missiles from any one of 32 mobile batteries during the terminal stage prior to impact. We would sacrifice the partial destruction of the U.S. in order to keep from destroying humanity. This action, the government believed, would be 78 percent effective in destroying all incoming missiles.

Since 1952, there have been 2,044 nuclear tests worldwide. Most have been underground at depths of 8,000 feet or underwater at depths of 2,000 feet. Each test has averaged 10.4 megatons of explosives or more than 500 times more powerful than the first nuclear bomb. The Hiroshima bomb, by today's standards, would be considered no more than a tactical weapon. The military has argued that if the environment could survive sixty years of explosions, then a small scale nuclear war is feasible. That way of thinking has never been accepted. But as Sen. Barry Goldwater once said, "Thank goodness America has a nuclear arsenal second to none." (26)

The President ordered the launch of seventeen Interceptors from Alaska's Aleutian Island base and another seventeen from Sacramento, California. It was imperative that the 11,000 mph interceptors reach their targets before the Russian missiles each launched six separate warheads towards predetermined targets. The President was informed that both sites were off line due to the seismic activity. President Datchet could feel panic grip his body. He ordered a launch from Langley Virginia but was told that the trans-continental launch would never reach their targets in time. The entire process has only twenty minutes to react.

President Datchet had already made contact with the Kremlin. Prime Minister Alexey Navalny pleaded for restraint. He reminded the POTUS that both countries vowed in 1962 to never use nuclear weapons again at the bequest of Pope John XXIII when the Pontiff read the third secret of Fatima to President's Kennedy and Khrushchev. Although Datchet had viewed himself as a War President, in this instance, he did show restraint. The Prime Minister, a banker-lawyer-blogger ousted his KGB predecessor Putin and his puppet Medved. Every six years, Putin and Medved alternated terms as president. Navalny acknowledged the launch but could not account for the reason it took place. It appeared that WWII ended with an atomic bomb and that WWIII would start with a nuclear one. President Datchet wisely chose not to respond to the bear by attacking it.

Minutes before the Langley Interceptors would have impacted their Russian enemies, the Russian missiles each launched their six multiple independently targetable re-entry vehicles (MIRVs) – effectively multiple warheads in a horizontal line and each detonated thirty miles apart. The 102 blasts occurred 3,000 feet above ground level and lit up the sky with an orange glow. Some thought it was the Northern Lights. The darkness of the long winter night was interrupted and the brightness of the sunniest of tropical days replaced it. The release of heat was enormous. An ocean of boiling water on top of miles of frozen ice formed immediately. The meltdown took place in a geometric progression expanding outward and downward into millions of years of frozen glaciers.

Washington and Moscow cheered in relief that the accidental launch had been unsuccessful prior to reaching the soil of mainland U.S.

As President Datchet and the Russian leader assured one another of no further retaliation, all communications were lost. The electromagnetic pulse or shockwaves from the blast had temporarily incapacitated all electronic and satellite use. An EMP above twenty five miles from the Earth's surface would destroy all satellites and fry our two trillion dollar electrical grid. Man's reliance on technology over the human condition had come back to haunt him. The information super highway had closed and with it any hope of knowing what was happening beyond ones immediate senses.

It was no different at the Pentagon. The U.S. 63 war room scrambled again believing the Russians were lying to them and readied for defensive measures. There was never trust between the two countries although they have worked together since the Trump Presidency.

A worldwide blackout followed as all power grids, Internet and cell phones, pumping stations, and railroad switching lines temporary failed. Without electricity, it would only take weeks before a society reverted back to feudalism. Luckily, the power outage only lasted for a few minutes.

Although there were no more launches detected by our satellite systems, the government once more had shown humanitarian restraint. This could not be said of everyone. There was uncertainty worldwide.

The ocean of warm water continued to expand over the North American side of the North Pole. In some ways, it was better that the world was unaware of what was occurring in the northern hemisphere. At times, uncertainty is better than body numbing panic. As Datchet prepared a State of the 63 Address for 7 a.m. over the emergency broadcast system, most of the citizenry were aware that something had occurred. What it was, they didn't know. They did know that the vermin that crawls out of their holes at a moment of crisis were already at work. The police already had their hands full. Criminals sensing a disaster began to prey on the unprotected. The few minutes of blackout had disrupted alarms and looting quickly proceeded.

There were unsubstantiated rumors about a massive asteroid blast having rocked the North Pole. The Pentagon had tried for hours to squelch the rumors. As the State of the 63 States Address approached, the President realized he may have to tell the citizens the truth.

As the ocean of water reached critical mass, the Prime Minister of French Canada was notified of this environmental disaster. He was informed by President Datchet just as the tidal wave of water was cresting free from its glacial walls. In the war room, the generals were beside themselves with this crisis. How do you stop the flooding of North America?

A stenographer said, "It's like mashed potatoes with gravy. You break it on the sides." The generals had an epiphany. They launched two nuclear missiles on each side of the snow encased ocean of icy water. Most of the water was released to the east and west into the Atlantic and Pacific Oceans, as the President said, "By the grace of God."

There was an overabundance of water which flowed south to flood the Great Lakes which became one huge fresh water lake, as well as flooding the Colorado and Mississippi rivers.

By daybreak, water levels had risen 10 feet all over the world and rivers were overflowing at unprecedented rates. India and China were experiencing massive flooding in their southern most regions along with London, Bangladesh and the Netherlands.

In the mainland states of the U.S., water rushed down Bourbon Street in New Orleans. The Big Easy of jazz bars, voodoo shops and the French market were washing away for the second time. The rebuilding of the city was even grander this time.

Although the city sits ten feet below sea level and ecologically makes no sense to have levees keeping the Mississippi river out, the rustic charm of the city had been restored. Sidewalk chairs were swept away from the famous Café Du Monde. The Cajun Queen riverboat crashed into the Jackson Brewery at Dumaine Wharf. Water spilled over levees and swamped the saucer shaped city with a toxic slush of heavy metal refinery chemicals, sewage and human bodies.

Many desperate locals again rushed to the Superdome for safety as others were stranded on roof tops. There was no evacuation plan for the prisons; so they were let loose on the locals. This time, citizens were armed as the police chiefs could no longer legally take weapons away from licensed citizens. As darkness approached, the electricity went out. These bayou residents were caught in the dome in the dark as water levels filled it like a bathtub. (26)

The more fundamentalist of the Christians would view this as a cleansing of the decadence of Mardi-Gras. The scientologists, who believe that people are basically good, had a hard time explaining the marauding looters and rioting and gangs of men that rape and plunder during a crisis. We seem to regress into a state of nature where there are no rules and we take what we need and want. As all the major cities on both coasts were inundated with water, the Christian theory of the Lord's cleansing began to take on an entirely new meaning.

Two hundred years after swashbuckler Jean Laffite defeated the British Navy in the War of 1812, the Crescent city succumbed to the ocean and truly became the gateway to the vast Mississippi delta leading to the Great Lake.

The Gold Coast of Southern Florida was under water. Manhattan was quickly becoming the "New Venice" of the world. Long Island's Fire Island and Jones Beach could not hold back the power of the ocean.

Worldwide panic had taken place. Highways were jammed with cars desperately trying to escape the rising waves. As cars began to stall along the coastal highways, due to the rising water, millions abandoned their cars and attempted to wade through knee-deep water. In the lowest lying areas, millions had already drowned before the sun rose on this new world.

In Pittsburgh, where steel once built the I-beams of the Empire State Building and girders of the Golden Gate Bridge and was the back bone of the Industrial Revolution; the three rivers of the Alleghany, Monongahela and Ohio meet. The swell of water washed over the fountain at Point Park and covered the playing fields of PNC and Heinz fields where the Pirates and Shalers play.

The football teams name had been changed a few years ago from Steelers to Shalers due to the boom in Marcellus Shale and the lack of steel produced in Pittsburgh. The swell of water slammed into the Southside where the theme parks of Sandcastle and Kennywood, along with restaurants, casino's and clubs at Station Square and the Boardwalk sit. The view from Mount Washington overlooking the Pittsburgh area was incredible.

In Austin, Texas, the 1.5 million bats that reside under the Congress Bridge were sent rushing from their daytime abode. In a rabid like frenzy, the startled creatures attacked anything that moved; humans included.

Hawaii twice in the past has been hit with a 1,006 and a 256 foot tidal wave caused by slabs of Mauna Loa sliding into the sea. It happened again funneling the water toward Honolulu and creating a 1,200 foot wave.

In Washington State, the Hanford nuclear storage site which houses 53 million gallons of high level radioactive waste was also flooding.

In Boston, the Distrigas liquefied natural gas depot ruptured and released enough gas prior to its exploding and caused a blast equal to fifty Hiroshima bombs.

It is estimated that if all the planets ice melted, the water level would rise 200 feet. The entire planet would not be covered with water. Since the blast melted ten percent of the planets ice, the water level would rise twenty feet. In fact, there had been three prior "great floods" experienced by mankind caused by pools of water bursting free from melted glaciers.

As the President's chopper escaped from the White House lawn to the Air Force One runway, no longer was there any thought of reassuring the country. The Potomac River had crested and overflowed. The Lincoln and Jefferson memorials were being invaded as the water rose, covering these bastions of freedom, one step at a time. The big cats of the Washington Zoo were going wild. The chimps climbed to the top of the bars in their cages.

Their screams of fear were mixed with the death throe gurgles of every encaged animal.

A second chopper headed for the Tomb of the Unknowns at Arlington National Cemetery where more than 400,000 men and women rest in more than 600 acres of the 190-year-old cemetery. Every thirty minutes, 24 hours per day, 365 days per year since 1930, a marine changes duty at the site. They take twenty one steps across the Tomb of the Unknowns; pause for twenty one seconds; and take twenty one steps back across the tomb. This alludes to the twenty one gun salute which the highest honor is given a soldier. For two years the guards live in a barracks below the Tomb. They cannot speak to anyone or watch TV for their first six months. They cannot drink or swear for the rest of their lives.

As the chopper approached, the pilot could see the two 6'2" soldiers changing guard in knee deep water. As the chopper hovered a few feet above the soldiers, the pilot shouted out, "You can suspend your assignment and get in the chopper."

The soldiers, waist deep in water reply, "No way, Sir. This is not an assignment but the highest honor afforded a service-person!"

The pilot replies, "Well then at least retreat to higher ground in the amphitheater."

"No disrespect, sir, but we are incapable of retreat."

As the water soaked their skin and the rain pelted their caps, the two saluted each other; paused 21 seconds; and turned in neck deep water.

The pilot knew that this was a cause worth dying for. The pilot read the inscription on the sarcophagus, "Here rests in honored glory an American soldier known but to God". A tear formed in the corner of his eye as he banked right and ascended his chopper.

In the midst of the massive death and destruction, there were many sad personal stories. One concerned a family of four. They had taken an early Christmas break camping trip away from the hustle and bustle of the city. They had left their lodge early in the morning for a trip to Niagara Falls. They wanted to see what was left of the Falls since the continental shelf was rising as the arctic ice shelf melted and the Falls were drying up as they tipped back towards Lake Erie. As they traveled along Route 490 in Rochester, New York, their son in the backseat asked if the Falls was up ahead. This occurred just as the car passed through a fog-laden area between two hills. The father jokingly said the Falls was directly up ahead. He realized that his son would easily mistake the dew and mist of early morning for the white foam which crashed on the "Falls" rocks. He smiled to himself at his little trick on his son. In a very serious tone he said,

"Everybody get ready, Niagara Falls is right around the next bend."

He looked in the rearview mirror to see if his son had believed his little joke. As their Grand Cherokee rounded the bend, the little boy yelled excitedly.

"There it is, Dad, I see it!"

The joke was on the father. As he dropped his gaze to the windshield he viewed a thirty foot wall of water coming directly towards his family. His fingers tightened on the steering wheel as he saw the white foam as the water broke on the blacktop of Route 490. The digital clock flashed 6:35 a.m. The sun had just begun to rise and for an instant, the father thought he might be in bed waking from a dream. That was his last thought; the force of water killed the entire family instantly. The little boy's last thought had been, "Why did Daddy drive over Niagara falls?"

On a national scale, it was decided to get President Datchet and key personnel to higher ground and to the underground shelter in West Virginia. The previous shelter was located under the Greenbrier Hotel in Lewisburg, West Virginia. It had been relocated and upgraded to the new facility beneath the FBI Fingerprint Center in Clarksburg, West Virginia. A plan for continuity of government at every level for any emergency and the suspension of the Constitution is in place. The new site, south of

Pittsburgh, sits on 1,000 acres with 2,800 employees and has a self-contained underground nuclear power source and medical facility. It has a television production area with a stage set up with a podium and the Presidential seal behind it so the President could broadcast to the people in times of crisis. It has its own zip code along with a private runway to the airport. It is a new government in waiting. When activated, it has the protection of hundreds of FBI agents and the third largest police force in West Virginia. There is no plan to reinstate the Constitution if enacted for a world crisis. The same agencies charged with protecting the people have used their powers to usurp the people.

What almost no one knew, including the POTUS, was that it was the only entrance point to an interconnecting maze of tunnels miles beneath the Earth's surface known as D.U.M.B.'s or deep underground military bases. Since the 1990's, billions of dollars had been siphoned off from the military budget to build these safe havens in case of a nuclear war or Earth changing event. It was much cheaper to go underground than to try and build a base on the moon. Advanced lasers melted rock to create the tunnels. CIA and military personnel were selected to live in these DUMBs since 1997. The personnel had to have no siblings or spouses and elderly or deceased parents in order to be selected for this permanent position. A third generation of "Under-grounders" had just been born. They have no connection to the Americans that reside above the surface; they have no connection to any humans that reside above the surface. They were a separate society raised on high tech voice activated electronics and artificial light and heat. This third generation was displaying albino like features. Their DNA had been altered to increase intelligence but decrease aggression. After learning about Hitler's search and infatuation with the Vril society in Antarctica, many teens referred to themselves as the Vril. There was room for 250,000 survivors in the DUMB's. Many CIA, DOD, NSA and other military and scientists had been preselected and were being "rounded up" and transported to the DUMB's. Satellite feeds would keep the "Under-grounders" informed as to what transpired on the surface.

President Datchet glanced back, as Air Force One ascended; he swore he saw the Capital Christmas tree floating away. He realized the public would need his reassurances that everything would be all right, but this was not the right time.

The U.S. 63 Weather Bureau was reporting numerous unusual weather patterns. There was rain falling in the Sahara Desert, El Nino was expanding across the Pacific Corridor, tornados were forming all over the Southwestern States. Global temperatures had dropped three degrees by morning.

The rush of less dense cold freshwater into the Atlantic Ocean lowered the temperature of the water in the North. This caused salt in the water to drop to the ocean floor, which then slowed the warm Gulf Stream from Africa. The start of a new mini ice age had begun due to abrupt climate change. The reason this was happening was because the conveyor belt of Gulf Stream currents control the temperature and weather patterns of the planet by bringing warm surface water north while returning cold dense deep ocean water south.

Greenland and the North Pole would soon be free of their polar ice cap and the lost civilization of Atlantis would soon be exposed from the 12,000-year-old ice that had covered it since the last ice age.

The famous seer, Edgar Cayce, believed Atlantis to have been the original Eden. He believed that it was destroyed in 10,500 B.C. Cayce also believed that many Atlanteans escaped and spread out into the regions of Egypt, Greece, and even Peru. Cayce had predicted that part of Atlantis would be discovered in 1968.

The Bimini Wall was discovered in 1968 under the ocean located southeast of Miami. In addition to this discovery in the Bahamas, manmade ruins have been found under the waters of Okinawa and Japan. (19)

The Great Pyramid of Giza is said to hold a repository of records from Atlantean times. The Atlanteans believed in the science of the paranormal. They were said to have possessed crystals that had destructive force.

Cayce believed that the demise of Atlantis was caused by Earth's close brush with a comet. It was somewhat fitting that the ruins of Atlantis would reappear after the Earth's most recent contact with another heavenly body. (3, 19)

The asteroid strike, or "event" as it was now being referred to, had caused other strange discoveries to appear.

In Norway it was announced that the melting ice in Greenland, in a fjord, had exposed an ancient cylinder. It appeared to be a time capsule. Even in this time of distress, scientists asked questions. Could there have been an entire civilization here on Earth long ago? Could time have destroyed all clues to our true ancestry? Amid this cataclysm occurring worldwide, a national newspaper begged the question; could the cylinder be alien in origin? The Americans put a time capsule aboard the International Space Station in 2008 in case something happened to mankind and another species was able to resurrect mankind. It is called the Immortality Drive. It contains the digitalized DNA of Professor Stephen Hawking. Many questioned using the geniuses' DNA since he suffers from ALS and if resurrected, all future humans may suffer from it since it is in his DNA.

The world as we knew it was changing rapidly. These discoveries would soon be short-lived. The thought on everyone's mind would soon be survival, theirs, their countries and their worlds.

The President and the Joint Chiefs of Staff were briefed on Air Force One that the Chinese military was beginning to mobilize. The Chinese Dragon was on Def-Con 3 and the possibility of an attack seemed imminent. The most urgent Chinese threat was from the use of their diesel power Ballistic missile subs which could surface close to shore and launch a nuclear attack. There would be no time to defend against such an attack. Our satellites tracked every sub and showed their entire fleet in home ports for the holidays. This was a custom that all nations abided by at the U.S. request during our holidays regardless of whether other nations celebrated them or not. Yet a rogue sub took out our newest aircraft carrier, the USS Barack Obama. The five year-old carrier, one of seventeen in our fleet, was one mile long and twenty stories high with over 5,000 troops on board. The ship had more fire power alone than most countries. The sub hid in the sea cliffs of the continental shelf 100 miles from shore. It launched short range Sea Sparrow missiles at the Obama who countered with anti-air fused airburst shells. Multiple missiles were launched against the Obama and met by the ships close range MK-15 Pahalanx weapon systems and infrared guided weapons. The incoming shrapnel and debris overwhelmed the Obama and the Chinese multiple missile attack struck its target. The sub must've been acting on its own since the USS George Washington was in port in Japan assisting Japan's newly formed military in the Pacific. Prime Minister Shinzo Abe reversed Japan's 85-year-old U.S. imposed pacifist constitution over odds with China over wartime history, resources and island territories. Abe believes in the lost values of bushido or the samurai warrior's code which emphasizes morality, loyalty, respect and honor.

Chinese spies stole military secrets during the Clinton years and had compromised our Aegis battle management system which is our cruiser and destroyer warship management plan. They also stole $1.9 billion worth of data on rocket technology from NASA. Their DF-21D missiles can change course in mid-flight to evade Aegis interceptors and can home in on a carrier from 930 miles off shore. The Chinese are also believed to have electromagnetic pulse guns which can disrupt aircraft electronics and disable fighter planes. The Chinese know more about our military than we know about their entire country. (26)

Between political correctness, corporate bottom lines, ethics violations, and lobbies P.A.C. money influence, we've sold this country out to our enemies.

Our last two battleships, the Iowa and Wisconsin, were turned into museums off the coasts of Stockton, California, and Newport News, Virginia. Even though Marine Corp Generals testified that the loss of naval surface fire support would place troops at considerable risk and that eighty percent of the 1,067 planes we lost in Vietnam could've been spared if we fought the war from battleships, they were decommissioned. Their replacement, the DDX destroyer, was introduced in 2014 at a cost of $4 billion each even though it only cost $250,000 to keep the old reliable battleships operational. The battleships each had eighteen guns capable of firing 51 one-ton shells per minute capable of taking out hardened targets 27 miles away on land. The new DDX is capable of firing ten shells per minute at a cost of $1 million per minute. It relies on 155 millimeter rounds that cannot reach shore and protect the marines. The DDG-1000 uses rail gun technology.

We even retired the F-14 Tomcat fighter jet because we believed that aerial dog fights were a thing of the past due to missile targeting systems from miles away. These ultimate fighter planes flew at 1,600 mph and were unmatched by opposing aircraft. (26)

The Joint Chiefs of Staff consist of equal numbers of officers from the Army, Navy, Marine Corp and Air Force. They are responsible for the unified strategic direction of the combatant forces under a unified command. Established in 1947, a statute prohibits the Joint Staff from operating as an overall armed force. They have no executive authority over the forces; that honor belongs to the President. (27)

It is for that very reason, executive authority that Army General Scrocoff of the Joint Chiefs, has conspired in this time of crisis to formulate a military coup to over throw the President and give executive power to the group most capable of carrying out its responsibilities.

George Washington Datchet had let power go to his head.

In 1777, the Continental Congress had offered George Washington the title of King prior to making him our first President. The current "G.W." had wanted his rightful place in history. Like Joan of Arc, Datchet believed he was in touch with God's plan. Most terrorist acts after 2020 were committed by a covert branch of the DHS with the President's approval.

A group of low tech terrorists in 2001 with box cutters got incredibly lucky but also gave us the opportunity to enact our Middle East and domestic spying policy. There had been too many missed opportunities and decisions made on faulty intelligence over the past years that has left the U.S. in a vulnerable position as world power shifted to the Pacific Rim. We should've partnered with the world's largest English speaking democracy, India, instead of China. We should've used them as a counterweight to China but were too slow to move because India never signed the Nuclear Non Proliferation treaty. The un-named President had stood with Mexico to denounce the Minutemen who thought they were patriots defending our border, because she knew there was no real threat. We had hostile foreign powers in charge of a majority of our 361 mainland sea ports yet we ousted allied Scandinavian countries from our airports when they owned the guard services that employed the screeners. Foreign ownership had increased in 53 of the 145 U.S. refineries; in the control of drinking and waste water services; in operating many U.S. toll roads; and in telecommunications.

General Scrocoff reached for a pen in his breast pocket. The pen, similar to the type that would be dipped into an ink well, had a clear plastic cap on it. Admiral Byrne watched the General as he moved closer toward the President.

General Scrocoff removed the cap from the pen, secured it tightly in his left hand and moved quickly toward the unsuspecting

President. His eyes marked the President for death. He muttered, "Let none but real Americans stand guard tonight."

U.S. Marine General Holden, Chairman of the Joint Chiefs of Staff, had also been watching the Army General closely. The marine, who was seated to the right of the President, extended his left hand to protect the neck of the "sitting" President just as General Scrocoff struck with his pen. The tip firmly penetrated the back of Marine General Holden's hand and wedged between the bones of the middle and ring fingers. General Holden jerked his hand pulling the pen from the grip of General Scrocoff.

The pen had been dipped in genetically enhanced ricin poison. The Marine General stood, through a left elbow to the face of the Army General, knocking him backwards and to the floor. General Holden then started to vomit as multisystem organ failure progressed. He quickly developed pulmonary edema and then respiratory failure as he fell to the floor as he took his next step towards the fallen General Scrocoff. General Holden was dead within two minutes.

Two armed secret service agents were simultaneously moving towards the fallen traitor. They pounced on the General and immediately cuffed him. The four remaining secret service agents all drew their weapons and pointed them towards the remaining staff looking for a sign of aggressive movement. The President took charge and called for restraint. He knew he could trust his Secret Service Agents since there has never been a traitor among its agents.

"The last thing we need now is an ill-advised coup of my Presidency. There are threats everywhere. The world seems to be draped in camouflage. What we need now is continuity of government"

He ordered the agents to question the General and secure him in the next cabin.

"In the game of chess, you are all pawns and pawns are easily sacrificed. Some pieces are more valuable than others and the king or President is the most valuable of all," said the POTUS.

As they took the General away, Admiral Byrne made eye contact with the General and gave an ever so slight nod like a fifth column in waiting. General Holden was covered with a blanket and moved to an adjoining cabin for analysis by the chief medical officer.

President Datchet ordered the use of the HAARP defense System. These 72-foot-highs, 48 antennas high altitude system would employ the Earth's natural shield or ionosphere to bounce microwaves off as a defense against an alien invasion or to disable enemy troops. Through Chinese birth control methods of favoring males which make up a disproportionate sixty percent of their population, China has an all-male army larger than the population of the entire U.S. It was decided that the HAARP would be a good defensive system. The microwaves had the capability to disorient living creatures. Once it is used, it takes hours for the enemy to re-metabolize. This would give us time to attack using either missiles or troops.

The President did not show restraint, in this case, by using the HAARP to disable the massive Asian army. He gave Admiral Byrne complete autonomy to use our submarine based Trident anti-matter missiles against the Chinese Dragon. These missiles were clean bombs that emitted gamma radiation which kills all life but doesn't leave the area a wasteland for years. Datchet harbored ill will against the Chinese since their invasion of democratic Taiwan and their alleged sabotage of Chinese made electronics during the Iranian attack. It was believed that China installed kill switches in their products as they awaited their time to attack the U.S. President Datchet had appeared weak in his compromise treaty. China called its military the new aggressive 2.0 version and boasted how it now controlled the American built Panama and Suez Canals. They had been covertly using their containerized shipping facilities to monitor and pilfer technology from the West. They also ran drugs and arms through the ports as they pleased. These maritime ports in every ocean also served as military bases to launch an offensive if needed.

President Datchet was quoted as saying, "Our allies should respect us and our adversaries fear us."

Admiral Byrne moved to a laptop computer with phone in order to make the necessary arrangements. The Admiral smirked with surprise that the President did exactly what he himself intended to do if General Scrocoff was successful with their plan. He knew that the General also had his own ricin poison in the cap of a ring on his finger. He would easily access it and Scrocoff would be dead in minutes leaving no other witnesses to their plot.

President Datchet, like all world leaders, had a bigger problem dealing with what was happening to their world. With 54 percent of all humans or 3.7 billion people living in coastal areas, people were drowning by the thousands in nearly every country. The survivors were looking to their leaders but to no avail. With communications failing all over the globe and their leaders nowhere to be seen, chaos reigned. The leaders, like President Datchet, were heading to where they could govern their people in safety. The people saw their leaders as abandoning them. All major institutions were in disarray. The Catholics couldn't turn to their church; thousands of years of teachings were gone in an instant. Without communications to connect them, the police were nothing but armed vigilantes. For all intents and purposes, people were awakening to a Darwinian world based on survival of the fittest. Some would learn to cope; others would be victims of this world in mere hours.

With the Catholic Church destroyed, will this give rise to the Antichrist to trick the populace in a time of crisis and move into a position of power? Will seven trumpets be heard?

Chapter 16

NEW JERSEY

"Pay no attention to that man behind the curtain."
(The Wizard of Oz)

Kirk had drunkenly slept through the night. He rolled over and began to slowly open his eyes. He could see three dark shadows flying counter clock wise around the ceiling fan. His head was a bit fuzzy but he had no other ill effects from his drinking. Suddenly, he sat up with a start. Where were the children?

He slowly lay back down and stared at the ceiling. He glanced over at the alarm clock which read 5:27 a.m. Kirk realized the children were fine. They were in their rooms sleeping. Christmas break had begun today and there was no school. Kirk had the day off, even though it was Christmas rush. He swore under his breath, "No wonder the boss gave him the days before Christmas off; they were trying to squeeze him out."

Kirk thought back to yesterday, and how he lost his promotion. After he left the admissions office, he called some friends from the gym to see if they would like to meet for a holiday drink. He felt no need to tell them of his problems but after Kirk downed three Long Island Ice Teas, they probably knew something was wrong.

Kirk took a Prilosec for his stomach and began to get dressed. Kirk hoped the children weren't angry with him because he went to bed around nine. Of course, they were getting older and didn't need him looking over their shoulders constantly. Kirk knew, after they finished their dinner, they would be in their respective rooms on their computers and phones until they were sleepy. The only thing he regretted was forgetting to kiss them goodnight. In actuality, the kids often slip out for a few hours to hang out with their friends when they know their father has fallen asleep.

Kirk didn't hear anyone walking around the house, so he turned the TV on softly to catch up on last night's news on FOX. The TV came on to channel seven, the Good News Channel where only good deeds were reported. The channel had no reception so Kirk switched to FOX.

The first image on the screen appeared to be hundreds of body bags on the ground in a Third World country. Live video from a helicopter showed a family trapped on top of a sand dune in Southern California as the water washed away the sand and quickly swallowed their Hummer and themselves. Kirk turned the sound up and heard a reporter talking about disasters occurring worldwide. The Science Reporter was now talking about.... Kirk shook his still fuzzy head and pushed the replay button. The reporter said the same thing. Something about, the Earth wobbling off its axis as the weight of the South Pole was making the rotation of the Earth uneven. Antarctica already contains 90 percent of the world's ice. Kirk was certain he was watching the Christian station and a special about The End of Days, and paid little attention to the news reports of worldwide devastation.

The picture on the screen was really fuzzy today; perhaps something was wrong with the digital cable signal. The phone rang before he had time to channel surf. Kirk quickly answered it so as not to wake the children. The voice on the phone was Kirk's father. He was crying. Kirk became worried that something was wrong with his mother. Kirk's parents live on Long Island in the middle class town of Lindenhurst. Kirk knew that he could get there fairly quickly if he had to. The phone was cutting out but he heard his Dad speak.

"Kirk! Kirk! Your mother and I always loved. . .", and sobbing, "We always will no matter what."

Kirk screamed into the phone. "Dad, Dad! My God, what's wrong?" The phone went dead. Kirk, in a panic, redialed his father's number. A recording said, "Sorry we are unable to complete this call at the present time, please try again later, if you need...." The phone was dead.

Kirk ran downstairs and turned on the HDTV. He was hoping to see the picture better. Many stations had nothing but snow for reception. The three major networks, ABC, NBC, and CBS along with CNN had news reports of massive flooding around the world.

Kirk grabbed his cell phone and saw it was full of text messages as the Nationwide Cell Phone Alert System had sent emergency alerts to everyone.

Kirk knew that his New Jersey home was located well above sea level. In fact, he often complained about being caught in the Pocono Mountain Snow Belt during winter storms. Kirk sat stunned in front of the TV, which was his lifeline to the outside world. Suddenly, it crackled a final death throe and went blank. He feared the worse had befallen his parents, his brother and sister, as well as their families who all still resided on Long Island. Kirk was still unaware of what had happened.

The Atlantic Ocean had rushed into Lindenhurst and all of Long Island. The water level rose over the beaches. The boats docked at the Montauk Yacht Club lifted and capsized as they were still tied to the docks. The water rushed over the docks and down the streets past Montauk Highway toward Sunrise Highway. The North Egg of million dollar homes in Manhasset and South Egg of Montauk Point and the Hamptons, as once described by F. Scott Fitzgerald, were rapidly becoming engulfed in salt water from the ocean. The Coast Guard's 140-foot Fast Response Cutters failed to save but a few hundred residents.

Kirk knew what he had to do for the good of his parents. He picked up the keys to his SUV and headed towards the door. Suddenly he stopped and turned around. He headed towards his trophy case and opened it. Kirk took out two large battle knives, placed them in their scabbards, and attached them to a belt that he then slung over his shoulder. There was time for a quick note to the kids that he'll be home in a few hours; he knew the dogs would protect the children with their lives until he returned.

He said, "Headed to LI. Be back for dinner. You two are supposed to pass me up. The student becomes the teacher; the parent the child. I was supposed to marvel at who you've become; smarter and stronger than me, safe in your hands as I get old."

He took one quick glance back at what had been his life, and then turned to face an unknown world. He knew that mankind had survived global catastrophes and genetic changes before. He knew that life would somehow find its own way!

Upon awakening at 10 a.m., Cole checked his blood sugar and scanned the refrigerator for breakfast through its glass door. Kirk had always been very cost conscious about turning lights off and conserving energy. He thought having a refrigerator with a clear glass door was a practical idea. In fact, the refrigerator compiled a shopping list of items not placed back on the shelf. The microwave could scan an item and cook it at the proper temperature and time. The washing machine could sense whether the wrong colors were placed in the load. And the media player in the house was linked to the car of the user so the same tune would continue when you left the house. Cole didn't find anything to his liking and decided to head to the Deli on Route 206 and get an egg sandwich and juice.

Upon arriving at the Deli, which was almost within walking distance, Cole exited his Jeep and witnessed a bazaar scene. Two of his friends from high school were beating a man with a baseball bat and a golf club. Cole ran over and yelled to stop. Beating homeless and seniors had become a sport in some urban areas. Usually they are shot with paintball or BB guns and pushed around for fun or out of contempt. But this wasn't a high crime "city" environment and Cole knew both of these kids from his baseball team.

As Cole got a closer look, he could see that the man was the store owner. He was bleeding profusely from his nose and his teeth were cracked as he grimaced at Cole. The man raised his arm up to

225

protect himself and Cole could see his broken wrist just flop around without control. This was all Cole could take and he rushed his two former team-mates.

The first turned and swung his golf club at Cole. Cole put his forearm up in defense and caught the club about halfway on the shaft. The club bent and hit Cole on the shoulder. This infuriated Cole and he stepped into his friends "personal zone" and clocked him with an elbow to the forehead. The elbow is the hardest bone in the body. The boy just crumbled to the ground.

The second boy turned towards Cole and raised his baseball bat. Cole took a step to his right and kicked the boy on the side of his locked knee immediately tearing his ACL and MCL tendons. The boy also crumbled and fell to the ground. He started screaming, "How am I going to survive now, you just killed me."

Cole thought they must be high on drugs. He turned to help the Deli owner only to find him pointing a gun at Cole and shouting that he better turn and leave now. Cole screamed, "But shouldn't we call the police?"

The man cocked the hammer on the revolver and told Cole, "The police can't help us now, just go home."

Cole jumped back into his Jeep and raced home. He couldn't believe how fast everyone seemed to be driving on this road. The drivers were passing Cole and turning their heads to glare at him with an insane intensity. Cole just wanted to get to the safety of his home and tell Rose to call his Dad.

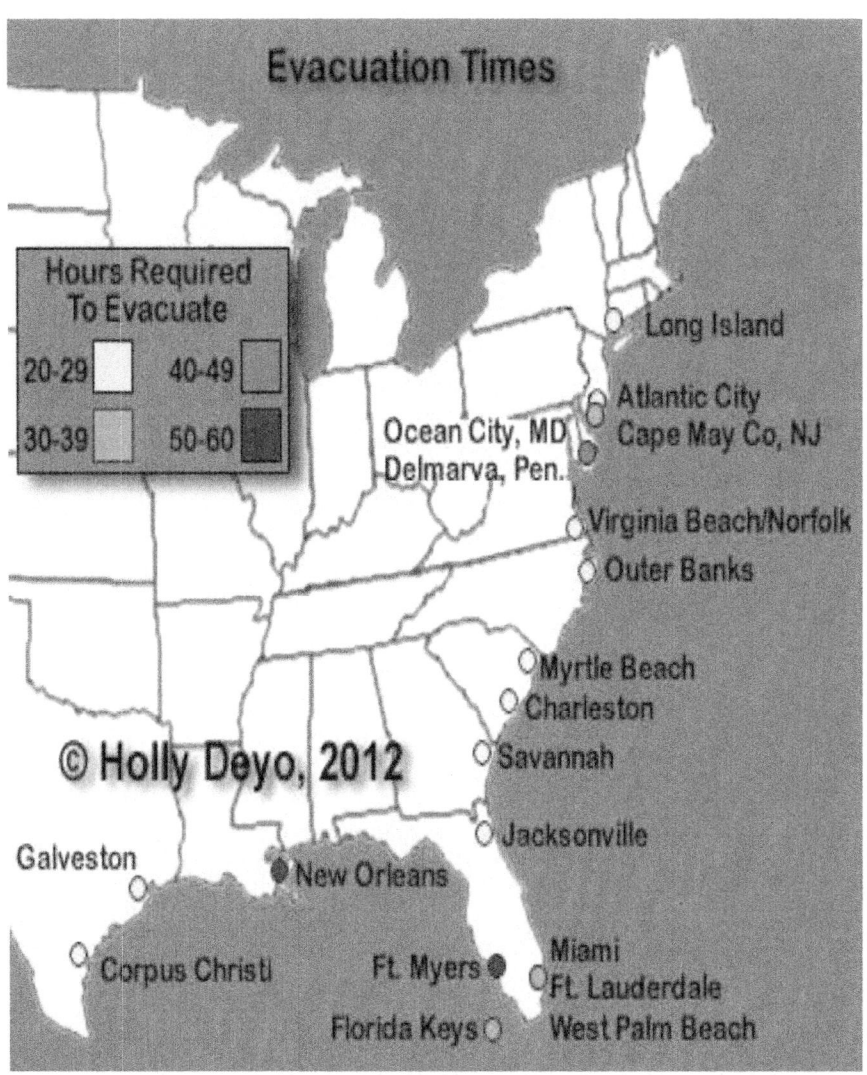

Evacuation Times

Hours Required
To Evacuate

20-29   40-49
30-39   50-60

Long Island

Atlantic City
Ocean City, MD   Cape May Co, NJ
Delmarva, Pen.

Virginia Beach/Norfolk
Outer Banks

Myrtle Beach
Charleston
© Holly Deyo, 2012   Savannah

Jacksonville

Galveston   New Orleans

Miami
Corpus Christi   Ft. Myers   Ft. Lauderdale
Florida Keys   West Palm Beach

227

Chapter 17

ARIZONA

**"After how it went for Jesus the first time,
I would expect something very different next time."**
(Prometheus movie)

Vespa Prada's alarm went off at 3:15 a.m. She had already awakened a few minutes earlier to strange tapping on the walls and ceiling. She planned on getting an early start on her trip to Sedona. Vespa smiled as she got out of bed.

She had lucked out; her parents couldn't make it for New Year's but were coming in on the twenty sixth. The desk clerk she spoke with said that Christmas week was usually dead because few people wanted to travel to celebrate Christmas in the warm Southwest. Vespa was able to change her reservation. If she needed companionship on Christmas Eve, she knew she could find a willing guy in Sedona. She was very excited to spend the holiday at her favorite place in the Southwest. To have her parents spend a few days with her was even better. Vespa had only worked a half day yesterday and couldn't wait to pack. Most of her neighbors had also left for the holiday and her street was nearly empty.

She always liked to have some quiet time before a vacation. The previous night, Vespa placed five CD's of Christmas music on her phone. She lit some candles, had a salad and some mineral water, and made herself her customary two strong bloody Mary's'. Vespa put one in the refrigerator. She then picked up a candle and the other drink and ran a hot bubble bath. She took off her clothes and admired herself in the mirror. The bathroom mirror displayed a digital clock and the inside and outside weather in the top right corner. It also helped the fashion challenged by reading the colors of the outfit worn and remarking if they matched and was correct for the outside temperature. Vespa's eyes moved to her breasts which were as round and supple as they were in college. She laughed to herself as she thought of a guy she met in a club in New York a few years back. His name was Gunnar Chesney. She invited him to her place. It didn't take long before she removed her top and bra. He referred to her breasts as "milk pillows." She smacked him in his face and never saw him again. If it had happened today, she would've laughed and proceeded with her objective.

Although they were short, her legs were well toned, and her stomach had a slight sexy curve to it from her nightly PX90 regimen. She couldn't help but smile as she thought about the kind of man she would spend Christmas with. Vespa knew that women had the upper hand in the dating game. She could "get it" anytime she wanted and enjoyed making desperate men beg and just walk away.

After her bath, Vespa had her second drink and as the Nutcracker played in the background, she fell asleep.

Vespa yawned as she remembered her blissful and relaxing night last night. Vespa was driving west on Route 10 towards Phoenix and north on 17 towards Flagstaff and the Grand Canyon. By 7 a.m., Vespa was only an hour outside of Sedona and decided to stop for breakfast at a familiar truck stop.

Vespa walked towards the glass door and saw her reflection in the glass. She nodded approval of her outfit. Her Daisy Duke shorts showed off her tan legs and her white wife beater T-shirt, without bra, showed off her nipples. She buttoned the two buttons of her denim shirt. A girl must have some mystery to her she thought. She paused for a second as she realized she had been looking at herself through a clear glass door. She went inside and peeked around the corner to see if there was anyone there. She grew uncomfortable when she saw the building was empty and turned to leave.

Vespa saw the sun peeking through the trees, and then, sudden darkness as her head hit the floor. The powerful blow that struck her head made her see stars for an instant. Her head pounded and a trickle of blood rolled from her nose. Vespa felt two sets of arms grab her legs and drag her far into the building. Her clothes were bunching up beneath her as her chin scraped the floor. The hands now grasped her waist and she felt her shorts being ripped down her legs. Then she felt the elastic of her lace panties push against her belly as they were also pulled off from behind. She was pulled almost to her knees now, her rear end nearly off the ground. Terror cocked the hammers of her heart as she realized what was happening. The first thrust into her hurt as her rapist put all his weight on her back. She nearly threw up from the pain and mixture of sweat, beer and cigarettes she smelled. Vespa realized her attacker was behind her but how could she smell him? As her hair was being pulled nearly off her scalp by her attacker from behind, she realized what she smelled. For her face had been pulled up to meet her second attacker. She didn't know what had become of her denim shirt, but the man had pulled the wife beater around her neck. As the man behind her grabbed it and pulled tightly, she could barely breathe.

The second attacker paused for a moment as if admiring her breasts. Then he grabbed her nipples, squeezed them, and pulled them sideways as hard as he could. The tears welled up in Vespa's eyes but she couldn't breathe enough to sob. Her lower lip began to wibble or tremble with fear. When she saw the man approaching her, she looked into his vacant eyes and prepared for the ultimate humiliation. The man behind her seemed to lift her for an instant. When she felt the man's slimy finger enter her rectum, she knew what would come next. Her second attacker said, "We need a second opinion" and pushed her backwards on the first attacker and proceeded to enter her from the front. Her legs were on his shoulders as she was held from behind in a "Full Nelson" suspending her arms in the air and pinning her chin to her chest.

She became the literal "piece of meat" in the sandwich. As the first spasm of pain hit her from behind, Vespa closed down her senses and waited for the end, however it would occur.

She first thought of how many male predators she had used or been used by, but never like this. As she was raped repeatedly, her mind wandered back to 2014.

She remembered her sister getting into a car accident. She remembered her parent's divorce, and how happy she had been working as a bookkeeper at a clothing chain. She even remembered being engaged.

When she passed out, she didn't recall. Once she shut down her senses and let her mind leave the horror of the present, she stayed in the security of the past.

If she had been aware of what had happened, Vespa would have felt her body being drug from on top of her first attacker by the second. She would have felt him dragging her across the floor by the wife beater wrapped across her throat into a darkened corner. He had grabbed the T-shirt and pulled down hard on it, banging her head against the floor. She would have seen herself nearly spread-eagled on the floor, and bleeding. Vespa would have felt the final indignity as the men nonchalantly turned and spit on her.

As it was, Vespa only knew that she woke up in great pain. Her body had curled into a fetal position and she was shaking from the cold and her injuries. Vespa didn't know if she was alive because her attackers wanted her to be or if they were incompetent and believed she was dead. Vespa only knew she was alive and planned on staying that way.

She warily opened one swollen eye and surveyed her surroundings. Vespa was in a corner behind the counter of the deserted truck stop. She dragged herself across the floor and peered into the restaurant area. It was empty and she heard no sound. Vespa had to assume her attackers had gone or else they were toying with her. She tried to stand but fell down from the slight dizziness she felt. Her lower body felt like it had been split in two. Her head pounded and she couldn't imagine what part of her body didn't hurt. Vespa shook her head to clear it and pulled herself up while holding the counter. She knew she was naked except for her socks and one stiletto shoe. But this was the least of her concerns. She felt wetness on her head and shoulders and realized there was blood coming from her head. Vespa used the counter to balance herself and with great disdain, tore the wife beater from her neck and tied it around the cut. Except for the gash in her head, the blackened eye and bloody lip, no bones were broken.

She was in great pain but whispered a quick thank you that she was alive. Whether to God or the incompetence of her attackers, she didn't know. How was Vespa to know, that worldwide, there was a harvesting of souls taking place at an unprecedented rate? She only knew she survived.

Vespa crossed the room and began to pick up her clothes. She grasped her panties and used them to remove the blood, fluid, and spit from her body. She dressed slowly as each movement caused a new yelp of pain to escape her swollen lips. The pain came from her ribs, back, breasts, stomach, neck, legs and lower body. Her soft cotton shorts even caused pain as they were pulled up her legs, across her thighs and even to her stomach. The soft denim shirt irritated her black and blue beasts and swollen nipples.

She grabbed a bottle of iced tea and drank it slowly.

Vespa had planned on washing thoroughly in the restroom when she heard a loud sound coming from outside. It sounded like a train but she knew there were no tracks in this area. She wasn't sure if she was totally awake.

As she rubbed her eyes and felt the pain, she knew she was fully awake. Vespa exited the front glass door and stopped for a moment to see her reflection in the looking glass and turned in horror as her swollen battered face appeared. She then crossed the lot to the front of the truck stop. The sky was a grayish blue hue and a few blocks away she saw a funnel cloud. It was close enough to grip Vespa with visceral terror.

A level five tornado ripped across Route 17 and reaped revenge on her attackers. Their pickup truck had been lifted into the air and the force of the 200 mph winds tore the two passengers from the vehicle and tore them into four or five parts that just floated in the air.

Vespa knew Arizona didn't often get tornados like this but the sight of a gigantic one that had passed just up the road mesmerized her.

Vespa returned to her car as soon as she was sure the tornado had headed east. She felt safe from its wrath as she headed north, away from the destruction. Although she saw two tornados in her rearview mirror, they were heading away from her.

Vespa may have said a little prayer of thanks if she could've seen the mangled corpses of the two rapists. As it was, she had no time to think about what had happened to them. She needed to get to a hospital.

She turned her radio to the "Hog", a local rock station, which gave news updates every hour. It wasn't on the hour but there was no music, just news reports.

Vespa was about to put on an instrumental Christmas CD to help soothe her. She stopped short when she heard the word, evacuate. Vespa listened intensely to reports of the Colorado River overflowing and warnings to head north to higher ground. The radio stated that all of the southwestern part of the original U.S. was in danger of massive flooding.

Vespa knew from the change that had occurred in the terrain that she was far enough north in Arizona to be safe from flooding. There was no longer rocky desert terrain, for pine trees had replaced it.

Vespa was somewhat concerned that the Colorado River flowed through the Grand Canyon only ninety miles north of her. She didn't know what new threat lay ahead of her, but she knew it couldn't be any worse than what she had gone through this morning. Vespa tried to force a sad smile through her swollen lips; she had survived and was proud of that fact. She felt that once she reached the safety of her condo in Sedona, things would improve for her.

Vespa believed that life is a test. It seems to push everyone to the breaking point; testing to see if one would commit suicide, which is the ultimate failure; the one test that you cannot give in to. Vespa knew she was very strong willed and would not give the devil his way. She'd like to give him his due!

Chapter 18

SURVIVAL OF THE FITTEST

"We deal now, not with the things of this world alone, but with the illimitable distances and as yet unfathomed mysteries of the universe....Of ultimate conflict between a united human race and the sinister forces of some other planetary galaxy."
(General Douglas MacArthur, speech West Point May 12, 1962)

Kirk drove his SUV east on Route 80 until he saw the waves of the Atlantic Ocean breaking on the shores of Secaucus, New Jersey. There were reports coming in, amid all the static, of water covering all of Manhattan, Long Island, and the south shore of New Jersey. Kirk realized, the farther he drove from his home, that his rescue mission to his parents was doomed. When he viewed the skyscrapers in Manhattan sticking out of the water with no streets visible, he had to accept the fact that his parents were dead.

The evacuation bridge from Port Jefferson to Bridgewater, Connecticut, was never built. The six million residents of Long Island were trapped like rats. As he viewed the buildings in their new watery home, Kirk imagined that the buildings could still function with generators on the tenth floor in a Venice like new city.

He mused about how property values just changed with the newly found ocean front property. Of course, everything had changed.

He no longer had to concern himself with PPS downsizing. He and the world had new problems to deal with. Kirk realized there would be all kinds of food and supply shortages to deal with. Already he had viewed the vermin, which always seemed to be the first to arrive when disaster hits, wading through knee deep water with their electronic prizes held above their heads.

On her way to Sedona, Vespa had already seen proof of what happens when there are more incidents than the authorities could handle. The scum rises to the top.

Vespa didn't care if her attackers had been law-abiding citizens before the disaster hit; all she knew was they were animals when she met them.

Things were not much better when she reached Sedona. The police had already been called to other areas of the state hit by tornados or floods. The few people she saw on the streets were no longer the friendly and fun people she remembered. Many were loading their belongings into vehicles. Some were armed with hunting rifles or carried pistols in plain view. A group of New-Agers were sitting in a circle chanting.

The clerk, Marie, at the condo was especially helpful to her as soon as she saw Vespa's injuries. She opened her condo immediately, and even helped dress Vespa's head wound. Vespa was grateful for her help and told the clerk how she had been struck with debris from the tornado. Vespa had no desire to divulge her ordeal even to a woman she knew. Marie had always been kind to her and they even had shared coffee and conversation on occasion. Marie's kindness then ended when she told Vespa, matter-of-factly, that she could only stay here through Christmas. The Verde River was rising and they expected the flooding to occur in Sedona after the twenty-sixth. She was closing the condos on that morning and heading south. When Vespa told her she was meeting her parents, who were coming from back East to visit her, the women's kindness ended. Vespa couldn't believe the words she heard from the woman.

"Honey, there isn't much back East to speak of anymore. And the nuclear waste repository at Yucca Mountain, Nevada, is flooding. You don't want to be around when that overflows."

The repository is larger than the state of Rhode Island. The mountain was selected due to its dryness and controllability by the military. One site was selected and guarded for the storage of all nuclear waste and weapons disposal. It is located 1,000 feet below ground and was to be safe for 50,000 years. Its inventory had substantially grown after the Japanese Fukushima reactor accident and the U.S. of 63 had convinced Russia to use this location so terrorists couldn't get their hands on the nuclear waste. The U.S of 63 had reduced its arsenal from 7,094 nuclear warheads to 1,550 and the Russians from 8,626 to 1,550 also with the signing of the New START Treaty. Each side also assigned unique serial numbers to their missiles so that verifiable onsite inspections could take place. All spent fuel rods are encased in anti-corrosion-resistant copper caskets and coated with bentonite which swells and seals when exposed to water. Once water seeps in, if the bentonite doesn't hold the underground drinking water supply for Nevada and neighboring states will be destroyed.

Marie knew some of what had occurred. Even more than most since her brother was an Air Force Colonel but like nearly everyone, she mainly concerned herself with what would affect her. At this time, worrying about yourself and your family's survival was the most a person could hope to do. Her brother had told her he had orders to take his fighter squadron South to the base at Roswell, New Mexico, and that she should prepare to pack up and head towards the Mexican border. She didn't know why they were going south when the news reports said to head north to higher ground, but she trusted her brother.

Marie looked at Vespa, who was trying not to cry. There was a good chance her parents were dead, and Marie couldn't help but feel bad for her. Her brother had told her to tell no one but family about moving south. As she looked at the physically and mentally beaten Vespa, she couldn't help but consider telling her. Her parents had always taught Marie that family must come first, but it was important to help others also.

Kirk instinctively pulled his hand closer to his knife scabbard. A feeling of hopelessness had overtaken him as he thought about what he and the children had facing them. It wouldn't be easy, especially with Cole being diabetic. Kirk knew that Cole was running dangerously low on his supplies. He also knew that in this new world, supplies would take months to be delivered if they would arrive at all as most drones were being shot down. Kirk made his decision. His family must come first.

Kirk realized his security clearance gave him the right to inspect all packages that flowed through the operation at work. He had master keys to all the buildings and trucks and headed to the nearest PPS terminal in Randolph that delivered to Morristown Hospital.

The gates and buildings were locked tight and there were no guards anywhere to be seen. Kirk was somewhat concerned that when he used his access card it would be monitored at the PPS Central Monitoring Station in Chicago, but chances were there was more to worry about that close to the Great Lakes than the security of packages.

Kirk thought about all the people who had sent their packages a few days ago, sure that PPS would make certain that their loved ones would have them to open on Christmas morning. Of course, any thought of happenings like that were a waste of energy. The minimum wage guards must have realized that also. Chances are, they were someplace huddled with their families, and Kirk couldn't blame them in the least for locking the place up and abandoning their posts.

Somehow, Kirk felt vindication for what he was about to do. Not only because it was helping his family but also because of what had occurred yesterday at work.

Kirk easily unlocked the barriers and disabled the alarm with his code. He searched feverishly for the truck that delivered to the hospital. Kirk found the truck and used a company issued razor knife, which he used to open and inspect packages, to pilfer what he needed. He found insulin, syringes, chem-strips and alcohol wipes. Kirk took only what he needed. Thousands of others would also need these items to survive.

Kirk felt a sense of power knowing that his top security clearance probably saved his son's life. Kirk had always valued honesty and integrity and hated thieves but his families' safety was the most important thing. So Kirk had done something totally opposite to his values. Kirk felt it was his only choice, and would have to live with it. The company would survive and no one had actually been hurt by his actions.

As he was getting out of the truck, he heard a voice. Kirk softly shut and locked the door and prepared to meet the person who had spoken. Kirk tried to look nonchalant and at ease. He knew PPS guards were armed and he didn't want to be shot. He had placed all the items in his large coat pockets, so nothing was visible. When the voice yelled again, he answered.

"Joe, is that you?"

The voice answered with another question.

"Yeah it's Joe, who the hell are you?"

"It's me Lolich, Kirk Lolich."

A light shone on Kirk's face as he blanched. It came from a flashlight held by a guard who looked to be in his late fifties. This guard was no Barney Fife type, for in his other hand; he carried a .45 with the safety off. The patch on his shoulder had a recoiled snake on it and read, "Sidewinder, Security that strikes back."

"Wow! Mr. Lolich, damn good thing you said who you were. With everything going on, I was ready to shoot first and ask questions later." He holstered his pistol. His chest was heaving like a bellows in anticipation of a confrontation.

"I can't believe you're here Joe. If I'd have known, it would have saved me a trip."

"Why? Is something wrong, Mr. Lolich?"

"Well Joe, with all the vandalism in the streets, I was worried about the place."

"Yeah, I can understand that, especially with no guards but me."

"Why did you stay?"

240

"Look, Mr. Lolich, I live alone. The others have families to worry about. I understand why they left early or didn't report. My shift was over at 6 a.m., no relief came, so I stayed. I take my job very seriously. I'm not a career man like you with stock in the company but my word is my bond. I'll go down with the ship!"

Kirk smiled. "I guess the scum out there know the reputation of PPS Guards; since nobody bothered you all night."

"It's not going to get any better is it, Mr. Lolich?"

"No Joe, it isn't. If the place doesn't flood, chances are pretty good some animals will show up to see what they can get. You know I can't stay, Joe. I have two kids that are going to wake up and need a father."

"Of course, I understand, you just wanted to check the place one last time."

"Right. You're staying, aren't you?"

"Yeah, Mr. Lolich, it's my job."

"I know this doesn't mean much. But if someone had told me a guard stayed through it all, I would have known it was you."

"It means a lot, thanks."

As Kirk prepares to leave, he stops.

"Joe, weren't you a marine once?"

"Yeah, Special Forces in Iran."

Kirk took one of his knives off his belt. "Here, you might need this."

Joe didn't argue. He knew when a man gave away a prized blade like that; it was an honor to receive it. He said to Kirk, "Thanks. Say hello to the kids for me. I know you must be concerned about having enough supplies for Cole's diabetes and probably had a shipment on the way." Joe thought to himself that he wanted Kirk to know who the better man was and it was better than shooting him in the back.

Kirk smiled a half smile and turned to leave. He knew that Joe cut him a break. He was sweating under his coat. The realization he had stolen was sickening to him. The thought that he may have

241

had to kill old Joe was something he couldn't bear to consider. But he knew he would have, for Cole and Claire. At times like these, family had to come first.

Vespa had waited at the condo for her parents until the twenty seventh. Marie had left the day before. She told Vespa she could stay as long as she wanted to wait for her parents. She also advised her to watch the river, and finally advised her to head to Mexico. Groups of rafters could be seen headed down the river but they would never survive the Grand Canyon. Vespa had waited till the last possible moment; already a few roads had flooded. Her cell phone calls were to no avail. She had valued her family greatly and hated to admit they were gone.

Friends and family were also important to Kirk and he wasn't surprised to see Arian Whitaker's van parked in front of his house. It also didn't surprise Kirk that it was filled with canned goods and camping supplies. What did surprise Kirk were Arian and the children coming out of the house with sleeping bags and knapsacks. The children must have let Arian in or the dogs would have ripped him to pieces. The dogs were docilely walking; playing the role of Cole and Claire's protectors.

Kirk felt very secure with his trusted friend and two powerful dogs with him. He knew there would be trouble; just like he knew that old Joe would be lucky to survive the week. When there is a survival of the fittest mentality, chaos rules and not the bravest or the strongest but the smartest and most well prepared will survive. Joe was the former; Kirk knew he must be the latter.

He knew they now had enough food and medical supplies to survive for months. Kirk felt secure that his two powerful dogs would warn them of intruders and his two athletic children could hold their own if attacked.

Kirk entered the house as Arian was going in for another load. Kirk was grateful he had his fantasy knife collection and his Samurai swords. Kirk and the kids had taken fencing and Korean sword fighting lessons. He knew their little band could defend themselves but he also knew they would need guns to protect themselves from all the private militia gangs that would soon be roaming the streets. Kirk thought back to how he occasionally had played the paintball war games and the way that some players would take the jungle warfare so seriously. He wondered if he would feel the same type of tension and excitement, when it would be for real. Arian tapped him on the shoulder ending his reverie.

"Pack shorts buddy."

"What? It's freezing out there."

"It won't be where we are going."

"Where the hell is that?"

"Mexico."

"Why there?"

"Listen to this. You remember I have a cousin who is a Colonel in the National Guard."

"Vaguely."

"He called me up in the middle of the night. Cousin Coulter wanted to talk to me about buying his assault rifle collection. I had asked him once if he wanted to sell, he said if he decided to, I'd be the first to know."

"Are they in Mexico?"

"Hell no! They're in my van."

"Why sell now? You would think that he would need them at a time like this."

"My thoughts exactly, but wait till you hear this. His brigade was called up. He thought, like I did, that they were called up to clean up or protect from looters. That's not the case; it seems our dear government feels this area is lost. They mustered the entire New York guard to go to Mexico. Whoever survives here is "on their own". He advised me to go to Mexico. I decided to take you and the kids with me. They are all set to go."

"Leave all this for good?"

"I hate to tell you this, but all this left you; washed away in the acid rain of reality. There is one hell of a snowstorm brewing up

North. We talked about this in November; this is the big one. Your damn Tigers had to win."

They both smile. Kirk was so wrapped up in his work problems; he had forgotten all the prophecies. It was happening.

"Kirk, don't zone out on me. Here's the best part of this, Colonel Coulter thinks Datchet is going to invade Mexico. He's in one of those underground bases calling the shots."

Good old G.W. Datchet had picked up the nickname of Global War Datchet.

"What is his reasoning?"

"How the hell do I know? Are you coming? We have supplies and arms. He sold me all his stuff. He said, 'All the arms he needs the army would supply,' and he would rather have cash. By the way, we bought two M-15's, three AK-47 and six Glocks. You owe me 3,000 bucks."

"Great. Will you take a check? So, your cousin thinks the President is ultimately heading to Mexico?"

"Yeah, I'm sure that will happen."

Kirk picked up his blades and headed to his SUV. It had begun to snow heavily.

In a war room deep in the bowels of the Clarksburg, West Virginia Mountains, decisions were being made that would affect two countries. A great chill had begun to sweep down from what had been Canada. Snow was measured in feet not inches while temperatures were dropping below the norm in large increments. There was no telling how far the cold would proceed south.

Washington D.C. had been destroyed; a new capital would be needed. With the approval of President Datchet, it was decided that Roswell, New Mexico, with an elevation of 3,570 feet, would be the place. There was also a separate meeting of the President and the Joint Chiefs of Staff where a plan was laid out for the invasion of Mexico. The U.S. 63 was no longer whole; there would be a need to replace the lost states. Datchet's plan for Manifest Destiny now pointed south toward warmer weather.

The idea of "manifest destiny" was first written in 1845 by Democratic Review writer John L. O'Sullivan. President Datchet quoted our right to "overspread and to possess the whole of the North American continent." (28)

The crisis continued worldwide. The water level had risen twenty feet and tidal waves seemed to come in every eight or nine hours. Two billion humans had died in the Earth changes. The temperatures had become very cold and snow was falling. The Great Lakes had merged into one Great Lake. A category two hurricane was reported on its cooler waters. San Francisco bay had expanded twenty times its size. L.A. was an island. The shoreline was approaching Dallas. Texas has twenty seven percent of our refineries and is the heart of our petrochemical production. The Colorado and Mississippi rivers had cut the eastern and western third of the country off from the central. Florida, Long Island and New Orleans were gone.

As Kirk, Arian, Cole, and Claire headed southwest from New Jersey, they noticed the constant snowfall. It was late December so this wasn't unusual weather for the Mid-Atlantic region. Little did the small group know that the cold and snow would persist for 30 years similar to the mini ice age that was experienced in Europe and North America in the 14th and 15th centuries? That cold spell actually lasted for over 500 years from 1300 to 1850. The average person only lived to 36 with 50 percent of children dying in their first year due to the severe winters. The difference this time was that the weight of the massage Antarctic ice sheet in the south was shifting the mantle of the earth like a weighted top trying to spin properly. North America was slowly being pulled south while Siberia and China were being pulled north.

Our history has always been marked by temperature fluctuations. In 6000 BC, temperatures dropped eight degrees. From 900 to 1300 AD, temperatures warmed by seven degrees and populations boomed. In 1815, Mount Tambora blew with a force 100 times that of Mount Saint Helens. Brown and red snow fell during the summer and 1815 became known as "the year without a summer". One could walk from Manhattan to Ellis Island to New Jersey on the frozen Hudson River.

By the year 2100, temperatures had been predicted to rise 10 degrees and cause severe draughts, powerful hurricanes, and the possible start of another new mini ice age as sea levels rise three feet; only it happened 70 years sooner.

The group stopped at an old gas station outside of Saint Louis. The sign read "Esso" and had never been upgraded to Exxon or Mobil. As the group stretched their legs, Kirk and Arian filled their vehicles with gas. Cole and the dogs slept, and Claire went to use the outhouse around back. A sign in the window read "no food or beverages".

As Claire reached for the outhouse door, two men stepped out from behind the structure. They were filthy unshaven men missing a few teeth and staring at Claire like hungry dogs. Claire could've sworn one was wearing a fur coat but then realized it was the skin of a very hairy man that he was wearing like a bear rug. She also thought she saw a figure in a hooded robe behind them. They rushed Claire and she screamed "Dad". Kirk dropped the gas hose, spilling valuable fuel on the ground. The men had Claire cornered against the outhouse door with knives drawn. Kirk already had a Bowie knife in one hand and a small axe in the other. The men turned toward Kirk and rushed him. Arian threw open the car door awakening Cole and releasing the dogs.

Kirk swung the axe with his right hand but missed and then spun around to his left, backhanding the man in the gut with the Bowie knife. As the other man extended his blade towards Kirk, he slapped it away with his axe. Kirk held the Bowie knife with the blade in a downward position. He threw a left hook, slicing the assailants throat and then threw an over-hand right, splitting the man's head with the axe like a piece of fire wood. Sixty to zero in five seconds. Claire stood stunned by the fierceness of her father's unflinching actions.

Kirk looked to his right at a sign that read, "Autumn Leaves, Jesus stays" and said to Claire, "Guess you're not Claire-Voyant after all?"

The dogs stopped dead in their tracks and turned back toward the car. They raced past Arian and Cole as the two said, "What kind of attack dogs are they!" The gas station attendant looked up from behind the lift gate of the Grand Cherokee and dropped the supplies he was pilfering and reached for his shot gun. As he grabbed the rifle, Mama Bear clamped down on his wrist. Papa Bear then locked onto his throat and the two pinned him to the ground. As the group returned to the vehicles to assist, it was too late. The attendant's throat had been ripped out and his body was twitching as the two dogs sat attentively and watched while waiting for their master's return.

Arian says, "Let's take everything we need and ransack the place."

Kirk says, "No, there are probably more relatives inside. Let's just fill up and leave unharmed." Kirk put a $50 bill under a rock on top of the pump and the group drove away.

On Route 66 through Oklahoma, Kirk noticed a fairly athletic black couple hitch-hiking along the road without any luggage. Kirk calls Arian on their walkie-talkie and says, "Hey buddy, why don't we pick that couple up. They still have a 600 mile walk up ahead."

Arian replies, "Why would I want them in my van? We'll be facing armed gangs of these people as soon as resources get low and they are unable to feed themselves. Let me tell you about these people. There isn't one Black Country that has ever sustained what white people had given them. Africa never invented the wheel, a calendar or even a written language until we showed up, because they couldn't. There are no important African discoveries or inventions and they hold virtually no patents. We spend more per capita on black students than whites and yet they still fail at an alarming rate. We gave them ten times more public assistance than whites and they responded by committing twenty five times more violent crimes on whites than blacks. Two out of every three white women that are raped are raped by a black man even though we out number them six to one. Ninety percent of homicides by gun are committed by blacks but we outlawed guns a few years ago in cities where we left white people unable to defend themselves against the very people who were most likely to use a gun. We don't need these people!" (29)

Kirk says, "Come on, technology was invented by colder climate countries because they had to and black crime stats are skewed due to the breakdown of the family structure. We need all the friends we can make. I saw a wedding ring. They're not going to hijack us."

Arian replies, "I don't know that I know you anymore. It's every man for himself."

Kirk says, "Pull over; I don't want to get too far ahead of them."

Arian says, "Good, I like to give people false hope. You know we had to put a stop to the death penalty for blacks because it was cruel punishment since they are genetically more aggressive than us and proven to be less competent."

"I know all about the argument that stopped black capital punishment because we are genetically different. It was the right thing to do since their serotonin levels were proven to be lower than whites and Asians which explained why we are calmer than they are and why they are less deserving of capital punishment."

"If you accept that, then you must also accept the fact that they score 200 points lower on SAT tests and fifteen percent lower on IQ tests. Only twelve percent of blacks outscore the average white. Most violent criminals have an IQ under 85. Twenty five percent of blacks have IQ's lower than 75 compared to five percent of whites and Asians." (29)

"And Asian IQ scores are ten percent higher than whites. Eskimos and American Indians have the same IQ as us."

"Yeah but almost all of the people with genius level scores above 160 are white. Every significant invention has been made by whites. Next are you going to tell me we owe them reparations? At least black kids were raised by both of their parents when they were slaves." (29)

"No, because there isn't one white American who is living that owned slaves and there are no living blacks that were slaves. They should take it up with the tribal leaders that sold them. Thousands of Northern whites died or were maimed in the Civil War to free them. Distant relatives were wronged just like in most other cultures. What I do owe them is respect. Respect for no other reason than they are human just like you and I!" (29)

"Not like you and me!"

Kirk says, "I'll tell you what. You wait here. We're doubling back to pick them up. I'll take my chances with my kids in the car that these are descent people. I have changed; I see the world with a different set of eyes!"

Kirk spins his Grand Cherokee around and picks up the couple in need. The man introduces himself as Mikal, an eye doctor from Tulsa and his wife, Halle, an endocrinologist also from Tulsa. They explain that they stopped for supplies and came out of the store to find their Escalade stolen. They greatly appreciate the help and were in Kirk's debt. Cole and Halle immediately start a conversation regarding diabetes. Kirk smiles and says, "God works in strange ways."

During the long drive, Kirk thought about how important family was. How people weren't meant to live alone. How he strangely felt a strong need for a companion. How his true feelings surfaced during this crisis. He had wealth but was poor and needy in the intimacy department. Like Maslow's hierarchy of human needs, as we meet each level of need we focus on the next; security, love, family, self-worth; the things that bring true happiness. What we do and how we do them are far more important than how much money we earn. (26)

It was just a nondescript Mexican take out on a dusty stretch of Arizona highway near the Mexican border. The sign outside read, "Flying Salsa, Out of this World Mexican Food" and had a large UFO with neon lights above it. The only thing that stood out was the SUV with New Jersey plates and the custom van with New York plates and an orange Challenger from New Jersey. Even this wasn't out of the ordinary. The word had begun to leak out and the Mexican migration had begun. As they exited their vehicles, a man with two women exited the store. He was a priest with two nuns. He wore his white collar and black shirt but also was wearing jeans and cowboy boots. The two nuns were dressed similarly. The man carried a flanged mace and made eye contact with Kirk who said, "Hello". The man replied with a New Jersey accent, "Father Hardt and Sisters Elizabeth and Laura. Stay clear of Phoenix. What's left of the three million Free Masons in the U.S. are claiming it as their Lodge and will be congregating there shortly. Heard they plan on forming their own government. May God protect you!"

Inside the restaurant-grocery store, Claire and Kirk were getting a few needed supplies while Cole, Mikal, Halle and Arian were waiting to use the rest room. Arian stepped in front of the couple and said, "Twelve percent."

Halle quickly scanned the shelves and noticed the Mexican beer sign that read "twelve percent alcohol" and she replied, "Potent and strong; maybe even superior."

Arian gave her a smug look.

Halle smiled and went out for a cigarette smoke.

Cole commented to Arian how ironic it was that they were planning to vacation next year at Japan's Ice Age Park located in Siberia. Japanese scientists had extracted soft tissue and sperm cells from frozen extinct species of woolly mammoth, rhino, deer and saber tooth tigers. They then artificially inseminated similar present day species and in just two generations, their offspring had populated the Safari Park. The mammoth's fur turned out to be blonde and red. Cloning of dinosaur soft tissue found in fossils threw the whole theory of evolution into chaos and was the next planned park exhibition. Like usual, Americans protested this ungodly creation but Japan and Russia ignored the protests and tourism at the park and snow mobile and dog sled rides nearby boomed. (26)

Cole also asked Arian if he thought the Crypto Zoo in Wild and Wonderful West Virginia would be completed. It was the American version of genetically engineered animals or "Chimeras" and was scheduled to open in 2030. It paired lions and tigers; bears and boars; rabbits and wolves; buffalo and chicken (really!); pythons and alligators; rhinos and zebras; eagles and turkeys; sharks and manta rays, etc. No cross breeding of chimps or apes would be permitted.

Arian, like usual, was oblivious to any conversation that didn't involve a skirt. His eyes were transfixed on a well-built 40-year-old brunette by the beverage section.

Kirk had placed a few items on the counter and was pondering what else to purchase when Claire called out, "Dad, look at this picture."

Kirk says to Claire, "We really need a map. Can you find one?"

"What's a map? My iPhone isn't working."

Kirk smiles and says, "OK, how about a Twinkie?"

Claire, looking confused, handed Kirk a newspaper. On the front page, there was a Boston picture of the statue of Paul Revere. It was half covered by snow. As Kirk looked at the photo, Cole hurriedly brushed past him. As he passed, he said, "Dad I think my blood sugar is low, could you add cheese crackers and an orange juice to the bill?"

Claire stared at the picture in the paper looking over Kirk's shoulder.

"Dad, when will this cold period end? It looks like snow-mageddon. How am I going to live without Facebook, YouTube and my IPAD?"

Kirk looked at his daughter. It was a good question but one he couldn't answer.

"When hell freezes over, Claire."

The woman looking in the cold drinks refrigerator stood transfixed when she heard those words coming from a man with a New York accent. She remembered the voice and how those words had hurt her years ago at C.W. Post College.

Her reflection on the past was interrupted as the door to the cooler next to her was flung open. It hit her hand, which held a Lipton Iced tea. Cole, in his haste to get his orange juice, hadn't seen the woman standing transfixed. The door knocked the iced tea from Vespa's hand and it crashed to the floor and shattered. When Cole saw the woman holding her hand, he immediately asked her if she was all right. She nodded she was. When Kirk heard the noise, he immediately rushed to the back of the store and reached for the Bowie knife tucked away near the small of his back. He saw the broken bottle, the woman holding her hand and Cole comforting her. Kirk immediately surmised what had happened. The first words out of his mouth were, "I'm sorry."

The first thought Vespa had was, how she would have loved to have heard those words from him back in college. But instead she simply said, "I'm okay; your son just startled me when he opened the door. I'm fine, thanks. Your son asked about me already." Her back genuflected as she spoke.

Arian also heard a loud bang outside and exited the store.

Kirk reached into his pocket and caught his left ring finger on his belt loop. He grimaced in pain as he pulled a five-dollar bill out of his wallet.

"Here, get yourself another one. I'll pay the clerk for the broken one."

Kirk handed her the five. Vespa took the cash and spoke.

"Thanks. I can tell from your accent you're from New York."

"Originally, we live or did live in Jersey."

Vespa was now sure it was Kirk. His appearance was different than what she remembered. He had less hair with gray side burns and a moustache. He was no longer wiry but had added around thirty pounds of muscle. He seemed to be a nice man now; he had two children and was kind. She didn't see a wedding ring, so chances were he wasn't married. Who knows, maybe she could have a real relationship with Kirk this time. When they met in college, he was engaged. She considered what she would do if he wasn't involved with anyone now. Although she had never had children, perhaps she could have a mother-daughter or mother-son type relationship with his children. Vespa had never grown up enough and had been too selfish to want children. If they had both been mature back then, these children may have been hers. It seemed now, that she and Kirk had both finally matured. Vespa stopped thinking in that vein. She knew that once again the timing was bad for them. After her rape, she wasn't sure if she wanted to talk to men, let alone have them touch her. She wasn't sure if she hated men. She just knew she didn't trust them. She began to make small talk.

"That was the worst six days of my life after the asteroid hit."

"Yeah, six days of nonstop destruction. Funny, it also took the same six days to create the world."

"I went to college in the East. You said, did live?"

"Yeah, a friend of mine said with what is happening that Mexico might be a good place to be."

"That is the same thing I was told."

"Are you going to Mexico also?"

Vespa felt a little bit at ease talking with Kirk.

"I guess I will."

"You're welcome to join our little convoy. It's just me and my two children, my buddy Arian from New York and two doctors from Tulsa. It might be safer as we get closer to the border."

Vespa didn't know what to do. It was nice to hear a familiar voice and he seemed nice. Maybe if she had run into him later, after she had time to heal, her answer would have been different. But right now, she knew what it had to be.

"I appreciate the offer but I'm in a bit of a hurry. I think I'll go it alone."

"Sure, I understand. Could you do me a favor though?"

"I don't know. What kind of favor?"

"Since you are leaving right now, we will be behind you. If you have any problems or need anything, don't be afraid to flag us down. In other words, if you don't mind, we'd like to keep an eye on you."

Vespa smiles a slight smile through her still swollen lips.

"A Jersey guy watching my back. I could do a lot worse. Sure, I don't mind and thanks for your kind words."

Kirk smiled back and handed Vespa his cell phone number. He had warm eyes but was unsure of what to say.

"No problem," he said shyly.

As Vespa walked out of the door, Kirk knew it was time to face the cashier who had been giving him dirty looks since the bottle broke. He reached into his wallet to try to appease the clerk.

Vespa found Arian in a fist fight with two young men. She asked Halle if they shouldn't get Kirk or her husband but Halle said the two men tried to attack her and Arian appeared in an instant. Before they ended their thought, Arian had knocked both men out cold.

Halle commented, "Arian, you're the last guy I thought would come to my defense."

Arian replied, "You're with us now, which makes it different."

Kirk hadn't realized that he had indirectly apologized to Vespa for what had happened years ago. But Vespa knew, and she also knew that an immature boy had turned into a good man. She remembered how Kirk had said, "When you have sex with someone, you're connected with them throughout eternity from lifetime to lifetime. It is a soul tie." As she sped onto the highway, she smiled to herself, grateful that she had survived. After what she had recently been through; grateful to see that a man could change for the better. She began to think, it might be nice to know someone in Mexico so she didn't have a repeat of Arizona. Vespa slowed her car's speed. She didn't want to lose site of the little caravan. Vespa wasn't about to kid herself. She knew she would be keeping a close eye on them in her rearview mirror.

The struggle for life was mirroring medieval times and conditions. As she drove, Vespa daydreamed of more chivalrous times of Camelot and knights in shining armor saving damsels in distress.

Vespa called Kirk on his cell phone, "Do you remember what the Bifrost is?"

"How do you know about the Bifrost?"

"I believe it has collapsed! Think about it."

Vespa slowed her car, waved Kirks SUV ahead of her, and followed him. She became filled with determination and possessiveness and decided that Kirk would make a fine "alpha male". The hunter got captured by the game.

Sometimes a man can meet his destiny on the road he took to avoid it. . . .

At 8:11 pm, the thirty by sixty mile wide super volcano at Yellowstone National Park erupted. The ash blew into the upper stratosphere while eight feet of ash fell on Wyoming, Colorado and Nebraska. The bread basket of the US will be un-plant-able for years. The warm air forced itself in all four directions and soon the warm air would reach the caravan heading south for a temporary reprieve from the cold. On this day, Mother Nature accomplished what the Japanese, Germans, Soviets, Muslims and Chinese failed to accomplish. Mother Nature effectively ended the 253 year reign of the United States.

Chapter 19

GUARDIAN ANGELS

**"The universe is not only stranger than we suppose,
but stranger than we can suppose."**
(J.B.S Haldane)

"Yuck!" the words voiced by the woman as she entered the room, said it well.

The room was once a Catholic school classroom; identified by the crucifix that hung from the wall. The room still held the customary desks, computers, and even the blackboards surrounded by four sturdy walls. What was out of place was an acrid odor of charred flesh; the sight of blood, and the hole in the center of the ceiling and floor. It was easy to see that there had been an explosion. There was a seared circular outline around the hole but the most disturbing part of the room was the burnt pieces of flesh on the floor and hanging from the ceiling. The next words spoken by a man who also entered the room were surprising.

"Can't you handle it? You never saw anything like this at Grambling, did you?"

"Of course I can handle it! Where did you learn to handle this? Was it at Northwestern or could it have been during your Master's work at Georgetown?"

The woman who spoke was tall and thin with a narrow upper body but her hips flared out widely; enough to easily rest her long boney hands on when she spoke. Her chin was as pointy as a stalactite. It was a wonder that she didn't harm herself when she looked down. She was dark haired and dark skinned. A Homeland Security Science and Technology I.D. hung beneath the lapel of her jacket. She took a pair of surgical gloves from her pocket and pulled them on. She bent down and picked up a charred piece of flesh.

"Damn, Walters, I thought you liked your steaks rare."

The African-American woman laughed as she dropped the flesh in a plastic bag.

"Agent Annie Etienne, part time comedian." The man who spoke was six inches taller than the woman and weighed 180 pounds. He had an athletic build with thinning blond hair and blue eyes. His face was chiseled and easy to admire. He was dressed in an expensive suit and like her, also had a Homeland Security Science and Technology I.D. hanging from his raincoat.

"The name, agent, is Anise not Annie. Get it right or better yet just call me Agent Etienne," The woman said with bitterness.

The man feigned a bow. "Milady", he said as he swiped a gloved hand across the wall.

"Nothing on the walls," he said as he pulled off his gloves.

"What do we have Walters?"

Walters began to read from a small note pad. "Two assailants entered the building and shot two teachers who were bringing in refreshments. They seated the kids in a circle around the perimeter of the classroom. Then they drew a circle in the center of the room, stood in the center of the circle, mouthed some nonsense about God and blew themselves to bits with plastics attached to their bodies."(25)

"The kids?" Etienne asked as she kicked a pile of ashes.

"Unharmed, fine, not hurt physically. Mentally I can only guess."

"How?"

"That's what we are going to find out. Maybe they suffer from hypnagogic or vivid hallucinations"

"Two nuts in a classroom blow a hole like this in the ceiling and floor and no one gets hurt?"

"Right. No flame, no blood, and no guts reach the children?"

"Maybe it was spontaneous human combustion?"

"No, that's when the body's fats somehow self-ignites to a temperature of 3,000 degrees and somehow leaves the arms and legs intact along with the surrounding furniture while reducing the body to ashes in a matter of minutes. . . .Probably from eating fast food!"

Walters steps back as a charred piece of flesh drops from the ceiling. He then continues to speak.

"The motive could be anything. My guess is, since it is a Catholic school and with Catholicism being nearly destroyed after what happened in Rome, there's definitely an anti-religious agenda at the heart of this."

A police officer enters the room.

"Agent Walters, we found this disc in a portable DVD player in the back hallway. It must have belonged to the dead guys."

"Did you watch it?"

"Yes sir, in the AV room."

Suddenly, Walters' phone rings. He hands it to Etienne.

"Could you take it, it's the Director's ring tone."

Etienne takes it. "Etienne here."

As Walters talks to the policeman, Etienne listens to the call and hangs up after a quick "Yes sir."

Etienne talks to Walters. "Excuse me; we've got a new assignment."

"What! This is getting good. I've got to watch that disc."

She shakes her head no.

"Fine, but listen to what he told me."

"I guess we can talk about it while we go to the airport. There's a military plane that's going to take us to Wright Patterson. Assistant Director Appomattox will meet us at the airport. That's all I know."

"Interesting, but listen to this. I was on the right track about religion. I used my old altar boy education and of course, what the officer told me about the contents of the disc. It seems that today is the Feast of Holy Innocents." As they walk past firemen and police, Walters stops talking. The agents get into a car and head down the highway.

Walters resumes speaking. "Holy Innocents, commemorates when Herod killed the children hoping to kill the savior right after Jesus' birth. If you read Matthew 2:13-18, it explains it all. Suffice it to say, the Christians knew he didn't succeed. The two dead guys belonged to the Herodians. It seems that they think the End of Days started and that soon the Antichrist will appear. Then in Revelation 14:1-5, John speaks of the lamb saving 144,000 virginal people."

Etienne looks at him incredulously.

"It's on our web page. Didn't you read it? Our friends the Herodians decided to put two and two together on their own and kill all the children. Since Herod screwed up, they decided to finish the job their own way; that part is on the disc. Luckily for us, their plan here didn't work. Hopefully, the others in their group will have the same results."

"I don't think the two incidents are related. They realize they can't kill all the worlds' children, I hope?"

"They don't have to; they only need to kill 144,000. I guess they figure that will piss God off enough."

"But they aren't dead."

"That's the best part. A miracle occurred here; or so the priest thinks. The guys blew themselves up but the kids were shielded."

"What could shield them from all that plastic explosive?"

"Angels!"

"What? I think you should leave miracles to God."

"The police report says the kids saw these shapes standing between them and the Herodians. The few kids who were willing to talk said that the shapes were of their dead grandparents. Also, the Captain said when he and the firemen entered the room; they saw silhouettes of angels on all four walls."(25)

"The kids had guardian angels? My Grandma Sadie would buy that."

"Not you?" says Walters. "I thought you were from Haiti and believed in voodoo. What race are you again?"

"Human! But no way, the Southern Baptist Ministers were too busy scaring us with hell to tell us about guardian angels. And my people were originally from Jamaica, not Haiti! I also have Russian, Irish and American Indian in me. How about you?"

"I wouldn't mind being in you. Better keep the Russian part a secret. You're talking to a lapsed Catholic. It would be a beautiful story and there is a basis for it. I've investigated plenty of cases and know plenty of people who believe that there is a spirit world or another dimension right around us. They believe a relative watches over us and guides us when it is our time. When I was six or seven, I pulled a plug half way out of the wall socket and touched it. I believed that the electricity would make me stronger. I felt the electricity jolt up my arm but nothing happened to me because it wasn't my time. Just like it wasn't these kids' time yet."

"Think about it, on the Feast of Holy Innocents, a group of kids are saved at Saint Nicholas School and Saint Nicholas happens to be the protector of children. Then you add to that, it occurs in Saint Joseph, Missouri, and Joseph was the protector of the child Jesus. The dead grandparents protected the kids from the Herodians like Joseph protected Jesus from Herod."

"Good story, it might even have legs. The only problem is it no longer involves us. It seems like this disaster has brought every nut out of their icon-infested hole. All the religious zealots and the gun-crazed militias can't wait for the world to end so they try to help it along. At least when Michigan was destroyed, the Michigan Militia went with it. That's one group of crazies we don't have to deal with."

"I can't argue with that but there were over 200 private militias in this country a few weeks ago. Now, about this new assignment."

"You're on a need to know basis agent."

"What the hell does that mean? I'm senior agent here."

"I can't tell you what I don't know."

"You didn't ask any questions?"

"No."

"It figures, I would have. Damn, I should have taken that call. See, this is what happens when they start using quotas to fill jobs."

"What the hell is that supposed to mean?"

Etienne angrily glares at Walters.

"It's nothing personal Agent Etienne. I'm sure down the road you'll be a good agent. But they take kids like you right out of college, send them to Quantico with a liberal arts degree; train them for about six months and think you'll catch public enemy number one. You 'fast trackers' don't even have to have six years of work experience like the rest of us! At 24, Etienne, I don't think you or anyone else is prepared for field work. Do you honestly think any white guy fresh out of college would get your job in this elite unit?"

"If you are disappointed with where you are in life with your BA in pre-law and Masters in management, don't take it out on me. I didn't write the old affirmative action law but I'll be damned if I'm not going to use it to my advantage whenever possible."

"Don't get me wrong, I'm not a racist, white women also have an advantage. You just have a double advantage."

Etienne speaks with sarcasm. "Oh, I'm sorry, I got it wrong. You're just sexist. I did hear that with all this global melting that 10 million-year-old micro-organisms are being released with DNA that is causing a bacterial evolution. Maybe women are just evolving and men aren't. Enough of this banter; you know how much I love you. The GPS unit says the airport is on the next street. Let's act professionally for Assistant Director Appomattox or perish the thought they might separate us."

"I thought the cross around your neck was your GPS unit?"

Etienne smiles sarcastically while Walters tries not to laugh.

"Yeah, who would want to have some forty year-old white guy as a partner? Or for that matter, a twenty four year-old girl or I mean, woman, just a year out of Quantico."

They pull into a small airport. An eight seat Air Force micro jet is already on the runway. A large middle-aged man walks towards the car.

Walters gets out first, extends his hand and speaks. "Why us, Director Appomattox, you didn't have any agents closer to Wright Patterson than two from St. Louis?"

"Walters, shut up and listen. Agent Etienne," he nods at her. She returns his acknowledgement.

"To answer your question, no one is as experienced as you. We've lost nearly a third of the 700,000 law enforcement officers in this country and half of our agents since that damn asteroid hit and the east and west coasts dipped into the ocean and disappeared like Sodom and Gomorrah. What with entire staffs across the country drowning in their offices, to pitched gun battles with every kind of militia available; not to mention President Datchet taking some of my best to some hidden base to prepare for the invasion. I'm left with you. I closed your case with the police in St. Joseph. This is more important."

Walters and Etienne both shake their heads in agreement. Appomattox begins to tell them their assignment.

"In 1960, NASA wrestled authority away from the military to investigate and explore space. This past month, a cylinder was found in Greenland; possibly of alien origin. NASA is very interested in this and somewhat concerned.

A team of four scientists are at Wright Patterson along with a team of eight Insertion Special Ops. The area will be secured by the time you arrive. Even though we are living in a time of geological and social upheaval, departments and agencies have to continue their missions. The scientists will investigate the findings.

All international coalitions have dissolved. China and India have banded together to protect their huge population centers. Turkey and Israel have become allies. Russia has closed ranks with Europe in order to ward off its dysfunctional neighbors. Brazil is hoarding its mineral wealth. We're not sure whom to trust! (26)

The Special Ops were sent for security because the U.S. government has long debunked UFOs. The back engineering that started with the Roswell crash made many companies technology leaders, which put our military years ahead of Russia and China. Whoever controls the technology controls the world!

The reason I'm telling you this is if by chance this cylinder is alien, it will be up to you to protect our countries' interests. No scientist is to bring anything out of that cylinder without your authorization. The Special Ops will control and protect the site from civilian or other nation's interference.

There will be a Naval Lieutenant Davis there to meet you. A Norwegian fisherman notified his ship of the discovery. Davis notified the navy, who notified us. Once you land, dismiss him and his crew. The final say so at that site will be you two. Got it! There will be winter gear awaiting you at the air force base. That's it. Here's your itinerary."

He points to the runway. Walters nods.

"Thank you sir, Agent Etienne and I will get this done."

Appomattox walks away and waves.

"Come on Agent Scully, let's go."

"You're thinking like me Walters; it sounds like an episode from that old X-Files show."

He looks at her as they prepare to board the micro jet and smiles a slight smile.

She returns his gaze. "Why do you think myself and thousands of kids wanted to join the Bureau? For most of us, it sure wasn't to catch terrorists." As her phone rings, she says to Walters, "I have to take this. It's my godfather, the Secretary of State."

"Oh, I forgot to mention nepotism," as Walters just shakes his head.

Chapter 20

Acapulco

"He, who defends everything, defends nothing."
(Frederick the Great)

On the southern shores of the Mexican Pacific near the stunning Condesa Beach, lie the spectacular cliffs of Acapulco, Mexico. The temperate water and pristine shoreline was a magnet for ancient Aztecs and now home to 13.2 million Americans who have "moved south".

On the cliffs, a pair of teenagers stands on the edge, bend their knees and push forward. Claire does one 360 before making a very nice dive into the water. Cole spins sideways and hits the water awfully hard on his side. On the beach, standing hand in hand, Kirk and Vespa lean backward and then bend forward as the kids hit the water. The couple has a weekend off from their jobs at Blackwater Security LLC. Kirk is the assistant director and Vespa is the finance office manager. As Cole and Claire swim to the dock, Kirk and Vespa are locked in a passionate kiss.

Vespa remarks, "I feel like we are a lifetime away from last year's disaster".

Kirk replies, "Don't talk, just kiss. The kids will be here in a minute."

Also on the beach soaking up the sun are Arian, Halle and Mikal. The couple work for the Red Cross now.

Mikal says to Arian, "I used to read a lot of sci-fi before the event. I read a book that said we were genetically engineered to be a slave species for a superior race. The book said that they would be back. What would you do if they came back and decided that a particular race was theirs, as slaves? The other races would be unharmed if they gave up one race. What would you do?"

Arian glares at Michal and says, "I would stand next to you, no, in front of you as brothers and fight with you as we did 200 years ago in the Civil War to end slavery. I believe all races would stand together."

A tear comes to Mikal's eye and he just nods his head in agreement.

Arian remarks to Mikal, "I'm going down the street to get a few six packs. Tell Kirk I'll be back shortly unless I meet a Latin lover. You know how the women can't resist me."

Mikal whispers into Halle's ear, "Funny how his other head is color blind now also."

Arian walks to the main strip to his favorite café Kookaburra, a modern café that won the hearts of the Americans by serving as much European as Mexican food and brewing their own cold beer. Arian loved the old nostalgic black and white movie posters on the walls. While crossing the street, Arian is signaled to by a mid-20's brunette that would pass for Miss Mexico. She turns into an alley and looks over her left shoulder to see if her stranger is following. Arian breaks into a speed walk and the woman smiles and motions with her finger to follow. Arian breaks into a trot so as not to lose her. As he turns into the alley, she is about 50 feet ahead of him. She bends forward; locking her knees, and pretends to fix her shoe. She has no ass, her buttocks and thighs were all one muscle.

Arian is fixated on the figure, no, her figure as the bat strikes him in the back of the head. Arian momentarily loses consciousness as he hits the ground. Two young men rifle through is pockets while taking his wallet and lose change. As one has trouble removing his watch, Arian gains his senses. Realizing what is going on, Arian throws a knee into the assailant's waist buckling him over. Arian scrambles to his feet but the larger of the two men has him in a strangle hold from behind. The man is at least six inches taller than Arian and lifts him off the ground. As Arian's feet kick, he feels the cold sliver of a blade slice his stomach. Like a boxer pounding the heavy bag, the shorter assailant punctures

Arian's waist seven times before plunging the knife into Arian's diaphragm and turning it. As Arian's body goes limp, the larger assailant drops him. Arian's knees hit the ground first, followed by his hip and he falls forward onto the knife. Arian can see his blood running on the ground and can feel his shirt moistening. As his vision dims, he can hear the female shout, "Gringo immigrant" as the three casually walk away.

WHITE PRIDE
DOESN'T MEAN HATE!

IT'S OK, YOU CAN SAY IT!
I'M PROUD TO BE WHITE!
THERE IS NO NEED TO FEEL GUILTY
BECAUSE OF THE PAST! ↑↑↑↑↑↑↑
↑↑IF THAT OFFENDS YOU, YOUR RACIST

WHY IS IT OK FOR OTHER RACES TO BE PROUD?

WHY ARE WE NOT ALLOWED TO CELEBRATE OUR CULTURE?

WHY CAN'T PRO-WHITE RIGHTS ORGANIZATIONS EXIST,
WITHOUT BEING LABELED "RACIST"?

WHY ISNT 'BLACK ON WHITE' CRIME LABELED A HATE-
CRIME?

WHY ARE OTHER RACES IN THIS COUNTRY
ALLOWED THESE RIGHTS, AS THEY SHOULD,
BUT NOT THE FOLK OF EUROPEAN ANCESTORY?

!!STAND UP FOR YOUR RIGHTS &
THE RIGHTS OF YOUR CHILDREN!!
AMERICAN FREEDOM PARTY

AMERICANVIKINGS.COM   AMERICAN3RDPOSITION.COM

Chapter 21

Exopolitics

"They became farmers in the seeds of the stars; they sowed, they reaped and they had to weed the universe."
(Arthur C Clarke)

The flight to Wright Patterson was totally uneventful. The air force micro jet covered the 700 miles at a rapid pace in spite of a constant snowfall.

Agent Walters comments, "What if these aliens have been monitoring American Bandstand or Soul Train for years and think all they have to do is play music and we automatically go into gyrations? It might be their way of disabling us and taking over."

Agent Etienne smiles and asks Walters, "Have you ever been to St. Paul?"

"No, but did I tell you I like my women to have IQ's higher than their body temperature?"

"There are over one million Asian residents there, mostly from Vietnam. How about the Amish country of Ohio or Pennsylvania?"

"Sure, I've been to Lancaster, boring!"

"How about the Cherokee Indian reservations of Oklahoma?"

"Nope but I want to go to the Cowboy Hall of Fame."

"Let's try the barrios of Tucson or the Cajun country of Louisiana?"

"I thought Mardi-Gras were a bunch of low life's, reminded me of Coney Island."

"So, you've been to Harlem then?"

"No, wouldn't go there unless ordered to."

"How about the Russian Jewish community of Brighton Beach, New York? They're white!"

"Not interested in Yiddish but I do like vodka."

"Little Tokyo in L.A. or Little Havana in Miami or Dearborn, Michigan's Arab American Museum?"

"What's your point, Etienne?"

"My point is that I'm twenty four and my parents took me to these places! When I look in the mirror, I see an amazing range of faces as an American."(26)

Embarrassed and looking like he was suffering from xenolexica or loss of words, Walters's replies very seriously, "I wasn't raised that way. Sometimes, no matter how hard you try, you revert back to what you learned first."

Etienne nodded her head, smiled, and closed her eyes.

A few minutes later, as Etienne started to doze off, Walters deliberately asks, "Did you know that up until recently, eco-terrorism was our biggest threat?"

"No."

"The Animal Liberation Front and the Earth Liberation Front actually commit more violent acts than al-Qaeda. They view mankind as a virus to Mother Earth."

"Did you notice a copy of Al Gore's old "An Inconvenient Truth" on the end table draw next to the bible in the hotel room last night?"

"No, but let me tell you something creepy about those movies from the 1970's, the *Omen* ones."

"Don't tell me, the young blond girl died in real life from an intestinal problem and her older sister in the movie was murdered by her boyfriend."

"No, that was *'Poltergeist'*. On the first day of filming the 'Omen', the director was in a car accident. After filming that day, he was in a second car accident where he got pinned against the car as he exited. There was also a scene which got cut where a lion actually killed an actor. Then on separate plane flights, Gregory Peck and the screenwriter's planes were both hit by lightning. The film crew also hired a private plane but cancelled the charter. A group of businessmen took the charter instead and it crashed upon takeoff. The plane hit a car on the highway as it descended and the car's driver was the pilot's wife. The special effects directors' girlfriend was actually decapitated in a car crash after the movie was released. And lastly, William Holden and the entire crew contracted influenza during the filming of 'Omen Two' and Holden's best friend was murdered in a bar fight."

"What the hell are you trying to do, give me nightmares? Next you're going to tell me that the Shroud of Turin is a fake."

"Actually, it has been carbon fourteen dated back to 1300 AD. They say that it actually belonged to the Grand Master of the Templar Knights who was tortured in 1307 by the church in a similar manner to Jesus. It is actually the blanket that he was wrapped in as he healed from his wounds," says Walters.

"Nice try but the Shroud was actually in storage at that time and suffered damage from a fire that threw the carbon fourteen dating off. Let me think. Did you know that in London they monitor traffic by motion sensing cameras in the traffic lights and issue tickets based on the digital recordings?"

"Yes, I was aware of that."

"And that recently, these cameras started picking up dark human shaped shadows that appear to have enough substance to trigger the cameras?"

"No, really?"

Etienne bursts out laughing and says, "Just kidding, got you."

"I knew you'd get into this. Did you know that John Adams and Thomas Jefferson were bitter rivals and that both died on the Fourth of July in 1826?"

"Yes. Do you know about the 9-11 coincidence?"

"Not really, I heard about names with 11 letters."

"Besides the President's name, the main terrorist and New York City having 11 letters; New York is the 11th state, flight 11 had 92 passengers which nine and two equal 11. The other flight had 65 passengers which again equal 11 and 9-1-1 also equals 11.

September 11th is the 254th day of the year and 254 people died on the three planes and again $2 + 5 + 4$ equals 11."

"Wow, and don't forget that verse 9.11 of the Quran says that a son of Arabia would awaken a fearsome eagle. The wrath of the eagle would be felt throughout the lands of Allah: for the wrath of the eagle cleansed the lands of Allah."

"That's right, I forgot that part."

"Did you know that over 80 percent of hospital deaths occur at 3 am? And that most UFO, ghost, paranormal, crop circle and alien abductions occur at 3 am?"

"That's because the sun is on the opposite side of the planet and causes a change in brain waves causing hallucinations at that hour!"

"Do you know what monument would be left standing in 500 years if all humans died?"

"Mount Rushmore because it was cut in granite."

"Do you know why one in 90 boys has autism?"

"Yeah, because kids are more sensitive to the other side and see 'dead people' when they are young and it frightens them so severely that they turn inward from the experience. Usually happens when "They" come back to abduct a fetus and a young boy witnesses it."

"Did you know that over 70 species of females have reproduced without a male partner recently? This parthenogenesis is capable in only a handful of species but scientists don't know why more and more are developing this latent ability or if it is a new evolutionary development. Some believe we are meant to keep evolving until we reach a state of orthogenesis or perfection, like God."

"I told you we don't need men. It would explain the Virgin Mary birth though."

"Remember when they claimed to have found the Ossuary of Jesus, I mean the burial place of his bones and family in Talpiot, Jerusalem?"

"Yeah"

"Wasn't it weird how they DNA tested his bones and then opened a web site where you could pay to find out if you were his descendant and the first 300 samples they received from around the world all matched?"

"Yeah and they closed the site down claiming it was an infringement on religious freedom. It's similar in a way to people who have been able to identify who they were in past lives and were granted permission to exhume the body and have it DNA tested only to find that their current DNA matched. They stopped granting permission to exhume the bodies."

After a pause, Walters speaks.

"Did you know that federal law still states that every able bodied man from 17 to 44 is a member of the United States militia?"

"No, but I do know that Americans possess one third of all the handguns on Earth; 350 million of them! That's why we're in this dogfight with militia groups. I've always believed that handguns should be outlawed."

"Let me tell you something. Freedom is lost in steps. The aim of government is to keep people alarmed about something and then lead them to imaginary safety. Jefferson said that liberty yields to government. Tyranny thrives when government has no fear of an unarmed people. The Second Amendment is a doomsday provision. Designed for when government fails. To take away our freedom of speech or right to bear arms is a mistake you only make once!" (26)

"Wow, well said. I'm going to sleep on that now."

The two agents get comfortable and slip into a light sleep. Agent Etienne rolls to her right and uses agent Walters left shoulder as a pillow. The two agents awaken to the seat belt chime and smile at each other.

Agent Etienne says, "Did I ever tell you that when I was young, seven or eight, my brother and I would go into our grandparent's room and play a game with a picture on the night stand?"

"No, what do you mean a game?"

"There was an uncle in the picture and he would smile at us and motion for us to come closer to the picture. As we got closer, his appearance would change. His teeth would grow and eyes turned bloodshot. The nails on his fingers would grow long and sharp as he reached out for us. One time, my brother extended his hand and touched the picture and he vanished."

"He was a changeling, I know all about them."

"Got you again, just kidding," laughs Etienne.

"You know the Federal Reserve is controlled by the Rothschild's, Bilderberg's and Rockefellers' and large banks?"

"No it's not. The Federal Reserve is part of the government."

"Wrong, the Fed is no more controlled by the government than Federal Express is! President Wilson formed the Federal Reserve in 1914 and handed financial control of this country over to the largest bankers in the world. No one even knows who is on their board. They pick the Fed Chairman and dictate monetary policy to the government."

"I didn't know that."

"People think I'm paranoid but I know there are conspiracies."

"Have your dreams become more intense and frequent lately?"

"Yes, and my cell phone messages are showing up a day or two later."

"Mine also, something weird is going on. My grandparents also had a picture that couldn't be explained. It looked like a poor man's Mona Lisa but when you looked close at the eyes, they reflected who was looking at them like a mirror. The strange thing was that if you used a magnifying glass to look closely at the eyes, you could see inside a room and if you moved to your left or right, you could see walls and a furnished room. How could you possibly paint with such minute detail with a brush?"

275

An Air Force Major greets the two agents as soon as their plane touches down. He takes them in a Humvee to a large jet already on the runway. He explains that there will be winter gear inside the jet for each of them and introduces them to the scientists.

The scientists are all dressed in lab coats and there is little to distinguish them. The first thing Walters observes is their lab coats. Although the scientists had winter gear near their seats, Walters found it strange that they would have their lab coats on at takeoff. This meant only one thing to Walters; they planned on working immediately so chances were there was easy access to the site.

Walters knew that when the Vikings discovered Greenland and Iceland, they reversed the names in order to preserve Iceland for themselves. Iceland has a small glacier but is mostly open land and a fishing community. Greenland, on the other hand, has only 60,000 residents and is three times the size of Texas or the size of Mexico. It was almost completely covered in ice one mile thick; at least before the events of the past month had occurred.

The micro jet was compact and had an open belly with two rows of eight seats. In the back of the micro jet, was an area filled with equipment. Walters assumed it was important because four Special Ops were guarding it.

The major had introduced the two agents as simply federal employees. Walters had watched the scientists for any noticeable reaction, but there was none. There was little to distinguish the scientists but the two agents studied them and memorized any distinguishing characteristics as well as noting their names.

The bearded scientist was Dr. Abrahams and he wore a parka that looked like it was made of aluminum. The one with glasses was Dr. Johan. The short one was Dr. Lai and the one with a moustache was Dr. Kaznir.

The only Special Op that was formally introduced was the commander, Captain Northrup, which may or may not have been his real name. They could have been members of any one of the four military branches consisting of 73,000 commandos or Special

Ops. The Navy Seals, Green Berets, Rangers and Delta Force all are assigned to operations like this. The Special Ops were already dressed in their all white winter gear; even their equipment bags were white. They all had black patches which symbolized which black budget project or secret government branch they represented. Four wore a dragon draped in an American flag whose claws gripped the Earth. Two wore a patch with a naked woman riding a killer whale. The remaining two's patch had an alien holding a stealth fighter in its jaws with the saying, "To Serve Man", written below it. Night vision goggles hung around their necks and Walters was certain he saw a Kevlar vest sticking out of one soldier's coat. They were all armed with side arms and each had a very advanced version of an M-15 complete with laser scopes and lights. Walters could see they were ready for combat but he wondered if they were ready for aliens. He doubted it because he wasn't sure he was.

Walters asked, "What type of knife is that that you are carrying?"

The Op responded, "A Wasp Knife. When I insert it, liquid nitrogen injects into the victim and freezes his internal organs. Death occurs pretty quickly."

As they neared what had been the East Coast, Dr. Johan spoke to break the tension of the flight.

"Did you know that Japan and Long Island, which is somewhere below us in that water, was formed by the expanse of glaciers? It pushed rock and soil from New England and deposited it in New York where the glacier ended."

Special Op Kayne Rockport spoke up.

"I'm from New York; no wonder our two areas always hated each other. Boston's been doing stuff to piss us off since the Ice Age but Japan was destroyed because of their Shinto belief in multi-Gods."

There were some chuckles among the soldiers and scientists.

277

Dr. Johan spoke again. "Soon there may be another glacier and another Ice Age upon mankind."

Dr. Abraham's then spoke. "Do you realize that there have been UFOs during the Ice Age and they definitely appeared as far back as in biblical writings?"

Walters did not like the conversation turning to UFOs. The scientists might divulge too much of the mission.

Dr. Johan answered Abrahams. "Of course, and the Air Force taught a Physics 370 course to cadets in the late 60's that had a chapter on UFOs that stated they have been here for as long as 47,000 years and that there are three or four species but I'm not sure everyone here is aware of that fact. Ezekiel described being taken up in a flying wheel in 593 BC and he returned with the knowledge of how to make steel. An Egyptian papyrus from 1500 BC describes a UFO. In fact, there are UFO carvings on cave walls to say nothing of their depiction in Renaissance era paintings and Sumerian and Hindu scrolls. There are many documented sightings prior to the invention of the airplane. Northern California even experienced a UFO wave in late 1896."

Dr. Kaznir remarks, "UFOs provide evidence for the reality of the bible such as visits by angels."

Special Op Kit Winslow then spoke.

"Doctor, my grandfather was a test pilot after WWII and he knew Kenneth Arnold."

Doctor Abraham's nods and then speaks.

"The soldier is speaking about the pilot in Seattle who in 1947 sighted a formation of saucer like craft flying over Mount Ranier. An article then appeared in the Seattle papers and the term "Flying Saucer" was coined.

Two weeks later, the infamous Roswell, New Mexico, crash occurred. That same week, prior to the crash, Edwards A.F.B. in the Mojave Desert experienced seven UFO flyovers. I was in grade school when UFOs buzzed the Capital for two weekends in a row. You must remember that this was in 1952, at the heart of the Cold

War, to say nothing of the Korean War. There was so much tension in the world at this time and with there being standing orders to protect the nation's Capital at all costs, nothing was done.

I doubt if any of you here are old enough to remember but there were front-page photos of the incident on the *Washington Post* and the *Times*. There were no investigations launched by the government. At that time, it was as if they knew our weapon capability was no match for them."

Virgil Huron, one of the remaining Ops with an Australian accent comments, "We had a pilot in the 1970s whose plane disappeared. His name was Valentich. He radioed in that a craft was flying by him at incredible speeds. He said that it was huge and that it was right above him. On the tape you could hear the sound of metal scraping and his plane disappeared."

Special Op. Rick Stone began to mutter to himself as Abraham's continued.

"In 1942, after the bombing of Pearl Harbor, L.A. had a UFO wave. General Marshall ordered the firing of 1,433 rounds by the 37th Brigade at the objects. Six civilians died. The *L.A. Times* printed pictures of the UFOs on their front page. There were thousands of witnesses. It was the first time we denied their existence, first time we fired upon them and first time we used the weather balloon excuse. (17)

In 1964, at Vandenberg A.F.B., the launch of an Atlas F-class missile was shot down by a UFO. It was caught on film, on multiple cameras, shooting four beams of light at our missile before it tumbled into the Pacific Ocean. (17)

In 1967 and 1975, UFOs shut down our nuclear missile silos at Malmstrom Air Force Base near Great Falls, Montana. They disabled our launch codes on twenty Minutemen missiles which sent a message to us that we were helpless. That is why Reagan and Gorbachov agreed to end the Cold War and began to use the Star Wars technology of particle beam lasers to protect the planet from attack."

Special Op Rick Stone then yells at Abrahams, "That's bullshit!"

Captain Northrup then spoke.

"Settle down soldier! The man is entitled to his opinion. Go on doctor, continue."

"Thank you, Captain, but I'm finished for now."

Walters made a mental note to keep an eye on the hotheaded Special Op. He could tell by the way Etienne looked at the soldier that she was doing the same.

Dr. Kaznir then spoke as if to change the subject.

"I hope there are no polar bears where we are going. Speaking of bears, I must tell you about an assignment I was involved with before I was called here.

In Alaska, Eskimo's discovered a cave after last month's cataclysm. It seemed the entrance had been exposed during the shifting. Inside the cave they found a national pale-ontological treasure. The limestone and clay cave had remains in it dating back 45,000 years. The remains of a short-faced bear that stood 14 feet high at the shoulders were found. When the bear would stand on his hind legs, it would be taller than the average home. It probably ran 60 miles-per-hour and had a bite of 3,000 pounds per square inch. This would have been the fiercest creature in North America at the start of the Ice Age. It was the T-Rex of the Ice Age. When one realizes that the average black bear can kill a tiger or lion, imagine what havoc this bear could have created. It is believed that the bears migrated to coastal waters to support their tremendous weight and eventually disappeared. (10)

Archeologists have always wondered why it took a small tribe of nomads from Asia so long to venture cross the ancient Bering Straits land bridge into Alaska. Now they know, nothing could escape the pursuit of this fierce-some creature. Population geneticists estimate that only sixty Amerindian immigrants were able to elude these creatures 8,000 years ago and push deep into the U.S. to escape these predators.

This mammoth sized bear resembled a Kodiak bear. At the time of my departure, the remains of the bear were being flown to a genetics lab where they hoped to clone its DNA with a Kodiak bear."

He smiles. "I just thought you might find that interesting."

Dr. Abraham's speaks to Dr. Kaznir.

"As we know, Dr. Kaznir, the Earth is a living organism capable of fighting off viruses. Some believe its reaction to pollution and deforestation has resulted in an increase in diseases like Ebola, AIDS, SARS, etc. We now find that male sperm counts are down 40 percent in the past 50 years."

Dr. Kaznir listens intently, unsure of what point Abraham's is trying to make.

Dr. Abraham's then poses a question to Dr. Kaznir. "In your genetic research, Dr. Kaznir, have you ever discovered why humans have more diseases or genetic mutations than any other species on Earth? Chimps have 200 defects, we have 6000. Why some are diagnosed with cancer, HIV and diabetes but have no ill effects? Are somehow immune? If I could make my question even clearer, would it have been possible that humans could have been genetically altered or spliced with another alien race?"

Walters saw that Dr. Abrahams was trying to restart the UFO controversy after Kaznir had tried to quell it by changing the subject. Etienne decided she had better keep an eye on Abrahams because he seemed to her to be an instigator.

Abrahams did not wait for Kaznir to answer but continued.

"Wouldn't this intelligent design concept then explain the 50,000-year-old missing link in our evolutionary process? The Bible states man was created only 6,000 years ago. Our nuclear DNA also shows a random chance mutation at both of these same times! The gene called ASPM showed a dramatic leap in human intellectual development at both these times. As a matter of fact, Neanderthals are more like the core of our family tree than we are. We're the only branch with uniquely distinct traits like shortened faces, reduced nasal cavities and lack of brow ridges. In the broader sense of human evolution, the more unusual group is not the Neanderthals, but it's us! Cro-Magnon man was only around 10,000 years during the Ice Age and developed after us. That can't be evolution. Was it God or an alien interloper?" (26)

Dr Kaznir says, "The only sign of evolution I can attest to is the 'men's hairy chest contest' on cruise ships. But seriously, I've always wondered why if there have been over 8 billion humans over our 200 million year existence, why can't we find the graves or bones? As many humans have died as there are presently on this planet."

"Were on this planet."

"Have you ever submitted your theories to peer review?"

Abrahams replies," I have no peers!"

Dr. Johan interjects. "When one brings the Bible into a discussion on genetics and aliens, Dr. Abrahams, one walks a slippery slope. The Bible was created just 6,000 years ago. In its history of mankind, we learned of Adam and Eve and their three sons. We know that one son named Cain killed the other named Abel. We also learn that Cain's wife had a child named Enoch. Where the wife originated from, we don't know."

"In the Bible's book of Enoch, it states that fallen angels had mated with human women. Genesis 6:1 tells of 'the Sons of God, looking at the daughters of men and saw that they were pleasing.' Some say that these 'Sons of God' taught us medicine, science and war. As sin and corruption spread across the Earth, God sent Gabriel, Michael and Raphael to destroy these children of evil with a 'Great Flood!' There are some who believe that angels are aliens. I am not one of them. I believe it all to be a divine mystery."(17)

Walters had been observing everyone during the discussion. The scientists seemed to all find the discussion interesting. The hotheaded Special Op listened and often could be heard mumbling under his breath. Two other soldiers listened intently. The other soldiers on the plane could care less about what was being said. Special Op Winslow again spoke up.

"The bible is full of high tech miracles. I don't know if this has anything to do with what you gentlemen are discussing, but I come from near the Great Plains area and sometimes they find crop circles in the grain fields. I was wondering if you knew anything about them. I did see an old movie called "Signs" that somewhat explained them."

Dr. Johan spoke to him. "Early in the millennium, that movie was made and it did in part concern crop circles, but they didn't explain much. It was actually based on the Kelly-Hopkins Kentucky UFO case in 1955 that was also referenced in the Air Force's Physics class that was mentioned. Did you know that over 300 crop circles have been reported in the town of Avebury in England? You probably didn't know that the base of the wheat explodes from within; this is similar to micro-waving. The wheat is then magnetized and has been found to undergo cellular changes.

"I can think of two instances when a black helicopter was filmed confronting a ball of light that was in the process of creating a crop circle. On film, the wheat can be seen falling under the ball of light as a pattern is formed. Using mathematical principles, the crop circles have been determined to be musical notes and a form of communication. Who that communication is between, I have no idea. It could be a secular form of communication or even a spiritual one."

Dr. Abrahams leans over and whispers to Walters. "Doug and Dave did us a great favor in 1978 in England by faking a few crop circles and debunking the whole topic. We were disappointed that we didn't think of that piece of disinformation first."

Dr. Kaznir comments, "What if the aliens took over the world in 1947 and everyone born after that date is a hybrid? There were an unusual number of important people born nine months later in March of 1948. The only real Earthlings left would be over 81 years old."

Walters blurts out, "And maybe the Hokey Pokey is all that it is really about."

Everyone laughs except for Dr. Abrahams who gives Dr. Kaznir a stoic glare.

Dr. Kaznir then says in a more serious voice that, "I read in a Roper Poll a few years back that two percent of the 6,000 people surveyed answered a series of carefully arranged questioned that indicated that they had been abducted. That would mean that forty million people worldwide have been abducted. These polls are always very scientifically accurate. Another poll indicated that eighty percent of Americans believe that the government is withholding evidence about UFOs.

And don't forget that news broadcast in South Africa three years ago where a salvage ship off of Table Bay near Cape Town was attempting to raise a sunken Galleon. Sonar identified a large mass and when they sent cameras down to survey, video clearly showed a large round damaged disk protruding from the ocean floor. Of course, it was deemed a hoax and the video footage was lost when FDX'd to London and the site could not be found again after a U.S. Navy ship left the area."

Dr. Lai asks a rhetorical question.

"We know life arose from the sea. What if a species of humans had always been here and had at times communicated with mankind? There have been numerous reports of USOs or unidentified submerged objects. What if they have bases on the ocean floor off the coast of Bermuda or Japan or Australia where most of the sightings have occurred? The Mariana Trench is 35,201 feet deep. Our best subs can only go 8,000 feet, yet we've tracked fast moving, large objects on sonar at 10-15,000 feet. Pilots and ship crews have reported for years seeing large glowing spokes of light under the water. The huge ocean light wheels rotate under the water and move alongside and under the ships. They could have evolved prior to us in their natural underwater environment. I also heard rumors of a confrontation that took

284

place. With the recent collapse of forty percent of ocean species and the stability of entire ecosystems at stake, there was a showdown between a USO and fishing trawlers that were aided by the coast guard. A clear message was sent that we are trespassing on their food chain and we had better become more responsible or face the consequences of full scale 'contact'. Aliens from space don't make sense because the temperature in space is minus 434 degrees and is a buffet of radiation that can boil blood and dissolve DNA.

"In Peru, Inca stones were found in 1961. The stones are hundreds of years old. The drawings on the stones depict an advanced prehistoric culture performing surgery and even flying. Species such as these could have lived inside of mountains or beneath the sea and had little interaction with other humans. They would have then in all likelihood, at some point, mixed with the human population. Upon their arrival, wouldn't this species be viewed and revered as Gods much like the Incas and Aztecs viewed the armored mounted Spanish soldiers 400 years ago? (25)

Cortez and thirty soldiers defeated the Aztecs because Aztec prophecies foretold of the return of a white skinned visitor. Kukulcan emerged from the sea and gave the Mayans mathematics, architecture, astronomy and medicine at a time when the Mayans had just discovered the wheel. He was a Caucasian male with blond hair, blue eyes and an elongated skull. He departed the Mayans by walking back into the sea.

What about the Dead Sea Scrolls? Fearing that the Romans would destroy the Bible, the parchments were hidden in jars in caves on the sheer desert cliffs. When the Dead Sea Scrolls were discovered in 1947, one document described a race of 'watchers' who watched over the planet. There is a Sumerian tablet from 3500 B.C. that depicts a race of reptilian gods who will return to this planet. A rock wall in Tanzania Africa, which was discovered by Anthropologist Mary Leakey, depicts carvings of thin alien like creatures. These carvings are 5,000 years old. I find one of the strangest discoveries to be a 3,000-year-old Sphinx in Colorado."

The interested soldier, Kit Winslow, spoke up again. "Excuse me doctor, I heard you talking about the Sphinx in Colorado. Where I come from in Wisconsin, we have a pyramid submerged in Rock Lake."

The other Special Ops' looks at their fellow soldier quizzically.

Dr. Johan speaks before Lai can continue.

"In New Zealand, 2,000-year-old pyramids have been found. Yet, the area was unpopulated until 700 A.D. (12) And in 2019, 600 gold chariots were found on the floor of the Red Sea!"

"As was the Flight 77 plane which was found off the coast of Virginia. That was the one that supposedly hit the Pentagon on September 11th!"

Dr. Kaznir continues the pyramid discussion.

"I find this fact the most interesting of any which concerns pyramids. In 1976, the Viking probe photographed the Martian surface. After the photos were made public, a face and pyramids were discovered in the Cydonia region. The truly amazing thing is the pyramids are the same size and alignment as the ones we find in Egypt. There even appear to be staircases up the front of the pyramids. On a second flyby in 1993, to re-photograph the surface, the probes camera system shut off only to restart once it had passed the Cydonia region. In 1996, a third probe photographed the region and found no face and no pyramids. I wonder how long the face and pyramids had been there before Viking shot the photos? In 2005, while searching for the wreckage of NASA's Mars Polar Lander which disappeared in 1999 as it landed on the Martian surface, more strange photos were seen. The Polar Lander and the Mars Climate Orbiter which was also lost four months earlier, were both found next to what looked like a larger ship. The 'mother ship' was the size of four football fields. Again, it was explained away as being shadows, rocks and camera angle."

Dr. Abrahams speaks with disdain.

"It sounds like a cover-up to me."

Dr. Johan speaks. "I hear that some scholars are insisting the Egyptian Sphinx is 10,000 years old because it shows severe water damage and erosion from that time period. Perhaps that coincides with the great flood of Noah's time which occurs early in the Bible."

Dr. Lai says, "Doctor, the Sphinx is only 4,600 years old. The time of Noah is prehistory. There are some scholars who believe that four great Pacific civilizations had been destroyed 800,000 years ago, 200,000 years ago, 80,000 years ago and 12,000 years ago. (3) This all pre date's history as we know it. One cannot combine creationism and history in a time line. It will not work. Maybe we should apply Occam's razor which states that, "All things being equal, the simplest answer is the best!

"An interesting fact, though, is this; every American Indian tribe has an accounting of a great flood. The Anasazi 'cliff dwellers' even built their cities high up in the mountains to escape the next one. I have also read that in the Ohio Valley, there were great stone mounds built that date back to 200 B.C. Ohio also has no natural lakes; they are all manmade."

Walters had seen the mounds in the past and had listened intently to the scientist speak of them. He felt that the scientists might be more comfortable around him if he acted interested.

Walters remembered something he had heard while at Northwestern.

"I was amazed to discover that a half million pounds of copper were excavated from Michigan's Upper Peninsula 5,000 years ago."(1)

Etienne rolled her eyes at Walters. When no one responded to him, she decided to make a statement to see if the scientists were excluding him or her on purpose.

Etienne spoke, "I have always wondered who lifted and fit the 100 ton blocks at Stonehenge."

Abrahams replied, "Please don't be obtuse."

287

Etienne knew her question was lame but she knew it was no worse than Walter's comment. She also had discovered what she needed to know she and Walters were definitely viewed as outsiders.

Winslow again asks a question. "I saw a show on golf where it explained that the dimples in the ball make it go twice as far as a smooth ball due to reduced resistance. I've always wondered why planes don't have dimples and whether alien ships do."

"They do." said Abrahams.

"And how big is our Milky Way galaxy?"

"It takes 27,000 light years to get from one end to the other."

Winslow again asks, "Is it true that right before we were preparing to shut down the Hubble telescope, that the view went blank? That it wasn't a mechanical failure but the telescope showed that all distant galaxies had vanished and that's why aliens were forced to come here?"

Abrahams smiles and says, "I've never heard that one but there is a theory that we are living in a hologram and everything we see is a projection. Maybe the camera shut down? Actually, in the end, the universe will stop expanding and contract into one giant black hole of gravity. It will compact everything into a ball the size of a house and when the energy gets so super-heated, we will have the big bang effect and start out all over again."

Op Virgil Huron asks, "Is it true that gargoyles and reptilians evolved from dinosaurs since some stood upright and had opposable thumbs?"

Abrahams replies, "No, they are not from here. Actually, the size of dinosaurs was determined by the amount of oxygen in the atmosphere. Our atmosphere is 21 percent oxygen, theirs was 35 percent."

Dr. Lai was a bit perturbed after having been interrupted so many times.

"It is as the soldier said when he interrupted me; there are so many instances of out of place artifacts found in geological strata.

288

These artifacts are found among ancient peoples' remains and are far too sophisticated and superior for their time period. I could give you examples all day. There are so many questions that need to be answered. If we could only answer these types of questions, we could probably explain many of our myths and religions of the world."

Dr. Abraham's speaks again.

"What if what we are finding and establishing as scientific historical fact is nothing more than past civilization's entertainment and story books like the fiction or fantasy section of a library or your DVD collection at home? We might be examining their trash! Perhaps the answers can be found in Hopi, Mayan and Tibetan folklore. They all tell of 'people' from twin stars that visit earth every 26,000 years. This occurs because of an alignment which causes a bending of the galaxy. This in turn, makes it a much shorter distance for them to travel than the distance a straight line would be. Think about this; Zeta one and two Reticuli are only 39 light years away and a billion years older than our sun. The twin star system of Sirius is only four light years away. A light year is approximately six trillion miles. Some believe that there is a 10th planet that orbits Earth every 3600 years. Its gravitational pull causes a pole shift, or the outer crust of the Earth to slide causing the oceans to wash over the surface which explains the Great Flood. (12)

"Einstein and Tesla proved that the laws of physics can be changed using electromagnetic fields. Maybe aliens are just time travelers who bend space or have mastered the gravitational pull of worm holes. (12)

"Yet we still use a product created 100 years ago, the radio, to search for life. In 1992, the U.S. spent 100 million dollars on the SETI Project to search for extraterrestrial intelligence. After a few hits, the project was shut down. Why did SETI search the universe using obsolete radio waves? Wouldn't you think the other worlds would be more advanced than this? Personally, I think we should lay low. They're bound to be more advanced than us and we have a long history of dominating inferior tribes.

"After billions of years, no two civilizations could evolve and be technologically equal. The search is not over though. I heard of a privately funded project which is carrying on the search. It is called Project Phoenix and is funded by Intel, Microsoft, Dell and Hewlett Packard. They discovered that radio waves break up into white noise beyond our solar system and search all spectrums of light and noise. It may have been forced to shut down after the events of last month. I'm sure its funding would be needed elsewhere."

Winslow also asks, "What country has the most UFO sightings?"

Abrahams replies, "I'll give you some facts. The U.S. 63, then France, then Brazil have the most sightings. Pennsylvania has the most by state. Eleven p.m. in October is the peak time and month. Most sightings have multiple witnesses and they get within 40 feet of the object before it whistles away leaving burn marks and tree damage. We've also had a UFO Officer assigned to all military bases since 1952!" (12)

Walters asks Abrahams, "Do you believe in heaven or hell?"

Abraham's replies, "I believe in what I can see and touch. Most of the biblical tales are just copies of older ancient Sumerian and Hindu stories regarding Adam and Eve and a savior. It's plagiarism! How about you?"

Walters's replies, "The Old Testament is only the story of the family of Adam, not the entire human race. There is no fossil evidence showing the morphing stages in between the changes to lead me to believe in evolution. Whole new species just appear. If we evolved from apes, then why are there still apes? There's no transition! In my heart, I fear the church is right about being the custodian of moral truth and that we all answer for our actions. I've seen and heard too many things that cannot be proven by science. One thing I do know; after how we treated Jesus the first time, I would expect something very different next time."

"It may have already just happened. Yet we have the exact same percentage of salt in our bodies as sea water," replies Abrahams.

Walters and Etienne were becoming very concerned with the path Abrahams was taking. They didn't want too much divulged to the soldiers and Abrahams seemed to have his own agenda.

Abrahams continued.

"If somehow a government could back engineer alien technology, they would be the superior power on Earth. That is why the U.S. 63 debunks and uses disinformation about UFOs and corporations continue to search privately. We have to dumb the populace down in order to protect our institutions!"

Walters swore under his breath. He had let Abrahams go too far and it was too late to pull him back.

Abrahams continued but in a different vein.

"As far back as 1954, President Eisenhower had a face to face meeting with the aliens at Edwards A.F.B. He had two more meetings in 1954 and 55 and we signed the Greata treaty.

In a speech to West Point graduates in 1962, General MacArthur spoke of an ultimate conflict between a united human race and a sinister force from another galaxy."

That was more than the Special Op could handle. He leaps from his seat to attack Abrahams. He shouts. "No U.S. general would ever say anything that stupid!"

The Captain grabs him by the collar and throws the soldier into his seat extremely hard. "Soldier, don't think I won't have you court-martialed if you do that again!"

Walters was glad for what occurred. It changed the climate from what Abrahams had previously said. His last statement made him lose all credibility with the soldiers. He had, in their eyes, attacked one of their own.

Walters thought about the footage of the Russian Cosmonaut that set the record for orbiting Earth. When they took him from his capsule, he couldn't walk. His arms and legs atrophied. They were spindly, like the way aliens are portrayed in movies. He couldn't help but wonder if the depiction of aliens wasn't correct since the cosmonaut lost bone and muscle mass being outside of the Earth's gravity.

Dr. Kaznir ended the entire discussion with a few well thought out sentences.

"I am not a very religious man but the Vatican made a statement I find very comforting. They believe that extraterrestrials are humanoids like us with both a physical body and a spiritual one. God's wisdom is infinite and so are the possibilities. In fact, the Pope made this comment that I will always remember. He said aliens are also the children of God. Do you think God is limited to this small planet? Do you think no others love the Lord? That they don't sin and fall as we do? That I believe we have in common with the ETs; a similar battle against Satan." (12)

Walters watched as a few soldiers and scientists and even Agent Etienne nodded their approval.

Abrahams leaned over and whispered, "The greatest story ever told!"

The silence was broken as the pilot spoke a few moments later, "Greenland, dead ahead."

Walters sighed, as he thought, "Not a moment too soon."

As he turned to his right he saw a cigar shaped UFO through the window. He turns to Etienne and says, "Look, do you see that?"

"I don't see anything."

"You have eyes but can't see it?" Walters slumps back and mumbles, "They probably view us like we view Iran. Like a cancer to be contained."

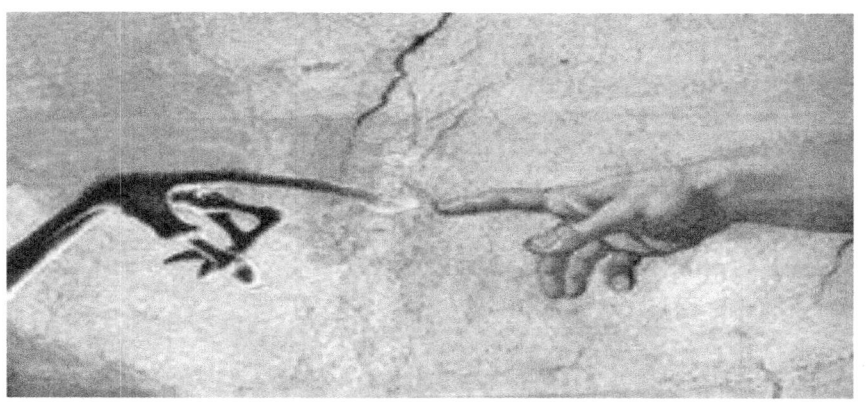

"Who's Your Daddy?"

In 1947, the Bulletin of Atomic Scientists created the Doomsday Clock in defiance to God's will that no man will know the hour or minute of the end and that it will come swiftly like a thief in the night.

Chapter 22

GREENLAND

"We must insist upon full access to discs recovered. For instance, in the L.A. case the Army grabbed it and would not let us have it for cursory examination."- J. Edgar Hoover - 1947

(Courtesy: Sandeep Karunakaran)

As the team's jet descends down to the runway, the group couldn't help but marvel at what they saw outside their windows. The heat from last week's blast had exposed much of the interior of Greenland, Alaska and the Arctic region. How fertile the land now looked. Dark brown soil had been exposed; soil from before the building of the Eight Wonders of the Ancient World. From before modern man and society as we know it existed.

As they exited the plane, Etienne says to Walters, "Look, a pack of wolves on the hillside; probably sizing us up for dinner."

Walters replies, "Funny thing about wolves. Wolves would scavenge off human scraps thousands of years ago and that's how we chose them to domesticate. Dogs were bred from wolves yet wolves won't make eye contact. Dogs do. Dogs hunt individually, wolves in packs. Wolves are smarter than dogs yet wolves have thinner skin which is odd since they live out here. A wolf the same size as a dog has a larger brain and 20% larger head and teeth. Wolves are problem solvers and can escape from cages. Dogs don't. Wolves..."

"Enough about wolves already!" Shouts Etienne.

The team flew by helicopter to the excavation site. At the base of the site which was on top of a hill, they found a team of six French "scientists" who had claimed the find for France.

Both Walters and Etienne look back in the direction they flew from almost like hikers that look back at the path just conquered. They both became suspicious of the French immediately. They looked awfully athletic for scientists. Walters figured they were probably members of the French Foreign Legions Intelligence Division. He could see they had some scientific demeanor, but he also knew enough to realize that an entire team of scientists could not be built like a team of U.S. Navy Seals. He wondered what kind of game it was that France was now playing.

The French had long been the United States' most vocal enemy. They viewed Americans as teenagers that should listen to the more adult European nations with their long histories of culture and civilization. They believed France should be the center of the world order and the U.N. of the world. They had convinced the other European countries into forming the European Union in order to stand up to the U.S. It had been quite a blow to them when Britain's 75 million citizens, and the world's sixth largest economy, had voted to accept statehood from the U.S. after withdrawing from the E.U. in 2016.

France had gradually become a Muslim nation. For generations, the French prided themselves on being a color blind society. Large numbers of North African Muslims immigrated to France. France's economic policies of limited work hours, social welfare, and restrictions on competition lead to joblessness and unrest in French communities. When rioting broke out, the French blamed unidentified structured gangs on the violence. They passed laws protecting the Islamic extremists and laid out economic incentives and social funding to spur integration. Soon, the same radical Muslim leaders who had been expelled from the country were leading an election in a French country of more than 70 million people where African and Muslim immigrants made up a majority of the population. (26)

The French had long politicked for a sharing of all alien technology. They knew the U.S. had possessed it and we weren't about to share.

After nearly an hour of negotiating, the two teams decided to work together and share the find with what had recently become a very desperate world. Advanced technology or a new medicine could be of great importance at this time. Both sides now worked together, albeit like a bad marriage, with both sides being wary of the others every move.

As they prepared to walk to the find, Walters heard the two teams of scientists talking.

The French were discussing a UFO sighting in Montreal where 40 guests at the Bonaventure Hotel had seen a 6,000-foot wide UFO pass overhead. It caused a nearby military base to experience a power outage. The French were blaming the U.S. for this. Abrahams was yelling something about the U.S. having better things to do than bother with an inconsequential area like French speaking Canada. Another French scientist then blamed the U.S. for cluster UFO incidents within the last forty years. Twice in Mexico in 1991 and 1992, and once in South Korea in 1996, the sightings had occurred.

Dr. Kaznir did not want the French to gain the upper hand and mentioned the Shag Harbour, Canada, incident of 1967. A UFO crashed into the water where it submerged and traveled underwater to the Shelbourne Submarine Listening Post. The U.S. Coast Guard cutter, Sir William Alexander, reported the sighting and a search and recovery mission was started. Fishermen reported seeing a large "aluminum" piece lifted from the sea. U.S. tracking satellites photograph everything from space.

Kaznir states that, "perhaps the French Canadian government stole it."

He also added that half of all UFO sightings have been made around water where the object enters or exits the water. Naval sonar has tracked solid objects in the ocean traveling at four times the depth and four times the speed of anything in our Navy. (25)

Walters froze as he recalled being on an investigation off Bodega Bay on a 90-foot dragger when it snagged something large. The object came up and bumped the hull with a loud metallic knock. It then twice dove pulling the stern about 20 feet under as a warning to cut it loose. The crew complied out of fear that the third try would submerge them.

As Walters listened, he couldn't believe how supposed learned men could get into a contest of he said-she said. The French were on the attack and blaming the U.S. for interfering in Tehran, Iran, on September 19, 1976. Walters smiled as he listened more intently.

As the disagreement continued, Walters remembered seeing film of a cluster UFO sighting in Utah in 1952. It showed a larger craft breaking into a dozen smaller craft which then flew, in formation, like a string of pearls. There were no contrails from the craft. He thought back to what he had heard a French scientist say a few minutes ago. Each time there were cluster UFOs sited, an Earth change or disaster then followed. He racked his brain trying to remember if any UFO reports had been made before the asteroid hit last month. He recalled none.

The U.S. 63 scientists were now trying to blame the French for a number of incidences at Air Force bases. They mentioned Wurtsmith in Michigan in 1975. Loring in Maine and lastly Malmstrom in Montana. They knew the French had nothing to do with these occurrences but they had to fight the French allegations as everyone calmed down.

The hike to the find was short as light snow started to fall. Walters had been right. The cylinder was only a few hundred yards from their touchdown area. He was glad that the great explosion had melted most of the ice for traveling to the cylinder was fairly easy.

The first group of four Special Ops reached the find followed by Walters and the scientists. The other soldiers and Etienne brought up the rear. Walters immediately walked up to Davis and six well-armed Navy MP's who had formed a perimeter around 30 yards from the cylinder. He shook hands with Davis and his men, thanked them and told them he would take over. Walters was glad Davis understood protocol and left without an argument.

The cylinder was about the size of a house, only wider. It measured at least fifty feet wide by thirty feet high and was partially buried. The cylinder was lava black with a satin finish. It seemed to be glass smooth and beautifully oval in shape; like an egg. The first four Special Ops set up a perimeter, which was now only twenty yards from the cylinder.

The ten scientists and remaining Special Ops approached the cylinder while the two agents stood back where they could better observe everything.

On the outside of the cylinder there was a charcoal gray seam, which resembled a doorway. It wasn't immediately visible. The scientists stopped and began to study some markings carved above the handle which appeared to be made of rubber or a polymer. (12)

Walters could hear the two groups of scientists yelling at one another. He also heard the click of four safeties being released from four M-15's. This was followed by the clicking sound of two pistols. As Walters reached the cylinder, he saw the Special Ops drawing down on two armed French scientists. He yelled at them to stop this foolishness and Captain Northrup, who had been on the perimeter, came running. He told his men to lower their weapons and the French did the same.

Walters was angry.

"What the hell are you soldiers doing?"

Doctor Johan turned to face him.

"The French are playing games with us. Read that inscription above the door and look at the fossilized boot prints in front of the door."

Walters was glad the nuns had made him take French at Sacred Heart. The inscription was written in French. It read "Amerique Terre" which he knew meant "American Soil".

One armed French scientist spoke.

"What kind of a prank is this? You can't claim this, it wasn't found on American soil! President Datchet has not yet annexed Greenland."

An angry Johan then spoke.

"What are you talking about? You set us up. It is written in French!"

Walters knew he had to calm the situation. He spoke to everyone.

"The U.S. 63 government gave me full control here. I can't tell you French what to do but let's look at this logically. It makes no sense for either of our countries to have written this. I can only assume it is a third power trying to cause discord among us; in the hopes of gaining this find for themselves.

Doctor Kaznir spoke.

"I know the Russians patrol these waters. Perhaps they came upon it but had no means to investigate it."

They all agreed and put down their weapons. It struck Walters as odd that no one made mention of the fact that the French scientists were armed.

Dr. Lai was looking intently at the metal that covered the cylinder. His axe made no indentation on the material and easily bounced off. He used a small scalpel to scrape off a sample. He put down his kit and shook his head and face palmed in disbelief.

"It's not the Russians. It doesn't correspond to anything in the Periodic Table. How could this be?"

No one responded to him, for they were all intent on opening the hatch on the cylinder. One scientist from each team grabbed the handle and pulled. The hatch groaned as it pulled from its place of confinement. It took two more scientists to pull it totally open. They stepped back as the smell of ammonia and the fear of poisonous gas gripped them. There were four gasps as daylight shone into the cylinder. They froze in amazement as Dr. Jones entered first but jumped back as if pushed by some unknown force. The air had cleared and was now cool and sweet smelling. Dr. Johan now stood behind Dr. Kaznir. As they entered, there was a soft hum inside like the ambient sound of the nature CD's you can buy at the mall. The floor was blue-gray and the walls had hieroglyphic symbols covering every inch of their black inner curves. The inside of the craft was huge; much larger than the outside should allow it to be. This is called the Nordwag effect.

Special Op Winslow accidentally discharged his weapon inside the cylinder as his hand flinched nervously. The report ricocheted off the walls causing green sparks.

As they shined their five million candle power Vector spotlights inside the cylinder, four bodies were displayed in glass beds in suspended animation. There were two males and two females. The most amazing thing of all was that they were human!

NASA had sent Dr. Kaznir because he was a noted medical doctor and the French had a doctor who had been sent from GEIPAN. The two worked together to see if they could provide any assistance to the inhabitants. Two were deceased and in a state of fossilized decay. The doctors worked in unison to revive the other two. The male awakened first. It seemed much warmer now inside the cylinder. A strange hallucinogenic sensation seemed to grip the entire crew as if caught in some vortex of new age energy.

Dr. Johan screamed loudly.

"My God! Those words above her pod, they are from the Bible. I believe from Isaiah 28:10, 'Caulacau, Saulasau, Zeesar.' What does it mean? Jesus whispered those words to the Apostle Thomas.

He said the existence of the universe depended on these three words. Thomas told the other apostles that they would stone him if he told them their true meaning. No one really knows what they mean. But him, he knows!"

Johan runs towards the male inhabitant like a madman. Kaznir holds him back with one arm while two Special Ops restrain Johan. He screams again.

"You know, what do the words mean?"

Kaznir yells angrily.

"Get him out of here, so we can help this man!"

As he is taken out of the cylinder, Johan yells again. "This has to be a hoax. This can't be real. What does this all mean?"

Etienne attempts to comfort Dr. Johan while the two soldiers stand next to him. Walters walks towards Dr. Lai, who had been doing a carbon-dating test with a portable version of the equipment.

"Any results yet?"

Lai eyes Walters suspiciously but then finally speaks.

"I guess it doesn't matter if I tell you, although I'm not sure if I believe these results myself. The results read 50,000 years old."

A French scientist heard Lai's pronouncement. He turned to face Lai.

"Do you think we are fools? First the writing outside the cylinder, then your scientist goes into 'histrionics' over supposed Biblical writings. Now you say this 'whatever' is 50,000 years old. The southern half of my country was liquidated by the blast nearly two weeks ago. Do you really think we have the time and resources to be treated like cuckolds by you? We don't need your games and your 50,000-year-old supposed alien or whatever you are trying to pass him off as. We are leaving now. Doctor, get your equipment, we are going. I'm tired of being the brunt of this U.S. 63 joke."

Walters smiles largely in hopes the French leave. The doctor aiding Kaznir protests to no avail. In 15 minutes the French had packed up all their equipment and were helicoptered to a waiting French ship moored along the coast.

Walter's team was glad to see them leave. Captain Northrup commented, "The French are only good for surrendering anyway!"

Walters was totally surprised by what occurred next. Captain Northrup had been sent recall orders for six of the Special Ops. The soldiers had been ordered back to their base in Iceland. It seemed to Walters that the French had been the militaries chief concern. Since they were gone, most of the Special Ops were also sent packing.

A few minutes later, a wild-eyed Dr. Kaznir burst from inside the cylinder.

"Northrop!"

The captain put down an advanced cell phone device he had been speaking into.

"What's the problem, Dr. Kaznir?"

Kaznir began to speak at a rapid pace.

"Where are the soldiers who restrained Johan?"

Northrup spoke calmly.

"They were recalled to Iceland. Why?"

"What is wrong with you military? Don't you read? FEMA lists UFO protocol in their manual in chapter 13. It states that, 'anyone who comes in contact with a UFO must be quarantined.' This would include your men and the pilot unless he is the one who returns for us. Call the base and make sure those men are quarantined and tell them to send us a helicopter with special medical equipment."

Kaznir asks Dr. Lai to help him inside the ship.

"Dr. Lai, besides humans, do other species wage war?"

"Yes, chimps and spider monkeys are the only other species that attack their neighbors besides man. Only, they never make peace. The feuds go on forever. And of course, ants. They are the most warlike creatures on Earth. Red ants will raid a black ant camp and steal the pupae to raise as slave workers."

"Do you think these creatures are trustworthy?"

"I think there is an order to the universe regardless of whether you believe in God or not. Good and evil battle every day. Plato and Socrates believed that there is a voice deep within our soul that guides us."

"Only some people listen better than others!"

"Yes, I'm sure there are greedy aliens and generous ones. Left wing and right winged ones taking bribes. Power always corrupts. I'm sure they are no better or worse than we are."

They both laugh as Kasnir says he'll be sure to look for their wings.

Etienne leaves a calm Johan and walks up to Walters.

"Did you know the UFO protocol?"

Walters looks at her.

"I wasn't playing solitaire on my computer on the flight here. Kaznir was partially right but his quote came from the FAA and NASA manual. As strange as it might sound, there is also protocol instructions found in the Air Force guidebook as well as the firefighter's guide in all 63 states. The information is there if one knows where to look."

Etienne shakes her head in agreement.

"I know, I read it on the way here, in the NASA guide."

Walters smiles as he begins to survey the scene. Johan was sitting on the ground drinking water and thumbing through the Bible. The captain was communicating with the base in Iceland. The remaining two Special Ops were stationed directly in front of the cylinder. Kaznir and Lai were inside continuing their attempt at reviving the two aliens. The only person missing was Abrahams. Walters cursed himself for letting him out of his sight.

Walters stepped into the cylinder past the two scientists and into an antechamber. It was in this chamber where he saw Abrahams feverishly pushing buttons.

Abrahams was talking to himself.

"There's nothing here, nothing!"

303

Walters speaks to Abrahams.

"There are two aliens in the next room, or don't you care?"

Abrahams replies bitterly, "Does it look like I care?"

Walters answers, "Definitely not about aliens."

Abrahams says, "Leave the physiology to the others, it doesn't concern me."

"What does concern you, doctor?"

"I think you know. I had an inkling on the flight here that you knew something. I'm not a fool, Walters; I knew you and Agent Etienne were watching my every move. What did you think I was a 70–year-old terrorist? No Agent Walters, you have nothing to fear from me. Just as I have nothing to fear from you."

Walters knew that Abrahams was not just a scientist. He could lie and manipulate on a dime's notice. The other scientists had a hard time not telling scientific truths aided by stats and data.

"How do you figure that? I'm in charge here; you have to listen to me."

Abrahams chuckles to himself.

"Don't make me laugh agent. My security clearance makes yours look like the equivalent of the federal employee you were introduced as; a postman."

Walters is seething and Abrahams knows it.

"Don't get angry, Walters; I'm not here to undermine you. You can tell the others what to do and they'll listen. I should probably explain why I'm even here today."

He points to a jutting piece of the framework.

"Take a seat, it's a long story. Don't worry about the others; it usually takes an hour to get the aliens coherent after we revive them."

Walters folds his arms and leans against the wall.

"Go ahead, I'm all ears."

"I know you are familiar with the Roswell incident. Shortly after the crash at Roswell, which was at that time our only nuclear base, the supposed 'weather balloon' was flat bedded to Wright

Patterson. The base was the T2 or technical branch of our military. One year after the crash at Roswell, an interesting thing happened. Three engineers filed patents for flying disks.

President Eisenhower commissioned the Jason Society in order to find out the truth regarding the alien question. It was made up of 32 of our most prominent minds in America. The control group inside the Jason Society was the Majestic Twelve Group. It consisted of 12 experts in their respective fields. All of which dealt with some aspect of this phenomena. The group was not accountable to the judicial or legislative branches and most definitely not the old FBI. MJ-12 ordered the Kennedy assassination along with the twenty two material witnesses that disappeared the following two years.

I'm sure you realize by now, that I am a current member of the Majestic Twelve. We funded our activities by controlling the drug trade throughout the world. We meet in Pennsylvania at the Country Club which is accessible only by air. We unfortunately also had to kill RFK when he threatened to expose us. The NSA was formed to protect the secrets regarding the flying disks.

You probably don't know that we have been trained in UFO retrieval procedures. I have done so many of these; it is becoming old hat for me. But with everything that is occurring now, we felt this might be a special find since it is so old. Alas, we were wrong. The technological aspects of this craft are nothing new to me.

In Area 51, we developed the U2, SR71 Blackbird and Stealth fighter. The Aurora fighter is a stealth bomber with a pulse detonation wave engine that flies twice as fast and high as the current stealth bomber. We're saving its introduction for when we might need it. There are still nine disks that are stored there and being back engineered. We used their communications system to make contact with the Tudors. They've given us some technology but they play games and are not reliable.

In 1953, our government made the release of any UFO info by military personnel a crime punishable by a $10,000 fine and ten years in prison. We obviously didn't prosecute for what doesn't exist, so we then go after the whistle blower by saying and staging that he's involved in terrorist acts and it's a matter of national security. I can tell this doesn't come as a big surprise to you. Why is that?"

"I read a lot. I assure you, you didn't waste your time and you definitely filled in the blanks. Still, as early as 1950, President Truman said, and I quote, 'I can assure you that flying saucers exist and are not constructed on Earth.' That kind of said it all for me."

"We've had numerous Projects in MJ-12. Project Aquarius documented the 50,000 year alien interaction with us. Project Plato opened up diplomatic relations with them and secured a treaty which exchanged technology for abductions. Krill was their ambassador. Project Sigma established communications. Project Sign was to determine if they were a threat to our national security. In Project Red-light, we flew a recovered craft but crashed it killing our pilots. In Project Snowbird, we built our own and flew it. In project Moonbeam, we proved that our moon and Mars' moon Phobo's are both hollow. I can go on and on."

"I take issue with the high number of UFO sightings and abduction cases reported. "They" would never need that many to accomplish their goal. I also don't think their similar physiology to ours could survive a deep space flight."

"Who says they're all from deep space? I hope you realize, Agent Walters, that this is not a James Bond movie where the villain relates his nefarious plot and then must kill Bond to shut him up. The world has changed in more ways than you can imagine. Your problems that were of utmost importance last month mean little today. Who knows if any of us will even see tomorrow? Feel free to relate anything I told you to your partner, if that would make you feel better. I have the feeling that the Majestic Twelve will soon go the way of the Vatican; relegated to the dust bin of history."

"So your trip here was a waste."

"For me, yes it was. There is no technology here that I hadn't seen before. I think the others are fairly excited. They have a new toy to play with. We should be getting back. Your partner probably thinks a big bad alien got us."

Walters and Abrahams walk to the front of the cylinder. The other three scientists had begun to talk with the alien. Etienne stood outside in front of the doorway. Dr. Johan had been allowed to rejoin the group.

Although the male was fully awake, the female was still in a coma. The man appeared to be totally human in his physiology. Except for the lack of body hair and his elongated skull with two odd small horns, he could have been a member of the team questioning him. Strangely, some saw him as tall; others as short. Some saw him as thin, others as stocky. Each seemed to have an opposite view of his appearance. This also happens to some people when reading the same passage from the bible. Some see completely different words in the passage.

Peru and Bolivia have the greatest number of ancient burial sites on Earth. Many graves have been found with artificially produced elongated skulls where boards are strapped to infant's skulls to create the effect. Prenatal elongated skulls were also found suggesting that the tribes were mimicking a ruling ancient race.

The three scientists were peppering him with questions. They were surprised to find that he understood English. This made them very skeptical of the man. The scientists wanted an explanation.

Dr. Lai played a trump card immediately.

"Your craft is 50,000 years old. How do you explain that to us?"

The man says, "I am prepared to explain everything to you. I always knew that the day would come when I must tell our story. I came to this world after leaving my home planet, which had annihilated itself. Ours was a female dominated society."

He pointed to the female in the coma and says, "That one, she was our leader."

The scientists could see the disgust in him when he referred to her. They simultaneously asked, "What are your names?"

The man answered, "I am Indrid. She is your Heiness."

He resumed his tale.

"There were thirty eight of us originally in the ship. When we crashed here, the ship was badly damaged but this pod was unscathed. Twenty three of us survived and we were able to salvage some supplies and medical equipment. We knew we could never leave this world. One hundred and twenty ships were able to leave my planet, Heaven, to colonize the galaxy. We were not fools that day we disembarked on our journey. We all had accepted the fact that ours was a one-way trip. Unfortunately, there was nothing to return to."

Dr. Kaznir then spoke. "What happened to your planet, Heaven as you call it?" Dr Kaznir could hardly contain himself.

"We had a vision, from the savior, Maria Christo. She gave us instructions, which we then followed. Our blind obedience resulted in a world war."

Dr. Lai interrupted him.

"That is the same thing that almost happened to my home country, China, a little over three years ago. Thankfully, cooler heads prevailed and our world survived at least till this point."

"I feel our results were different than yours because ours was a false prophet. We were tricked by her and our need for a higher power to govern our lives. She said we must follow her instructions if we were ready to finish God's work. We must branch out to the four corners of the galaxy and spread God's word like missionaries."

Dr. Johan could not contain his excitement.

"His world also believes in God! His world goes by the name of Heaven!" He excitedly told the others. He then asks Indrid, "What do these three words above everyone's pod mean?"

Indrid replies, "Caulacau, Saulasau, Zeesar mean that the Kingdom of God is found within you."

Indrid smiles a wry smile and continues.

"Prior to Maria Christo's arrival, we experienced a season where storms and severe weather were alive. Tornados would chase our vehicles and turn when we turned. They would target homes and people who were fleeing. We sensed that something ominous was about to occur. Upon her arrival, she gave us the advanced technology to travel beyond our planetary system. We had been to Marto and Vento but not to Junto or Sato. When we got out to the edge of our solar system, our shields were not safely keeping out the radiation. Reports were also being received from Amerique Terre that war had broken out. She was the false prophet, the Antichristo!

All 120 ships with 4,560 crew members of our world's best scientists, athletes and doctors raced back from this mission. We lost communication upon entering the atmosphere and upon landing, everything was different, primitive. Our world had vanished or was on another plane or dimension. Each ship had only members of their own culture and three political systems; democracy, socialism and communism. We were instructed that this was the divine way. I can see from your crew that all races mix and work together. Upon landing, we were able to communicate with the other ships. Based on their coordinates, our people with dark skin landed here, yellow skin here, ourselves here."

Dr. Johan pulls up a global map on his phone and Indrid points to Africa, China and Europe. Johan exclaims, "That's amazing, our races are in the same locations!"

Indrid says, "That's because we are your parents; your progenitors! We were your first civilization. You are more than a unique accident. You were engineered! Rather than constructing monuments, we incorporated the proof in your genome which will last as long as you do. There is a coded message in your DNA from us."

Dr. Johan exclaims, "What gave you the right to manipulate another species? How could you know the consequences? Were we not more than just cattle to you?"

"When we landed here, we set up camp. The species of human we found were not much more advanced than the animals. We genetically engineered our DNA with theirs. You are undoubtedly the product of our work. We used our advanced knowledge to speed up your evolutionary process. The species we had first encountered were dangerous and of low intelligence. We felt we needed to advance them. We felt the need to make them more intelligent so we could co-exist. Soon, they worshipped us like Gods. Everything that happened; storms, lightning strikes, failed crops, were all attributed to us. To them, we became the Gods of air, fire, wind, reproduction. It was pathetic. We even gave some thought to ending the experiment and starting over again with more of our DNA and less of theirs. Some of us even took advantage of our new found power. We mated freely with their females. Their off-spring was even more advanced than we made them. They were semi-Gods."

Dr. Johan asks, "Could you cure all diseases and give us clean, free renewable energy?"

Indrid responds, "I could but I won't. That's your test to ethically help yourselves. I fear we've done too much. Over there on the wall; we cut a tablet with our lasers. Just in case none of us survived. It contains all the knowledge and technology that you could dream of. It appears to be a brief legacy of our race and history. But, when you are technologically advanced enough and take another look at it, you'll find that there is a three dimensional science manual hidden inside this tablet. Of course, you'll need quantum computers to decipher it. Until then, you are still evolving."

Dr. Lai turns toward the others and says, "Like the Bible, no human could've written it. Were the miracles of the Old Testament made by advanced technology? Is the Bible a Rune stone, a

Rosetta stone or better yet, an alien artifact? An extraterrestrial time capsule!" (6)

Indrid says, "I know not of your Old Testament. Once a society enters the digital age, there is no longer a written record of their history. When an advanced society collapses, it's like hitting delete. I suspect that there have been many societies on this planet and others but they have left no primitive written footprint. Many societies lose the ability to manually write. That's why we cut you a tablet."

Dr. Kaznir spoke.

"We must take them back to the base in Iceland; there we can help the woman."

Dr. Abraham's spoke.

"Do you even begin to realize what this would mean? This would tear the fabric of society apart. In December of 1960, the Brookings Institute in Washington D.C. published an analysis of the Implications of the Discovery of Extraterrestrial Life. They wanted to know if the public could handle the discovery of alien life forms. Guess what? They concluded the public couldn't."

Lai answers him. "That was almost seventy years ago. We hadn't even been to the moon. Things change and there's not much society left to be torn apart."

Abraham's responds. "People don't change. Also, look at what you are going to ask them to believe. Not only are there flying saucers with aliens piloting them. That is just the tip of the iceberg. Now you want them to accept the fact that not only did they evolve from monkeys but that little green men provided the missing link. Try telling that to the Fundamentalist Christians. They wouldn't boycott the news agencies; they would burn them to the ground."

"As a Christian, Dr. Abrahams, I see your point. You must realize, the more open minded of the Christians have accepted a hybrid evolution/creationism."

"You mean "Intelligent Design". The open minded Christians, Dr. Johan, are not the ones I fear."

311

Kaznir mediates. "Let's get them to the base and then we can debate later. You have to realize this operation was clandestine from the start and the base couldn't be more remote. If we don't want this find released, believe me, it won't be released."

Indrid had been mildly sedated for the flight. The scientists felt it best that as few people as possible know the whole story. The pilot would be briefed later when they were all in quarantine. Indrid and the woman were taken to the base's medical facilities. It was there that Indrid continued his story for the four scientists as well as Walters and Etienne. Walters noticed that Abrahams seemed bored by this all; chances were that Abrahams had already heard many stories like this.

"I can see by the fact that all but one of you is male, that yours is a male dominated society." says Indrid.

Etienne whispers to Walters. "He can sure say that again."

Walters responds to her with a wink.

"As I said before, ours was the opposite. Your species here was also male dominated prior to our intervention. I can also see that your technology is based on what you can see and create. There is another form of technology based on vibrations, antigravity magnetic fields and the power of the brain."

Dr. Johan can no longer contain himself and blurts out, "You mentioned God before. If you believe in God, how could you tamper with us and leave our souls intact?"

Indrid responds to him, "Yes, we believe in God. Life is abundant in your universe. We once believed we were the beginning and the end of everything. How ignorant we were to think that God would only create life on one planet. We began to pick up electromagnetic impulses all over the universe. When our time came to depart, we went in all directions; navigating to the nearest planets. There are 1000 billion galaxies out there with 200 billion stars each. As I said before, life is abundant and each will be tested. It's all a test. How you react during the test is all that counts. What you do will define the person you are. Your soul lives many lives on many planets. How could you develop your soul in just one lifetime? Everything you do, you say, you learn, is accumulated in your soul. That is why you find some people to be better than others. We all live every type of life. That is why there is so much diversity. You mentioned the soul. God is in you. You are his church. Advancing your evolution here didn't alter your souls. That is because you will live every type of life eventually. God gives you your soul; your mind which is separate from your brain. He doesn't concern himself with your body or appearance. Does that answer your question doctor?"

Dr. Johan can handle no more of this.

"I can't listen to any more of this. You have totally disavowed everything I ever believed in. I can't process all this change in my belief system. I need time to think and I need a drink."

Abrahams speaks. "I too doctor, let's go to the officers' mess and have a couple of stiff ones."

Walters grabs Abrahams' arm.

"You can't go there, you're under quarantine."

Abraham's roughly shakes his arm free.

"You're right Walters, I forgot, forgive me."

He begins to walk away but turns back toward Walters and whispers, "It's really much ado about nothing. There really is no need to quarantine. We found that out long ago, but I'll play along for you."

As the two scientists slip from the room, Walters hears Lai ask a question.

"Indrid, not to be rude but why does the female have a bulge in her pants? This is very unusual."

"Yes we noticed the difference with your females. Our females have their vaginal tube on the outside. It protrudes ten to twelve inches as well as another eighteen inches on the inside. It is lined with flowing veins and follicles that pulse and contract. It is not unusual for us to stand and face each other and couple without

313

even moving our bodies. We call it 'tubing'. Your species was different and your DNA was dominant in that area."

"Tell us about your society?"

"In my world, the females were always the smarter and more aggressive of the sexes. They also retain the memories of the past three generations. They know everything their mother, grandmother and great grandmother experienced. As with the laws of nature; female insects and fish are always larger and more aggressive than males. They control everything. The more power we gave them, the more they took and abused. Although the males were stronger, our gender was more docile, more dependent. We were obviously needed for reproduction and as workers.

"In our world, we lived by the 20/40 rule. At 20, a male or female will live with a more experienced 40-year-old. This was important training. The 20-year-old must learn all they could from their mentor. This lasts for 10 years. Our DNA is made up of our experiences and those of our ancestors. At 30 and 50, you are free to mate with whomever you are compatible with at that age difference. We have four mates in our lifetime. Children are abundant and there can be no divorce. If you harm your mate physically or psychologically, you lose all privileges until the ten years are up. That is why I am so angry, and so unhappy. This female took me from my mate.

"We had detected a comet on a collision course with your planet. It was visible in the daytime sky. We made a decision and formulated a plan to attempt to survive its destruction. To survive, we would climb into the pod. A problem arose because there were only four chambers in the pod and twenty three of my people. All of us were previously evaluated for overall breeding and superior traits and genes. My wife was number six. Therefore, she would not be amongst the saved. The two superior males, I and another male, and the two superior females would be saved. The other 19 had to be left outside to perish. I had no say or choice in the matter. I argued that all of us should enter the safety of the pod and emerge

314

after the strike. We would take our chances as a group. The females calculated a low probability of success and that the four would certainly survive. Tears streamed from my eyes as I and the other male climbed into the pod. The two females would be last to enter, as befit their place in our society, since they were in charge. The 19 we left behind tried to be brave but their sobs and cries of mercy rang in my ears as the hatch to our chamber slowly closed. The two women, who were to be saved, were very mentally strong and the cries of mercy didn't affect them in the least. As I waited for the blessed sleep to come, I damned that woman to any hell that there was on your world or for that matter, the entire universe."

He became quite agitated and tried to get off the examination table. Dr. Kaznir gently held him down.

Indrid yelled now.

"It is a cosmic joke that we are the only survivors. I would rather have perished than be with you woman! Do you hear me? Death would have been better than a life with you!"

Dr. Kaznir feels he has no choice and gives Indrid another mild sedative. Indrid begins a restless sleep.

"Dr. Lai, I fear we have no choice. If we are to save the woman, she will need a blood transfusion. Based on my tests, Indrid's blood will be compatible."(14)

"Kaznir, I hate the thought of using this man's blood to save the life of the person he despises the most in the entire universe. But for the sake of science, and what we can learn from this species, I'll help you."

"Good, the less people who know about these two, the better for all of us. She is strong, evidenced by the way she fights to keep from slipping back into her coma."

The doctors then wheeled their two patients into an empty operating room.

The female was still clad in her neoprene outfit with full headgear and her breathing apparatus still attached. Dr. Lai looked at the woman's terrific shape and wondered if this woman could still be beautiful without any hair on her head or body and that strange elongated skull. After they completed the transfusion, the two doctors left the room to allow their patients to rest. Walters had been standing outside the door as the doctors left.

Walters was surprised they had both left and yelled at them.

"Where the hell are you going?"

Lai answers, "We haven't eaten in 24 hours. We are famished. There's no need for quarantine."

"What about them?"

Lai answers, "They are sedated. We're only getting a snack and we will be back in 15 minutes. The door is unlocked if you want to look in on them."

Walters shook his head. He would never understand scientists. They had made the discovery of a lifetime and all they cared about was feeding their faces. He hoped Etienne would return soon and went down the hall to look for her but never let the door to the operating room leave his sight.

Indrid's physiology was so advanced from the trans-alien upgrades given to him in order to make the space trip that the sedative wore off much earlier than it would on a human of this current generation. He got up and locked the electromagnetic door to the operating room. He then disconnected the gas jets in the room. Once he had done this, Indrid then opened all the valves and filled the room with gas. He glanced at a framed document on the wall. Upon closer inspection, he read the words, "We hold these truths to be self-evident, that all Men are created equal, that they are endowed with certain unalienable Rights..." He then smiled and said, "I have seen the reel of life over and over again and civilization always repeats itself. We stole the light from the Gods and were punished. We were then punished by kings and then big government and then socialism but individualism always wins out." He then laid back down on his gurney and looked towards his adversary. Indrid mumbled an unintelligible curse towards her and then his eyes welled up with tears. The tears were not caused by the gas but were tears for his long dead wife.

The female then awakened from her coma and leaned to her right. Her helmet came off from her sudden movement and crashed to the floor. The sudden noise temporarily stopped the man's sobs of despair. He raised his head to see what had occurred. The woman turned to her left. As she began to cough, she saw a face she had longed for. She saw the face of her husband. The male was astonished to see his wife and began to panic. He realized that somehow she must have overcome the chosen female leader and had taken her place after the other three had gone into suspended animation. (14)

Kaznir and Lai returned in twenty minutes and tried to open the locked door. Kaznir was puzzled when it wouldn't open.

"Walters, did you lock this door?"

Walters became alarmed as he approached the door.

"No. Why, what's wrong?"

Dr. Kaznir says, "It's locked. It's not a problem. The commander gave me this access card to open the doors in this wing."

Dr. Kaznir took the access card and slid it through the entry slot. The lock electronically sparked and disengaged.

They had slept through our Middle Ages and Renaissance Period and they had no knowledge of Shakespeare or Da Vinci. Like the heartbroken Romeo who could not live without his Juliet, so to the alien male could not live without his true love. As the operating room exploded, their hands attempted to touch one last time. It was to no avail. Their love that had lasted through nearly the entire history of mankind on this planet, while they were locked in their separate cubicles, ended as it had been throughout those 50,000 years. So close but never touching. (22)

The truth about our past, and life in space, went up in a blast of fire. Lai and Kaznir assumed it was an equipment malfunction that had caused the destruction. Walters, who was troubled by the locked door, felt that Abrahams had some role in it. None of them would ever know the true reason that our fore-father and mother, and the hope they provided, would not be revealed to mankind. Amidst a world filled with hate and fear, it was only fitting that the absence of love in the end kept a world from discovering a much needed hope. As humanity prepared for the next mini Ice Age, we continued to repeat the same mistakes over and over again.

The team, including the pilot, was released from quarantine.

Walters spoke softly to Abrahams as they were walking out.

"I guess all your concerns are moot now. There's no proof that any of this ever happened."

Abrahams smiled sarcastically.

"To everything there is a season; a time for truth. The pod will be reported as being a French hoax. SETI will announce that it has located a verifiable, repeatable signal very far away and that no contact has been made or is possible. I told you, they couldn't handle it."

Walters snickered. "I guess we'll never know."

"If there is one thing I've learned, Agent Walters, it is never say never. Remember, UFO stands for a Un Funded Opportunity." Abraham's walks away.

Etienne walks up behind Walters.

"What were you talking about?"

Walters turns to face Etienne.

"I guess they had a dark secret they didn't want us to expose. No pun intended, Anise."

Etienne couldn't help but smile a slight smile. She didn't appreciate what Walters had said, but he had actually used her given name. Etienne knew she could cost him his job on any given day for remarks like that. But she understood his bitterness. With his credentials, Walters should have been a Director long ago. Instead, she knew he fought a glass ceiling for white males.

As the two walked outside, Etienne says to Walters, "Did you know that Hitler had commissioned Buffalo Bill's Wild West

Show for a shooting demonstration by Annie Oakley? He put a cigar in his mouth and she shot it out of his mouth. Years later, during WWII, she wrote him and asked for another try."

Walters laughs and says, "College grad. That's a true story but it was 1889 and Hitler would've been a child. It was Kaiser Wilhelm II that she used her Colt 45 to shoot a cigar out of his mouth. If she had killed Wilhelm, history may have played out different for Hitler who was in the infantry in WWI and might have died or never had any of the opportunities he did."

"Guess you just can't alter destiny."

They approached a crowd looking up at the moon. Etienne slipped her arm inside Walters'. As they reached the gathering, they looked up at a sliver of perhaps one eighth of the moon illuminated. The moon had been full a few days earlier and the agents had forgotten that the world was awaiting a view of the "dark side of the moon" since it had completed a slow full rotation; it's first due to the asteroid impact. They saw nothing special but could hear the others shouting that there were lights on the "dark side of the moon"; perhaps a city.

One man said, "It's been over sixty years since we landed Apollo on the moon. Funny how we never went back. Not even the Soviets who were in space before us or the Japanese. No country has gone back."

Another woman in the crowd said, "I saw a documentary where they said that the moon landing was staged in New Mexico; it never happened! It sure did happen, one time only and we were told not to come back or risk the repercussions of violating their territory!"

Walters took out a small pair of binoculars and focused his sight. He turned to Etienne with an ashen colored face with a big smile and gave her a full frontal hug and said, "Let's go. You're not going to believe this."

"Where are we going to go? We're in Iceland! Don't tell me that those cris-crossing jet contrails in the sky are a defense shield against UFOs!"

He took her hand and quickened their walk pace. Etienne looked at Walters in a different light. Her thoughts raced.

At Joint Chief Admiral Byrnes' bunker, he sat alone sipping a martini and watching the 1939 "Wizard of Oz" classic movie on DVD. As the phone rang, he reached for the TV controller to lower the volume just as the Wizard said, "Pay no attention to the man behind the curtain". . . .

In 2003, the Trilateral Commission had met with the entertainment, newspaper and television industries. Their findings concluded that in order to avoid the race riots of the 1960s and build up female and minority self-esteem, all mass media needed to show females and minorities successful in traditional white male roles. There would be no bias towards gay or inter-racial relationships. This plan became evident in sitcoms, news commentators and even sports announcers. All TV shows further portrayed all groups interacting as equals. The school system also followed suit in order to get their federal funding. The EEOC and Affirmative Action also fell in line. The demographics of the country were changing. Divorces were up, women were heading households, and minority birth rates far exceeded whites. The most effective way of changing the structure of society was to do it silently. Manage the media and you can change everything; as long as you do it covertly. No announcement was made, just a simple policy change to go from conservative to liberal and break down barriers with the politically correct mix with respect to race and gender.

How times had changed in the last thirty years. To make up for past mistakes and guilt, society thought two wrongs would make it right.

Etienne wondered who would have to pay for these mistakes in the next 30 years but had other thoughts on her mind at present.

More importantly, the days of trivial arguments, frivolous lawsuits and racial tension were over as we moved towards a North American Union where there is no majority race and limited federal government. The states through their Governors ruled for the people. The U.S. Congress and Senate was no more. The Governors voted on the Administrations Bills and Governors would run for the Presidency ending the non-productive two parties in-fighting and wasteful spending. The federal government's role was solely defense and trade policies.

Numerous cement trucks and workers worked around the clock to seal off the entrance to the 129 DUMB's where the POTUS and many others fled to in safety. They were viewed as betrayers who left the "above grounders" alone to die. Pulse weapons and lasers were setup all around the hollows of Clarksburg, West Virginia and at all locations in wait for the return of the POTUS and his Vril society and the ensuing war with them.

The "aliens" would clean up the environmental damage, teach us their religion, cure our immune systems and set the stage for the *Great Deception*.

Etienne recalled President Ronald Reagan's 1987 speech to the former U.N. General Assembly where he said, "I occasionally think how quickly our differences worldwide would vanish if we were facing an alien threat from outside this world". He was right. We faced our alien threat, only it came from the forces of nature. The time to unite as one human race is now!

"1,000 years of peace and tranquility will follow for the human race". . . Nostradamus

Chapter 23

THE FUTURE

**"Our faith in the present dies out long before
our faith in the future."** (Ruth Benedict)

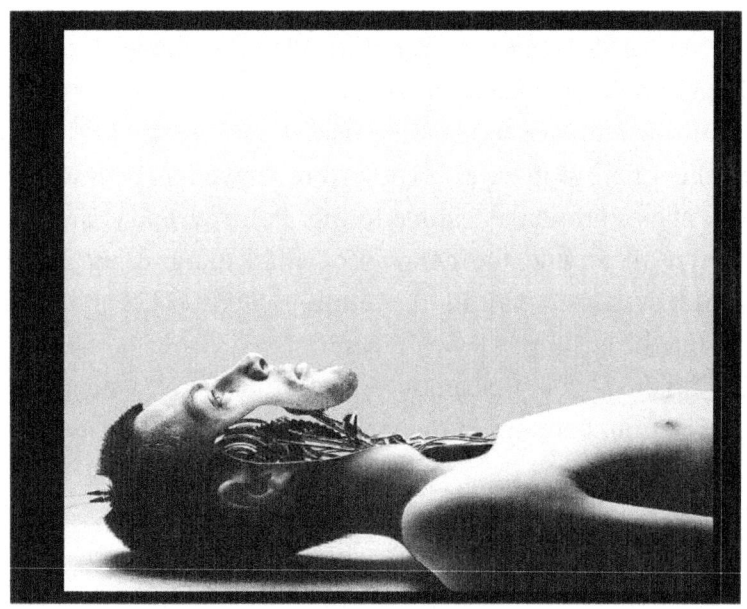

Life in post apocalypse will either usher in a new era of improved living or a new crisis that ends humanity. Cities and public transportation will be green and efficient or they will look exactly like they do now since there is no money for massive reconstruction. A golden age of trans-humanist nanotech and biotech will follow. Alcohol, tobacco, firearms, drugs and prostitution will all be legal since that is what the masses want; not what the federal government or God wants. Decriminalization always results in less use, not more and reduces the high cost of prisons for victimless crimes.

Newspapers, magazines, bill boards, food boxes, stop signs, menus and applications will all use electronic paper that is fully animated and will direct your attention. Holographic entertainment will be in everyone's living room. Simulated reality will allow travel and shopping anywhere in the world. Artificial Intelligence will replace the need for lawyers, accountants, banking and internet inquiries.

All genetic diseases will be eliminated by DNA sequencing scans and Nano therapy that will direct tiny particles to attack cell walls of cancer and other diseases. Nano weapons will be used to disorient but not destroy. Nano robots will be programmed to build and software will be a family's largest expense. Life expectancy will grow to 130 and all families will adopt a one child preference. Seniors will be respected for their memories and life experiences. Spare body parts will be grown and extinct creatures will be resurrected.

Bionic athletes will compete against pure humans and then against robots as robots are advanced to perform dangerous jobs and their hard drives and mobility surpass our brains and reflexes. Generation "Cyber" will break all Guinness and sport records. Robotic concerts will perform perfect music. The robot industry will dwarf the auto industry. Astronauts will be transhuman since it is the only way to make the long flights.

All vehicles will be self-driving using auto pilot and electric then solar then hydrogen as water will be used as fuel by burning the hydrogen and releasing the oxygen. The reason dinosaurs were so large was because there was a higher percentage of oxygen in the atmosphere. Desalination plants and pipelines will be built to make water abundant for all. The use of water for fuel will offset rising sea levels due to global warming. Vehicles and homes will have solar skins to power them and cars will be driven by GPS and later will hover over roads using electromagnetic.

Biometric scanners will be used everywhere for security and contact lenses will activate search engines as a built in I-Cloud in your eye in this PG or post Google era. Bathroom mirrors will perform complete DNA scans every morning. Brain to brain chips will create a singularity and be as common as business to business. TV news will come from YouTube and Facebook not CNN since people will prefer and believe the unverified version rather than the sensationalized TV version. (31)

Our greatest challenge will be the genetic modification of humans. It will start with the military in response to the Chinese military upgrades. First we will create a humanlike robot and then design a human brain. We will simultaneously upgrade humans for war by slicing genes from other creatures that upgrade us against cold, heat, injury and increase our strength and speed. (33) This is where the moral questions will arise if the public is even made aware of the programs. How hard is it to recruit soldiers whose parents have passed on or have no siblings? How hard would it be to use unwanted children for this purpose? Thirty thousand people a year disappear in the U.S. and are never heard from again. Where do they go? They can't all be abducted by aliens or kidnapped for human trafficking into sex trade. What if 32,000 or 33,000 disappeared? Who would notice the increase since there are 225,000 "missing persons" reports yearly?

As far as employment, three and four day work weeks will be the only way to have full employment if there isn't a natural or man-made disaster that reduces population. With 150,000 people entering the job market and millions still looking for work, a non-manufacturing consumer spending economy will not support full employment with the technologies that are coming. Most jobs lost recently were mid salary while most jobs gained have been low salary. Our military will downsize by 500,000 through the use of drones and rapid deployment super soldiers. Automation, high tech and Internet based solutions will also replace many workers. If we don't deal with our immigration situation or have the courage to make major social service changes, we will have a twenty percent real unemployment problem for the next twenty years until the baby boom generation passes on. All citizens will be given a living wage or "social security now" at age 18. It will pay for minimum food, clothing, legal drugs and housing. It will be up to the ambitious to find work which will be difficult due to automation and robotics.

I used to think that our future cities will look totally different and that progress keeps moving forward like the lie of evolution but I now realize that that will never happen here in the U.S. due to social spending programs. I suspect that NYC will look exactly the same 100 years from now. The only changes will be technology not structural. No culture can have the top 20% supporting the bottom 40% and expect to advance forward. The U.S. will stagger along unless there is a natural or man-made disaster that forces us to re-construct. We seem to be becoming comfortable with handouts instead of motivating people to succeed.

The greatest threat will be in a non-belief in God and that we already have.

THE MUFON FILES (PT. 1)
AN INTERVIEW WITH JOHN VENTRE

Photo: Los Angeles Times, February 25, 1942 - "The Battle of Los Angeles"

Chapter 24

WHAT IF

By Andrew P Napolitano (courtesy)

**"People should not be afraid of government.
Government should be afraid of its people."**

"What if freedom is illusory? What if our rights didn't come from God or from our humanity, but from the government? What if the government thinks we are not unique individuals with immortal souls, but just public property? What if we were entitled to our natural rights only if it pleased the government? What if our rights can be stripped away anytime the government considers us to be the enemy?

What if this could all be accomplished with the consent of the people? What if the people's own representatives subverted the Constitution? What if the people were so afraid that they accepted the subversion? What if government demonizes an external enemy and uses fear to suppress our freedoms? What if people are afraid to protest?

What if threats become imminent dangers because the government allowed them to happen?

What if the government can lock you up indefinitely? What if government has passed laws that allow you to be detained without a lawyer or hearing? What if you were speaking out and the government came to silence you? What if the government could declare you its enemy and kill you?

What if the real war was a war of misinformation? What if the real threat to your freedom is an all-powerful and all seeing government?

What if when the danger got more threatening, the government asked you to give up more freedoms? What if you fell for it?

What if you ended up in an internment camp? What if the government broke its own laws? What if I'm right and the government is wrong? What if it is dangerous to be right when the government is wrong? What if the government is wrong?

What if this is actually happening? What if freedom is the ultimate target of the war on terror? What if that includes you? What would you do about it?"

. . . . From Andrew P Napolitano "It is dangerous to be right when the government is wrong".

Authors note: I would add; will the U.S. Government confiscate all guns, gold and silver during the coming pandemic? Will the U.S. military fire upon U.S. citizens that resist? They did at Kent State and Waco! I believe the NSA and CIA are the biggest threat to the domestic America I grew up in. Who is John Galt?

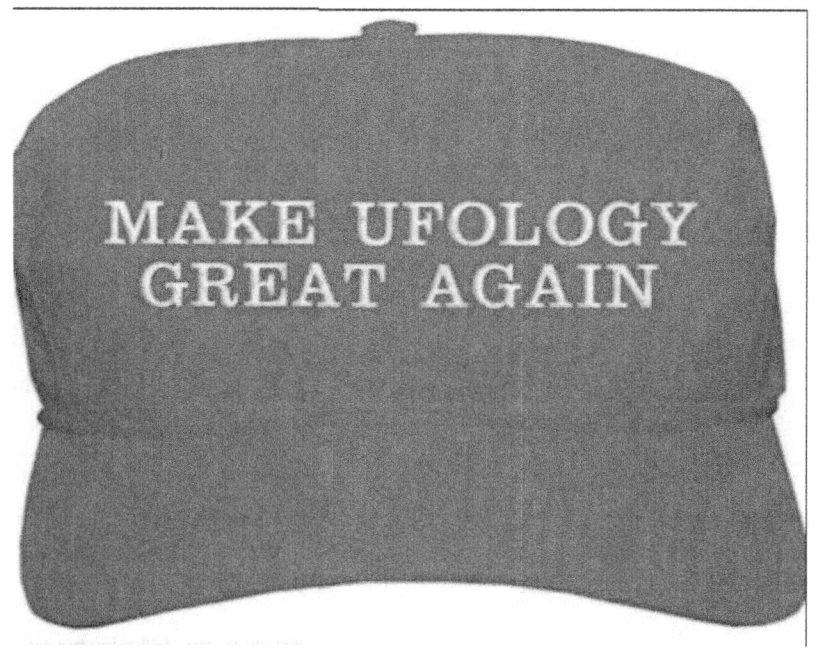

Chapter 25

About the Author

"Success can be measured by the obstacles overcome."

John Ventre was born in The Bronx, New York in 1957. He attended college at S.U.N.Y. of Farmingdale and C.W. Post. In high school, he had a 91 average and maintained a 3.8 during his time spent in college. John never finished his senior year. He elected to get a full time job and get married.

John married his first love who he had met while in high school. They divorced sixteen years later. While married, John was blessed with two children; Nolan born on Long Island in 1984, followed by Vanessa, also born on Long Island two years later. John would have liked to remarry and have two more children. He would've named them Cole and Claire.

John has lived in New York, Oklahoma, New Jersey, Pennsylvania, and has traveled most of the U.S. and Europe. He grew up poor in The Bronx, Brooklyn, and Queens. As a nine year old, John used to write his own Star Trek stories after watching his favorite weekly show. He would love to role play and act out his own scenes from movies and play fight. His first job was as a paperboy at age eleven and he has worked ever since.

John retired in 2012 as the PA, VA and WV State Security and Public Affairs Director for UPS and is a member of the FBI's InfraGard group and the DHS Regional Business Coalition. John was the PA State Director for the Mutual UFO Network for 10 years. John is also a lifetime member of the NRA and his Rotary club Pres. John sits on the Board of Directors for JDRF and the Westmoreland Economic Growth Connection and was his companies' liaison to Congressman Tim Murphy and was elected to the Republican Committee. John is also a Tocqueville Society member for charitable giving. John is the co-inventor of the Thor Wood Splitter and owns the UFO themed Mexican restaurant trademark for "Flying Salsa".

John appeared in the Discovery Channel's *"UFOs over Earth"* series in 2008, the History Channel's *"UFO Hunters"* in 2009 and the *Anderson Cooper show* and Discovery Canada in 2012, Destination America's *"Alien Mysteries"* and History's *"Ancient Aliens"* (cameo) in 2013 and H2's (History) *"Hangar 1: The UFO Files"* and PCTV21's *"UFOs over Pittsburgh"* which changed its name to *The String Theory of the Unexplained* and "Close Encounters" for Discovery Science in 2015. John has appeared on numerous radio shows and hosts his own show on *Liveparanormal.com* and is a speaker at various UFO and Paranormal conferences such as the *MUFON* and *Paradigm* Symposium's, *UFO Congress* and *Fortean* Conference's. John has also lectured at Duquesne and Drexel Universities on UFOs along with the *Wizard World Comicon* in 2015. John gives eleven different lecture presentations: *End Time Prophecy, The Case for UFOs, UFOs in Art and History, The Chronology of UFOs, Anderson Cooper and the Case for UFOs, UFOs and the Media, My Haunted Life, Kecksburg Solved, the String Theory of the Unexplained, Eerie Pa* and the *2008 Pa UFO Wave.*

John plans to donate some of the proceeds from this book to the Juvenile Diabetes Research Foundation. He doubts the controversial content will be widely published and intended this work for friends and family. He doesn't recall ever reading a book from a divorced male's viewpoint. John still hasn't gotten over the trauma of his unsuspected, unnecessary divorce and never fully trusts in a relationship. That's how he protects himself.

Although he was raised Roman Catholic, John firmly believes in God and Jesus but also believes in Saint Thomas' Gnostic view that God is found within us. One does not have to go through a church to have access to God. John believes that all religious institutions have completely missed the point. There is no reason to fear God. We need to fear Satan who is real but the church seems to have edited him from their sermons. Religions, and some people, are more interested in what they can get from God instead of just protecting their soul. No religion can murder over differences in religion.

John is of the belief that one chooses their life based on their past mistakes. A person lives many lives. We shed our bodies like clothes and just put on a new life. He believes that predestined roadblocks will be thrown in your way throughout life but that you have the free will to make a choice. He believes we are not human beings having a spiritual experience, but spirits having a human one, over and over again until we get it right. The fact that some people can "speak in tongues" may prove that we have lived many lives. John actually learned more about religion by researching this book than in years of catechism. John also wonders if we are not just a vessel or body being used by someone else. Our mind or consciousness might not be our own. The split personality between the animal and angels inside us is the soul which enables higher thinking.

John originally wrote a version of this story, in 1996, while working on assignment in Florida. He sent copies of this story under the title "Khrushchev's Revenge" to ghostwriters and movie studios, only to be rejected.

Books with similar themes were published in 1999. A movie also followed with many similarities to his original storyline. Since he didn't copyright the original story, he made a grave mistake.

John had chosen the title from a phrase, "Hitler's Revenge", which referred to society's downfall from becoming diversified and mixed. There are racial and religious overtones to the story for the purpose of making it more controversial; similar to the "Passion of Christ" movie.

Lately, there doesn't seem to be free speech in public or in schools or workplaces due to political correctness even though nearly everyone might privately hold the same opinion. Truth seems restrained in public. This deeply disturbs John and goes against the very grain of this country. In 1789, James Madison said, "The People shall not be deprived or abridged of their right to speak, write, or publish their sentiments. The freedom of the press shall be inviolable." One would think that new ideas should be as intoxicating as a new lover.

John believes that in our lifetime and prior to 2029, that there will be a man-made influenza outbreak that will kill fifty million Americans. Many of these victims will be the elderly and sickly with weak immune systems. This is how we will "get out" of our debt with legacy and social service spending. There will be many questions as to whether it was an engineered outbreak or natural.

In 2005, John rewrote Khrushchev's Revenge with the aid of Ronald Draftina, and fashioned it into "*12/21/2012 A Prophecy*". There were only five other 2012 books listed on Amazon.com at the time but that evolved to over 200 by the year 2012. John references this book at his UFO conferences and as a guest on various radio shows. After being asked numerous times, "What are you going to say when nothing happens in 2012"? John replied that he was working on a new book called "The Day After 2012". John liked the title and published his second book in 2011. The strange thing about his first book is that eight of the predictions in that book actually came true. They are:

On page 2 the main character is watching a TV show named "Switched at Birth". This show actually aired on ABC in Sept of 2011.

Page 8 discusses $5.00 per gallon fuel which occurred in 2009.

Page 12 discusses the Supreme Court ruling that the Second Amendment is a right and not a privilege. The actual Supreme Court ruled 5-4 that same way in 2010.

On page 14 John wrote that the housing and financial markets would collapse in the summer of 2008 and they did.

On page 30 the main character reminisces about a movie where all the old time action stars; Stallone, Schwarzenegger, Willis, Van

Damme, and others unite in an action movie. That movie, the "Expendables", actually was released in 2011 and 2012.

On page 44 John discusses the problems with Wall Street greed which we all experienced during the 2009 recession.

On page 160 John described a craft that is found that resembles the one found by the Swedish Ocean X dive team in the Baltic in 2012.

On page 346, the legalization of drugs.

In chapter 9, John quotes a January 2012 *Wired Magazine* article regarding the NSA's data center. He brought this up on the April 2012 *Anderson Cooper Show*. Anderson scoffed at the government monitoring our emails and calls. All media and politicians said the same when the story broke in the spring of 2013 yet the first publishing of this book was Dec 21, 2012 and the story is here four months before it broke. Why didn't the media and politicians know or were they lying?

John also mentioned building a wall that Mexico will pay for. Did President Trump read the first edition of this book for his campaign?

John's life has on many occasions crossed into the realm of the paranormal. In the scientific and medical communities; "the paranormal" is believed to be the mind playing tricks on you. Could a mild form of psychosis, like in the movie "A Beautiful Mind", be the answer for millions of believers? Many times in his life he has asked his guardian angel for non-financial help. Each time, he received his wish. John believes you can visualize and ask for help and receive it when the intent is pure.

In 1988, while working in Europe on assignment, John tried to move his return flight up by one day from December 22nd to December 21st. He had spent Thanksgiving in Germany and wanted to get home for Christmas a day early. Due to the cost of changing the flight, John decided to stick with his itinerary. The next morning when he boarded the flight, the passengers were abuzz about the flight that crashed the previous day. John was out of touch with the news. He later learned that the flight was **Pan Am flight 103**, the same flight that he tried to change his flight to! During that same week John turned down a promotion to Europe as UPS's Security Director for Spain and Portugal since his wife refused to move to Europe. The man who took his place went on to become UPS's International and later Corporate Security Director in Atlanta.

Since this was John's first book, he initially believed in ancient alien theory that we were genetically upgraded since evolution doesn't add up. He viewed the soul as separate from the body and belonging to God. That opinion changed in 2014 and 2015 after a demonic attack upon him in his home. John came full circle back to God. My theories cannot be found in scripture of which I am poorly versed.

"Some of the most important men in the U.S. are afraid of something. They know that there is a power somewhere so organized, so subtle, so pervasive, so watchful, and so complete, that they better not speak above their breath when they speak in condemnation of it."- - - President Woodrow Wilson

John J Ventre
Pennsylvania, USA
2012

A Letter
To My Great Grand Children:

Hopefully you know of me. God bless you because God put you here. As long as you have grandparents, parents, children and pets, you'll be loved. The world you inhabit is vastly different than the one I grew up in. You have better technology and medicine. The one I grew up in was a white male dominated America that got things done and was the world's super power and believed in God. I hope China is not in charge in your time. China is a communist dictatorship where people have very few rights. America is gambling that we can build up China and increase trade yet China increases its military while we have fallen into debt and our people want socialism which kills motivation. Politicians need votes so they give the people what they want; not what they need. Your parents and grandparents grew up under the threat of terrorism. Their parents grew up under the threat of nuclear war. I hope you have better leaders and are not living under the threat of bio-engineered and nano-technology threats.

My America was white male dominated who were hard on everyone including themselves but we had low crime and an exaggerated media fake news belief that racism was rampant. Affirmative Action was a quota system where the ends justified the means and discriminated against Asian and white males in violation of the 14th Amendment. Instead, what was needed was the elimination of race and gender questions from all applications. Everything this world is was created by Europeans and Americans. As I write this, whites seem to be on the decline population wise due to their own birth self-control and common sense and your world will be well on the path of multiculturalism and diversity. I was a third generation immigrant and my two children, Nolan and Vanessa, were the first Ventre's to earn a college degree. I attended excellent public schools on Long Island and my children did the same in Northern New Jersey which now seem to be in decline again due to quotas and a lack of discipline. My generation and my parent's generation had pride in America yet it now seems to be under attack by left wing liberal groups and minorities. The school system and media seem to rewrite history or ignore the truth only to attack America which is the freest and kindest country on the planet. We rebuilt Germany and Japan after WWII; no other country had ever been so generous. We contribute more per person to charities than any other country. We are portrayed as greedy hostile racists by the media and academia. The media sells out for viewership and Politicians for votes. They are the two ends of the same stick and both are corrupt. I believe a patriotic President will arise. Do the research and find out the truth for yourself. Believe your lying eyes. America has been good to the five generations that got you here; stand up for America, freedom and your Constitution! I am a self-made millionaire who started working at eleven and is at peace with himself and with what I have accomplished; mainly on my own. I have never received any government assistance and I hope you never do either.

My father's side of the family was butchers and cooks. My mother's side of the family was steel workers. Always work hard and never lie, cheat or steal. Compete; be a little better than the next person but don't brag. Everything you do comes back at you. Trust no one but family. Most people are like floor wax; shiny on the outside but lacking depth. People vote for who they like and then require no more from them than themselves. Stay away from gambling, drugs and alcohol. Respect the Ten Commandments and the Bill of Rights. The Kingdom of God is within you. When you do things for the right reasons, you are in the Kingdom of God. Respect the police, military and adults. Love your parents and children. Protect your inheritance even though nothing given to you is worth as much as something earned and work to live; don't live to work. And I hope I was able to see you get born. (32)

LOVE,
Your Great Grand Father
John J. Ventre

"The world is neither good nor evil; it's just controlled by money"

My dog Apophis can sense spirits and has alerted me.

My Child...

You may not know me, but I know everything about you. Psalm 139:1 I know when you sit down and when you rise up. Psalm 139:2 I am familiar with all your ways. Psalm 139:3 Even the very hairs on your head are numbered. Matthew 10:29-31 For you were made in my image. Genesis 1:27 In me you live and move and have your being. Acts 17:28 For you are my offspring. Acts 17:28 I knew you even before you were conceived. Jeremiah 1:4-5 I chose you when I planned creation. Ephesians 1:11-12 You were not a mistake, for all your days are written in my book. Psalm 139:15-16 I determined the exact time of your birth and where you would live. Acts 17:26 You are fearfully and wonderfully made. Psalm 139:14 I knit you together in your mother's womb. Psalm 139:13 And brought you forth on the day you were born. Psalm 71:6 I have been misrepresented by those who don't know me. John 8:41-44 I am not distant and angry, but am the complete expression of love. 1 John 4:16 And it is my desire to lavish my love on you. 1 John 3:1 Simply because you are my child and I am your Father. 1 John 3:1 I offer you more than your earthly father ever could. Matthew 7:11 For I am the perfect Father. Matthew 5:48 Every good gift that you receive comes from my hand. James 1:17 For I am your provider and I meet all your needs. Matthew 6:31-33 My plan for your future has always been filled with hope. Jeremiah 29:11 Because I love you with an everlasting love. Jeremiah 31:3 My thoughts toward you are countless as the sand on the seashore. Psalms 139:17-18 And I rejoice over you with singing. Zephaniah 3:17 I will never stop doing good to you. Jeremiah 32:40 For you are my treasured possession. Exodus 19:5 I desire to establish you with all my heart and all my soul. Jeremiah 32:41 And I want to show you great and marvelous things. Jeremiah 33:3 If you seek me with all your heart, you will find me. Deuteronomy 4:29 Delight in me and I will give you the desires of your heart. Psalm 37:4 For it is I who gave you those desires. Philippians 2:13 I am able to do more for you than you could possibly imagine. Ephesians 3:20 For I am your greatest encourager. 2 Thessalonians 2:16-17 I am also the Father who comforts you in all your troubles. 2 Corinthians 1:3-4 When you are brokenhearted, I am close to you. Psalm 34:18 As a shepherd carries a lamb, I have carried you close to my heart. Isaiah 40:11 One day I will wipe away every tear from your eyes. Revelation 21:3-4 And I'll take away all the pain you have suffered on this earth. Revelation 21:3-4 I am your Father, and I love you even as I love my son, Jesus. John 17:23 For in Jesus, my love for you is revealed. John 17:26 He is the exact representation of my being. Hebrews 1:3 He came to demonstrate that I am for you, not against you. Romans 8:31 And to tell you that I am not counting your sins. 2 Corinthians 5:18-19 Jesus died so that you and I could be reconciled. 2 Corinthians 5:18-19 His death was the ultimate expression of my love for you. 1 John 4:10 I gave up everything I loved that I might gain your love. Romans 8:31-32 If you receive the gift of my son, Jesus, you receive me. 1 John 2:23 And nothing will ever separate you from my love again. Romans 8:38-39 Come home and I'll throw the biggest party heaven has ever seen. Luke 15:7 I have always been Father and will always be Father. Ephesians 3:14-15 My question is...will you be my child? John 1:12-13 I am waiting for you. Luke 15:11-32

Love, Your Dad
Almighty God

Courtesy Barry Adams

337

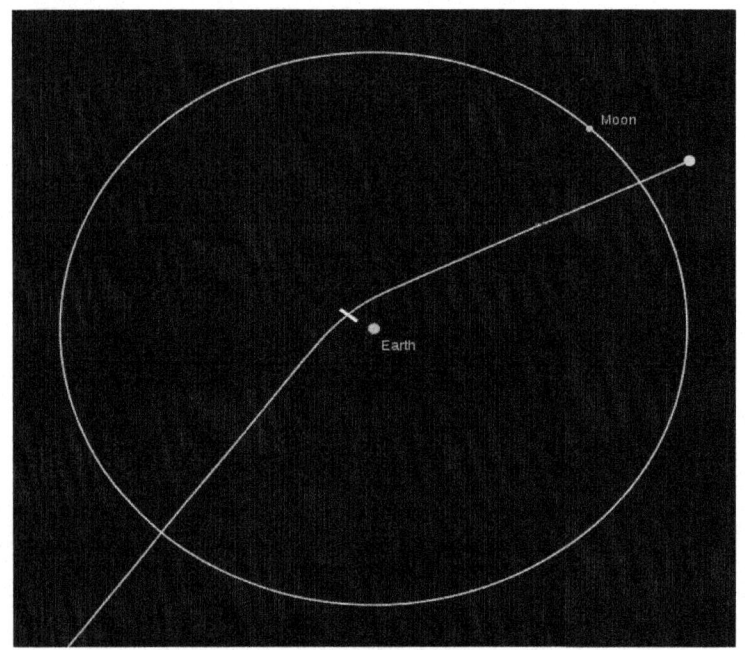

Path of Apophis in 2029

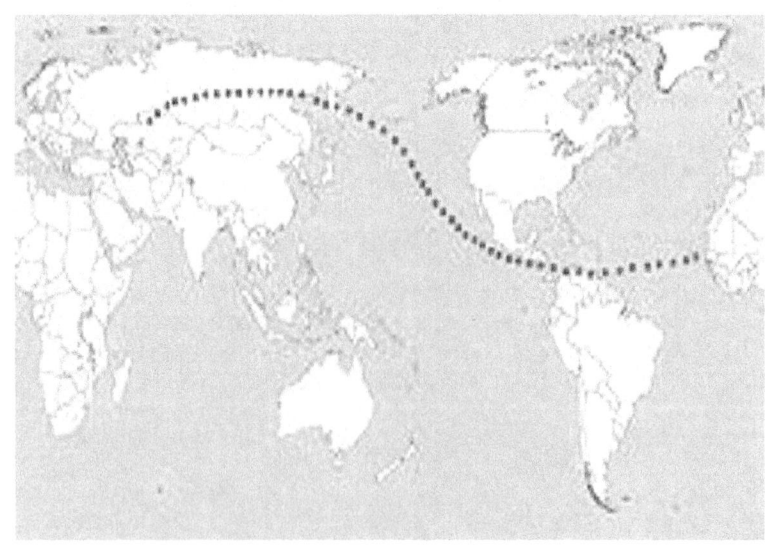

Path of Apophis Impact

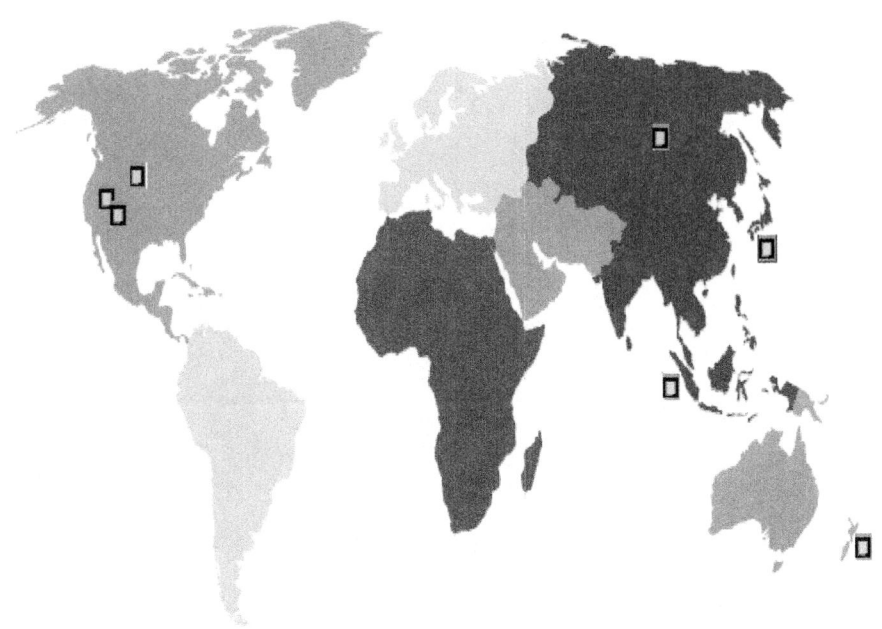

Super Volcanoes around the World:

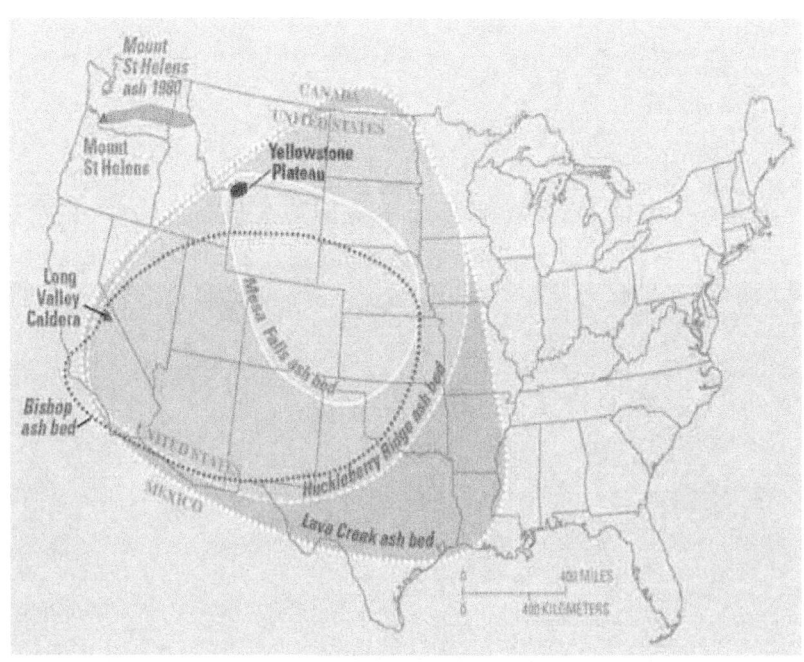

Potentially Active Volcanoes of Western United States

Bellingham

▲ Mount Baker

Seattle ▲ Glacier Peak

WASHINGTON ● Spokane

Great Falls

▲ Mount Rainier

MONTANA

Mount St. Helens ▲△ Mount Adams
Portland

Billings

▲ Mount Hood

△ Mount Jefferson

Three Sisters ▲ Bend
Eugene ▲ Newberry Crater

IDAHO

△ Yellowstone

△ Crater Lake

OREGON Boise △ Craters of the Moon

Casper

Mount Shasta ▲ ▲ Medicine Lake

Pocatello WYOMING

Cheyenne

Lassen Peak ▲

Reno

Clear Lake △

NEVADA Salt Lake City Denver

Sacramento UTAH COLORADO

San Francisco

▲ Long Valley Caldera

CALIFORNIA

Coso △ Las Vegas

Santa Fe

△ San Francisco Field

Albuquerque

| ▲ | Volcano active during past 2,000 years |
| △ | Other potentially active volcanic areas |

Los Angeles ARIZONA △ Bandera Field

San Diego Phoenix NEW MEXICO

0 100 200 kilometers
0 100 miles

Tucson

USGS

Topinka, USGS/CVO, 1999, Modified from: Brantley, 1994, Volcanoes of the United States: USGS General Interest Publication

Credit: BBC, USGS.

340

OR

(Courtesy Stanley Simmons)

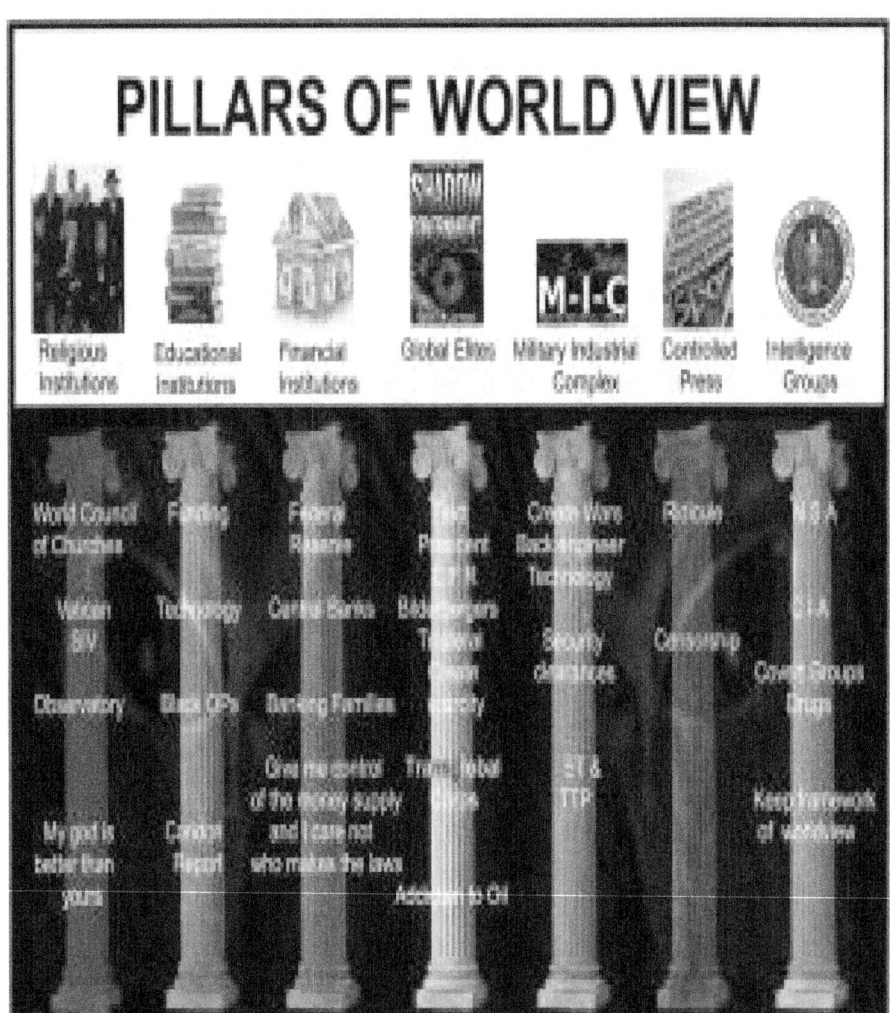

PILLARS OF WORLD VIEW

1. Religious Institutions

- Planetary division though belief in a <u>God spell</u>.
- Religious leaders acting as intermediaries between man and the Gods just as they did during the Sumerian era.
- Religious dogma used to keep people in a state of fear and obedience.
- The Catholic Church once believed the Earth was flat, the solar system revolved around Earth; control of 1.2 billion minds.

- The unsavory behavior between priest and children; "do as I say, not as I do".
- My God is better than your God.

2. Educational Institutions

- Every museum has 2 doors.
- The removal of historical artifacts.
- Promote Angels, not ETs
- Elite control over Universities.
- Carry out religious agendas in schools
- Carry out policies formulated within the <u>Condon report</u>, <u>Robertson Panel</u> and other false flag operations to demystify UFOS.
- Only brightest students are recruited into <u>Black Ops</u> or special military programs.

3. Financial Institutions

- <u>CFR</u> – Control of the Federal Reserve.
- <u>FED</u> is privately owned.
- <u>Fiat currency</u> – world loans for geopolitical control.
- Central banks control transfer of world money, drawing governments into debt.
- <u>US $ 1.7 Trillion</u> drawn from US treasury by military – Black Ops; without congressional oversight.
- Elites leverage humanity into a predetermined worldview.

4. Global Elites

- Weave between the Politics, Economic and Military structures, holding interlocking directorates.
- Economic, Politic and Military have an uneasy alliance based on a community of interests "Military Metaphysic" creating a permanent war economy".
- They are members of CFR, Bilderberg, Trilateral Commission and secret societies.
- Create scarcities; maintain our addiction to oil and a world of shortages.

- They receive the benefits of back-engineered ET technology; some used as exotic weapons.

5. Military Industrial Complex

- Made up of military subcontractors – some are household names.
- Guardians of back engineered ET technology.
- Operate without congressional oversight.
- Part of the Shadow Government
- "Can take ET home" – Ben Rich – CEO of Lockheed Skunk-works

6. A controlled Press

- Censors and directs world news on behalf of the elite.
- Promote elite's favorite election candidates.
- **Used to ridicule break-through discoveries that threatens 'elitist' interest's i.e. cold fusion**
- Ridicule UFOs and contactees to protect the oil industry.
- Keep humanity in a state of fear and obedience.
- The Press shapes society's Worldview.

7. Intelligence services

- Operate a world wide web of ET craft surveillance, telecommunications and anything that poses a threat to the elites.
- Operates counter intelligence programs against contactees, including military abductions [MILAB]
- They comprise of several covert agencies within their compartmentalized organization.
- NSA has remote neural monitoring systems that can track the electromagnetic footprint of individuals as well as influence brain patterns.

(With permission from Neil Gould)

"I CAN ASSURE YOU THAT FLYING SAUCERS, GIVEN THAT THEY EXIST, ARE NOT CONSTRUCTED BY ANY POWER ON EARTH."
PRESIDENT HARRY S. TRUMAN,
April 4, 1950, White House Press Conference

"BECAUSE OF THE DEVELOPMENTS OF SCIENCE, ALL COUNTRIES ON EARTH WILL HAVE TO UNITE TO SURVIVE AND TO MAKE A COMMON FRONT AGAINST ATTACK BY PEOPLE FROM OTHER PLANETS. THE POLITICS OF THE FUTURE WILL BE COSMIC, OR INTERPLANETARY."
GENERAL DOUGLAS MACARTHUR
October 8, 1955, New York Times

"I WOULD LIKE YOU TO ASSUME PERSONALLY THE INITIATIVE AND CENTRAL RESPONSIBILITY WITHIN THE GOVERNMENT FOR THE DEVELOPMENT OF A PROGRAM OF SUBSTANTIVE COOPERATION WITH THE SOVIET UNION IN THE FIELD OF OUTER SPACE, INCLUDING THE DEVELOPMENT OF SPECIFIC TECHNICAL PROPOSALS."
PRESIDENT JOHN F. KENNEDY
November 12, 1963
National Security Memorandum
#271 sent to James Webb,
Administrator, NASA

"I DON'T LAUGH AT PEOPLE ANY MORE WHEN THEY SAY THEY'VE SEEN UFOS. I'VE SEEN ONE MYSELF."
PRESIDENT JIMMY CARTER
Remarking on his sighting
January 1969, as remembered by
ABC News, January 22, 1999

"THE PHENOMENON REPORTED IS SOMETHING REAL AND NOT VISIONARY OR FICTITIOUS."
GENERAL NATHAN TWINING
September 23, 1947
Chairman, Joint Chiefs of Staff, 1955-1958

"...I STRONGLY RECOMMEND THAT THERE BE A COMMITTEE INVESTIGATION OF THE UFO PHENOMENA. I THINK WE OWE IT TO THE PEOPLE TO ESTABLISH CREDIBILITY REGARDING UFOS AND TO PRODUCE THE GREATEST POSSIBLE ENLIGHTENMENT ON THIS SUBJECT."
PRESIDENT GERALD FORD
In a letter he sent as a congressman to the Chairman of the Armed Services Committee, March 28, 1966

"WHEN THE LONG AWAITED SOLUTION TO THE UFO PROBLEM COMES, I BELIEVE THAT IT WILL PROVE TO BE NOT MERELY THE NEXT SMALL STEP IN THE MARCH OF SCIENCE, BUT A MIGHTY AND TOTALLY UNEXPECTED QUANTUM LEAP." 1

"WE HAD A JOB TO DO, WHETHER RIGHT OR WRONG, TO KEEP THE PUBLIC FROM GETTING EXCITED." 2
DR. J. ALLEN HYNEK
Scientific consultant
for Air Force Project Blue Book
(1) The UFO Experience:
A Scientific Inquiry, 1972
(2) On camera shortly before his
death in 1985

THE TRUTH

"I OCCASIONALLY THINK HOW QUICKLY OUR DIFFERENCES WORLDWIDE WOULD VANISH IF WE WERE FACING AN ALIEN THREAT FROM OUTSIDE THIS WORLD."
PRESIDENT RONALD REAGAN
Addressing the United Nations
General Assembly, 1987

"I HAD THE EVIDENCE THAT A CRASH DID HAPPEN... I ASK [YOU] THIS, WERE YOU THERE WITH ME? DID YOU HAVE THE CLEARANCES? THEY CAN'T ANSWER THESE QUESTIONS. THEY SIMPLY CRITICIZE WITH NO EVIDENCE."
COLONEL PHILIP CORSO
Former head of the Foreign Technology Desk for United States Army Research and Development, National Security Council member, Eisenhower Administration on camera shortly before his death, 1998

"UNKNOWN OBJECTS ARE OPERATING UNDER INTELLIGENT CONTROL... IT IS IMPERATIVE THAT WE LEARN WHERE UFOS COME FROM AND WHAT THEIR PURPOSE IS..."1
"BEHIND THE SCENES, HIGH-RANKING MILITARY OFFICERS ARE SOBERLY CONCERNED ABOUT THE UFOS."2
ADMIRAL ROSCOE HILLENKOETTER
First Director of the Central Intelligence Agency
1947-1950
(1) Statement for National Investigations Committee on Aerial Phenomena, 1960
(2) New York Times, February 28, 1960

"I AM CONVINCED THAT THESE OBJECTS DO EXIST AND THAT THEY ARE NOT MANUFACTURED BY ANY NATION ON EARTH."
AIR CHIEF MARSHAL LORD DOWDING
Commander-in-Chief, Royal Air Force Fighter Command
WWII, London Sunday Dispatch, July 11, 1954

"THE EVIDENCE POINTS TO THE FACT THAT ROSWELL WAS A REAL INCIDENT AND THAT INDEED AN ALIEN CRAFT DID CRASH, AND THAT MATERIAL WAS RECOVERED FROM THAT CRASH SITE."
APOLLO ASTRONAUT EDGAR MITCHELL
UFOs: 50 Years of Denial, airing on the Learning Channel, March 4, 1999

"...THE POSSIBILITY OF REDUCED-TIME INTERSTELLAR TRAVEL, EITHER BY ADVANCED EXTRATERRESTRIAL CIVILIZATIONS AT PRESENT OR OURSELVES IN THE FUTURE, IS NOT FUNDAMENTALLY CONSTRAINED BY PHYSICAL PRINCIPLES."
DR. HAROLD PUTHOFF
Director, Institute for Advanced Studies at Austin, in Physics Essays, Volume 9, No. 1, 1996
Author of Fundamentals of Quantum Electronics

"...I MADE AN EFFORT TO FIND OUT WHAT WAS IN THE BUILDING AT WRIGHT PATTERSON AIR FORCE BASE WHERE THE INFORMATION IS STORED THAT HAS BEEN COLLECTED BY THE AIR FORCE, AND I WAS UNDERSTANDABLY DENIED THIS REQUEST. IT IS STILL CLASSIFIED ABOVE TOP SECRET."
SENATOR BARRY GOLDWATER
In a letter dated March 28, 1975

INTERNATIONAL SPACE SCIENCES ORGANIZATION

www.TheWordIsTruth.org

REFERENCES

1. Ancient American
2. Ancient Manuscripts
3. Alexander Higgins
3a. Atlantis and Lemuria
4. The Bad Popes
5. The Bible
6. Bible Code
7. Breaking the Godspell
8. COMETA Report on UFOs
9. The Day after Roswell
10. Discovery Channel
11. Execution
12. Fate Magazine
13. History Channel
14. The Ice People
15. Learning Channel
16. Lipman Report
17. MUFON
18. Nostradamus and Other Prophets
19. Paranormal Sourcebook
20. The Plain Dealer
21. Prey
22. Romeo and Juliet
23. Sci-Fi Channel
24. The Secret Sayings of Jesus
25. Sightings
26. The Tribune Review
27. Webpage: Homeland Security, Joint Chiefs
28. Why Do People Hate America?
29. Why Race Matters
30. UFO quotes by Steve Myers (2002)
31. Michio Kaku, Ian Pearson and Dick Pelletier.
32. Paraphrased from a NewsMax article by Ben Stiller.
33. Initiative 2045
34. King James Bible
35. Wired Magazine

Printed in Great Britain
by Amazon

47564082R00195